I0580826

The Blood Rises

ALSO BY JAMES K. MCVEY

Children of Ennaris
The Children Return
The Blood Rises
Ennarisi Unite
Children of Destiny

The Blood Rises

Children of Ennaris II

James K. McVey

James K. McVey

Copyright © 2024 by James K. McVey

All rights reserved.

This work is copyright. Apart from any use permitted under the Copyright Act 1968, no part may be reproduced by any process, nor may any other exclusive right be exercised, without the express written permission of the copyright holder.

ISBNs:

EPUB: 978-1-923211-05-6
Paperback: 978-1-923211-01-8
Kindle: 978-1-923211-09-4

This novel is entirely a work of fiction. The names, characters and incidents portrayed in it are the work of the author's imagination. Any resemblance to actual persons, living or dead, events or localities is entirely coincidental.

First Printing, 2024

Book Cover Design by M. Yankevich, Novelized, at https://www.novelizedbookcovers.com/

CONTENTS

CONTENTS

CONTENTS

For Stephanie, whose support and encouragement made this and many
other things possible.

Captain Jord made his way to the bridge. *Starfire* was at general quarters and Jord was pleased to see his crew moving with quiet purpose. No panic. No rush. Positions were occupied at speed. The ship was ready for whatever was thrown at it.

He took a moment to think of the team on the surface of this planet, designated AX-365T by the astrological staff. The name had been corrected to "Ennaris" by the Grand Admiral. They had been down there for weeks now, and there was no way to reach them. Communications between the surface and *Starfire* were out for some reason, and their sensors were not showing anything significant. In any event, the team's communications capabilities were limited by the need to try to blend in, so they probably hid or de-activated their communicators when they arrived. The amount of Empire activity around the planetary environs indicated that something of importance was attached to this place, so the Union fleet had to hold them off. Simple, but far from easy. Luckily, *Starfire* was the best of the best, much more so than the enemy knew.

He reached the bridge to find Colonel Kiri, *Starfire's* executive officer, occupying the command chair. He waved her back as she started to get up, and instead moved to place himself in front of the large screen that dominated the bridge. The screen showed the entire system in the main view and the segment of the galactic arm in a second segment. On the main screen the relative positions of the Union fleet were displayed in green, while those of the enemy Empire fleet were displayed in red.

When the Empire fleet had arrived the fleet strengths had been slightly in the enemy's favour. That was until the strange energy ball had destroyed the dreadnought that had been the Empire fleet's flagship and one of its most powerful vessels. Now, the Union fleet held a significant advantage and the commander of the Empire fleet had backed his or her - his probably, knowing the Empire - ships away slightly. That state had held for several weeks now, with odd incursions attempted by smaller Empire vessels, seemingly more to irritate than to make any tactical gains. During those minor actions, at least one of the smaller Empire ships had been rendered inoperable and had drifted away, engines dead, while a second was badly damaged if not also incapacitated. Damage had been done to Union vessels. One light gunship had been lost with heavy casualties and several other ships continued to undergo repairs but were functional. One of the larger attacks, though, had damaged the fighter bays of two of the Union's capital ships. *Starfire* carried above her usual complement of stingers as a result, but there were many pilots whose craft had been destroyed in the attack.

Jord could not see the reason for the actions that had resulted in the damaged vessels, but then, he often struggled to understand the tactics of the Empire commanders. Often, the Union had achieved a victory where they probably should have been defeated because of what, to Jord, were irrational actions by Empire commanders.

He shrugged to himself. If it helped then all to the good, except when it cost him people and ships.

Meanwhile, he could now see the cause of the alert, as a new set of markers were flashing on the smaller viewscreen. Additional Empire ships were coming at speed and would soon be close.

"Do we know which ships they are?" Jord asked Kiri.

"Aye, sir. It's the *Zirkuk* battle fleet. Two cruisers, five destroyers and eight smaller vessels, apart from the *Zirkuk* itself. They're coming through the Dead Zone, sir."

"The Dead Zone? Really? They must be in a hurry. Have they lost any yet?"

"No sir," Kiri replied. "But I've never known a group of ships of that size go through the Dead Zone at speed, so maybe that's a way to avoid it."

As she spoke, one of the vessel markers for the incoming ships flashed bright red three times and disappeared, followed seconds later by another.

"Or not," Jord said. "They must be in a hurry, but I can't see why. We've had no activity on the planet that would indicate a reason for such haste."

"The loss of the *Xcrute* may have done that, though," Kiri said. "It was their flagship for the entire sector and their last dreadnought except for *Qorv*. And I bet the Empire command didn't believe that it was caused by an energy ball flying through space. They probably think we did something."

"Yes, quite likely. Mr Rork, estimated time for the incoming ships to get here?"

Rork turned from his console to face Jord. "About thirty minutes, sir, at the way they're going. They'll have to transition to normal space close to this system, I think, in the next two or three minutes or they risk blowing past. Then about twenty minutes or more to get here at flank speed, which I assume they will use."

"Hmmm. Okay, Admiral to the bridge, please. Um, both of them," Jord instructed, and the communications officer turned to her task.

"Signal all ships not to do anything without instruction, please. Let them know we expect *Zirkuk* to arrive in a hurry and they may try to bluff us out. By the same token, they may come in all guns blazing so let's be ready. Rork, I want their weapons conditions as soon as you can get them for those ships. Kiri, keep a watch on the current fleet vessels. I want all shields to be at half strength immediately and ready for full strength on command. We'll be outnumbered when *Zirkuk* gets here."

"Aye sir. The Empire fleet vessels are powering shields and weapons."

"That may just be in response to us. Keep watching though." Jord continued to stand and watch the large screen.

"Sir, *Zirkuk* has exited hyperspace and has transitioned to flank speed. Shields are up, weapons are charged and on-line from what I can see at this distance." Rork concentrated on his instruments as he spoke. "They are separating into a standard attack formation, sir. One of the cruisers in front, *Zirkuk* in the middle, and the second cruiser behind. Destroyers and scouts are deploying above and below as usual."

"Sir, the fleet ships are moving," Kiri reported. "They're moving above the plane of the incoming ships. Making room I would say to allow them to go through."

"No imagination," Jord muttered. "Very well, direct our smaller ships to move behind *Starfire*. They'll be the first targets and we may as well save as many as we can. *Starfire* fleet to configuration zeta-four."

"Zeta-four?" Grand Admiral Mavin Serra asked from behind Jord.

He turned to face her. "Aye, Admiral. The standard attack formation they've been using recently is a vertical plane, with the capital ships in a centre line and the support ships above and below. It works against small numbers of ships where there's only one larger ship in the defending group."

"And zeta-four?"

"Well, we have four capital ships and three small frigates of the newer design, that probably seem to be destroyers to the Empire scanners. To minimise risk we'll go vertical also, but with a difference. It's a tactic Admiral Bard worked out, sir. *Starfire* will take the *Zirkuk*'s fire and our other ships will deal with the rest."

"And that works?"

"It has several times so far. They just don't learn very fast."

"That's because any captain who deviates from the defined formations and plans is executed," Admiral Denton Bard said as he made his way to the small group standing at the screen. "This tactic will fail at some stage when they issue a new attack doctrine, but it looks like they're sticking with the same one for now."

"Odd," said Serra. "They were not quite that rigid in the past. They always lacked imagination and were held to task for not sticking to plans, from what we were able to learn, but there was some slight leeway."

"Intelligence believes the emperor has taken direct command over the Fleet recently, so that may have something to do with it. And he, um, dislikes his commanders taking any real initiative."

"All ships acknowledge zeta-four, sirs. Shields to full on all ships. The smaller ships are feinting forward ahead of withdrawal. Empire ships have reconfigured above the path of the incoming ships. *Zirkuk* has slowed but still is coming at speed."

"Very well. All weapons deploy, hold for the command." Jord stood quiet, aware Serra was watching him with a small smile playing over her face. He turned to her and raised one eyebrow. "Admiral, you may want to watch this. I think you will recognise some of our armament."

"Very well Captain, Admiral. I will be on the observation deck. I leave this engagement in your capable hands."

She smiled as she walked calmly from the bridge to the elevator bank, smiling even more broadly as the crew took no notice, concentrating wholly on the upcoming engagement. She enjoyed seeing her former junior officers taking charge so effectively.

"*Antar* reports smaller ships are withdrawing behind the capital ships," Rork reported. "*Zirkuk* fleet will be in range within two minutes. They can't stop at the velocity they carry."

"Very well, Mr Rork. Kiri, all main guns forward, orient front on, configure the shields for an umbrella." Jord paused for a moment as adjustments were made. "Roll the ships." Jord was a rock, rooted to the spot in front of the screen, his voice calm as he shot orders. "Kiri, you have firing control."

In unison, the capital ships of the *Starfire* fleet turned to present a small front-on cross-section to the incoming vessels, which were moving too fast to change course significantly. As they came to their new orientation, each ship started a ventral roll. Artificial gravity made it seem like the world turned around them but, in reality, the ships rolled like a corkscrew in space. Gun ports on each capital ship opened to allow a massive rail gun to be thrust forward, and smaller energy weapons from all vessels were trained to the front.

The ships of the *Zirkuk* group commenced firing as they came within range. Their speed and changed angle of attack worked against accurate fire, while the spin of the Union ships disoriented those seeking to provide targets. Railguns operated but most rounds missed, and those that hit were glancing blows that caused damage without incapacitating their targets. Power weapons discharged and met massive shields that were shaped like an umbrella from the front of the ships. These shields were much more powerful than any encountered by the Empire ships before and were capable of absorbing or deflecting enormous quantities of energy. The Union fleet remained passive, absorbing the impacts as the *Zirkuk* group thundered through the system.

Kiri was watching the tactical screens intently, completely absorbed in her task, unaware of anything else around her. She watched the markers line up in the computer simulated attack sequence, glanced from time to time to see how much the actual track deviated from the simulation. She nodded to herself and five seconds before the computer's suggested time gave the order.

"*Starfire* hold fire. All other ships, zeta-four sequence. Fire!"

Space was ripped apart as the Fleet's capital ships fired to pre-specified target locations. All ships except the flagship fired all weapons to where the enemy ships were expected to be, and then walked their fire forward or backward. An enormous quantity of high-tensile metal projectiles was emitted from the massive railguns of the capital ships and the smaller versions carried by the rest. The velocity and volume of the projectiles were such that they smashed through the energy shields like they did not exist, shredding external fixtures on the enemy ships and punching holes through the thinner pieces of armour plate. As the railguns exhausted their energy reserves the powerful energy blasters took up the battle, hammering the now unshielded vessels in salvo after salvo. The two enemy cruisers were heavily damaged while four of the destroyers were rendered inoperable. *Zirkuk* had been targeted by two of *Starfire*'s cruisers as it swept past them but had fared better than the smaller ships.

"*Starfire*, fire all guns!" Kiri rapped out as *Zirkuk* moved across *Starfire*'s rotating bow.

Starfire was celebrated as the largest and most powerful ship ever built by the Union, a fact that Serra would have disputed had she not been floating through space at the time it was launched. It had the most powerful weaponry the Union had ever devised, weapons that were in development for decades using designs located amongst Grand Admiral Serra's papers after she went missing. The Empire had little that could compare to its raw power. Nothing the *Zirkuk* possessed could protect it for any length of time. *Starfire*'s single large and multiple smaller rail guns smashed apart any remaining defences *Zirkuk* retained after the cruiser barrage, and then enormous energy pulses tore through the enemy battleship. Bolt after bolt rained on *Zirkuk* as it passed by, now carried by its velocity rather than its engines.

"Cease fire!" Kiri ordered and all guns of the *Starfire* fleet fell silent. Her mouth was dry as she looked on at the destruction her orders had caused.

Jord turned to Kiri and nodded grimly, then turned back to the screens. One of *Zirkuk*'s destroyers retained manoeuvring capability and was slowing, making its way to the relative safety of the survivors of the *Xcrute* fleet. Several escape pods were emerging from two of the destroyers, but because of their relative velocity Jord knew they would be lucky to survive intact. Some of the smaller vessels of *Zirkuk*'s fleet had escaped relatively unscathed, as their lesser weapons had posed no threat to the *Starfire*'s capital ships. Still, two had been destroyed completely and one was limping. The rest had continued through the system, following the *Zirkuk* and the heavily damaged cruisers.

"Mr Rork?" Admiral Bard called. "Status of the *Zirkuk* and those cruisers, please."

"Sir, *Zirkuk* is going critical. I make it a minute to core detonation. The cruisers are dead in space but are going too fast to be saved. I estimate they will reach the asteroid belt in about four hours." He did not have to say what would happen when helpless ships met asteroids. "The damaged destroyers are also drifting in the same direction but will have lesser momentum. They may be able to be reached by the Empire forces before they reach the belt. However, none of the *Xcrute*'s ships are in motion."

Bard nodded. "I'll be with the Grand Admiral," he said, turning towards the elevators.

As he passed Kiri, he placed one hand on her shoulder and squeezed gently.

"Well done, Colonel!" he said quietly but in the shocked silence on *Starfire*'s bridge his words carried clearly. "Very well done to your crew."

On the observation deck Serra observed the result of the battle from the huge viewscreen that looked more like a window on space. Bard stopped by her side and remained silent, taking in the enormous destruction.

"My heavens," Serra breathed after a short while. "When did you get those designs? I never dreamed they could be used this quickly in a smaller ship than *Sunburst*."

"When you were reported lost, some of us had duplicates of your papers, if you recall. After a while we started to review them and came across the uprated railgun designs, as well as the upgraded blasters. It took us a while to work through them, and then we had to devise a new way to power them, which is why *Starfire*'s cores are so over-sized, but we did it. *Starfire* and its fleet are so far ahead of anything else we have in terms of armaments that it's a little scary. How did you work them out? The plans we found were fully formed, and there were only a few working papers."

Serra shrugged.

"I had been working on them for a long time, a very long time," she said.

"Well, wherever you got the inspiration, you can see the result. We even managed to keep them secret, up until now anyway."

"Yes. It may give our people on Ennaris some additional breathing space. I think they may need it. And I think we can expect more company, with better tactics."

"We'll be ready."

In the northern wastes of Ennaris, atop a small knoll standing above a rocky and barren plain, an old man stared at the bright lights playing across the skies. He was no stranger to the powerful energies available for use in space-based vehicles, although his experiences with them were so far in the past that he sometimes could not recall them. Still, he knew a battle was under way. He also suspected that the battle was similar to that about to be undertaken on Ennaris, as the forces supporting Goroth met those supporting the Council.

He wondered which side had won the space battle, but he had no doubt about which would win on Ennaris. For Goroth's forces had something the Archmage did not have. They had the Children of Ennaris, without whom no side could win, according to the Prophecy of that old fool Halfgar. Still, that Prophecy seemed to be tracking truly so far. His efforts over the long cycles were coming to fruition at last.

He had also worked out with his latest reading of the Prophecy - how irritating that its meaning was revealed only in snatches - that the bar on advanced technology would drop in the near future. Exactly when that would be he could not tell, but every indicator was that it would occur when the Children met the enemy in battle, or shortly before. That seemed to be some sort of signal that certain events would happen. He looked to the small pavilion erected below the knoll, where three Andorethi stood, being fawned over by his private ghazrak guards. He needed to establish what they had to do in order to fulfil the Prophecy, but he was sure he could do so. After all, he was Goroth's loyal and most valuable lieutenant, and had been for eons.

And the time was coming. He knew the Guardians had been returning, and almost all had done so. As he had long suspected, they were not myths. He also had a clear understanding that they would not be able to take part in the battles to come, and he intended to take advantage of that. For, as always, the fools of the Council relied on the Guardians for their support. Drewflin had always referred to the Guardians as though he was a stary-eyed true believer, and that would be his downfall. Likud had always felt that Drewflin did not believe in the Guardians but he, Grensor, was not fooled.

He drew his cloak around himself as the chill deepened. When the technology ban fell, Goroth would be released and the true battle would begin. For Drewflin could not stand against the battle skills of Goroth and, he was reliably informed by his spies, he no longer had Marjory to call upon. Without the pre-eminent Battle Mage by his side, and with Goroth having the Children by his, this matter would be settled and they could get back to ruling the galaxy. Likud would be coming soon - he had mixed feelings about that - and Grensor had more Ghazrak being prepared. Drewflin would have no chance this time.

The final flashes faded away in the deep sky. Grensor gave a final glance, wondering again who had won.

Corm stood atop the battlements of the Citadel of the Faeronar, watching the interplay of lights in the sky. He had no idea what they meant, but he knew they had significance for himself and his people. Probably for Ennaris as a whole. Most things seemed to have such significance these days. And he was about to be in the middle of it.

He had come to terms with losing his father, Intika Ramesa. The Faero would die from his wounds, and already preparations were under way for his funeral. Corm grimaced at the thought that the high priest of the Temple of Amra was to conduct the service, but Amra was the chief of the current pantheon of gods and so the high priest of his order was the designated one to send the Faero on his final journey. Corm did not trust Presart to be anything more than a self-serving climber, and most of his priests were thugs rather than people interested in helping the Ennarisi to live well. But Corm did not feel that he could say much, especially after Creely, the erstwhile Chamberlain, had been found to be in the pay of the northers. The amount of red gold that had been found when Creely's quarters were searched left no-one in doubt, for red gold only came from the north, beyond the Skyrim mountains, and was the usual currency for payment of kingdom spies. The kingdoms of Kresh and Ingten were a blight on the northern continent, and reports were that they had started to raid again. That would be likely to restart some of the tensions between Escar and the clans of the grasslands.

Corm was suffering a personal crisis. He knew the people of the Citadel, and the Faeronar as a whole, did not consider him to be suited for the role of Faero. He also knew, and was shamed to think it, that he had ignored the lessons that he should have been taking, spending his time in drinking and gaming, whiling away the days with women who valued his available funds rather than himself, and believing that he had all the time needed to enjoy his youth and then knuckle down to his responsibilities. And now he had no time at all.

He knew his father had valued the counsel of Clofta, the healer of the Citadel and of Flin, the old storyteller and sometime conjurer who had been revealed during the recent fight as an ancient Mage of power, as well as others, but he felt little connection with them. He was drawn to the three travellers Flin had brought with him, and had watched with awe as they had stepped into multiple breaches voluntarily, as though made for the purpose. He especially was drawn to Varna Barr, the yellow-haired woman, but her exploits had become stuff of legend in the Citadel and Corm was reluctant to seek her out for advice. She would see him as little more than a dilettante, and she would be right at that. Corm sighed. He would have to change that, he knew, but did not know how.

He looked into the skies as the lights faded, like the final stage of a battle of the gods, or perhaps the mythical Guardians. He smiled wanly to himself at the thought, and wondered who had won.

Varna and Flin joined Jalor and Blaine in their now customary haunt, the larger tavern of the two on the main square of the Citadel of the Faero. Two tankards of ale appeared as though by magic as they sat, and Varna smiled broadly to Marla, the serving woman who they had all come to know well. At least she was not overawed any more.

"Intika is almost gone," Flin said sadly.

"You knew him well, I take it?" Jalor asked.

"Yes, although he knew me as an old story-teller from his childhood, and one who his father trusted enough to have in council from time to time. I provided updates on what was happening around the different lands of Ennaris, and what some of the other leaders were thinking."

"Was he a good ruler? The people in the Citadel seem to love him," Varna asked. "At least, most of them. It seems he did try to make their lives easier, even though there remains quite a lot of inequity."

"In general, yes. He had some blind spots, and probably could have done more to ease poverty. His father was not that inclined to worry about the poorer people, and I think Intika took some time to realise that they were his people, too. Once he did, though, he started to make changes, but they have a way to go yet."

Varna nodded. "Yes, they do, and that has opened the way for some people to try to take advantage. I think it goes further than that though. The Citadel's watch has been allowed to deteriorate, from what I can gather."

"Probably the work of Creely," Flin said. "He had charge of the Citadel and its services, including the watch."

"Not many of them are worth much. None of the watch arrived to help out, just the remaining guards. Not that the watch is trained, but I would have expected them to be there, at least." Blaine scratched his head. "I'll have a word with Almin Bor. Everyone seems to know him here and they listen to what he says."

Flin nodded. "We'll have to be leaving soon. I see why Balgor wanted you to remain here, though. Corm is going to have a tough time of it, I think. He'll probably be the new Faero, but many think he's not up to the task. And he won't have an experienced Chamberlain to rely on, either. Plus, the Guard seems to be much smaller, probably Creely's influence again, and will need to be rebuilt if my guess about the future is correct, and the Prophecy comes to pass as I think."

"This Prophecy," Jalor said after a moment of silence. "You've mentioned it a few times, and I know you had to go back to wherever to grab your copy and check your understanding. You were telling us about it, and I think we need to have more understanding before you go."

Flin nodded. "Yes, I think so. Well, no time like the present."

The Mage became the Teller as Flin settled himself and took a sip of his ale.

"So, as I said, the Prophecy is the work of Halfgar, who turned out to be the oldest and probably wisest, and possibly most powerful, of the Guide Mages. Thinking back, it was never really clear what he did day to day, where most of the Guides worked to improve the lives of the Ennarisi in many ways. Anyway, Halfgar seems to have guided the Guides. In the last days of the rebellion that caused so much destruction, Halfgar created the chamber that holds Goroth, and the barrier to technology that allowed us to end the rebellion. But he died as a result of over-extending himself, as he had warned us many times would happen. I know he knew what the result would be and he proceeded anyway.

"But it was when we got around to clearing out his things that we found the Prophecy, which seems to have been written over many, many cycles, perhaps thousands. It was a series of writings that predicted the events of the rebellion, as well as the confinement of Goroth. It also predicted that some of Goroth's minions would not be found and would cause problems for Ennaris, and the wider universe. I gather that you may have seen some of that."

"The Shadows," Blaine said, with a twist of the mouth. "We know that they have what we've always thought of as a hereditary ruler, who always took the same name of Likud. Could it be that there has only ever been one ruler?"

"Likud was a strong second level Mage and one of Goroth's key lieutenants," Flin nodded, frowning. "That could mean that he's behind some of the trouble we have now. He's vicious and unprincipled, and what you describe of these Shadows would suit his way of thinking and doing things. It's unlikely that he created the ghazrak, though. They're genetically modified from men and are the results of Grensor's experimentation with the dark arts, as well as his advanced science. Assuming Goroth remains held in stasis, that means another lieutenant is at large. I assume it's Grensor."

"And it may mean Goroth can communicate with them," Varna said thoughtfully.

Flin considered and nodded. "I hadn't thought of that. Yes, it seems likely, or at least possible. Anyway, to return to the Prophecy. Halfgar wrote that a time would come far in the future when the Guardians and Guides would be all but forgotten, when the protectors were reduced and when the old evil would arise afresh in the lands of Ennaris. At that time, in the hour of need, the Children of Ennaris would return to provide aid, preceded by the one champion plus three. And that the Nine would be called forth to fight the evil and return Ennaris to its position amongst the stars."

"So, if we are the Children prophesied, as you believe, then Clay and his party could be this 'one champion plus three'," Jalor mused. "But are you sure we are the Children Halfgar spoke of? And exactly what does it mean to be the Children?"

"I believe you are the Children of Ennaris," Flin said confidently. "More to the point, so does Balgor and, despite the legends about his mischief I very much doubt that a true Guardian would mislead us about that. And to answer your questions, the Children are generally agreed by all who attempt to decipher the Prophecy to be three of the Nine but there is no real lead as to which three."

"How is that?" Blaine asked.

"The Prophecy says the Nine must take the message through the lands of Ennaris to gather the people and oppose the evil. But the Nine are described by roles. Some of them are ancient and legendary roles, where some I am sure are for this mission only."

"What roles?" Varna asked, watching Flin's face intently.

He smiled. "The Guide I think is likely to be me," he said with a shrug. "That's logical I guess and there are few of us left. The Seeker I'm sure is Varna. The Seeker is an ancient and legendary person who has many gifts, but the seeking part refers to knowing how to locate items or people when required to do so. Or perhaps even knowing what to do and when to do it. The legends are vague about the specifics but we do know that the Seeker displays multiple strong gifts. I have yet to see evidence of Varna as a Seeker but she is displaying multiple gifts and I think that is right."

Varna grimaced. "You mean I have to go through more of this gift stuff?"

"Probably," Flin said with a smile, "but at least you know what to expect."

Varna poked out her tongue at him.

"The rest are less sure," Flin said, laughing. "There are the Protector and the Defender. For some reason the Defender is also referred to as the Golden Defender in some tales. The Protector is a legend also, reputed to be one of the best warriors of all time in any age in which he or she lives. The Protector acts as a defender more than an offensive warrior in most tales, although that is a matter of degree, of course. Most defenders see attack as a valid form of defence at times." He paused while Blaine and Jalor both nodded. "The Champion we have discussed before. There is no real information about that one. It seems to be part of the Prophecy that a Champion will be found but there is no information as to who that is."

"If Clay is alive, he would be over eighty cycles old," Varna said to Jalor. "He was the youngest Champion by far but that would be a big ask, still."

Jalor nodded. "Yes, but there are things at play here that we don't understand. Let's keep an open mind. Part of our mission was to determine what happened to that earlier team, and we still need to do that. If Clay remains alive somewhere, we still need to find him. That may shed some light on this. Of course, it may also mean that somewhere in the future someone will become this Champion."

"Then," Flin said, continuing, "we have the Eye of the Dark. The Eye is one of the old legends and usually is described as being able to detect and combat certain negative forces. Then there is the Warrior, again a fairly generic sort of name and that could be anyone. It could refer to Blaine, for example, given his skills in battle. Were Marjory alive still I would expect it to relate to her. With all respect to Blaine's skills, my Marjory would have wiped the floor." Flin reflected for a moment before shaking the thoughts away. "The Dreadlord is one of the legends, though."

"That sounds fearsome," Varna said. She was fascinated at what she was hearing.

"Indeed. It's said that the last Dreadlord became a hermit once the need was done. The Dreadlord leads or commands or calls the legions of the dead, but beyond that we have no real idea of what it truly means. Tradition of the Guides says there have been four Dreadlords in the times of Ennaris' greatest need but none have written down anything of what it means." Flin shrugged. "The final one is the Arbiter. It's not a role of legend, so we must assume it will be someone for this task only."

"Do you have any idea about those roles? Does the Prophecy include any factors that allow you to determine who they may be?"

"Not really," Flin replied. "What I do know is that you don't choose the role. It chooses you. From the Guide archives, I have some information about three of the legendary roles. The Seeker was not so much looking for some object usually as seeking the truth. That sounds fairly odd," Flin continued as Varna cocked her head to one side and raised an eyebrow, "but you should know that the truth can be especially difficult to handle for many people, especially those who follow the wrong path. The Seeker apparently reconciled those people to the true path, not always with happy consequences for either party, I'm afraid.

"Which may be where the Defender comes in. This is also more than it seems. Most people think of the Defender as one who protects individuals, and that has been the role at least once. That may be the intent here. But the role also has at least once worked to save the entire planet of Ennaris, when we were invaded by a hostile space-faring race in the early days. That race subsequently destroyed itself.

"Finally, the Dreadlord reputedly provided support and assistance to the dead, even though the idea of an overlord of the dead has remained associated with the legend. As I said before, none of them wrote anything about their experiences, so that also is guesswork."

"What about the Guide. You're sure it refers to you. What were, or are I should say, the Guides? You talked about Guide Mages more than once, but the way you spoke suggests there were non-Mages also?" Jalor asked after a moment of reflection.

Flin nodded sadly. "The Guides were a group that stood apart. Early legend says they acted as the link between the Guardians and the Ennarisi. As I said, in my time I never met a Guardian, nor saw any sign that they were here. Balgor tells differently, and I'm not going to doubt him, but that was not my experience. So, the idea of the Guides being go-betweens may have been in much earlier days. The Guides worked to assist all parts of Ennarisi society to function, using their gifts, and not just of magery. Some gifts took the form of assisting plants to grow, allowing crops to flourish even when there were inclement conditions. Others helped the healer scientists to achieve incredible results from advanced surgery techniques when melded with the Guide-healers' abilities. Some could see auras and interpret them clearly, which is what I think Almin Bor's daughter, Aldar, may be able to do in the future. Every expedition to other planets took a handful of non-Mage Guides with them, although most participants were full Mages of varying strength. The gifts came in all shapes and sizes and each played a role in one way or another with assisting the Ennarisi. The Guide numbers were never more than a small fraction of the population, though. And as a group, they were wiped out during the rebellion and the aftermath."

"And no idea about the other roles?" Varna asked.

"None. We probably can guess that the Champion plays a part in the battles to come, and the Eye is likely to have some sort of quality that assists at a crucial time, but really all of that is guess work. I will have to go over the Prophecy and see if anything else comes out. Each time I read it some new thought arises, almost like it's exposing only what I need to know at the time I need to know it." Flin stopped, a speculative look washing over his face. "I have often wondered if that's possible. Is the Prophecy revealing only what I need to know when I need to know it? Increasingly I'm inclined to believe that's the case."

"That's pretty imaginative!" Varna exclaimed. "But if it is the case then we each may get additional insights as we read through it also."

"Now that's a good idea," Flin said excitedly. "We should try that, possibly in the Council chambers. It has access to old records."

"Does the Prophecy indicate what the Nine are really trying to do? Just roam around and try to get people interested in what's coming? That sounds like an exercise in frustration." Blaine glanced to Flin.

"No," Flin replied. "Not beyond drawing the people of Ennaris together and then playing their own roles in the final battle. If the Prophecy truly is revealing itself in stages, then we may get a better idea as time goes by."

"Is there any idea as to when this final battle happens?" Jalor asked thoughtfully. "How long we have to get ready?"

"No. There is mention of the third lights of the heavens as a marker, though."

Blaine nodded and looked at Jalor. "Space battle," he said succinctly.

"Likely," Jalor replied with an answering nod. "So, we need to keep an eye out for that, and hope the Admiral is able to hold out."

"Admiral?" Flin asked.

"Grand Admiral Serra," Varna explained. "She was the one who dropped Clay at Ennaris and then her whole battle group was destroyed. She was found adrift and in stasis a short time ago and is in charge of the fleet that's in orbit now."

"I would like to meet this Grand Admiral," Flin said. "When all is done, she appears to have done a great service for Ennaris and its people, even if she does not know it."

Jalor nodded pensively. "It's always hard to know what the Grand Admiral knows," he said. "And it's always more than you think."

2. Varna's Dream

Varna was adrift in a fog, lost, alone, unable to sense anything. Not again, she thought, I thought I was over this. She tried to push through, to awaken. But the sensation persisted and, if anything, became deeper. She struggled, then remembered what Balgor had told her about taking control of her gifts and accepting them, making them part of her. She tried to relax and let the gifts become part of her, but that did not seem to work. She started to grow desperate, feeling herself dwindling, her sense of self shrinking inward. There were no points of reference any more, and the fog was darkening. She knew she had to get out, to wake up, or it would consume her. But nothing stopped the growing sensation of nothingness. She felt that she was approaching the point where she, Varna, would unravel. When that happened her spirit would join in with the great nothing that one of her more spiritually-inspired tutors taught was at the core of existence.

At that point, where she thought she was past saving, where her mind was about to become so many mental atoms, Varna felt the presence approaching. This presence carried the sense of great authority, but it also exuded enormous compassion and patience. She sensed rather than saw a brilliant aura, such that she was unable to describe the colours or the intensity. It was overwhelming. She could do nothing about its approach, as she was unable to function effectively in this strange world in which she found herself. Her old fears were revisited as her self-confidence, not yet fully rebuilt before this mission and shattered again and again at being unable to control or even to understand what was happening to her, was shredded all too easily in the presence of this massive personality. The weight of the presence settled over her, but it was soothing, calming.

Varna's sight cleared somewhat and the fog dissipated a little. It became more like a veil that obscured her vision. Somehow, she remained aware that she was on Ennaris still. However, Varna now could see a dull grey plain stretching away in all directions. Looking down Varna saw that she was dressed in strange robes, with patterns of greens and golds interweaving through the material, with a golden rope belting the material around her waist, and plain sandals on her feet. Approaching her was a man of uncertain age, clothed in flowing robes that shimmered as he moved, with all the colours of the rainbow and more but, rather than being garish, the colours blended into a whole. A long, silver beard and shoulder-length silver hair framed a friendly face, with sparkling green eyes, a long, pointed nose and bushy silver eyebrows. A wide smile turned what could have been an austere, serious mien into an open and friendly one. She could only stare, dazzled still by his over-powering aura.

He stopped in front of her, regarding her carefully, still smiling broadly. After a moment, Varna felt a brief surge of power from the being, and the veil that she still could not penetrate was swept aside. She found herself standing in an enchanting glen. Soft green grass edged a pond with lily pads. Silvery fish swam in the crystal-clear water. Birds sang in the surrounding trees and flitted from branch to branch. The pond was fed by a brook, chuckling as it passed over a few stones. Varna saw wild-flowers edging the far side of the pond, with butterflies and small bee-like creatures moving from flower to flower.

A feeling of wonder suffused Varna. She could feel the glen, and without thought to the being in front of her she closed her eyes and opened her senses to her surroundings. She felt the peace emanating from this place wash over her. She could now sense the birds, the fish in the pond, small frog-like creatures that hopped across the lily pads. She could even feel the lily pads, the trees and the grass. There was no fuzziness or head-ache. It was like she was back in Balgor's Garden, but even more so. She revelled in the sensations, and drank in all she could. Even with her eyes closed she could see the glen, the gentle rise in the land around the pond that formed a sort of bowl in which she was standing. She sighed in a sort of rapture.

She floated on her senses for an indeterminate time before becoming aware of a voice calling to her, and with great effort she opened her eyes and pulled her attention back to a point of focus, the being still standing in front of her.

"Well met, Varna," he said, his voice warm and friendly.

"Um," Varna said, feeling foolish at being tongue-tied with this being whose aura again threatened to overwhelm her.

He laughed and she saw how that enormous aura was tamped down to a level that she could manage. It still shone brightly and told her of a presence that was so much more than she had considered possible, even having experienced the presence of Balgor. But at least she could handle it now.

"My apologies," the man said. "I have not worried about hiding my aura here for a very long time and I'm surprised that you could get the full sense in this place. I think Balgor may be correct about you and your potential."

"Balgor? Then you are a Guardian?" Varna asked without considered thought.

"Indeed," he replied with a laugh. "I have been known by a few names. I am Odruf. However, in the world of Ennaris I was known as Halfgar."

"But you're dead!" Varna gasped, realising even as she said it what a stupid statement that was.

Odruf laughed.

"Oh, not so dead," he said, "although it was necessary for others to believe it so."

"But are you the same Halfgar Flin talks about?"

"Indeed I am." He smiled as she worked through the revelation. "But you must not tell him. Not yet anyway."

Varna's mouth opened and closed without saying anything as the import of Odruf being Halfgar sank in.

"Flin and the Guides truly were never alone! You were with them all the time!"

"Oh, yes. The Guides and the Mages were assisted in doing their work, as they were in dealing with Goroth and the rebellion, as much as we were able to do. We cannot intervene directly in the affairs of Ennaris' people, as much as we would like to. Not yet, anyway. Apart from some relatively small things, that is."

"Like Balgor protecting the Faeronar and the Citadel?"

"Indeed so. And even Balgor had to work through you to make that happen. Which is why we are having this chat." Odruf smiled again, moving to a stone seat that did not exist a moment before. "Please, sit and be comfortable."

"This is all in my mind, isn't it?" Varna said, looking around.

"No, actually I have created this space so we can talk. I have brought your spirit here for a brief period. You are in no danger. Balgor will ensure your physical body remains safe." Odruf looked around. "But I like this place. I have used it in the past a few times when there was a similar need."

"Why have you brought me here, then?" Varna looked at Odruf, amazed.

"Well," Odruf paused and gave a wry smile. "I needed to be close to you to ensure your injuries were not too severe. You see, you were hurt by the release of power that Balgor pushed through you. You were not ready for that, although there was a need. Even though he tried to shield you from the effects, there was damage done."

Varna thought back to the moment when Balgor unleashed the power of a Guardian to disintegrate the ghazrak and men who had been charging up the gateway tunnel. She could sense the immense pressure that had passed through her, and the huge surge of energy but could recall nothing beyond that.

"He was concerned that he had caused you significant brain damage," Odruf continued. "He is quite distraught at the moment, no matter his ready smile. You have become quite special to him, I feel." The latter was delivered with a sly smile. "However, I am pleased and somewhat surprised to say that there seems to be no such damage. But there may well have been. You carry a block to your gifts, something that you have built around your abilities. I expect it was caused by some form of trauma in your youth, possibly something quite small but with large consequences. In setting a block the power of your gifts has been shunted around and through pathways that may not have been meant for that purpose."

"So, whatever this block is has meant that I am unable to access my gifts properly?"

"Yes, so it seems to me," Odruf nodded. "But you will recover from this episode, as you have from the minor ones since you have arrived on Ennaris. You will need sleep and rest, which you are getting as we speak. Balgor has already suggested that you visit the Forest. You need to do so soon. Your gifts are seeking a way through and we must open the way. Hollow Branch is the best at doing such things."

"Hollow Branch?" Varna giggled. "That doesn't sound very Guardian-like, or even Ennaris-like."

"He is Fernis," Odruf said with a grin, "but he has lived as Hollow Branch for so long that he even thinks like a tree."

"He's a tree?" Varna said, astounded.

"You'll see," Odruf said with a laugh. "He's looking forward to meeting you. He and others will be able to help you to break down your own barrier and to understand your powers better. Balgor has made a small dent in that barrier but you are too powerful for him to break through."

"I'm too powerful for a Guardian?" Varna asked sceptically. "How can that be."

"We're not all-powerful, you know. In fact, we were all corporeal beings like you a very long time ago. We are among the ones who were moved beyond those limitations. But still, we have our limits. You demonstrate one of those.”

“So, you can’t do anything for me?”

“Oh, I didn’t say that. Fernis will be able to help you, but it always is you who must make it happen. We never get away from taking personal responsibility in this world, or any other.”

“And where is this Forest? How long will it take for us to get there from the Citadel?”

“It is some distance away from the Citadel of the Faeronar. But you must come without your two companions. They are required elsewhere. For a time, your paths will diverge but if things go as I expect you will join together again to battle the evil at large on Ennaris. I suggest that Drewflin should accompany you. I believe there is unfinished business with him.”

“Is that from your Prophecy?” Varna asked with a sideways smile.

“It is, as a matter of fact. And I am somewhat ashamed to say that the Prophecy is real, and even we are not completely sure of the meanings of some of it. But it was the Prophecy that made many of us depart this planet, our home, for eons.”

“You made the Prophecy but don’t know what it means?” Varna asked, askance. “How does that happen?”

“I told you we’re not all-powerful. We are, after all, merely far more advanced people. We’re not gods, and will never be gods. The One guides our paths, as we guide those of the Ennarisi and others. And for all we know there are more advanced beings that guide The One. There are such powers throughout the known universes that it makes my brain hurt just to think about them.”

“Universes?” Varna was intrigued. “Really?”

“A discussion for another time, perhaps,” Odruf said with a smile. “We have an immediate set of problems to get past first. If Goroth and his ilk take over Ennaris then they may well use the inherent powers available to them to conquer this galaxy. And who knows what happens then. The stakes are high.”

"But surely your people would act to stop them doing that?"

"I and my fellow Guardians are not of this galaxy," Odruf replied gravely. "We have never been a very populous people, and there were relatively few of us when we were given this task by The One. We have lost contact with our former kin."

"I understand," Varna said before shaking her head. "Actually, I don't understand, but as you say, for another time. The bar to technology? That would limit things, surely."

"That bar will drop in the near future. We, the Guardians, will try to shield the Ennarisi as well as we can, but we can maintain that bar for only a short while longer. So much the Prophecy tells us. Flin must be aware of that, for it does set a time limit." Odruf grimaced. "The results would be terrible if the old weapons were used again."

"They exist still?" Varna was appalled. "I thought they had been destroyed."

"Destroyed? No, merely rendered inoperable." Odruf shook his head sadly. "Some of the stockpiles exist even after all this time. Most were stored in a form of stasis and I had to allow that to remain functional. Had the weapons deteriorated without such controls in place then Ennaris could have been destroyed. They remain a grave threat. They are much worse than anything your Union or the Empire have come up with."

"And you were not permitted to destroy them? And you know of the Union and the Empire?"

"The fate of their old weapons of colossal destruction remains the responsibility of the Ennarisi themselves. There are opportunities in the future if success comes to the Children. And yes, of course we know of you and your main enemy. We have, after all, had members of the Guardians striving on behalf of rising species across this galaxy. And we are aware of others who you do not yet know, who may prove to be friend or enemy in the future."

"Oh? Other empires?"

"Another time, also," Odruf said with another smile. "It is time, Varna Barr, for your time here to end. For now. Say little of this to Drewflin, and nothing of Halfgar. But do inform him that the Prophecy provides a deadline when the technology bar will fall. And make sure you come to the Forest."

"Just Flin and me alone?" Varna asked.

"Not necessarily only you two, but Jalor and Blaine are needed elsewhere. Remember that also. Rest well, Child of Ennaris, for you will face trials that will test your resolve. Have faith in yourself, and have faith in the Guardians and Guides, those of the lands of Ennaris and those of the seas. We will speak again."

With that Varna found herself fading back into dream. The fog reestablished itself and the glen disappeared. As she drifted away, Varna found herself with a startling thought.

The seas?

3. New Faero

Varna awoke - again - in the infirmary. This time bright light showed through open curtains. Windows leading to an inner courtyard were open and the sound of birdsong carried through, doing battle with the normal sounds that she now associated with the Citadel's healers' domain. Her movement was noticed by a guard standing just inside her door, and he darted out into the passage, doubtless to inform someone. She looked around to find herself in a single room, with a comfortable bed, soft sheets and somewhat less utilitarian fittings. She snorted to herself and flung back the sheet, only realising she was naked as she did so and, with a squeak pulled the sheet back over herself, just before the door opened and the senior healer entered.

"Back again, eh?" he said with a smile. "You do seem to make a habit of collapsing dramatically."

"I'm trying to do something about that," she replied with an answering smile. "Why am I here?" she asked as she gestured around the room.

"Oh, something about the saviour of the Citadel not being put in with the riff-raff," the healer replied. "My name is Clofta. Are you feeling okay? Is there anything you need? Last time this happened, if I recall, you were unconscious for a couple of days."

Varna considered her condition, alert for the inner turmoil that was so prevalent before her meeting with Balgor. She felt a slight buzz, which told her the effects were not completely removed as yet, and that she needed to fulfil her promise to visit the Forest of the Guardians. She now knew it would not be relieved until she could speak with Fernis. She also realised she was able to recall her dream clearly and in detail.

"I feel fine, as a matter of fact. How long was I out?"

"All of the afternoon and the night. It's mid-morning now. Clever of you to sleep while everyone else cleaned up."

She smiled again, liking this man with his friendly bedside manner.

"Part of my training," she said light-heartedly. "Never do what you can get someone else to do for you."

Clofta laughed.

"Well, if you're okay you'll find your clothes in that cupboard. I am intrigued by the materials used in the under garments. Don't worry," he said quickly as her eyebrows asked the question, "it was not me that undressed you but the head nurse. I brought them in after they were washed and was surprised at both the quality and material."

"It's a technique from my country. It may make its way here before much longer," Varna told him, thinking forward to the time when Ennaris may be part of the Union. "How many injured are there?"

"Quite a few," Clofta said seriously. "Most of them are doing okay, although I have two who will need limbs to be removed later today. There's one I'm worried about. He's not responding to the usual treatments. But I know all would appreciate a visit from the Lady, which is how you are being termed now, by the way. Just the Lady." He smiled again. "It seems you have admirers."

"Well, I'm not too sure about that, but if it would help then I'm happy to meet them. Let me get dressed and I'll accompany you?"

Nodding, Clofta signed for the guard, who was regarding Varna with something akin to awe, to step outside, and then followed suit. Varna swept the sheet back again, standing in a single motion and feeling a little dizziness but otherwise no ill effects at all. She wondered if Balgor had visited while she was sleeping, the thought accompanied by a slight smile as she dressed in the undergarments from *Starfire*, followed by the tunic and trousers that she had obtained in a local market during her walks. She finished with her belt, snapping her staff to its loop so it rode easily to hand. She picked up her cloak, took one look around the room and stepped through the door.

Clofta escorted her through the halls towards the common room. They passed a small number of infirmary staff, all of whom bowed or curtsied, to Varna's embarrassment. She was uncertain how to respond. Clofta was amused.

"You may need to get used to that around the Citadel," he said with a chuckle. "Just nod to them so they know you acknowledge them, which is what Intika does. Or rather, did." He sighed.

"The Faero is dead?" Varna asked.

"Not yet, but shortly. Even Flin's herbs can't help him, and he seems to be able to do some wondrous things with them. Although he does appear to be more than a Teller."

"Yes," Varna said, keeping her voice neutral. "The herbs do seem to be effective, and he definitely is more than a Teller. How are my friends?"

Clofta glanced at her, sensing that she was holding back but unable to determine what that may be.

"They're fine. The big one took no injuries, even though he and Helt turned the battle with those huge swords, and him without armour." Clofta shook his head, then grinned. "Helt took a couple of solid clunks but, luckily, they were to her head so she didn't notice. The other one has become quite the talk of the Citadel, the way he took charge. He has a few more scratches and is exhausted, but otherwise unharmed."

They turned a corner and entered the long ward, where beds were lined up along both walls, with a wide window at the far end. Several muttered conversations stopped as Varna entered, the occupants of about two-thirds of the beds all turning to stare at her. Varna stopped, looking at all of the injured men looking at her, with the same awe evident. She decided she did not want that, not from these men anyway, so drew on her barracks room experience.

"What? Haven't you ever seen a woman before?" she demanded into the awkward silence. "Given the way you're staring it's either that or I have horns and a tail, which I'm pretty sure weren't there the last time I looked."

The men smiled and most relaxed, and Varna moved to the first bed in line.

"How are you soldier?" she asked, turning to Clofta, who was standing beside her.

"Gresh," Clofta said.

"Gresh," Varna repeated. "Where did you get it?"

"Lady," Gresh replied, bobbing his head and regarding her sheepishly. "It's nothing. Just a scratch. I'll be up and about before you know it."

Clofta harrumphed. "Not likely. Gresh will be here for a while and then will be on a stick for a while. That scratch went through his leg and just missed the important bits."

Varna smiled. "Well Gresh, you just concentrate on healing. I have a feeling the Faero may need you and all of your comrades in the future."

"Yes, Lady," Gresh replied with another nod.

"Hmmm," Varna said and then turned to the room, where they all still stared. "Right. Let's get a few things clear. I'm not 'Lady'. My name is Varna. I don't care what stories you may have heard or what happened, but you have no need to treat me any different to anyone else."

Clofta pulled Varna aside.

"You may think you are nothing special but they all know different. They saw you destroy all of those things, whatever they were."

"But I don't want to be seen as different."

Varna's anxiety sparked Clofta's interest.

"It's actually not your choice if they see you as a hero or not," he said gently. "And believe me, these people need a hero. Intika is going to die very soon, and his son is untried and not really thought to be up to the task. So, for their sake if nothing else, accept that you are now something more and just let it take its path."

Clofta was sympathetic but firm. Varna just nodded, before sighing and nodding again. All she ever wanted was to be part of the team, not someone standing alone. Being alone always seemed to cause her pain and strife.

"Good, let's let these boys and girls meet you. Then I have been asked to take you to Intika's room. He has asked to meet with you."

Clofta delivered Varna to the Faero's room in the infirmary. The healer walked up to the bed on which Intika Ramesa lay, while Varna moved to stand at the foot of the bed. Flin was sitting in a chair against one wall.

"Well Clofta, you've not been able to get rid of me yet," Intika said gruffly, wincing slightly as he moved, "but I don't think it will be too long now."

"I'm afraid not, my Faero," Clofta replied gravely. "As you requested, I have brought Varna to meet with you. She has already charmed most of your men."

"Hmmpf, they'd be charmed by anything wearing a skirt half the time," the Faero said, a small smile playing across his pain-ravaged features.

"Aye, perhaps so, but I think this was different. Can I get you anything? More pain relief?"

"No, I want to speak with her, and I have Flin here for company as well."

"Ah, yes, Flin the storyteller with his herbs," Clofta said with a twist of his lips. "I always knew there was something not quite right about that, and what we saw during that battle told me I was right. I take you are one of the lost Mages?"

"Lost? I have always known exactly where I am," Flin replied loftily, then smiled. "Yes Clofta, I am a Mage."

"Just a Mage? I think not," Intika interjected. "Archmage, I think would be a better title. Yes?" His laugh turned into a cough and another grimace of pain.

Clofta stared from Flin to the Faero and back. "Archmage? Drewflin?"

Flin nodded.

"I am Drewflin, but not the Archmage, and let's keep that to ourselves, eh? There are too many people who blame us still for the rebellion."

Clofta shook his head.

"Legends return, miracles are seen. And Varna?"

Flin gestured to her, standing at the foot of the bed and watching the proceedings with interest.

"If I am not mistaken, Varna is one of the Children," Flin said softly.

Intika nodded, while Clofta stared once again, eyes wide, before turning to Varna and according her a deep bow. Varna sighed again.

"Not just like everyone else," he said.

"What was that?" Flin asked.

"Just part of a conversation we were having," Clofta said with a smile. "I'll leave the three of you now. I expect you have things to discuss."

He bowed to all three and left the room.

"There is one of the best," Intika said to Flin. "Confide in him, my friend. Most do not know but he has been one of my closest advisers for the last fifteen cycles. He knows as much about the Faeronar as anyone. And now," the Faero continued, looking to Varna, "please come closer. I would greet you properly."

Varna moved from the foot of the bed to occupy the space alongside the bed just vacated by Clofta. She clasped the offered hand of the leader of the Faeronar, noting his aura was fluctuating, a dim golden colour shot through with the red she associated with pain. The gold dimmed slightly as she watched, and she knew the Faero had little time.

"I am most pleased to meet you, Varna, Child of Ennaris," Intika said formally. "I would that I was able to do this in a better time, but it seems I am not destined to share your work. I must ask this though - will you fight for Ennaris, as the Prophecy tells?"

"I don't really know the Prophecy," Varna said, "and the whole Children of Ennaris bit is new to me and my companions. We fight to protect the Light, and right now that seems to include the people of Ennaris. I can offer no more than that at this time."

"Honest and forthright," Intika said. "I like that. It will have to do. I have a feeling about you. Balgor, is she the one?"

Flin started as Balgor stepped from the wall with a flare of golden light.

"Indeed, Intika, Varna is one of the Three, we think." He bowed to Flin. "Drewflin," he said in greeting, and then turned and winked to Varna.

"You knew about Balgor?" Flin asked Intika Ramesa, stunned.

"Most Faeros have been introduced to Balgor on assuming the position," the Faero said. "He has been with us all these long ages, and has been friend and confidante to us all, including some I expect who were not worth the effort."

"I have protected the Faero and the Faeronar within the Citadel as I was bid to do," Balgor said gravely, "but many of the Faeros have I considered to be a friend. You, Intika, are amongst the best of those, and I will miss you."

Intika smiled. "And you think Varna is of the Three?"

"I do."

The Faero tried to rise, excitement causing him to over-exert, which in turn caused him to cough, face twisted in agony. "Then she is ..."

Balgor gently held him down and Varna saw Intika's aura strengthen slightly. She knew Balgor had provided some additional energy.

"Dharmoney, I think," Balgor said simply. "Perhaps Dharmoney to come."

"Dharmoney," Intika breathed, his face showing wonder. "At least I have lived long enough to meet her."

Varna was mystified. This was the second mention of this Dharmoney, but this time applied to herself. Odruf had said nothing about that in her dream. She looked to Flin and Balgor in turn. The former was stunned while the latter shook his head and indicated she should wait.

Balgor turned to Flin. "It is time, Archmage," he said sadly.

Flin nodded and stood, deciding not to correct the Guardian about his title.

He bowed deeply to Intika Ramesa and said, "Intika Ramesa, as leader of the Council of Mages, I bid you farewell. Know that your name will live through the long ages to come as the one who prepared the way for the return of Ennaris to its position in the universe. I have been honoured to know you and to call you friend."

With that Flin left the room.

Varna reached for the Faero's hand and squeezed it gently.

"You are not of Ennaris, are you?" Intika asked, his voice weak now.

"No", Varna replied. "My world is far from here, but from what I have learned we were lifted to civilisation by the Ennarisi."

"Thank you for your help, my child," the Faero said. "And I feel my time is come. I must say farewell to my son. I wish I could assist you, but that falls to another. May the Guardians watch over you."

Varna nodded and left to join Flin outside the room. A young man was approaching, flanked by two Citadel guards, both of whom bowed to Varna as they passed. Obviously distressed, the young man entered the room as Varna and Flin made their way from the infirmary.

4. Flin and Balgor

Drewflin was troubled. Events were moving faster than he could explain, even with the Prophecy. Especially with the Prophecy. What he thought would be a gradually mounting set of actions leading to a climax where the legendary figures of Ennarisi history returned in the form of Ennarisi people who, he imagined, he would be able to influence if not shape had become something both more and less.

It was more because he had missed the reference to the Nine in the Prophecy, but when he returned to it after Balgor's message via Varna he was able to find it readily. That implied that the idea of the Prophecy being revealed in stages may well be right. Ennaris did not have a strong history of such prophesies, so Drewflin was not sure whether to feel aggrieved or not. In any case, it mattered little because if that was what was going to happen then that is what would happen. Probably. Maybe.

It was less because he may not be the guiding force that he imagined. For so long he had led the little group of Mages who remained, and for so long he had puzzled over the Prophecy and made plans for as many eventualities as possible that he had felt sure of his role. That certainty was gone, which took his sense of balance with it. He found himself fighting once again against his own anger, which increasingly moved closer to pure rage, at what had been done to his planet and people, even as he tried to deal with the sequence of surprises and revelations that kept coming. There were some challenges that were to the fore.

Varna was one of the challenges. Understanding that she, Blaine and Jalor were the Children was not hard. In fact, as soon as he understood that the returning Children may not be of Ennaris, other references made sense - references to fires in the sky, for example, had to relate to some sort of space battle that either had already occurred or would occur as part of the Prophecy being fulfilled. But the fact that two of them would appear seemingly without gifts, and the third would have a mighty struggle to accept her gifts, threw up problems. Having not believed in them for such a long time, now Drewflin hoped that the Guardians could help her because, without the Children being as powerful as legend stated, Drewflin could not imagine how they would defeat Goroth and his supporting forces.

The Guardians themselves caused Drewflin pain. For his whole life he had not believed in the Guardians. He had imagined them as nothing more than mythical figures to be brought out at times to help people to accept their lot, to assuage grief with the thought that a loved one was with the Guardians, or to provide contemplative examples of better times for Ennaris and hope for what could happen when the Guardians returned. He could talk the talk, of course, and speak of them with enthusiasm and conviction, but in truth he had not believed a word of it. He believed in the ideals represented, of course, but not them as people.

And now they had returned, or so Drewflin was told. He did not doubt that Balgor was the Balgor, but the thought that he had been watching over, protecting the Faeronar and the Citadel for all the ages since the rebellion's nadir was something Drewflin still struggled to take in. That and the fact that he had never revealed himself to Drewflin, knowing who he was, while ensuring that every Faero knew who he was, was the largest source of pain. Drewflin could accept Balgor's explanation, barely, but in his heart he felt hurt. He and his companions had fought and died with no inkling that they were being watched. Were they also being judged? Was he being judged and found wanting? Did Marjory know the Guardians existed all that time and not tell him?

And Varna had told him of Odruf's intervention. Varna definitely was the one, and Drewflin felt both elated and deflated. Elated because he would be able to play a part in the final chapter of Ennaris' descent and recovery, or so he hoped and prayed. Deflated because he had hoped and expected to play the lead role - he snorted at his own pride, definitely leading him to that fall - and it looked like he would not be front and centre. He sighed and smiled wryly as he considered that he had made sure that people did not know of the Guide Mages' continued existence and now felt put out that they did not acknowledge him. He was deflated also because, from what Odruf told Varna, there was a deadline, but none seemed to know what it was.

This was where he needed Marjory. Not just as his soul-mate and life partner, but because she was the greatest Battle Mage that Ennaris had seen. Her knowledge and mastery of advanced weaponry was what had allowed the Guides to hold out when Goroth laid hands on one of the stores of terrible weapons as the rebellion escalated, and it was her knowledge that allowed whole cities of millions to be protected from the weapons themselves, only for them all to suffer in the final stages as the planet's surface groaned in pain. She also was ruthlessly logical. Marjory would know exactly what to do when the time came for the block against advanced technology to be lifted and for both sides of what would be a sizable conflict to regain access to such weapons.

Drewflin's thoughts shifted again, shying away from thoughts of Marjory, of his last memory of her as they both re-entered stasis after a period of touring the lands of Ennaris, laying her hand in his and giving her crooked smile before both took their places on the stasis couches.

Now he thought of the weapons. He knew of two more caches of advanced weaponry held in stasis, intended for planetary defence. Both, to his knowledge, had been unknown to Goroth but perhaps not to others who had joined him. It was hard to know what Goroth knew. He was fully trained as a Battle Mage, after all, but had spent much of his time with the explorers rather than the defence force. There would be other caches, he knew, and not just on Ennaris but possibly scattered through this sector of the galaxy and beyond. Marjory would have known - another twist in his emotions. So, not only would Drewflin have to make sure that Varna got to the Forest of the Guardians, and that Jalor and Blaine did whatever they would have to do, but he had to ensure that the old weapons did not fall into Goroth's hands when the time came.

And Varna had said something else that caused Drewflin some pain. For Odruf had mentioned Guides of the land and the sea. Drewflin had no idea there had been Guides of the sea that survived. The thought caused him to grimace uneasily. What else did he not know? While his own power was great, he had inherited more of an acting Archmage role during the rebellion, largely because all of the more senior Mages of power had died. Were there things that he missed? Did the fact that he was not elevated formally mean that he did not have a full picture? Despite his misplaced sense of pride a moment earlier, Drewflin knew that he was not privy to everything earlier Archmages had known. But then, those earlier ones had access to many other senior Mages as supports and mentors, as experts in various fields, and with knowledge of various episodes of Ennaris' history and lore, as well as their own capabilities that formed a whole. Drewflin, with his much reduced and far less experienced cohort, did not have that.

And speaking of his much-reduced cohort, where were the twins? With Marjory gone - the heartache was stronger each time he thought of that - the Mages boiled down to Drewflin, Trabor and the twins. Their talents were varied but relatively limited, although at times they were surprisingly effective at extracting information about events around the two continents of Ennaris. That information would be needed in the coming days, if Flin's reading of the Prophecy was correct.

He wandered the Citadel alone, mulling over so many different aspects of the situation. He was doubting his own judgement now that he had been proved to be misguided in so many things. He had been wrong about the Guardians' existence. He had not even known there were other Guides surviving than those on land - an inexcusable lapse of knowledge that he had to remedy as soon as he could do so. What else did he not know that could prove to be crucial? The twin kingdoms in the north were stirring up trouble. New forces of ghazrak were being much bolder, coming into the open where recent stories suggested that previously they had stayed to the borders where the northlands met the wastelands. His thoughts roiled as he walked, his expression one of such a forbidding mien that even the footpads, those who did not know of his recent very public exploits, stayed away.

Suddenly, he passed from strife and turmoil to serenity and calm. The change was so abrupt that he stopped and stared around himself, taking note of his surroundings for the first time. He stood on short, soft grass, with a tinkling fountain to his left and a garden with tall trees, fragrant shrubs with bright flowers at their feet, and birds singing in their branches. A stone bench stood amongst the garden, with stones leading the way to it. Flin was astonished. He had walked the Citadel for a lifetime of lifetimes and had never seen this place, tucked against one wall in the poorer and less reputable part of the fortress. His heart lightened and for the first time in a long time a smile flickered on his face as he watched the birds flit from branch to branch.

He recalled Varna's tales of finding a place of solace where she could relax and leave the difficulties of adjusting to Ennaris behind, where she could speak with Balgor. Looking around Drewflin realised that this was Balgor's place, probably brought into being when required. As though that realisation was a trigger, Balgor appeared, seeming to walk from the Citadel wall against which the fountain was built.

"Well met, Drewflin," Balgor said. "Please, take a seat. You're troubled and we need you to regain your focus for the times to come."

Drewflin nodded and made his way to the stone bench, sitting and resting his back against the Citadel wall. He could feel the tension seep away, and the various troubles seemed less insurmountable.

"Balgor," he acknowledged as he sat. "I thank you for allowing me to see this place. I know you helped Varna, and do still, but I didn't realise what she meant when she said you had a haven of peace."

"Varna is not alone in experiencing this place," Balgor said, "for I've used it at times when events threatened to overwhelm those who needed to retain perspective."

"As I do at this time," Flin replied, with an incline of his head. "I have lately been plagued with doubts and uncertainties."

"You've had several shocks, my friend," replied the Guardian. "You've had legends come to life before your eyes, have realised that you don't know as much as you thought you did, and now you're faced with the Prophecy coming true. It's enough to make anyone doubt."

Flin sighed. "All true. I've been trying to maintain a confident front, but I'm worried. You will know that I'm not a warrior. While I am powerful and can perform some of all known Mage skills, my real strengths lie in healing and repairing all living things. Of encouraging growth and regeneration. I will not be able to stand up against Goroth with only the twins and Trabor to aid me. Or can the Guardians assist?"

"Alas no, we remain forbidden to take active roles in the battles to come. Don't ask me why, for I don't know, and it really irks," Balgor said with some heat, to Flin's obvious surprise. "Oh, don't look at me like that. I keep telling everyone we're not gods. We may have more talents - gifts - than you but that's a matter of degree and type, and believe me we do have our irritations and gripes."

"You maintain those limits yourself?"

"To some extent," Balgor nodded, "but the limits were imposed before we even came to Ennaris. I guess it's to stop any of us from becoming enamoured of that power and using it ill-advisably. Which is the same reason for you having the same policy for client planets and their races. It becomes very easy to lose perspective, to become that which we fight against, to fall into the evil that arises when you consider yourself before others."

"As Goroth and his followers did," Flin nodded.

"Yes, an illustrative example if ever there was one. There have been others, of course, but they pale against Goroth." Balgor paused for a moment, watching the brightly coloured birds in the branches. "What are your main concerns?"

"Ah, where to start," Flin said. "My pride was injured when I found that you had been here since the rebellion and I was not made aware.

In fact, that the massive destruction occurred at all, with the resulting death and suffering of the common Ennarisi, quite apart from the destruction to the planet and the Guides who tried to hold it back - that I still find hard to fathom. It raises my ire just thinking on it. Even if you had limits applied, I would have expected help."

"Would it help if I told you, again, that you have never been alone? Would it help if I told you that we wept long and bitterly for the damage, destruction and loss of life that the rebellion caused? Would it help if I told you that we were also trying to hold back the destruction, within the limits imposed on us?" Balgor asked, his tone almost one of idle curiosity but Flin knew he was being watched keenly.

"No," he replied, "no, it doesn't help. I feel anger and resentment. That's too light. In fact, I'm furious and struggling increasingly to hold it back. I'm not sure if it's because the Guardians are revealed to be less that omnipotent, or that you have been revealed at all where I believed we were alone. Or if it's because I've been left to face what will come with few resources, and without Marjory. Or if I'm just feeling old and tired and lacking in hope." Flin rubbed his face wearily. "For I am feeling tired now, I admit."

"You will have to find your centre again," Balgor said. "For you are what Ennaris has. You have the Children, don't forget. Varna is likely to prove to be vital to your work, but you need to get her to the Forest where Fernis dwells."

"Fernis? Fernis stayed also?"

"Indeed. The Forest of the Guardians is called such because of Fernis and Pio. You know that Forest I'm sure but perhaps have not truly seen it for what it is. When you arrive at the Forest take particular note of the trees, for they have lived with Fernis in particular for so long that many have evolved themselves." He laughed at Flin's quizzical expression. "No, you must find out for yourself. What else are you feeling?"

"Fear." Flin grimaced. "Fear that I will be found wanting and will not be able to overcome Goroth and so will ensure that Ennaris falls into evil. Fear that in doing so we open the galaxy and perhaps more to the same forces of evil. Fear that this will come to pass because I'm not strong enough, because I have no such support as my predecessors had available to them, and I seem not to be aware of many things that I should have known. I am not the Archmage, and I am unaware of so many things. How could I not have known that there still were Guides of the seas?"

"Well, the lack of knowledge is something you can remedy, and I suggest you take the time to do so. Review your records of the Guides and you should find what you need. There is a thing or two that I can do there also to make it easier. As for failing, we all risk failing every time we try something. Fear of failing may make us cautious but should not stop us from chancing our hand if the goal is worthwhile." Balgor smiled. "We made some huge mistakes as we were preparing Ennaris for the emergence of the Ennarisi. Luckily, we did have each other to support us and were able to rectify most of the problems we caused."

"Most?"

"Yes, well, we could not undo some things. I'm not going to go into details because some of my brothers and sisters still feel shame at them." He grinned to Flin. "Sometimes it's nice to remind them that they're not always right! But don't stop striving because of your fears, or your discontent at not being aware of everything, or because your pride has been hurt. You've worked long and hard for Ennaris and its people, even though they didn't know you existed and didn't acknowledge you for what you did. This is the same Ennaris, and these are the same Ennarisi. And you may find support where you do not expect it."

"You know what's to come, then?" Flin asked with hope.

"No more than you do, I'm afraid. None of us do. I don't know how the Prophecy will come out, nor what the future holds. Not gods, remember?" He shrugged.

"A pity. A little omniscience would be useful right about now."

"Yes, I've often thought that, actually." Balgor fixed Flin with a steely gaze. "And you need to get started. Intika has gone and Corm is left behind. He's raw and immature but has good qualities that must be forged. I think that may be Jalor's and Blaine's jobs, at least for a while. If you go back to the Prophecy you may find reference now, where you did not before. I hate that, by the way - getting information piece-meal is irritating!"

"I've noticed that," Flin replied dryly.

"No doubt," Balgor replied with a quick grin. "Time is wasting. Varna becomes your first priority, as is deciding on the remainder of the Nine. Ennaris must be brought together under the Faero, and most of the peoples will not readily accept any sort of overlord after so long being independent. Varna must get to the Forest safely. You should be with her, by the way. And you have to find your lost knowledge. You have the Children, and you need to get started before the block is lifted. Goroth is almost certain to be freed when that happens."

"Yes," Flin said, smoothly standing and straightening, feeling his mood lighter despite the weighty conversation. "Yes, it's time. Thank you Balgor."

"Oh, don't thank me. You have a hard road, I'm sure. We will do what we can, but it remains up to the Ennarisi to defend Ennaris, as it always has been."

5. Decisions

It was early morning of a mild autumn day and the Citadel was starting to stir when Flin sat in his now customary chair in the tavern. His lips quirked as he tried and failed to work out how he had managed to have a customary chair in any tavern, let alone this one. He usually came and went without staying for any length of time.

Now, he watched the Citadel come to life. The blacksmith drew open his huge door with little effort but great care, massive arm muscles not even twitching. Flin knew that Ragten did everything with care, for he found it very easy to break things inadvertently because of the strength built up over years of swinging the huge hammers that were so much a part of his trade. In the shop next to the tavern old Martek was placing her baskets just so, as she had done for more years than many could recall. Flin, however, could remember a winsome young girl helping her mother do the same thing, in preparation for displaying the array of wares to be sold from around the lands of Ennaris. Further around the square Grolper, the leather-worker, was hanging out on pegs driven into the wall of his store a range of bags and other leather goods, helped by his young apprentice, one of the children saved recently from the ghazrak.

Flin found himself looking over the familiar Citadel with new eyes, for he now knew that the troubles for which he had prepared for so long were coming, and that neither he nor the people of the Citadel, the Faeronar on whom so much of Ennaris' fate would hang, were ready for it.

His eyes were drawn to a small group making their way across the square. Two young men each leading a tired and bedraggled hrss headed his way. The two men stopped to tie their hrss at the hitching rail by the fountain before walking to the tavern. Both stopped at Flin's table and dropped into chairs with matching sighs of relief.

"Ragnor, Raglin," Flin acknowledged as though he had not been in the least concerned about their welfare yesterday.

"Flin," they replied in unison, each making exactly the same sign to the serving woman, to Flin's amusement.

"I see you've finally stopped finishing each other's sentences and just gone for a chorus type of approach," Flin said, mock serious.

"Well," both said in unison again, before stopping and glancing bemused at each other.

All three laughed, and Flin reached out to grasp hands with the twins, one after the other. Finally, he thought, he would get some answers about what was happening. He waited while Marla placed welcome tankards in front of all three, and followed that with a plate of meat, vegetables and fruit, before speaking.

"How have your journeys been?" Flin asked.

The twins tucked into the food as though they had not eaten for days, which, Flin thought, may have been the case. They had been known to ignore their physical needs for long periods. Ragnor waved a fowl leg to his brother, indicating that he should start.

"Well enough, to start with," Raglin said after a final draft from his tankard. "We did the storyteller routine mostly when we were doing the rounds of the middle lands. When we went towards the northlands we fell back to conjurers - they relate better to that up there. There's a lot of worry through the midlands. Some of the religions have taken harder lines to what they consider to be corrupt practises. I think a few actually believe it, too. For most, though, I think there's a recognition that something is happening and they're trying to grab as much as they can and get away. But there've been some strange things too."

Ragnor took over seamlessly as Raglin went back to his food. "Around the Vale in the approaches to the waste lands a sort of cult of Tanga has grown up. A man named Murk has been talking up miracles that he claims to have seen where the land bloomed again, with water flowing and trees and flowers and food crops. He says that it's happening in the Vale of Tanga. That's a large valley in the middle of nowhere, although legend tells that before the rebellion it was lush and rich. Which of course it was."

Flin nodded. "I remember the Vale. It was one of the loveliest places but the changes caused the river to move underground and the land just dried to a husk. So did you visit the Vale?"

"No," Raglin said, taking up the tale again. "We were on our way across the waste at the time and had little food, so didn't go up there. Trabor was going there anyway. We headed across the top of the grasslands and dipped into the wastelands a bit. Then we headed for Hensert as the closest sure source of supplies. Which brings up another oddity. The people up there are telling of an increase in activity of the leviathans, with the smaller long-noses also being seen a lot more. It seems the leviathans are closer to the shore than anyone can recall. A couple of temples to Ana have been rebuilt and one old fellow claims the leviathans have been talking to him, telling him of the return of Ana. We thought he may have been a little touched until we spoke with him." Raglin stopped and looked intently at Flin. "Flin, he has a gift. He truly can speak to the leviathans, and to the long-noses when they stop jumping above the waves and playing around long enough."

Flin stared. "An old man, you say?"

"Yes, and we never saw him before and have not seen anyone that old openly displaying a gift for a long time. Not in those parts of the world anyway. It was a leviathan that told him that Ana had returned. We could find no trace of a talking leviathan, though. We tried. As for Ana, well we didn't even know what to seek there."

Flin looked into the distance.

"The Guardians are returning," he said, almost to himself.

Ragnor laughed.

"So it seems. You never did believe, did you? Needed to see for yourself before taking it on faith. Well, we have always believed but have never seen signs. We still haven't seen any, but have been hearing about them for some time now. And then there are the Rocs..."

Raglin chuckled at Flin's expression. "Yes, the Rocs. They live still, apparently. There have been sightings reported in the foothills of the Reaches. People are talking about huge birds swooping down and grabbing enormous stones, taking them somewhere no-one knows."

"We told the stories of the Rocs of old," Ragnor took over, "how they came in time of need and helped the Ennarisi. We told how the cities and towns had maintained Roc ledges suitable for them to land on and perch, and how Rocs had taken part in councils. The villages in the shadow of the Reaches have started to build their own ledges after so many people saw the Rocs."

"There are stories of Pio saving a group of Quatoz people from creatures. Also, what looked like an effort to revitalise the old cannibal cults in the jungles. Rumours of Lak returning to the steppes in the centre, although the tellers were pretty confused about what was happening." Raglin stopped and sighed. "I think it's starting, Flin. I truly think it's starting."

Ragnor grimaced as he said, "The northern kingdoms are stirring. More than stirring, actually. They're causing trouble with raids to the icy north and their scouts are venturing into the grasslands. And there are stories of ghazrak being seen through many lands. Children are being hunted especially, but whole families are being killed. They're accompanied by northers and perhaps easterners. I have no idea how the easterners are getting across, if they are."

"That's what happened here, too," said Flin. "I think we managed to halt it, though. The common theme was that the children all displayed some sort of gift. And I don't think there are easterners, just different northers."

"Gifts?" Ragnor said around a mouthful of food. "There are gifts being found here, too?"

"Yes, and quite a few among the Faeronar," Flin replied. "There seems to be a resurgence, just as the Prophecy foresaw."

"You said 'we managed to halt it'. You and the Faero?"

"No, my friends. Me and the Children of Ennaris." Flin spoke quietly.

Ragnor stared at Flin, mouth agape, all thought of eating fleeing. Raglin slowly returned his tankard to the table as he stared likewise.

"The Children?" Raglin said in shock. "The Children have returned?"

"They have," Flin said, nodding with a smug expression.

"Where are they? Who are they?" Ragnor asked.

"They are not of Ennaris, but were from a planet they call Earth, which we think was the colony of Ordoreth that Goroth's crew tried to rule." Flin shrugged at the twins' identical grimaces. "As to where they are, look behind you."

Blaine led Jalor and Varna across the square towards the tavern. Blaine, from where he had been waiting for his colleagues, had seen the two strangers greet Flin and settle in for a discussion. So far, Flin had not demonstrated any real fellow feeling for many of the people of Ennaris, but he obviously was both familiar and comfortable with these two. Stands to reason, Blaine thought, because with his long lifespan, he would have seen so many Ennarisi come and go, so it was likely to be a defence mechanism. Still, it made Flin less effective, to Blaine's eyes. It always paid to understand the people around you at a more personal level, rather than as potential tools.

Blaine considered the two men with interest. Both had the same young-old look that Flin had, although they appeared to be quite young men. And they were identical twins, even down to the unruly mops of dark hair. They were clean-shaven, lean and somewhat angular in appearance when they stood, which they now did, and quite tall, probably close to 1.9 metres. From what Blaine recalled of Flin's stories, these would be two of the other three Mages.

The two men gazed on the three Warriors of the Light with a mix of anticipation and something close to awe. They bowed formally as Blaine reached them, the graceful bows taking in all three. Blaine sketched a salute and glanced to Flin, as Jalor manhandled a second table across to join with Flin's original one and Varna slid heavy chairs across.

Once all were seated Flin performed introductions.

"These two are my friends," Flin said. "Their names are Ragnor and Raglin" - each nodded as his name was said - "and they are two of the remaining members of the Council. My friends, meet Jalor, Varna and Blaine." Again, each of the Warriors nodded in turn. "We have much to discuss. I was starting to wonder if I would miss you" - this to the twins - "before I have to leave again. Varna and I must go to the Forest of the Guardians, and I need to go to the Council chambers."

"How soon?" Ragnor asked, or at least Blaine thought it was Ragnor. Yep, Ragnor, Blaine thought, remembering the introduction order.

"Very soon. I have been advised against dallying," Flin said dryly. "And that by someone I did not believe existed not that long ago."

"Balgor," Raglin said, and the twins nodded.

"You knew?" Flin's expression twisted as though in pain. "You also knew Balgor was here and didn't say anything?"

"Well, that rumour wasn't a secret amongst the Mages," Raglin said. "Those who paid attention to Halfgar, anyway."

"I don't recall Halfgar talking much about the Guardians at all," Flin said evenly.

"Really? Well, you younger ones didn't have as much time with him, I guess," Ragnor said with a frown.

"Wait, younger ones?" Varna looked from Ragnor to Raglin to Flin. "You two are older than Flin?"

"Oh, by about ten thousand cycles or so," Raglin said with a grin. "He always was a little impetuous and didn't listen all that well. Just wanted to get on with learning how to improve his skills and make things better. Mind you, that's what made him one of the most useful of the Guides, yet alone the Mages."

"But it does mean he probably missed out on a lot of the lore that tended to get passed along by the older Mages," Ragnor continued, with exactly the same tone of voice. "And then during the rebellion we lost so many of the older ones, including two Archmages. So much lore lost, so much knowledge lost."

"So, when Flin took on the Archmage duties there were not that many of us," Raglin said as he picked up the thread again. "I guess we just assumed you knew things like that. Did Marjory never discuss it with you? She will have known, being Halfgar's favourite."

Flin growled, which amused Jalor.

"So, the all-knowing Flin really doesn't know it all because he didn't pay attention to his lessons?" Jalor bantered.

"Yes, alright, so I was more interested in doing stuff then sitting around at the feet of the elders listening to stories." Flin paused, exasperated. "But in all of the last five thousand cycles no-one thought to mention that one of the Guardians remained on Ennaris?"

"Um, three or four of them remained, I think," Raglin said, glancing at his brother.

"Maybe five," Ragnor rejoined. "None of us were quite sure. They never advertised what they did after all. If you didn't know they were here you wouldn't have guessed at all."

"Five? There were five Guardians on Ennaris since the rebellion's end?" Flin's voice was quiet, almost glacial in tone, which Jalor thought should have been a warning to the twins.

The twins, however, were unconcerned.

"Probably five," Ragnor said. "Of course, it could have been six."

"Or seven, even," Raglin said thoughtfully. "There was that odd time, remember, when we thought we saw ..."

"Enough," Flin yelled, loud enough to elicit looks from other patrons of the tavern. He looked about, abashed, as the twins laughed, and lowered his voice again with an effort. "So, I need to learn about a few things and I have been told the Council records have what I need, so I'm heading there, with Varna and Dalresar, either before or after the Forest. I have yet to decide."

"I still want to know how you two can be older than Flin," Varna chimed in. "You don't look it."

"Why thank you," Raglin said, inclining his head to Varna.

"Always nice to know a pretty lady notices," Ragnor said. "Of course..."

"... we do take trouble from time to time with our grooming," Raglin finished, as Flin growled again.

"One of the simpler abilities all Mages seem to have is to be able to adopt an appearance and maintain it without significant effort. One Mage can tell another, despite the disguise, of course, but usually it helps to appear somewhat different." Flin glared at the twins. "Or not that different at all."

Varna thought back to Intika Ramesa's request for Flin to reveal himself, and nodded. "So, you two don't really need to look identical, do you?"

Both brothers wore the exact same smug expression as they said, "No, not really."

"I hate it when they do that," Flin said through gritted teeth, causing the twins to grin at what was obviously an old routine.

"But it fits our own purposes usually," Raglin said.

"So Flin, you said that you and Dalresar would be going to this Forest and your chambers, but what about Blaine and me?" Jalor asked. "We've been here for some time now and apart from fighting those half-man things have managed to make little head way in our mission."

"Yes, I know." Flin looked from Jalor to Blaine and back again. "I need you to instruct Corm. He has neglected his studies quite a lot and has to be brought up to speed in many things." Flin stopped to stare as Varna tried and failed to suppress a fit of giggles at Flin, who had just admitted to missing his own lessons, complaining about the same from Corm. "Don't say a word," he said warningly as the brothers grinned broadly. "Anyway, I think Jalor might be able to give him some strategy training, and Blaine weapons. Raglin and Ragnor, I would like you to instruct him in the history of Ennaris, such that a Faero needs to know."

Jalor considered and glanced to Blaine, who grimaced slightly before nodding, obviously not happy about doing so, and then Varna who simply nodded.

"Okay, so I guess we become part of the Faeronar," Jalor said.

"You have been that from the time you faced down the first of the ghazrak in defence of those families," Flin said seriously. "And your actions since then, all three of you, have only served to make that more evident."

"I think we need to be brought up to speed on a few things," Ragnor said, as Raglin nodded.

"Later," Flin said. "I will do that later this evening. For now, we have things to do in preparation for leaving tomorrow. I'm afraid I must miss Intika's sending, but he wouldn't mind that. I feel time is running out and there's much to do."

6. Sending of a Faero

Intika Ramesa's sending ceremony took place two days later. Flin, along with Varna and Dalresar, Flin's apprentice, had departed the Citadel early the previous morning, after the planning session of the night before. Jalor and Blaine had watched preparations with practised eyes, having seen many such events in their careers.

Of particular interest was the antics of a corpulent man who made a display of directing the raising of a pyre, with a bier laid out atop. With much waving of hands and loud directions to the workmen that, the two Warriors were amused to see, were completely ignored, he made a production of being seen to take charge.

Ragnor snorted as he watched with Jalor and Blaine from the tavern. Jalor and Blaine turned to him, the former quirking an eyebrow.

"That's the High Priest of the Temple of Amra. They're all the same, right across Ennaris," Ragnor said scornfully. "Well, that's not true - there's one fellow at the temple of Eresh who may be the real thing. At least, he survived Eresh's return, so she thinks he is. Made him her first disciple. And then he dissolved the temple as a religious centre but turned it into a haven for the poor and desperate. But as a rule, the priests have become the worst sort of parasite. It's even worse when you think that they are setting the Guardians up as demigods for their own purposes, usually extracting money, food and gems from those who are gullible or desperate. Amra, who really is Odruf by the way, probably is horrified. I'm not sure why they felt they needed to rename him, but everything points to them being one and the same."

"So, what can you do about it?" asked Jalor.

"Not a whole lot with the constraints we have. We can do a few things from time to time to make people see them for what they are, but otherwise we've been trying to limit the damage they do." Ragnor grinned. "Raglin likes to close in the opening to their strong-rooms, which we can do fairly quickly. Our talent is to do with building things. We are in tune with stone, rock and wood."

"Wait," Blaine said, holding up a hand. "You wall in their strong-rooms?"

"Oh yes," Ragnor said, his grin taking on a mischievous bent. "Sometimes we can make the stone walls lose cohesion, if they're not that well made, and then the strong-room just fills with rock dust."

"What good is that?" Blaine demanded. "It's just dust."

"Not when we rebind it to rock again, it's not. It just happens to have all the gold and gems embedded in it. All those priests with their vows of poverty climbing the walls because their riches can't be retrieved without hard work."

Jalor laughed while Blaine stared.

"You can do that?" Blaine asked. "Just by thinking about it?"

"Oh, it takes some planning and a lot of concentration but yes, pretty much."

"That's pretty amazing."

"Oh, it's nothing much really. You should have seen some of the buildings we worked on in Carpath. Spires with dozens of floors, floating pathways joining them together that looked like strands of gossamer threaded through the city. There were public squares of such beauty that your eyes would pop, and even the most basic of buildings were sculpted into such amazing shapes! All gone now, of course. All gone."

"Where is Carpath?" Blaine asked.

"Beneath the waves now, far beneath. It was a prime target of the rebels and took the brunt quite early of Goroth's anger and hate. Don't ever doubt the depth of hate that Goroth and his kind felt for the Council, and that spilt over to the common Ennarisi. Should you ever have occasion to doubt anything about Goroth and his followers, remember that it was pure hatred that caused them to use the most destructive weapons we had available, without care for the consequences."

"I don't think I have ever experienced hatred such that it would cause that outcome." Jalor was pensive, idly watching the fat priest cajoling the workers to greater efforts when any person watching could tell that the job was done. "I can think of a few who may have done likewise, though."

Blaine nodded. "Yes, there have been a few who would happily destroy their whole world rather than submit to justice. We have dealt with several of them."

"Oh?" Ragnor prompted. "And what happened to them?"

"All but one that I can think of are dead," Blaine replied, glancing at Jalor who nodded agreement. "Generally, they were killed by the citizens of the world they sought to destroy, mostly after trials. Not all of them were trials by the book, perhaps, but they were trials. The exception was allowed to live but with heavy penalties on him and his family, and close confinement. Of course, those were the really bad ones. Most of the people we dealt with were confined for periods of time and are likely to have been released back into their societies by now."

"You were with Flin during the fight to catch and pen Goroth?" Jalor squinted slightly as he watched the workers finish the Faero's pyre and walk away, followed by the priest who strutted away.

"You could say that. Remember we're not suited to battle, but we are very strong in our talent, so we provided strength to Marjory as she fought Goroth. She may not have needed our strength to augment her own had she not been exhausted. But she had been fighting to hold back the effects of the weapons being used by the rebels." Ragnor was looking far into the distance, or perhaps far into the past. "Marjory was the most powerful Battle Mage Ennaris has seen, but Goroth had mastered the dark arts, or a good portion of them. Flin tried to hold off Goroth's minions, supported by Hanfer and Krandol, and managed to do so, but the strain was too much for Hanfer and she died. Krandol joined us in stasis but it seems his chamber malfunctioned sometime about a thousand cycles ago. After all this time, he was killed by a malfunction."

"How many of those who sided with Goroth made it through to the end? How many survived?" Jalor turned to look at Ragnor. "And how many of them may still be alive to cause us trouble?"

The Mage waggled his head as though undecided. "There were three of power who survived, we think. Neither of the other two entered stasis with Goroth. We haven't been able to do anything against them, so we'll have them to deal with should Goroth break free. Or rather, when Goroth breaks free. They were never found and we assumed they escaped Ennaris. Likud was a moderately strong talent in battle gifts, but the talent was not paired with a great sense of tactics, thankfully. But Grensor was very strong in his talents. He was able to exercise a form of compulsion against weaker or vulnerable minds and could handle several at a single time. We have often thought that it may have been Grensor who caused many of the lesser Mages to side with Goroth."

"So, we have three of them to four of you." Blaine shook his head as he spoke. "The odds should be good, but they're not, are they?"

"On the face of it, no. Goroth was not quite as talented as Marjory but without any constraints was hard to stop. That strength will not have faded, or will regenerate quickly. Likud and Grensor probably are more than a match for the two of us and Trabor. But you never know," Ragnor said with a sly grin. "Flin has a few tricks that he always keeps up his sleeves. But," he continued with a grimace, "the odds are not great. Flin is not a Battle Mage, no matter than he probably holds his own with the greatest of the Archmages, or would if there were enough of us to make him Archmage. He doesn't believe that, of course, but I have confidence that such is the case. Halfgar told me exactly that not long before he left us. But against a rampaging Goroth? That will be difficult."

"Hmmm," Jalor said. "Well, here comes Raglin. I think we'll have to wait until after the funeral before we can start with Corm. I hope Raglin has been able to get his agreement to that."

It was the following day when Jalor and Blaine watched the priest wind up his long-winded speech. They felt a presence and turned to see Balgor coalesce from skeins of light.

"Balgor," Jalor said, calmly acknowledging the Guardian.

"Very impressive," said Blaine. "Do you appear like that all the time?"

"Oh no," said Balgor. "I'm trying out different methods of appearing. Last time I kind of faded into view but only Varna could see me. Did it work okay?"

"Yes," said Blaine, appearing to consider, "but maybe a little too long in getting through the whole routine."

"Ah, I'll think about that. Thank you." He turned to look at the bier where the priest was sprinkling some sort of liquid on the Faero's body. "That fellow is very tiring, you know. And his version of his god doesn't exist, which I'm fairly sure he knows."

"These people need something to believe in, I'm guessing. It's a shame you can't appear to them and show them what the Guardians can do. Almost all of the citadel's Faeronar are here, so it would make a good trigger for a revival of that religion or belief or whatever you would call it."

Jalor turned to Balgor with a raised eye.

"Oh no, I'm not permitted to be seen yet. Against all the rules. Would be very bad form. Besides, we're not gods, so a religion based on us would not be a great idea."

Jalor considered. "Well, how about if you were not seen but felt?"

Balgor looked at Jalor for a moment, and then grinned. "Well, I'm sure something may be possible, if only to make that pompous ass look stupid." He glanced at the bier, which several men were approaching with lighted brands. "I'll need you to help though."

The priest started another speech, telling the assembled crowd how the mighty Amra, his god, would take the Faero to his palace in paradise with the smoke from the bier, and finally directed the men to light the bier. As one, they thrust the brands into the pile of timbers on which the Faero had been placed. The priest stepped back and raised his hands, calling on Amra to take the Faero.

The lower levels of the bier took fire and burnt brightly, and stayed burning brightly, with no smoke and without burning any of the higher timbers. The priest frowned, his raised hands still held high. Someone in the crowd chuckled.

Jalor looked at Balgor, who grinned back.

Meanwhile, the priest called additional men forward with lighted brands, and they were thrust into the higher levels of the bier. However, the flames were extinguished as soon as they touched the timbers. The priest started to falter, his hands dropping to shoulder level. More brands were brought out but again they died as soon as their flames met the bier's timber. The crowd started to laugh, with comments called out about the priest's god being unable to burn wood. The priest started to sweat, and his eyes darted around as he tried to find a way out of the situation. The fire continued to burn on the lower levels of the bier, still without smoke or damage to the wood.

"Okay," said Balgor after a little more time had passed, during which time the priest was becoming frantic. "Jalor, would you announce me, please?"

"Me? I'm not from around here, remember? And I'm not sure I want to be remembered as the one to reignite the old religion."

"Reignite? Very good," said Balgor, and Blaine laughed, then laughed again when Jalor fixed him with a baleful glare.

Jalor stepped forward, still regarding Balgor grimly, until he realised that anyone watching him would only see him staring at empty space. He sighed.

"Hear me!" he declaimed, as he moved towards the bier. The priest watched him warily, gesturing for his cronies to deal with Jalor. As Blaine moved up to stand with Jalor and rested his hand on the hilt of his sword – the normal one, the broadsword stayed on his back – they stopped and shuffled uncertainly. The priest glared.

"Hear me!" Jalor called again, his voice seeming to boom out across the citadel. Jalor directed a glacial glance at Balgor who smiled innocently, "The Faero has been called to the Guardians and must be honoured as tradition demands."

He waved his hand negligently over the flames, hoping Balgor was paying attention, and was relieved when the flames guttered and died. The wood remained unburned. The priest goggled and the assembly murmured to themselves, and then the murmurs turned to gasps.

Jalor suddenly realised he was bathed in the last rays of the sun. To the watching Blaine, who found himself holding in unwonted laughter, Jalor appeared to have a golden nimbus. Jalor sighed to himself.

"Amra is no god. The one you know as Amra is Odruf, one of the Guardians of Ennaris, one of the helpers of the Ennarisi. Odruf," said Jalor, suddenly realising he did not know if Odruf was male or female, "has returned to assist the Ennarisi in their times of trial, as have the other Guardians of old. Intika Ramesa has been a strong and dutiful servant of the Faeronar and the Ennarisi, and has been recognised so by the Guardians. I call on the Guardians to take Intika Ramesa to them, to receive the reward earned by his devotion to duty." He halted as the beam of light moved to cover the still form of the Faero atop the unburned bier, accompanied by a collective intake of breath by the crowd. "Take your servant in glory, O Guardians, and show the Faeronar the true worth of their Faero."

Jalor stepped back as the light flared to a blinding incandescence. As it slowly faded, a coruscation of bright motes swirled from the bier, lifting through the air in spirals and swirls, going ever higher until they were lost from view in the now deepening gloom. Every watcher was held spellbound until the light faded away, and then the assembled crowd called out in shock and awe as they returned their gaze to the bier. It now was without its burden of the Faero's body but still stood with unburned timbers intact.

The priest moaned and moved away from the bier as fast as he could, surrounded by his men as though he was in danger, but the crowd were paying him no attention at the moment. Almost as one they knelt to the bier and then, in unison, turned to Jalor, who regarded the throng grimly.

"Stand, people of the Faeronar," Jalor said quietly, his voice carrying easily in the shattering silence. "Remember this day and tell all who ask that the Prophecy of the Guardians is at hand. Stand ready to support your Faero when he is called."

With that, Jalor turned and walked away from the crowd, accompanied by Blaine and Balgor.

"That was impressive and I must say quite moving," Jalor said quietly to Balgor without looking at him.

"It was appropriate," replied Balgor quietly, responding to Jalor's tone. "Intika was a good one. He would have fit in during the glory days. It's a shame he was not the one called. And he hated all priests of the false religions. He will be honoured though. I promise that, and he shall return to a life commensurate with his reward."

Jalor looked at Blaine and they both stopped in their tracks.

"Return?" said Blaine, as they looked at each other in shock and then both turned to Balgor. "What do you mean, return?"

But they were speaking to thin air.

7. Hooded Saviour

The day was young as the tall stranger walked into the village. He was clad in a heavy woven shirt and tough breeches of a dark hue, almost black. Sturdy boots were visible under the rim of his travelling cloak. The hood of the cloak was up and his features were obscured. It was enough to give watchers the impression of a young man, but nothing else.

He walked confidently, looking to neither left nor right as he made his way through the outskirts to the centre of the village. He knew where he was heading, having scouted the village for the last day and night. Nearing the centre of the village he slowed, eyes darting all round to see if anything had changed. Nothing had. All was as he expected.

In front of him, chained to a post in the centre of the square, were two children, a boy and a girl. Both showed signs of having been beaten. The boy sported a black eye and a split lip and the stranger could see a range of bruises. The girl had a similar array of bruises to arms and legs, and what appeared to be a welt of some sort across her face. Probably an attempt at disfigurement, the stranger thought. Both were dressed in little more than rags. A small bowl of water was placed on the ground a short distance from where they leaned, exhausted, against the pole to which they were chained.

Keeping his rising anger under tight control, the stranger walked up to the children and crouched low, so he could examine them better. Both cringed away from him. He made no gesture, nor did he say anything to them, merely examined them closely from head to toe. Each was about twelve cycles in age and were obviously related to each other, probably brother and sister, possibly twins. The stranger took note of others approaching but finished his examination before rising and turning.

Five men lined up facing him, with belligerence oozing from several of them. The stranger merely waited. The silence stretched and the five men started to feel uncomfortable, looking at each other. The truculence melted away in the face of the stranger's seeming lack of concern at being confronted. The tension stretched. Nerves stretched with it until finally one of the men broke.

"What do you think yer doin'," he demanded of the stranger.

"Why, I'm checking to see that the children" - emphasis on children - "are being treated well. I see that is not the case. Why are these young ones chained and why have they been beaten?"

The first man sneered. "They're bein' held for the constable. He'll know what to do with 'em."

"That does not explain why you big brave men are beating young children, or why they are being held in the first place."

The disdain with which the stranger addressed the men rankled, even as one of them looked somewhat ashamed.

"'Tweren't my idea to hit 'em," that one said.

"Shut it, Fres," the first man snarled.

"Won't," Fres replied. "I tol' you they shouldna be beaten, Grew. I tol' you I didna take to that."

Grew ignored Fres and turned back to the stranger, who still stood calmly, facing them. There was something in the back of Grew's mind, something he had heard. It would come to him sooner or later.

"If ya know what's good for ya yu'll leave now," Grew said, with bluster replacing truculence as the man seemed to be unmoved by his threats.

"Well, I think I'll await the constable then," the man said agreeably. "Meantime, these children need food and fresh water, and they need medical care. See to that, would you?"

The man turned his back on the five and bent once more to the children. Grew, nonplussed, realised he had been dismissed by this stranger. His anger grew but, again, there was something. Never a brave person, being much more at home with beating children, Grew decided that he would leave the stranger to the constable.

Fres, on the other hand, felt his guilt rise. Turning, he walked away from the small group of villagers and made his way to his small cottage. Why he joined with Grew and the other trouble-makers he could not say. Had his Nresa still been alive she would have stopped him, he knew. Shame turned his face red as he walked, thinking of what Nresa would have said to him now. She would have been one who would be out there standing with the stranger, feeding and caring for the children. Fres had been aimless since she had gone and had fallen in with Grew and his friends, none of whom were his own friends, he knew. They would allow him to buy their drinks, which he did on occasion, but they were not friends.

Arriving at his cottage, Fres rummaged through the few stores he had, pulling some roots and fruit from the cold store dug into the floor. He bundled them up and then walked to old Hulla's cottage where he purchased some of her baked pastries. Finally, he returned to his own cottage and pulled out two drinking mugs. All went into his sack, which he slung over his shoulder. Fres left his cottage and made his way back to the small village square. Grew and his friends were standing by one side, glaring at the stranger, who was bent over the children.

"Now," the stranger said to the girl and boy, looking from one to the other, "I need you to stay calm, no matter what happens. You will be safe with me, and shortly I'm going to take you somewhere safe. Okay?"

The children stared at him, uncertain. Safe was not a clear concept for them at the moment. And they did not know this man who stood up to the village bullies as though they meant nothing.

"So, tell me your names, please," the stranger said. "You can call me Maf. That's what my friends call me, and I think you'll both be my friends."

The boy was unsure, but the girl narrowed her gaze as she stared at Maf and then nodded. She glanced to her brother and nodded again.

"My name is Hulse Borm," she replied. "My brother is Kronse Borm."

"You have had your true naming days," Maf said, nodding at the names. "Well met Hulse Borm, Kronse Borm. You are of the Blood?"

Both children lifted their heads and the boy, Kronse Borm, spoke for the first time.

"We are of the Blood," he said, pride pushing through the fear.

"One of those men comes," Hulse Borm said to Maf.

Maf stood and turned to confront Fres, who approached the three carefully. He looked from Maf to the two children and placed the sack on the ground. Bending, he extracted the small wrapped pastries and handed one each to the children, and then the two mugs.

"You will need fresh water to drink," he said, and walked to the well.

Maf showed a small smile and looked to the children.

"Not everyone is evil in these matters," he said to the children. "Some are misguided, as I believe this man is."

"He's Fres," Kronse Borm said around a mouthful of pastry. "He's the village thatcher. My da," he choked a bit as he thought of his father but continued with a smaller voice, "my da said he was one of the better ones."

"Your parents," Maf said. "Were they killed by strangers?"

"They were," Hulse Borm replied, wiping her hands on her tattered clothes to remove the greasy residue from the pastry, and her eyes filled with tears. "We were not at home and returned to find them both dead."

"When was this?"

"Two tendays ago," Kronse Borm said, a tear running down his cheek.

"And you have been alone, fending for yourself, since then?"

"Hulla has helped us sometimes," Hulse Borm said. "But we have been alone. Grew and his friends beat anyone else who tried to help us.

And he made up stories about ma and da, accusing them of things they never did."

"And you," Maf said gently, "can you do things?"

The two children glanced one to the other and stayed quiet, which gave Maf his answer. At that time Fres returned with two mugs of water, which he placed on the ground in front of the children.

"I'm sorry I took part in this," he said to the children, before looking to Maf. "I'm not sure why I did."

"There are times when evil overcomes the best of men," Maf said. "Do you have the key to the shackles?"

"No," Fres said. "Grew keeps it with him all the time."

"Ah," Maf said. "Never mind. We don't need it anyway."

Smoothly, Maf reached out and touched the shackles where they were locked around the children's wrists. The grips unlocked and the shackles fell to the ground with a soft clatter. The children and Fres stared at the shackles and then at Maf, who merely smiled.

"Now, we're going to have a problem here shortly, for the so-called constable comes. I want the three of you to stay here and stay out of the way. Okay?" Maf turned his earnest gaze on all three, starting with Hulse Borm, then Kronse Borm and finally Fres.

"We can fight," Hulse Borm said. "Our da was teaching us."

"I don't doubt that," Maf replied, nodding seriously. "You are of the Blood. But you don't have any weapons and these men have swords and knives. And there are only six of them."

"Six?" Fres looked at Maf as though he was crazy, but the man seemed to be confident and there was nothing Fres could do.

"If Grew and his friends don't take part," Maf said, rising and turning.

He faced the end of the square where six men had appeared and were striding across the square carrying their own importance with them. Grew hurried across to them and had a brief and obviously uncomfortable conversation before bobbing his head and scuttling back to where his three friends stood against a cottage wall. The six came towards the children, hands on sword hilts.

"Northers," Maf said, looking down at Fres. "Your constables are northers."

Fres stared, turning to look at the oncoming men. Northers? How could the constables be northers? He looked back to where Grew and his gang were watching, grinning broadly in anticipation.

Maf watched the oncoming men. The six arranged themselves so that they walked as a single line. They stopped some distance away from Maf and stared at him. Maf merely gazed back. His face was composed and calm, almost bored looking. After a slow count of twenty the leader of the six took a single step forward.

"Hand over the abominations," he snarled, "and we might let you live."

"Ah," Maf replied, nodding. "If you refer to these children, then no, I will not be handing them over. And who are you to make this demand, norther?"

The leader's eyes widened and his men shifted slightly, for Maf had spoken loudly, loud enough for onlookers to hear. There were now quite a few onlookers whose interest had sharpened at those words.

"I am Grelmas. I am constable of this region. I am the law!" Grelmas' jaw tightened, as a lawman's may do when faced with someone defying his authority. "I order you to step away or face the consequences."

"You and your friends are norther spies," Maf replied easily, "sent here to create discord and chaos and to kill as many children who display the old gifts as you can find. You have no authority here. And you will not have these children."

Grelmas was shocked. Who was this man to know those details? No matter. But it meant he had to die now. Grelmas looked left and right and nodded, then turned back to Maf and paused again. In the moment when he had turned away Maf had shrugged out of his cloak, which now lay in a puddle near his feet. He was a tall, lean, young-looking man, with pale brown hair tied back by a thong so that it tailed partway down his back. His clothes were a uniform almost-black. The shirt had sleeves that extended three parts of the way to his wrists, and had a deep V-shaped neckline that was loosely held together by a cord. His trousers were well fitted but not tight and he wore soft boots of the same colour. Thin and plain sword scabbards hung from his belt to each side. Suddenly, this man did not look like an easy target.

Maf took two steps forward, creating some separation from the children and Fres. He raised his eyebrows questioningly as though asking: what are you going to do?

Grelmas pulled his sword from his own scabbard, and from his other hip he pulled a knife. Neither were of good quality but Maf knew they could leave you just as dead. The other five northers did likewise. Maf nodded, observing as the six adopted a posture he knew well. These were partly trained, as many northers were, but their stances were sloppy, their swords were held too low and their knives were not in the right position to defend or attack. They were accustomed to superior numbers winning out.

With a fluid motion Maf crossed his arms and extracted his swords, the sound of perfectly tempered metal being released ringing across the square. Where the six swords facing him were dull and pitted, Maf's slender swords gleamed, shone in the light of the twin suns. The six stared at the two swords, held away from Maf's body at forty-five degrees to each side, as he had been taught so long ago. They seemed to be too narrow to be of any real use. Grelmas snarled and looked back to Maf, seeking to intimidate. Maf smiled.

"Shall we?" Maf asked politely.

Grelmas snarled again and charged across the square with his sword and knife wavering as he did so. His companions were slower off the mark but followed. Maf took another step forward and then pivoted smoothly and, taking two quick steps to his left, placing himself in front of the two to Grelmas' right. Those two shouted and swung their swords hard at Maf's unprotected body.

Maf was no longer there. With lightning quick actions, Maf knocked aside the two swords, one to each side, avoided the knives that were being wielded with energy if not skill, and darted between the two. His own swords flashed to left and right as he did so, their razor edges easily slicing through the boiled leather breast and back plates and leaving deep cuts into the sides of his two opponents. Both stopped and stared at the blood bubbling from their sides before Maf's swords pierced them both from behind. The two fell.

Grelmas and the other three were well out of position. This was a dangerous point, for in making his move Maf left the children and Fres unprotected. However, as he expected, the northers were now fixed on destroying him. Grelmas swung around when he found himself charging at air and gaped as his two men collapsed, unmoving. The other three stumbled to a halt and tried to charge back but now they were well out of position and got in each other's way. Into the melee Maf darted, his swords flicking out to inflict painful cuts on Grelmas and the closest of the other men. He darted back again to create clearance and waited.

Grelmas looked at the blood running from the cuts to both of his arms. He pushed the pain away before lifting his sword and charging at Maf again. This time Maf took two quick steps and launched himself high in the air, pushing himself against the air behind while drawing himself into the air in front, for one of his lesser gifts was working with air. He landed lightly behind the rear-most of the four and wiped his right sword across the exposed throat before thrusting the left into the chest of the next closest as he turned back.

Once again, Maf stepped back. Grelmas stared at him, knowing he faced someone who was in a league so far above his own skill level as to be laughable. He had no choice, of course, for he would be dead if he returned with his mission a failure. He glanced to Beles, the only other one of his troop who was still alive. They separated to attack Maf from each side, seeking to hem him in and harass him until one could force an opening to cut him down. They were faced with a dazzling series of sword strokes. Each of their own attempted strikes were batted away by those apparently too slender swords and a growing number of nicks and cuts appeared on their arms and legs. The edges of Maf's swords sliced through the northers' clothes without effort. Both were bleeding from numerous cuts. Maf continued to block them both and then Grelmas stepped back to free his arms further. Unexpectedly, he found Maf had followed him and as he swung his sword back, he felt the bite of one of those slender swords. Looking down he saw the tiny trickle of blood start from the middle of his chest.

Maf had already turned both swords on Beles, who could only back up. A sequence of strokes that were so fast that Beles could not follow them caused him to swing blindly. Maf's two swords flicked out one last time. Beles was pierced through the neck and the body. His last sight was of Grelmas falling, face first, into the dust of the village square. His own lifeless body followed a moment after.

Maf stepped back and glanced one by one to each of the six. He could tell that all were dead. These six had been better than any of the others he had encountered. Maf shook the swords free of any remaining blood and sheathed them smoothly. Then a shout caused Maf to turn. Grew and his friends were running from townspeople who had tried to detain them. Grew ran with a knife in one hand. Maf pushed a hardened skein of air at them, tripping them so they all fell in a heap. The townspeople fell on the bullies. But they had been running from where the children were being held. Maf spun. Fres was on his knees in front of the children, holding one hand tight against his side. He locked eyes with Maf before collapsing.

Maf was at Fres' side in a moment, rolling the man on his back. A gash leaked blood copiously.

"Grew tried to kill the childers," Fres said weakly.

"And you stood between them," Maf said. "You protected the children."

"Wasna right what we done," Fres sighed. "At least done the right thing before dyin'."

Maf squinted as he looked down and examined the wound, saying nothing in reply. After a few moments he laid both hands over the deep wound and concentrated. Fres gasped as new pain swept through him, but then he felt warmth and the pain lessened. Looking down he saw the wound had closed. The blood that had flowed out still ran down his side, but no new blood appeared.

"How... who..." Fres stammered.

Maf smiled.

"I'll be back to continue that," he said. "Just lie easy now while I deal with the others."

He looked to the two children, both of whom were watching with wide eyes.

"Would you both stay with Fres for me, please?" Maf asked them. "I will heal your hurts shortly, and then we can leave."

Without waiting for nods, Maf stood smoothly and walked to where Grew and his bully gang were being held. The townspeople watched Maf approach with apprehension, unsure of what he may do or say. Maf ignored them as a whole, concentrating on Grew.

"You were in league with norther spies," Maf said.

"You don't know what yer talkin' about," Grew sneered. "And you lot'll get your beatin's when this one is gone, let me tell you."

He looked around the gathered crowd, and his confidence took a dive. No-one looked away from him. No-one spoke up for him. Finally, one of the villagers did speak.

"Can you prove what you say, stranger?" a man in the stained clothes of a tanner asked of Maf.

"One of you go over to the so-called constable and take a look in his pocket," Maf directed, gesturing to the bodies still lying in the square. "I'm betting you will find a purse filled with red gold. That's what I have found other northers carrying."

The tanner looked at him, understanding what was unspoken that this stranger had met and defeated others like this. The tanner walked to Grelmas' body and gingerly felt through the clothes, finally pulling a leather purse from an inside pocket of his shirt. He walked back to the crowd of villagers, tugging the drawstring of the purse open as he did so. He glanced inside and pursed his lips. Wordlessly, he turned the purse upside down. Red gold coins cascaded from the purse and formed a pile on the dirt at his feet.

Grew struggled to get free, while another of the villagers roughly tore open his shirt, exposing a smaller purse on a drawstring tied around Grew's neck. With a disdainful tug he snapped the drawstring and pulled the purse open, glancing inside. He, too, turned the purse upside down. The coins that spilled forth were a mix of copper and small silver coin, and amidst them were ten red gold coins, identical to the norther coins.

"These men have been looking for children who display signs of the old gifts," Maf said to the villagers while gesturing to both the dead northers and the bullies being held. "Throughout this part of Ennaris children are being hunted, because the gifts are returning. The old enemy will return, so the Tellers say, and in preparation they seek to ensure that none of the gifts are available."

"Who are you?" one of the villagers finally asked.

"I am one who protects this part of Ennaris, who protects these children. I am one who will find these agents of the enemy where I can and stop them. But I need you, each and every villager, to keep a watch so that you don't fall back into this evil. I'm taking these children with me to safety, but I will be watching, and others will be watching." Maf looked around the villagers, many of whom failed to meet his gaze. "Some of my friends are not as forgiving as me."

With that veiled threat given, Maf left the villagers and returned to where the children crouched. Fres still lay at their feet but Maf was impressed as the children stood over him protectively. Behind him, the villagers roughly threw Grew and his gang to the ground while they were bound by some drawstrings that the tanner produced. Maf gave them no further thought as he crouched by Fres. Once again, he placed his hands over the site of the injury and the remaining damage melted away. The site of the cut could no longer be seen.

"Be careful of this for a few days," Maf said to Fres, "as the healing may not be complete inside, although I feel that it is. But then you should be good as new."

"I thank you stranger. After what I did, I'm not sure this is deserved." Fres looked abashed as he spoke.

"That you stood for the children speaks more for you than the prior actions," Maf said. "But my warning to the villagers must be taken up. Any children who display the old gifts are to be protected. They are to be valued. If there is concern then pass the word through the villages that Maf is wanted and I will return."

Maf turned his attention to the children.

"Now then," he said cheerfully. "Let's get you two back on your feet and then you can come with me. I have many such as yourselves under my care, and two more will be more welcome than I can tell you."

8. After Sending

Jalor was frustrated. He had spent the morning waiting for Corm to appear and was waiting still. This was the third day in a row when the Faero-elect had slept late after what Jalor assumed was another late-night carousing session. With Flin having left the Citadel, and Clofta being engaged with an outbreak of some form of fever, there was no-one who could influence the young man to start training for his responsibilities.

Ragnor and Raglin had left the Citadel on some form of mission that Jalor did not learn of until they had left, although he had received a brief note promising a speedy return to assist with Corm's lagging education. The guards were being re-organised following the departure of the former chamberlain, amid further revelations of red gold being found in his quarters and those of his key lieutenants, proving that much of the administration of the Citadel had been compromised and at risk. In turn, the standing of Jalor and Blaine was raised even further. Both had been amused that their heightened reputations had been because they were companions of the Lady.

Blaine had decided to take over some of the training and had developed a coterie of his own, starting with the first day of training. Jalor still smiled when he thought about it. The remaining members of the guard and the Citadel watch, plus a number of new recruits, had been brought together by Almin Bor, who had accepted the position of Captain of the guard until such time as he could return to his farm. To understand what material he had, Blaine had demanded that every man should shoot ten arrows at targets, followed by demonstrating the basics of sword-play. To his dismay none of the guards had been able to hit the target at a distance of fifty paces more than three times out of ten, and the swordplay of many was poor, including some of those who had been involved in the recent fighting.

What was worse, one of the new recruits - there was always one, Blaine said afterwards - was belittling the efforts of the others. He was one who managed to hit the target three times, and scored the best over-all although without hitting anywhere near the bulls-eye. Blaine was not impressed and let them know it.

"Is that the best you can offer?" he challenged the group after the archery display. "If you have to fire at an enemy and you can't hit a target only fifty paces away, you'll be dead before you know where you are." He turned to Almin Bor. "We will have to make target practice one of the more important parts of training."

"Oh, come on," said Weltar Gorth, the new recruit. "Not everyone is that bad. I hit the target three times from my ten shafts, and missed by the barest margin so would have hit someone other than the one targeted. Some of these others need more practice, I agree, but I think not me."

"Is that so," Blaine said evenly, looking into the smirking face of Weltar Gorth. "And if they are separated and coming at you in a stag-gered skirmish formation you just miss. If there are four of them and you have ten shafts, you're dead, and that's if you can keep up the fire as you are attacked."

"Well, I've not seen you do anything except criticise," Weltar Gorth said dismissively. "I doubt you can do better, and I don't want to follow someone who is all talk."

Almin Bor stared at Weltar Gorth at this statement, recalling Blaine downing ghazrak one after the other during the retreat to the Citadel with the Blood families. Some of the veterans just shook their heads, then smiled knowingly as Blaine calmly nodded and picked up the very bow that had been used by Weltar Gorth.

"So, if I can beat your three from ten, you'll take part in the practice sessions?"

Seemingly without serious thought Blaine was plucking shafts from a quiver-full that he emptied in front of the group, although Almin Bor knew he was selecting the straightest of the ones available.

"If you can beat my three? I was the champion in my home town of Fregnor, not beaten for the last three cycles. At fifty paces you won't beat me."

Weltar Gorth almost strutted as he spoke. His arrogance caused frowns to appear on the faces of many of the group gathered, veterans and new recruits alike.

"Hmmm," Blaine mused. "You haven't answered my question. Will you agree to my training if I shoot better than you?"

"Sure," Weltar Gorth said blithely, waving one hand as though to dismiss the idea, and then smiled confidently. "But if you don't then I am made lieutenant."

"Well, that's not my call," Blaine said in return. "Almin Bor is the captain, and that will be his decision. Almin Bor, if I lose will you accept Weltar Gorth as your lieutenant?"

Almin Bor appeared to seriously consider the idea.

"Well," he said judiciously, "if he shoots better than you then I guess he deserves it. In fact, if he shoots better than me, he can be Captain."

Blaine nodded seriously, while Weltar Gorth grinned again. Several of the veterans hid smiles behind sudden coughing fits, while others seemed to be having difficulty breathing.

"Maybe you should shoot first, then," Blaine said. "Just to make that decision clear."

Nodding, Almin Bor stepped up to the mark, taking his bow from where it was slung over his shoulder and extracting the first shaft from the quiver sling across his back. He fitted the shaft, aimed and let fly, to see his arrow fly just over the target. Weltar Gorth smiled expansively, a smile that faltered when Almin Bor's second and third shafts found the target in the third ring of five around the bulls-eye. The smile evaporated when Almin Bor's remaining seven arrows all found the target, with two brushing the bulls-eye.

"I guess you stay captain," one of the veterans remarked to Almin Bor. "What happened to the first one?"

"New string," Almin Bor stated. "This was my first shoot with it."

Blaine now stepped up to the mark and fitted the first shaft. He raised it to aim and then hesitated. He looked around as though considering and then called out one of the veteran guards who had been with the small group defending the families.

"Bunter, would you move the target another thirty paces back, please?"

With a knowing smile, Bunter did exactly that. Weltar Gorth was eyeing Blaine uncertainly now, and watched intently as Blaine stood relaxed at the mark. Blaine nodded his thanks as Bunter returned to the ranks, ostentatiously took aim at the target and let fly. The shaft flew true and hit the bulls-eye dead centre. Weltar Gorth stared, while several of the new recruits looked at Blaine in awe. The veterans merely nodded - having seen Blaine's skill with a broad sword they knew they were in the presence of a master. Still, the accuracy with a first shot surprised most of them. Bunter merely smiled. A short time later all of the watchers were looking at Blaine in awe. The second shaft was fired with almost nonchalant ease, followed in such rapid progression by the rest of the ten that at any one time there were two or three in flight. Jalor had seen Blaine do that before, for it was one of his training routines, but he remained impressed every time he saw it. The result was a cluster of ten shafts in the bulls-eye.

"So," Blaine said to Weltar Gorth as he returned the latter's bow, "I expect to see you at target practice each day until I say you are skilled enough."

Weltar Gorth merely nodded, still staring at the target.

"Now, swords," said Blaine as he moved towards the practice area that had been established for the purpose. He was followed by the group, several of whom turned to look at the target again.

But Corm had not taken part, nor had he responded to the overtures of Jalor. He was considering ways and means of doing something when he saw the Faero-elect enter the square with a group of hangers-on, laughing loudly and slapping each other's backs. Corm was slightly unsteady on his feet, as were several of the group. Coming from the opposite direction was a smaller group of four men who, Jalor knew, were visitors to the Citadel. All were heavily armed and were quietly discussing something between themselves.

Jalor watched as one of Corm's party deliberately shouldered his way through the four men, who stopped as one. The last in the smaller group grabbed hold of the interloper and, with nonchalant ease, threw him to the ground, holding him down with one boot to his chest. The rest of Corm's group took umbrage and, with what they thought was a threatening air, confronted the four men, loudly demanding the four let their friend up or face the consequences.

"As soon as he apologises," one of the four said, "he gets up."

He looked at the one pinned to the ground, whose struggles to rise had no effect on the boot holding him in place.

"Are you going to apologise?"

Bravado brought a sneer to the face of the one on the ground and he spat on the boot holding him down, only to receive a slap across the face by a leather glove. Stunned, he looked for help to his friends.

The group looked a little uncertain until one of them loudly shouted, "You can't do that. Don't you know who this is?" He pushed Corm forward. "This is the Faero of all of Ennaris, and he commands you to let Arfor up."

"This is the Faero? This one can't piss in his own shoe, I expect." The speaker of the four looked at Corm, who squirmed under the gaze, uncomfortable at being pushed forward and now realising he may face trouble. "Well, boy? Are you going to order us to let him go?"

"Y-yes," Corm stammered, "I am. Let him up or face the wrath of the Faero," he concluded, looking for support at the grinning faces around him.

The grins evaporated as all four men drew swords and knives. The boot still held Arfor down.

"Make us," the speaker said calmly, holding his sword under Corm's chin.

Corm swallowed nervously, staring at the blade pointing directly at his throat. He lifted his eyes to the speaker of the four, who was calm still but whose gaze in return was implacable.

"Um, my friends won't let you do anything," he said weakly.

"Friends? What friends," the speaker said, dropping the sword slightly so Corm could look around.

With a start, he saw the last of his group running around the corner of the square, leaving Corm along with the four men, and Arfor still pinned in place.

Jalor sighed and stood. He saw Balgor appear at a point behind the four men but gestured to him that all was well. He knew the four men would not do anything to Corm but humiliate him. Jalor started across the square, aiming to come upon them from Corm's side so the four were not surprised, not that he thought they would be.

"You think you're pretty big, being Faero an' all, but I think you're too small for those britches," the speaker said. "I think you should drop them."

Corm stared. "W-what?"

"You heard, drop them britches," the leader of the four men said, still calm, still implacable.

With nervous fingers Corm undid his belt and opened the top buttons of his flies, after which his britches slid down to form a puddle around his feet. Unfortunately for Corm he was wearing nothing beneath and his manhood was on display for all to see. Two of the four men laughed openly, while the leader merely regarded Corm with pity.

"Not much to play with, have you?" he asked as Jalor finally made it to Corm's side.

"Enough I think," Jalor said, standing beside Corm, hands well clear of his sword.

"And you are?"

"Vinca Jalor," Jalor replied, "and I would appreciate it if you ended your little demonstration now."

"Jalor," mused the man holding Arfor down. "Are you the one who led the resistance to the attack?"

"Yes," said Jalor, "although the Guard did most of the fighting."

"But you took on two by yourself, as I heard it."

"At the end, but the fight was won by then," Jalor said.

The four men shared glances and then, with one accord, sheathed their swords and knives. Arfor found himself freed and immediately crawled away before jumping up and running as fast as he could from the square. Corm remained standing.

"Cover yourself," Jalor said to Corm, not bothering to hide his disgust, and then turned to the four. "Can I buy you a drink? You look like you may have built up a thirst."

The four grinned and nodded.

"Teaching is thirsty work," the leader of the four said, "and we would be glad to drink with the Hero of the Citadel."

Jalor grimaced. "The what?"

The four laughed as one, clearly appreciating Jalor's reluctance to be seen as a hero.

"The Hero of the Citadel is what the songs are calling you. And your friend is the Blademaster. Is he here by the way?" The leader looked around the square.

"Over by the corner there," Jalor said, nodding in the direction where he had seen Blaine take up station. Blaine was returning arrows to a quiver, with a long bow standing by his side.

"How far would we have got if all of that was for real?" asked the one who had held Arfor down.

"You would have all been dead or seriously wounded before you had the chance to swing at Corm." Jalor made the statement matter of fact, without any arrogance or change of intonation.

"But you would have gone down anyway," the leader said thoughtfully. "Is he worth that?"

"He may not be yet but his position is," said Jalor as he led the way to the usual tavern. "What songs?"

Corm was left where he stood, red-faced with humiliation, struggling to do up his belt.

The next day saw a change of heart for Corm. The realisation that his supposed friends were not the sort to stand with him, but were the sort to drink his money quite happily, and the scorn with which he had been treated by Jalor, who Corm knew was held in high regard in the Citadel, had stung. The sheer lack of capability that he had displayed when confronted by the four men showed him that he was unable to defend himself, let alone the Citadel. Finally, as he was trying to move quietly from the square he was followed by laughter and crude comments from many of the onlookers, those who lived in the Citadel and should have been looking to him for leadership.

To his credit, he spent the night in soul-searching. His thoughts were in turmoil still the following morning when, after a poor night, he decided to take a walk around the Citadel. He knew all of the seedier parts of the Citadel where he preferred to roam, and endured a few comments from the earlier risers as he walked along the path inside the wall, thinking and re-thinking of the events and what he could have done better. The first thing, he realised, was that he should not have been with that group of hangers-on anyway. The second was that the four men would not have done anything to him beyond severe embarrassment, but if they had wanted to then without Jalor's intervention, and probably in spite of it, they could have killed him easily. Without even raising a sweat, he thought sourly.

He walked through the usual haunts and into an area where he did not go in the normal course. The buildings were even more derelict here. Dark alleys were issuing noisome smells as he walked past. Corm took a fresh interest in what he saw. He realised that he had never really given thought to the people who were struggling to live in the Citadel.

His father had always said that you cannot help everybody, and he had never really stopped to think about where that policy can lead. The parents or parents' parents may not have wanted help but Corm was seeing children, almost naked and showing signs of being malnourished. Some of the dwellings probably were not fit for habitation. The earlier generations who did not want help consigned the later ones to filth and squalor. And that did not consider those who never wanted to live like this but were forced to by whatever circumstances had overtaken them.

Corm began to feel ashamed that he was not aware that these conditions existed but as he continued to walk, and as he continued to take notice of his surroundings, he began to get angry. By the time he turned a corner and came upon two men who were casually stripping another, who was obviously dead, of any useful goods, Corm was angrier than he had ever been. When the two men looked at him and then dismissed him as a problem his anger exploded. Picking up a discarded length of wood he yelled at the two men and charged at them.

"Get away from him," he shouted as he swung wildly at the nearest thief, missing him entirely and barely missing being impaled on the knife swung in his direction.

"Go about yer own bizniss, mate," the second thief said in a low threatening tone, pulling his own knife from the back of the dead man. "Or you can join Bogger here. In fact, you look like you might have some coin, and we can always use that, eh Cred?"

The other thief, Cred, gave a malicious grin and said, "Yep. Looks like he might be well heeled. And him with only that little bit o' wood."

Both thieves turned to Corm, who now suddenly was feeling foolish and not a little scared, but tried to hold firm. His father always said that confidence would get you further than you would think. But then again, Intika Ramesa usually carried a rather large sword and knew how to use it.

"Move away now, and put down those knives," Corm said, holding the length of wood in front of him defensively, or what he hoped was defensively.

"Or what?" Cred said derisively. "Ya gonna wave that wood about a bit more? Hmmpf," he snorted, "you've bitten off more than you can chew, and now ye can chew on steel."

"Oh, I doubt that will be necessary," said a fourth man as he strode forward, followed by an enormous slavering red demon with one great big eye and huge fangs like tusks emerging from its wide mouth. A pair of wicked looking horns stuck up from its forehead and, oddly, it wore a loin cloth. Gigantic knuckles at the end of thickly muscled arms dragged on the ground as it stumped along on legs that were the size of tree trunks.

The two thieves took one look at the apparition and fled. Corm, transfixed by the sight, merely stood in place as the sandy-haired man walked up to him and smiled sardonically.

"Well, that got their attention," he said, waving one hand negligently. The demon disappeared. "I think Varna would have liked that one. I made a few changes," he continued, as though Corm would know what he was talking about.

"Wh-who are you?" Corm stammered, still holding his piece of wood.

"Well, that's something we need to discuss," said the stranger. "I think you can drop your, um, weapon. We can go to my place. It's not far from here and there are some things you need to know. It's my job, or part of my job, to tell you."

"You know me?" Corm was struggling to make any sense of the events that had just occurred. "And what was that thing? And where did it go?"

"Well, yes, I know you. Have done since you were born. And your father and his father and his father and so on. And that was my demon. Pretty impressive, eh? I've been making improvements since Varna left so she has something really impressive when she comes back. He's not real, of course, but most people don't realise that. I let him go back to where he comes from."

"Where's that?" Corm continued to reel, but curiosity overcame his fear.

"Why, from in here, of course," the stranger replied, tapping the side of his head.

"I'm not going anywhere until I know who you are, and you can't make me." Corm said belligerently, trying to establish some form of power base for himself in the exchange, which promptly evaporated.

"I am Balgor," said the stranger with a shrug. "And if I wanted to put you on another planet I could do so with a thought - for real - but that would upset Varna and she's pretty special to me, so I don't want to do that. Actually, it would upset a whole lot of people."

Balgor? The Guardian? Corm was completely lost now.

"Balgor? The Guardian?" he said, his voice rising in shock.

"Yes, that's me." Balgor sighed. "Yes, I know I don't exist and neither do the rest of the Guardians and the Mages and the evil Goroth and so on, and so on. Except that I do, and they do, and you need to understand a few things. So, can we go now? I promise you it's not far, and then you can find Jalor and apologise to him and the twins and they can start on your proper education, the one you've neglected for the whole of your life."

Jalor was at the training ground, watching Blaine put several members of the Citadel guard through their paces. Weltar Gorth was one of the men working on the use of his sword and was putting up a pretty good showing. Now that he had lost his attitude of superiority, mostly, he was proving to be a likely recruit. Several of the veteran guards had improved their sword-play as well, while most of the rest could at least hit what they hacked at, which often was enough. In another section of the yard pike-men were going through their own training motions, with Almin Bor overseeing them. Jalor had taken one look at the shields the Faeronar were using and decided they needed to be replaced with something more likely to stand up to the sort of battering they may get from the ghazrak. So, in a third part of the practice field a group of men were being sized for shields, which would be larger and heavier than what seemed to be the ceremonial ones they already carried. Several archery targets showed the effects of a practice session, each of them sprouting a small forest of shafts, although a number of arrows littered the ground still. Jalor shrugged. Not everyone would be an archer but the ones who could use a bow were getting better.

He grinned as Helt berated one of the swordsmen recruits and with a blistering tirade informed him in no uncertain terms that he was not doing what he had been told - or words to that effect. She then pulled her great sword from its back mount and laid into the same bollard he had been using. Where the padding previously had been lightly marked by the impacts of the recruit, it now suffered almost total destruction as Helt unleashed all of her pent-up aggression, and that was a lot, Jalor considered admiringly. Pieces of padding went in all directions as she gave great overhand and underhand blows, the edge of her sword ripping chunks of padding off the pole. The wood of the pole itself showed gouges where the padding had not quite stopped the impact. She finished, breathing heavily from the exertion, and with a growl directed the recruit to another padded pole.

With a start, Jalor saw Corm walk onto the practice ground. The Faero-elect wore padding and carried a practice sword, which was actually a bundle of withes made to resemble the length and basic heft of a normal sword. Corm saw Jalor and, with a small hesitation, altered direction, striding up to him and halting at arm's length.

"Jalor, I wish to apologise for my behaviour of the last few days," he said, in what was obviously a rehearsed speech. "It was unwise of me to, um, to behave ... well," he sighed and shook his head as he went off script, "frankly, to behave like a fool."

"That seems to be a change of heart," Jalor said carefully. "What caused this?"

"Oh, a number of things. Not just the fight yesterday." He snorted. "Fight? No, the humiliation I suffered at the hands of those four men. I realised a few things about the people I was with, as well as some things about myself that I didn't want to know. Then I spoke with someone who made me realise a few more things about myself." He grimaced. "That wasn't very nice," he muttered.

"Well, those four would not have actually hurt you unless you did something truly stupid," Jalor said. "In fact, I've asked them to help train the recruits and Almin Bor may try to get them into the guard. They would be assets. And who was this person who gave you some home truths?"

Corm hesitated. "You'll think this silly," he said, "but it was a Guardian. Balgor." He watched Jalor and when there was no reaction continued, "Apparently Balgor has been watching over the Faeronar since the rebellion. I had no idea but my father did. And Balgor was not very complimentary."

Jalor laughed. "He is very direct, isn't he?"

Corm stared. "You know Balgor?"

"We've met several times. He wants me to do something but I'm not sure what. Did you meet his demon?" Jalor said with a sly smile.

"The big red thing? Yes. It, or rather he, saved my life." Corm's face turned red at the memory.

"You've had a big couple of days, haven't you?" Jalor said.

"I didn't think I would lose my father as soon as I did. And I didn't realise what sort of burden he was carrying, and that I didn't make it easy. But apparently my father charged you and the twins with my education for the office of Faero, whoever the twins are. Balgor made it clear that I was to listen to you and the Children, whoever they are. Balgor said the Children have returned to save Ennaris, but did not explain." He quirked his lips in frustration. "He said you could do that."

"How old are you, Corm?" asked Jalor, seemingly ignoring most of what Corm had said.

"I have had my seventeenth name day," Corm said. "That was almost a full cycle ago."

"Seventeen, almost eighteen. Quite a burden to take up." Jalor seemed to consider, although he had already decided on the course of action for Corm some time previously. "Okay, first we need to get you fitter than you are now. Blaine can take care of that, along with Almin Bor. Then we get you into some weapons training. Blaine and Helt will do that. And while that is going on the twins will bring you up to speed on Ennaris and its history, and your place in it. As for who the twins are," and here Jalor smiled, "they are two of the remaining Mages of the Guides."

"Mages? Guides? Most people I know have thought they were legends or no longer around at any rate. Balgor made it clear that I will rely on them, so I guess I need to meet them."

"Most people you know have no idea about the realities of life on Ennaris. Nor do I for that matter. Which is why Blaine and I probably will sit in on your sessions with the twins."

"How is it that you and Blaine don't know about Ennaris? I know why I don't, other than old stories I used to listen to from an old story-teller who used to visit, but I don't understand why you don't. I expect you've seen much of Ennaris and would know a lot about it."

"Not as much as you might think," Jalor replied with a smile. "And that will become clear as your lessons with the twins progress. But that will have to wait. They're off somewhere doing something, slaying dragons for all I know."

"Dragons?" Corm asked. "Do I need to fight these dragons?"

"Dragons are old myths from where I come from," Jalor said with a laugh. "Not for you to worry about. You do have other things to concern you, though. Meanwhile, drop that practice sword and I want ten laps of the practice ground, running not walking. Then I'll introduce you to Blaine, and your training can start."

9. Council Chambers

Varna was not sure if she should be worried or not. Two days out from the Citadel and she, Flin and Dalresar were walking through the edge of the thick forest that surrounded the Citadel. The day was bright and clear. A few wispy clouds were drifting leisurely across the sky. Visibility was good and the air was clear, crisp and fresh, as it can be on a planet where the heavy industrial past was so remote that the planet had recovered its own good health, despite the trauma of the rebellion's aftermath in most areas. Pristine was Varna's thought as she walked along. It was a lovely place on what seemed to be a lovely planet. Well, if you discounted the evil seeking to take it over and destroy it. If that's what was happening.

And that was one source of Varna's concern. She, and Jalor and Blaine, had been exposed to some ugly behaviour by the ghazrak and their allied men and women, but all of the context they had been given was from Flin and the Faeronar. Admittedly, for Varna especially that was also from Balgor and Odruf, and she could not feel anything but confidence in what they told her, but the sharp demarcation between right and wrong was something that Varna had always sought to see through. In her experience, which admittedly was less than that of Jalor and Blaine, lines rarely were drawn that precisely - all good people on the left, all bad people on the right.

No, that was too neat. Yes, she was well aware that there were truly bad people, those for whom others were merely sources of profit or worse. She was well aware of the case that one team of Warriors uncovered sometime in the past where the weak were sources of food for the predators, a thought that made her shudder just to consider it. But in general, bad things were done by people whose conditioning had led them to it, or where circumstances drove them to desperate acts. Even self-interest at times could take people further into the dark than they had ever considered, and then they were unable to find a way back. Perhaps this is what had happened with Goroth - extreme ambition thwarted by the Council that led to a sequence of outcomes that resulted in outright civil war and massive destruction. After all, Goroth had been a trusted member of the Council for a long time, to hear Flin tell the story.

Varna knew that she did not have the full story, and she knew that Flin did not have it either, which was a revelation that both made him more approachable but at the same time was worrisome. For they would rely on Flin for what was supposedly coming at them. Increasingly, she realised that Flin was very frustrated as he learnt more and understood less, and that probably was a mild description of what he felt. He had, it seems, been thrust into the leadership role because of major losses to the previous Council leadership, and was unprepared for it, more because he lacked background than through lack of talent. Again, that was based on what she had picked up. But that also did not really make a lot of sense, for he had led the remnants of the Council for thousands of cycles, including overseeing the end of the civil war. Or was the end of the civil war brought about by this Marjory, who was the greatest Battle Mage ever seen - whatever that meant - and Flin just picked up the pieces?

Then there was the whole point of this mission, to locate Clay, if he lived, and other members of the original landing party. That mission was about fifty standard years earlier, though. And if they located Clay, what were they to do? Technology did not work on Ennaris, except where it did, she considered with a mental grimace. And just how did that happen? Logically, it happened because someone wanted it to happen, but who would that be? Was it Odruf-Halfgar, who she had 'met' in one of those strange half-dreams? Or some form of automated shield that was failing and so unable to maintain coverage as it had done? But then the technology shield would fall when Goroth was freed, so that implied someone would relax control at that time. Unless the act of breaking out would also destroy the shield generator or whatever it was. The argument could go in circles, she knew, and she did not have enough context, again. She wondered if Jalor had any better ideas?

But back to this mission - the Grand Admiral seemed to have some knowledge of this planet before sending them out. Of course, she had been the one to send out Clay and his party also, so she probably had some surveys and such. And, with her having been in stasis for so long, those events were very recent to her relative to the actual time since they had occurred. But still, the more Varna thought back to discussions the more she concluded that Serra had some other ideas in mind. Perhaps she had known of the technology block? Had she intended them to choose sides, and put them in a situation where they would choose the Faeronar side? If so, that indicated some form of manipulation and she would have to be aware of that, as she did not doubt that Jalor and Blaine would be also. Once again, not enough context.

Finally, over the last two days, since leaving the Citadel, she could feel tendrils of the same malaise reaching out to her. They were not debilitating, not as yet anyway, and she now knew what they were - assuming that what she had been told could be trusted, she thought with a surge of irritation - but they were there and she knew that they would grow stronger as time passed. She had not mentioned it to Flin yet but she knew that she would have to shortly, if for no other reason than she would slow them down. She thought back to the discussion over the small camp-fire the previous evening, where Flin had laid out his plan for her to consider, with Dalresar as an interested onlooker.

"I know you want to get to the bottom of your gifts, Varna," he said as they sat by the fire after a spartan meal, "but I feel that I need to get a better idea of what I'm missing. I don't want to be dramatic but it bothers me."

"Are you afraid of Goroth?" Varna asked.

"Afraid of him personally? No. Afraid of him as a talent tuned for battle, even after so long in stasis? Yes. I know my limitations, or some of them at least. I have a feeling there are others about which I have no idea." Flin shrugged, as much to himself as anything. "But it's not just Goroth. There are the others and, for all I know, newer gifted who have cropped up since that we don't know about. Most of the Ennarisi who showed gifts were singled out for persecution for a long period and so the gifts have diminished. Lately they seem to have been on a resurgence, but it won't be enough to make a difference. But what if Goroth's supporters didn't drive them out or kill them? What if they actively sought them out and trained them. It's been many, many cycles since the end of the rebellion. For all we know we may face an army of gifted, all perverted to Goroth's designs."

"Well, on the plus side there seems to have been no indication of that happening or I'm sure you or the twins would have heard of it. But I see your point. So, what are you thinking?"

"I would like to get to the Council chambers and see if I can go through the Mage archives. I'm missing too much background, and it's obvious that I have to get better knowledge of the things that Goroth is likely to throw at me. And then we go to the Forest."

"What sort of time are we talking about?"

"It will take us about three days to get to the Council chamber from here, so four to five from the Citadel. We were not that far away from the Faero during the, um, better times, but without those forms of transport it takes longer." Flin considered further. "I'm not sure how long I will be in the chamber, but I expect two or three days. And then it will be another four days to the Forest."

"So that means around ten days. I guess we can do that. It really only changes the order of things a little."

"Yes. Thank you. By the way the Council chamber is shielded so you may not suffer any ill-effects while there. I'm not sure of that, mind you, but it is possible."

"So," Varna said while Flin relaxed following her agreement, "where does Dalresar come into this?"

Dalresar, reclining on the opposite side of the fire, raised himself on one elbow and looked from Varna to Flin. "That's a good question," he said. "I'd like to have an idea of that myself. I thought I may have been better with Corm. At least I know him, where Varna's friends don't."

"Yes," Flin agreed, "but Balgor made a strong suggestion that you should be with us on this trip. I'm not sure he knows why, either. I think he was acting under instruction. I can only assume it was from other Guardians."

"The Prophecy?" Varna asked.

"Maybe, Balgor didn't say."

"Well, I'm here, so I guess we just get on with it. What do you want me to do while you're reviewing your records?" Dalresar glanced from Flin to Varna. "Or Varna here, for the same matter?"

"That's a good question. There's not much for you to do and the archives are keyed for certain DNA sequences that indicate Mage potential. Anyone without that must be accompanied by a Mage." Flin pondered for a moment. "Perhaps the history of Ennaris will assist Varna to get a better understanding of how things stand. There remain numbers of sensors working, for whatever reason, probably because they are needed to hold the stasis in place."

"Which indicates that this block against technology is held in place by someone," Varna said.

Flin waggled his hand and almost winced to show his uncertainty.

"Maybe, or maybe it was set with specific exclusions. Halfgar did not confide in me any sort of detail about the block. I've thought about that often. There are some devices we had that would make people's lives much easier, but they're useless now. Anyway, for now sensors in orbit keep us in some sort of touch with what's happening around Ennaris. You may be able to see what's going on in a few places."

"Sounds exciting," Varna said with no enthusiasm at all in her voice.

Dalresar nodded.

Flin grinned.

"Yes, well it's the best I can do at short notice. We'll find out if there's anything else available when we get there."

So now, walking along as she pondered, Varna remained unsure of what they were trying to accomplish beyond Flin getting a better understanding. She might as well settle for taking a look at what she could find of the state of play around the planet, depending on how well the remaining sensors worked.

Dalresar maintained his silence as they walked. He was something of a mystery to Varna. She guessed him to be about thirty-five years of age, and Flin had called him his apprentice at one stage. The two of them had the sort of comfortable interaction with each other that spoke of long association. Varna also noted how he moved with a grace and economy of motion that indicated excellent physical condition, but there was something else and Varna considered it as she walked by Flin's side. And then suddenly she recognised it - it was the sort of flowing movement that Blaine had, that spoke of a relaxed but controlled position that could explode into action at a moment's notice. Varna determined to find out more about Dalresar when the opportunity permitted, which would not be while Flin was within hearing distance.

It was the evening of the fourth day from the Citadel that Flin stopped by the side of the road that they had been following. They had passed several people over the four days, but traffic was sporadic at best. Those few passed had been wary but invariably nodded a greeting, a simple gesture that Varna found comforting. Only one small group had given cause for concern. Three men who were dirty and unkempt had scrutinised them, paying particular attention to Varna, but they, too, had passed by. Dalresar had seemed to be amused at the time. Varna, on the other hand, recognised the type and knew they would cause trouble. They did.

"Those three have been following us since mid-afternoon," Flin said conversationally. "We're close to the Council chambers, so we need to do something about them, I suppose."

"Bandits," Dalresar replied. "The one who stared at Varna is known as Mop. He's a known rapist. I'm guessing the other two are no better. They're not about to apologise and go on their way."

"I thought not," Flin sighed. "Well then, is here good enough?"

"No, the small clearing over there," Dalresar said, pointing into the woods, "That will make a better spot to deal with them."

"Okay, lead on."

Dalresar led Flin and Varna through a small gap in the trees, along a short but winding path to a clearing that Varna estimated would be slightly smaller than the main plaza of the Citadel. Dalresar found what he felt was the centre of the clearing and removed his cloak, dropping it at his feet before kicking it to a point where the packs were stacked. Varna was re-evaluating the relationship between Flin and Dalresar - this was not Flin leading, but deliberately passing control to the other.

"Are we going to give them a chance to leave," she asked as she also dropped her travel cloak on the pile, making sure that her staff was attached to her belt.

Dalresar laughed shortly. "When they see you there will be no chance of that," he said with a wry grin.

Varna realised that without the cloak she was more obviously female, and sighed. Flin nodded and flung his cape back. All three took easy stances in the clearing centre, waiting calmly. Dalresar was closest to the trail opening. Varna was surprised to note that Dalresar adopted the same form of parade rest that she had done, but then realised that it probably was almost universal as the best way to stay alert on your feet but allow your muscles to relax slightly. Flin merely stood with his hands tucked into the opposite sleeves of his robe.

They could hear them clearly, now. The three men entered the clearing, looking around furtively and, seeing no-one else around strode arrogantly towards the three travellers. All of them held naked swords in firm grips. Apparently, none of them thought to ask why their intended victims had stopped to allow them to catch up. Varna glanced to Dalresar who merely shrugged and shook his head. His meaning was obvious. Like Varna, he had a low opinion of these three and their tactics.

The one known as Mop stopped in front of Dalresar, who still was standing empty-handed with his sword still in its sheath slung on the left side. Mop smiled viciously.

"Nice o' ya to wait for us," he said through blackened teeth. "We'll be takin' what yer got, includin' the little lady there."

His two companions sniggered as they surveyed Varna's form. Dalresar merely raised his eyes to the heavens and sighed.

"It's not too late to head back the way you came and try your luck elsewhere," he said, almost as a matter of form rather than with any expectation of them heeding the implied warning.

Mop laughed. "Now why would we want to do that? We got ya right here, and there's three of us to one o' you."

"Well, first, there are three of us also. Second ... oh why bother," Dalresar said with a resigned tone. "You have no intention of leaving us alive when you are through here, correct?"

"Correct," Mop said through clenched teeth, not accustomed to his victims talking back.

"And you intend to take this woman and all three of you take turns?"

"With me first," Mop said, almost snarling. He actually licked his lips while the other two sniggered again.

"And I'm not going to let you do that, and nor will my friends," Dalresar said evenly. "And I know you, Mop, and I know that this world will be better off without you. And you can't better me on your best day and my worst."

Mop's eyes narrowed and he tensed. His every move telegraphed his intentions. With a roar he drew back his sword and swung at Dalresar only to encounter nothing, and then his eyes opened wide as Dalresar's long knife ripped through his abdomen and up through the rib cavity to his heart. Mop stopped quite still, dropping his sword and looking down to where the knife still protruded before collapsing. But Dalresar had, in one smooth move that Varna later was unable to recall clearly because it was so fast, caught Mop's sword and danced - there was no other word for it - between the other two, dealing death with each of two swipes before they had even moved. Within moments the three would-be bandits were dead, and Varna was standing with her staff in hand but still not extended. Flin merely stayed standing as he had been.

Dalresar surveyed his handiwork before dropping Mop's sword on top of his body. He was breathing easily and was completely calm, as though this was a commonplace event.

"I'll dig a hole over there," he said, pointing to the side of the clearing furthest from the road, "and bury them. Varna, do you want a sword? Mop's is quite a good one. I'd guess he took it off some poor soul who could afford a good sword but never learned how to use it right."

"No," said Varna. "I'm close to useless with a sword. The staff has been my choice for a long time now and I'll stay with it. But I'll help you drag these over there when that hole is dug."

"Okay," Dalresar replied, pulling a crude collapsible spade from his pack, then picking up Mop's sword and walking towards the clearing edge.

Varna watched for a while as Dalresar used the captured sword to dig through the top layer of soft grass and earth. She turned to see Flin watching her with mild eyes.

"I don't think Blaine could have done that as well," she said, still a little startled at what she had seen. "Just where is he from again?"

"I don't know," Flin said. "He suffered some terrible trauma quite some time ago, before I found him, and his memories of the past are gone. Some form of amnesia, I guess, but his fighting skills have remained and, if anything, improved. By the way, how old would you guess him to be?"

"About thirty-five cycles," Varna said.

"Yes, about what I would say also. I found him over forty cycles ago, in a slavers camp. I managed to get him away and get him a job working as a labourer for a local farmer. He had wandered into the slaver's camp shortly before, injured and not knowing who he was or where he was.

Anyway, he stayed with the farmer after healing - physically, anyway - and I took him away from there almost thirty cycles ago. His language skills had almost returned and have done so completely now, and he is one of the most logical thinkers I know."

"Forty cycles ago? But ..." Varna stopped talking as she turned to watch Dalresar continue to dig with the sword blade and the small spade.

"Yes?" Flin prompted, drawing Varna to consider further.

"You said that people with gifts often can extend their lives considerably. Is that what is happening with Dalresar?"

"Those with strong gifts, yes, that's what I said."

"What gifts does Dalresar have?"

"None, to my knowledge," Flin said, watching Dalresar shovel dirt from the burial hole. "I've not been able to discern any gift, and he hasn't mentioned anything happening that is different."

"Perhaps battle skills are his gifts?"

"Perhaps. But on Ennaris battle skills have tended to include more than merely physical skills. Marjory, for example, could project attacks at long distance, or raise shields to protect from attacks with her mental powers alone. She was exceptionally powerful and skilful, of course, but Dalresar shows none of those abilities." Flin shook his head. "So, we're perplexed. But there's something about him that causes people to have confidence in him. The farmer who took him in was very careful in all things but had no second thought about Dalresar living with him and his family. Intika Ramesa often asked for Dalresar to assist his men when they had difficult jobs to do in the surrounding country, and Intika was a very good judge of men. It's a mystery."

Varna nodded. "But the fact that he hasn't aged as other Ennarisi have done indicates a gift or some sort, yes?"

"Yes, in the normal course. Perhaps it's his amnesia that is causing the blockage, or perhaps something else. I've been waiting for something to show up. Again, I may find out more when I review the older archives."

"Well, the sooner we get this done the sooner you can start to look for answers."

Varna reached down, grabbed hold of Mop's clammy cold hands and dragged him to where Dalresar had finished digging the hole.

Flin nodded thoughtfully as he tried to think of the right questions, let alone the right answers.

Not very much later, the three travellers gathered by the side of the road once more. Flin stared back and forth intently before crossing the road and walking confidently into the wood. He followed no trail that Varna could see but, evidently, he needed none as he skirted fallen trees and wended his way along or across small gullies. The ground was rising gradually, Varna could tell, with occasional steeper slopes. She thought they would have to be several hundred metres above the road when Flin called a halt. Standing under the shade of a knobbly, old-looking tree with needle-like leaves sprouting in clumps along scrawny limbs, he pointed forward to where the land seemed to come to an end.

"We will be going down into that valley. The Council Chamber is entered via a rocky shelf that walls the far end with a small stream running through a channel cut below it. During the wetter times the floor of the valley is a watercourse, and there are some uneven patches, so watch your step. When we get to the end, touch nothing," he warned. "I don't think there would be danger but the makers of the Chamber were a little paranoid when it was originally built. Ennaris was under attack from a superior force at the time, and the protections have remained intact from that time. In fact, they have been improved from time to time. Marjory made further changes during and after the rebellion, also. We're always careful when returning by this path."

After nods from Varna and Dalresar, Flin turned and led the way once more, entering a sloping track running through a dry watercourse that skirted the edge of a drop-off on one side while hugging a low wall on the other. The wall ended at a corner and Flin suddenly turned left and descended quickly. Varna reached the corner and saw a descending ledge that ran along the side of the valley wall, which was a nearly vertical cliff. She took one look around before following Flin. Her foot-steps were sure even though the brief look showed that they were on the wall high above a deep valley. Where they had turned the corner would become a waterfall when the dry stream was running with water, she guessed. The valley floor was dry and lightly wooded, with various plants growing between large rocks. Trees started about one-third of the way up the walls of the valley, which indicated where the water level may be when in flood. Saplings that were growing below them told of few such floods in the near past.

The ledge clung to the side of the valley, slowly descending. Round-ing a slight bend, Varna stopped short and stared. The valley was closed in by a sheer rock face that stretched from one side to the other, without apparent break for the lower two-thirds until it reached the cave-like opening into which the stream ran, although it was merely a trickle now. There seemed to be fissures and rents in the rock face for the upper third. Above the wall facing her Varna could see little detail. Trees bent over the edge, as though peering down on them from high above. The ledge opened to become a path wide enough for two or three to walk abreast, still following the valley wall. It went all the way to the wall that blocked the valley.

Dalresar stopped alongside Varna as he, too, regarded the sight.

"Impressive, isn't it?" he said quietly, moving past to follow Flin, who was striding towards the wall. "I've never been inside. I've usually been left at the Citadel or a close town so this should be interesting."

Varna took another look around, wondering where the defences may be. There was nothing visible but, she realised, there would not be anything as obvious as a gun-emplacement. She had the feeling that she was about to enter a place that would test her, and not just because her mental buzz had been getting stronger. This, she thought grimly, could be like going down the rabbit-hole.

Flin stopped at the wall, waiting for Dalresar and Varna to reach him. Varna could feel something examining her and she abruptly turned and walked away from Flin, moving about ten metres away before she stopped again and half-turned back towards the wall. The feeling of being examined had fallen away as she moved away from the wall. She closed her eyes and walked back towards Flin and Dalresar again, both of whom were watching her closely. When she was around five metres from the wall, she was again aware of the scrutiny and, with her eyes still closed, she turned in a slow circle. The feeling of being watched peaked and ebbed as she turned, so she turned back and forth until she knew where it originated. She opened her eyes to see nothing but bare rock, although the feeling persisted. She walked toward the rock, reaching with one hand. Dalresar moved to stop her, but Flin held him back with a touch.

Varna reached the rock wall. There was a brief flare and a section of wall disappeared, showing a passage into the wall itself. Varna turned to Flin with an uncertain smile and a tilt of one shoulder to further indicate her uncertainty about what to do next. Flin merely indicated that she should move into the passage. After a moment of indecision, she squared her shoulders and walked into the wall passage. She had gone no more than three steps when a female voice stopped her in her tracks.

"Genetic survey complete. Please state your name for the records." The voice was unemotional, impersonal and yet warm of tone.

Varna considered, then replied clearly, "I am Varna Barr, Major of the Warriors of the Light of the Union of Sentient Planets."

"Welcome Varna Barr. The Chamber of the Council of Mages recognises you and your bloodline."

Varna turned back to Flin, confused, but he merely nodded to proceed. She did so, pausing while Dalresar entered the passage. He likewise took only two or three paces when the same challenge was made.

"My name is Dalresar," Flin's apprentice replied, with a quirk of his lips.

"Welcome Dalresar," came the reply. "The Chamber of the Council of Mages recognises you and your bloodline."

Dalresar stared at Varna and then turned back to Flin, as Varna had done. The Mage was regarding Dalresar with satisfaction. Again, he nodded and Dalresar turned to proceed through the passage.

"Welcome back Drewflin," was the greeting accorded Flin. "Quarters have been prepared for the new Mages. There have been several events of which you need to be aware and the records are available for your viewing in the library."

"Thank you," Flin said as he proceeded down the passage. "Seal the entrance, please. We may have been followed. I have some research to do. It seems I'm not aware of several things that Archmages of the past knew, and I must catch up."

"Well," the disembodied voice replied, and Varna was unable to discern the source, "you had the responsibilities thrust on you without adequate preparation. While you have not been raised to Archmage, in the circumstances I am permitted to provide you with the requisite briefing. Would you like to review the briefing prepared for Archmage Hardus on his ascension? Then perhaps you will be able to direct targeted research."

"You mean there is a standard form of briefing for new Archmages?"

"Yes, Drewflin. However, as you did not request the briefing updates were not performed."

Flin grimaced and scratched his head. "I didn't request it because I was not aware such existed. I gather the Archmage usually was advised by people who were aware of all of these things? Who advised Hardus and those before him for, say, the hundred millennia leading to the rebellion?"

"Yes, to your first question. As for the second, Hardus had the support of Halfgar, as did Belthars and Broden before him and Prosfin before her. In fact, Halfgar advised all Archmages through the hundred millennia you refer to."

"All of them? Halfgar advised them all?"

"Yes, Drewflin."

"Can you update Hardus' briefing for me, please?"

"Yes, material has been gathered for such a purpose. It will be ready for you shortly."

Flin entered a large chamber to find Varna and Dalresar waiting for him.

"I've discovered one flaw in the process of initiating a new Archmage," he muttered sourly. "It relies on someone who knows what's happening to ask the right questions. In my case, there was no-one who knew the questions to ask. Not that I'm the Archmage, but I'm the closest we have." He had a quick look around the chamber. "This is the home chamber. Think of it as a shared space for preparing food, eating with fellow Mages, conversing and so on. Over there," he said, pointing to a passage leading from the opposite side to which they entered, "are the sleeping quarters. The Chamber assistant will direct you to your allocated quarters. It will also answer any questions you may have while I'm reviewing the briefing. I don't know how long that will take, though."

"Almost a full day, Drewflin," the Chamber assistant said.

"So, almost a day, then. I suggest that you don't leave the Chamber. In fact, at the moment you can't because I've sealed it. The assistant recognised you both as being Mages, not just Mage potential. That was a little surprising but also confirms something I suspected. It also means that it will answer you more fully that it may have done otherwise. Varna, you may get a lot of background from the information stored here. Dalresar, I suggest you see if there is anything to jog your memories, or to identify what your gift or gifts may be. The assistant is fully conversant with all known gifts, as far as I know."

Both merely nodded.

"Okay then, something to eat. Can we have three meals, please? No specific dietary requirements. Are there sufficient nutrients available?"

The assistant responded instantly. "Yes, Drewflin. Three meals will be ready shortly. Nutrient tanks have been maintained as normal."

10. Champion's Fate

It was some time after the brief meal that Varna and Dalresar found themselves back in the home chamber. Varna had explored her quarters, finding them spacious and comfortable, much more so than she was accustomed to on Ennaris. But then, she reasoned, this place had been built long before the rebellion that led to Ennaris' regression.

What surprised her was that the technology resources were active and functional. Wall lamps that ran from an unknown power source activated as she approached, and she had a personal vidscreen that she decided she would explore later. There was hot running water, the first she had experienced since leaving Starfire, and a quiet ambience that she could only describe as relaxing. The Mages' chambers were designed to help then recharge, she guessed, and, while they were not in any way decadent, they most certainly provided comfort.

Flin, she knew, would be in his chamber reviewing the briefing he had missed on being handed the responsibilities of Archmage, albeit without the title. Varna was bemused that he could have such little true context into the position, which would be something to check more completely. But, for now, she planned to explore her surroundings. This was not what she expected when the mission started, not that she ever had any hard expectations for any mission, but Ennaris was proving to be something different.

She decided to start from the home chamber and see how far she could get.

"Show me a map of the Chamber of the Mages, please," Varna said as she arrived in the home chamber, feeling slightly self-conscious at speaking to thin air.

"The map is now displayed on the viewing wall," the chamber assistant said.

Simultaneously, one wall of the home chamber shimmered and then held a schematic diagram of the Chamber of the Mages. Varna was both surprised and a little dismayed to note that the extent of the construction was relatively small. She had expected a rich confusion of passage-ways, chambers and she knew not what. What she saw was the home chamber with five passages heading off at angles like spokes, each passageway having twenty or more chambers attached. By far the majority of them were living quarters, with most of the rest being shown as store-rooms, or so she thought the icons attached to each meant. The home chamber was the largest by far, and had a marker displayed inside it, like a 'you are here' indicator, Varna thought.

She was puzzling over the relatively small extent of the Chamber when Dalresar arrived in the home chamber. He stopped by her side and examined the schematic for a short time.

"Where's Flin," Dalresar asked, seemingly taking this technological environment in his stride.

"Drewflin is in the Council chamber," the assistant replied immediately.

"Show the Council chamber on the schematic."

The display changed to show the Chamber of the Mages from a side view, with the home chamber marked still. Now, however, it showed in the centre of one of a huge number of levels. Dalresar whistled softly as he took in what was now a huge structure buried inside the mountain, with much of it below ground. Varna nodded to herself. She had been looking at the current level only.

"How many levels are there?" Varna asked.

"Fifty-seven," was the reply.

"And how many sleeping chambers?" Dalresar asked.

"One thousand seven hundred and fifty."

"There were that many Mages?" Varna asked in amazement.

"No," said the assistant. "At the height of the Ennarisi civilisation there were slightly more than twelve thousand full Mages. Most of them maintained lodgings in the communities they served, or were off-planet for long periods. The Chamber of the Mages usually provided lodging for about one thousand Mages at most."

For a long moment Varna found herself standing staring at the diagram with her mouth hanging open before she recovered from the shock. That many! And that counted only full Mages.

"What defines a full Mage?" Dalresar asked.

"A full Mage is able to draw on her or his powers on demand and consistently. A full Mage also has a dominant gene that has been shown to be present in the longest-lived Ennarisi. A full Mage is not defined by strength of power or type of gift."

"So, you can have someone with a strong gift who doesn't have this gene and that person would not be a full Mage?" Varna asked.

"Correct," the assistant replied. "However, there have been only two recorded instances of Ennarisi with strong gifts who did not have the gene. And both were found to have parents with the gene and both were inconsistent in application of their gifts. The last recorded instance was almost thirty-five thousand cycles ago."

"So, there would have been many Ennarisi with minor gifts who could apply them only sometimes and then not on demand," Dalresar mused.

"Correct," the assistant repeated. "It was calculated by the Mage Hyrus that in his time approximately thirty-eight percent of Ennarisi had access to one or more gifts to some degree."

Varna was struggling to understand how many people may have had these super-human capabilities. Almost two in five people had some sort of gift.

"How many people did Ennaris have at that time," Dalresar asked. His expression showed he was sharing Varna's struggle.

"Approximately three billion people," replied the assistant.

"Over a billion people with gifts," Varna breathed.

"But only twelve thousand full Mages at most," Dalresar said.

"Which meant that to be a full Mage was to be of the elite. In fact, probably the elite of the elite." Varna paused to consider. "So, when they went to other planets the ones who wanted to be seen to be elites could act out their desires. And I guess they became accustomed to doing that."

"Well, that's interesting," Dalresar said, "but it doesn't really help us today. We know that there are only a handful of Mages left, and they will be facing a superior force, although again only a handful that we know of. The number of other Ennarisi with gifts is so small as to be counted on one hand, as far as we know, and none will be of assistance. We have you and Jalor and Blaine, but with no real idea of how much power you bring to bear, nor what the other two bring. Goroth's supporters obviously have delved into the darkest arts to produce the ghazrak, and we will have to build a formidable army to hold them out. Each seems to be worth four or five of our normal fighters, just because they don't seem to feel pain or stop until every one of them is dead."

"Berserkers," Varna said. "Some of the oldest traditions of my home world tell of fighters who worked themselves up before each battle such that they did not feel injuries and were able to deal out great destruction for short periods."

"Hmmm, but the ghazrak are like that always. From what Flin said, they've been bred or made like that."

"They seem to be men made into beasts," Varna said. "I could sense a strange aura at one stage, like I can sense from most Ennarisi men, but it was overcome by the beast as they went into battle. At least, I think that's how to read it."

"Hopefully, Flin can shed some light on that," Dalresar said with a frown. "Meanwhile, I'm going to see if I can find out what's going on in other parts of Ennaris. I think Flin will need to know that. He thinks there may have been some sort of watchers still operating, so who knows. I think I can do that in my chamber."

"Sensors," Varna said. "They would be sensors of some kind. You may not get a clear image of people if that is the case, although their technology is very advanced."

Dalresar nodded as he turned to leave, then paused.

"More advanced that your own?" he asked, still facing away from Varna.

"Perhaps so," Varna replied, thoughtfully. "Some of this is very recognisable, which is a surprise, and some not so. The fact that this is running so long after the rebellion killed so many of the Mages and their support teams says something. I'm not sure we could expect that to be the case."

Dalresar grunted with a nod and left the home chamber. Varna considered. Her primary job as part of the mission was to locate Clay and the team. She knew where they were dropped, or near enough, because her own team had been dropped to the same location.

"Show a map of the area around the Citadel of the Faero, please," she instructed.

The schematic diagram was replaced by a topographic map of the southern continent, which then zoomed into a position she recognised from her briefing.

"Centre on this location," she said, walking to the screen and touching a spot near the screen's edge that she was sure was near the landing site. "And magnify ten times."

The screen shifted again. The point Varna had touched was drawn to the centre of the screen and the magnification level was increased greatly.

The topographic display did not tell her anything really, though.

"Can you display the same area showing the land as it is, not just in topographical terms?"

The image changed from showing the topology to a crystal-clear view of the land, the rise and fall of the hills replacing lines and circles.

Varna realised that she was viewing the planet from above. What was more, she could identify the landing zone, slightly left of centre. Once again Varna stepped to the screen and this time placed her finger on the centre of the clearing, on the tiny patch of green surrounded by the larger circle of blackened land.

"Centre on this spot, please."

The screen obligingly shifted slightly to centre as Varna requested.

"Do you have any sensor readings for this spot stored on file?" Varna was not sure she was asking the right questions, but reasoned a set-up as advanced as this was likely to have history stored. But how much?

"Yes," the assistant required. "However, observations are not taken more frequently than twice daily unless there is a reason for doing so."

"How far back do your readings go?" Varna asked, then considered what she was seeing. "And how much of Ennaris is covered by your sensors?"

"Most of the planet is covered to some extent. Several sensors have failed and gaps exist, however I estimate almost ninety percent of the inhabited planet is able to be monitored. Readings are available for the last two hundred thousand cycles only."

Twice daily images of the entire planet? For two hundred thousand years? Varna tried and failed to work out just how much data that represented. Advanced indeed.

"Can you go back around fifty cycles. No, make that fifty-five cycles, and allow me to view this location for ten cycles?"

"It will take approximately thirty minims to retrieve the data," the assistant said, almost apologetically.

"Okay," Varna said, trying to sound as though that was normal. Again, if the Union had technology that could do this, which it did not to this quality, then it would take much longer to bring it up on screen, she was sure. "Meanwhile, can you explain to me Ennaris' geography and the types of people? I know there are two continents, but are there countries or states? Is the level of civilisation the same across the planet?"

The screen shifted again. The view of the clearing shrank and drifted to the bottom left corner and the main view now showed Ennaris in a flattened view. The two continents occupied almost half of the planet, with a huge area of open ocean surrounding them. The continents were joined by a fairly narrow neck of land at the far right side, such that a sizable sea was formed between the continents. The sea opened to the ocean at the left side, which Varna thought of as west, and seemed to straddle the planet's equator. Varna knew Ennaris was close to Earth size, so she was able to put some idea of scale to the image.

The northern continent was very green at the lowest point, where it met the sea. Varna could see a line of tall mountains running north-south about four-fifths of the way across the continent, closest to the east coast. On the eastern side of the mountains was a smaller expanse of land that looked like a plain shaped somewhat like a fist starting in a huge bay and with a curving spit of land running into the ocean to the north-east. On the western side of the mountains, several major rivers wended their way across the continent. Three rivers flowed into the western ocean and one from the mountains ran to the eastern ocean. Which, Varna reminded herself, is the same ocean! Another three rivers flowed into the sea between the continents. Above the green band was a darker, browner stretch rising to what could be foothills of an east-west mountain range, but that instead led into what appeared to be a void where there was no detail. Above that, at the top of the continent was what was obviously icy reaches covering the whole northern coast and reaching partway down each side.

The southern continent was smaller, with a similar but much smaller green band running from the sea on the north-west for around one-third of both the width and length of the land mass, but with an ochre-yellow area occupying most of the rest leading to what seemed to be rocky extents running down each coast. At the southern extremity was a broken coast-line with the area coloured a pale blue, which Varna could not interpret. At least three rivers were evident which, given the very low level of detail offered by the view, indicated they were large.

Two of them ran north into the sea, and the third west into the ocean. A range of mountains covered much of the westernmost side of the continent below the green stretch.

The land area that linked the two continents, to the right - east - side of the sea, was a mottled green and extended the short distance to the eastern coast. No large rivers were evident but Varna guessed that there would be smaller streams. She already knew this was a tropical forest or jungle zone, and her experience was that most such areas would have streams.

"As you can see," the assistant began, "Ennaris has two continents. The northern continent is significantly larger than the southern one. The sea that divides the two continents was formed as a result of the damage caused by and following the rebellion. The indiscriminate use of highly destructive weapons in the region directly destroyed two great cities and resulted in significant tectonic movements. They caused a large land bridge at the western end of what was a deep valley with small enclosed lakes to collapse. At the same time several large islands in the ocean off the western shore of the south continent were almost destroyed, with little visible now but the tops of what were steep mountains. Ennaris had been a rich and verdant land prior to the rebellion, but afterwards the conditions changed sufficiently that what was a large tropical and temperate zone shrank to a smaller zone. A region of desert developed in the south and the grasslands grew markedly in the north over a single millennium. River courses were diverted, which moved sources of water. Mountain ranges were damaged, causing severe loss to smaller communities outside the cities that were attacked.

"Politically, Ennaris changed from a single polity to many disparate communities, each with their own ruling method. Organised government collapsed entirely in the aftermath of the rebellion, and chaos was the norm. It was during this period, which lasted for more than two thousand cycles, that most of the remaining Guide Mages lost their lives. The population of Ennaris was reduced to no more than a tenth of what it had been very quickly, and that continued to shrink during this period. The temperate areas were the first to re-establish organised government, only a hundred cycles after the rebellion, largely due to the efforts of the Guide Mages. The cities now were gone from this area, so new settlements arose, centred on farmland. The Citadel of the Faeros had survived and for a time the Faero seemed likely to be the centre of government. That did not happen, and warlords arose across the land, carving out holdings for themselves by force of arms.

"The current political layout of Ennaris has held in most ways for nearly five hundred cycles, although warfare remains a threat in several parts and changes of leadership continue to occur suddenly at times. In general, the warlords have been succeeded by leaders who drew together multiple small holdings to form larger domains and princedoms. There was the period of the kings, which saw kingdoms rise as holdings were drawn together, and several of those kingdoms remain in some form. In other places forms of citizen-rule have been established on various models."

Varna was trying to absorb the information being presented dispassionately, but she was seeing beneath the words to the horrors that must have been visited in this planet. More than nine people in ten perished during and after the rebellion! That single figure reverberated through her continuously. She had no idea as to what advancements of the Ennarisi civilisation had been lost, but the sheer scale of destruction of the people left her staggered. That the result of such damage was a total breakdown in government was therefore no surprise, especially given that technology was found not to function, and the subsequent rise of strong-men likewise was no surprise.

"Can you show me the changes to the land-masses caused by the rebellion?" she asked.

The vidscreen changed. The geographical layout remained but was overlaid by another transparent representation. Varna could see that the sea between the two continents was little more than a set of large lakes, held together by what looked like man-made canals, with the rivers heading in slightly different paths for the most part. The major changes occurred in the southern continent where the western coast was significantly changed, while the rendering of the tropical, temperate and arctic zones was very different. She could see how the tropical zone had shrunk, as had the temperate zone, while the area between temperate and arctic ones had expanded, with desert filling much of the gap in the southern continent and the strange void in the north.

"The area of the northern continent that has no detail," Varna said. "How long has there been that lack of detail? What does that area cover?"

"Detail has been lacking since the rebellion," the assistant replied. "That is the region of the twin northern kingdoms. The available sensors were destroyed in the last days of the rebellion and could not be replaced with the resources available."

Where the red gold came from!

"Were they targeted for destruction?" Varna asked, curious about the quite clearly defined zone that had been established with no real information for the Mages.

"Potentially," the assistant replied. "The available records show a definite pattern of attacks on sensors covering that region during the final stages of the conflict."

"And that would have been directed by Goroth?"

"Yes, or one of his lieutenants. They all launched from the last of the ground-based sites controlled by the rebels, as well as one of the space-based sites."

Varna was silent, considering. She was sure that the sensors had been targeted deliberately, which implied intent to render the area invisible to the remaining sensors.

"When did the ban on technology come into force?" Varna asked quietly.

"Two days after the sensors were destroyed," was the reply.

"Was that before or after Goroth was captured?"

"It was five days prior to Goroth's capture."

"How did the Archmage capture Goroth?"

"Archmage Hardus led the remaining Mages to the point where Goroth and his army were camped. The Battle Mages held a screen over the site while the Archmage and Goroth engaged in combat. Archmage Hardus fell at that time. Mage Drewflin was able to capture him and bind him with the assistance of the Battle Mage."

"Wait. What about Halfgar?"

"No. Mage Drewflin was elevated informally by the remaining Mages at a special session of the Council of Mages in the days following the capture of Goroth and the end of the rebellion. However, the formal appointment to Archmage did not occur. The Mage Halfgar perished while setting the ban on technology in place prior to Goroth's capture." The impersonal voice of the assistant seemed to take on a pensive tone. "Of course, Halfgar's physical remains were not found, as he expended all of his energies in the effort."

"So that's why no-one was here to advise Flin. None of the previous Council survived, did they?"

"On the contrary. Mages Drewflin and Marjory were the surviving Council members. However, both had been appointed to the Council for only a very short time before the rebellion commenced."

"Can you show me a picture of Goroth?" Varna asked.

"Yes," the assistant replied as the screen changed and the geography of Ennaris was replaced by a scene that Varna guessed was the capture of Goroth. "This is the last image of Goroth before he was bound in the stasis chamber. It was taken shortly after he was captured and bound."

Varna examined the man standing before two figures who had their backs to the imaging point. He was quite tall, with dark brown hair parted in the centre and flowing to his shoulders, a lean face without facial hair leading to a strong chin. His mouth was a thin slit, as though expressive of anger. He stood straight, with arms held by his side. He wore robes of deep green, edged in blue and some form of sandals could be seen. But it was his eyes that transfixed Varna. Even as a still image the force of personality showed through, and he was glaring at the two figures who had captured him, a haughty expression despite being held fast by bonds that the image did not show. Varna guessed the two were Flin and Marjory, although a Flin who was much younger, she guessed, based on stance. Varna pursed her lips as she examined the image. She could imagine this one leading the rebellion, and also not caring overmuch about the damage caused.

"What happened to Goroth's army?" asked Varna.

"The main army was disbanded at Drewflin's direction, after Goroth's sentence of banishment was announced and carried out."

Varna was getting a better perspective now. Flin had been made virtual Archmage of a tiny remnant of the Guides, with such massive changes to his world that he was powerless to save. He had lost all but a small number of supporters and the remaining people of Ennaris were struggling to survive let alone rebuild any form of civilisation. In any event, Halfgar's last act had been to deny them the benefit of advanced technology that would have been required to create such civilisation. Flin was not ready for such an elevation and, she suspected, had not been considering the likelihood of it. There was no-one to advise him, so he made the best of it that he could, without adequate context. And that lasted thousands of years - cycles, she reminded herself. It was the arrival of the Children of Ennaris, and the revelation that the Guardians existed, along with meeting one of those Guardians for the first time, that caused him to re-question aspects of what had happened, so that he would now get some of the training he may have needed then.

She felt sorry for him. This person who wished to help the people had been thrown into a position of being blamed for the destruction. In addition, his friends and helpers were being pilloried and killed as they worked to protect and provide succour for the remainder of the planetary population. She imagined his emotional pain as the planet degenerated into warring bands of people, resistant to his messages of peace and assistance toward each other - she had no doubt that would have been his message. And then the loss of Marjory, not just his life partner but the most powerful of the Mages available to him as he prepared for an encounter he knew was coming at some time, based on the Prophecy.

"The images of the requested location are ready for viewing," said the assistant, interrupting Varna's musing.

"Okay," she said, rousing herself again. "Please show them in sequence until I ask for them to pause."

The site where the three Warriors had found the circular scar was green and verdant in the images that flicked past Varna's sight. A small mound of vegetation, as though a tree had fallen and been cut into sections, was visible part-way to the edge of the site, but little else of interest. Image after image passed showing the passage of time - trees could be seen to grow on the fringe of the land, creatures were caught in single frames as they moved across the opening or grazed on the lush grass, some trees lost their leaves and regrew them. Image after image sped past, obviously a daytime shot and a night-time shot. The effect was soporific, and Varna's attention started to drift as the site showed almost no change.

And then suddenly it did. The frequency of images increased rapidly and started to play through a single day, or so it seemed to Varna.

"Stop," she called out. "Are there more images for this period than usual?"

"Yes," the assistant replied. "An unusual observation occurred that caused the governing assistant to increase surveillance on that site. Records indicate that a force of unknown beings were located near to this site and so enhanced tracking was established. For the next three days observations are at the rate of every five minims."

"Backtrack to the point where the unusual observation was made and show that area also, please."

The screen zoomed out and Varna could see that the landing site was marked by a small indicator. To the north and west of that site was a second indicator. The distance between the two was only around three klicks, she estimated, based on her memory of the team's landing site.

"Zoom on the second indicator, please," Varna said as she stared at the screen.

An area of woodland was brought into focus. At first Varna could see nothing of interest but then she was able to discern shadowy figures amongst the trees. She picked out one and placed her finger on the figure. Without being asked the image zoomed in, blurring slightly as the imaging sensor was taken past its point of clear resolution for the figure shown. However, Varna could not be mistaken and she sucked in a breath. It was a Shadow, partly hidden in the gloom of the trees. The Empire's Shadows were already on Ennaris when Clay and the first team were dropped.

"Damn!" she muttered bitterly.

"I don't recognise your request," the assistant said. "Please rephrase."

With a snort Varna said, "Return to the previous resolution, please, and forward the images one every ten seconds."

She watched the stop-motion as the Shadows filtered through the trees, definitely heading for the clearing. They knew that someone was coming and where! How? Her emotions were roiling as she watched the screen. There was a flash at the lower edge of the screen, captured at the point in time when the first team was dropped. Four images later Varna could see four figures at the edge of the clearing, and she watched as they moved into the space. Three of the figures obviously checked sensors and one of the figures was hanging back. That would be Clay, she thought. Why would they go into the clearing anyway? That made no sense. In the normal course a clandestine team would have found a place to observe before venturing out to make contact with the local people or to do whatever they needed to do.

With a sinking heart Varna saw the Shadows filter into position around the clearing. So many of them! She had to stop herself from calling a warning. In a rapid sequence of images, she saw one of the figures down, with two others standing and the fourth amongst the mound of what she thought were tree trunk segments - that spoke to very fast reaction by the fourth, hardening her suspicion that it was Clay - followed by a second being down and then the third among the tree segments. The next image showed the fourth figure bending over the third figure, with coruscations appearing on the body.

"Stop and zoom," she called again and examined the image more closely.

With a start she understood what was happening. The fourth figure was rescuing the third and was being fired on by energy weapons. How was that possible with the technology ban? And the coruscations must be the effects of a personal shield being impacted by blaster bolts. Normal Warriors did not carry such shields. In fact, they were forbidden to carry them. She was sure now that she was watching the Champion.

"Next image," she said.

Clay was standing with the third figure clasped in his arms, upright as though being supported. So, one of the others had survived so far. Coruscations showed that the Shadows were firing on them still. He must have extended his shield to cover the second figure. His left hand held a blaster - against regulations again - and was firing.

"Next!"

Clay and the rescued team member had moved towards the centre of the clearing. There were no coruscations and Clay had holstered his blaster. Shadows could be seen around the clearing.

"Next!"

Clay and the other Warrior were in the centre of the clearing, surrounded by a ring of Shadows. So many of them! Varna tried a quick count and reached fifty before giving up, as more were emerging from the woods still. She tried to understand what Clay was doing but could not. What was he feeling? What was he planning? His reputation was as the greatest of the small number of Champions that had existed, although still young when he was lost. Looking down from above as she was Varna could not make out any features but his stance was one of confidence, challenge. He was standing straight and his gaze was directed to a spot where the still image showed the Shadows separating.

"Next!"

The Shadows had parted to allow a single Shadow to move through and stand in front of Clay, separated by what she thought was about five metres. There were no Shadows in the trees at all, but they were clustered around the figures in a circle. What was going on? Why had they taken so long to attack Clay? Varna examined the image for clues and then, with a shock, she knew. Clay was speaking to the Shadow. While the leader was gloating about capturing the Champion Clay had drawn them all into the clearing! They all wanted a close view! He still had one arm around his fellow team member, and the image showed a faint glow around the two. His shield!

"Next!"

The next image showed a tableau such as Varna had never seen before. Every Shadow was looking up. Their barely glowing eyes were concentrated on a point above Clay. A small shape could be discerned high above Clay and with a thrill, and a chill, Varna saw that his blaster was in his left hand and was firing at the moment the image was taken. It was aimed straight up, at what Varna knew from Blaine's analysis was a blitz mine. But Varna could also see that Clay was not looking at the mine. Rather, he was looking down at his colleague and, if anything, was holding that figure tighter. Varna's eyes opened wide as realisation struck.

"Next!" Varna whispered.

The next image showed the black circle that she expected to see, with no trace of any Shadow, nor of the downed Warriors or the mound of tree segments. The small green patch in the centre of the clearing was clearly visible, empty.

"Oh!" Varna moaned as a single tear leaked from one eye.

Half-way across the blackened ring, heading for the trees, was a figure in white, obviously hurt, carrying a second figure over his shoulder. Clay had survived! The Champion had survived!

11. Revelations

Jalor was impressed by Corm's efforts. For the last seven days the young man had applied himself to the training program that had been devised for him, and was showing himself to be capable of understanding strategy, although starting from a very naive level. Almin Bor had taken him through some of the battles that had occurred over the last two or three generations. Jalor was surprised to find that Almin Bor had taken part in several of the later ones at quite senior ranks, and the strategic outcomes were consistent with what Jalor would have expected.

The lack of technology and the forced reversion to much more primitive weapons had the twin effects of reducing the number of outright casualties during warfare, which may have been the thinking behind it to Jalor's mind, and making warfare much more personal and direct. Generals were much closer to the action than Jalor had seen in his other missions, but the scale of engagements was smaller. A huge battle on Ennaris may involve five thousand combatants on each side, which paled into significance when Jalor thought of engagements like the Battle of the Frew Confederacy, which pitched over one hundred thousand soldiers into the fray on each side and resulted in the vast majority of them being killed or severely wounded, which in turn was dwarfed by the size of the collateral damage to the systems involved and the citizenry of those worlds.

Corm, Jalor thought as he brought his wandering thoughts back to the subject, was looking fitter than he had, with Blaine's constant driving having an effect. His sword skills remained rudimentary but were improving quickly, and his archery skills were poor overall. Helt had introduced Corm to the great sword, which immediately showed that he had a lot of work to do on strength and fitness still. Interestingly, rather than complaining about it, Corm had laughed at himself and determined to do the work required. Jalor was pleased at the progress in Corm's overall disposition, while worrying about whether they could get him up to a reasonable level fast enough, and whether he would stay the course.

Also interestingly, there were occasional spectators to the training sessions. There were not as many as when they had started but still it was a moderate number. Some of those watching were the ones who had derided Corm after his embarrassment in the main Citadel square, and Jalor thought that he could discern a shift in sentiment towards Corm. He had not been surprised to find that Corm was held in poor regard by those who would have to accept him as Faero, despite his father making it clear that Corm was his successor. But the need for acceptance was not merely form without substance. The Faeronar held to their rights to approve the succession and, while it had not happened for many cycles, stories were circulating about other Faero successions where the direct line was not carried forward, but where a branch of the family was brought back into favour. If Corm was made nervous by those stories, he did not show it, but Jalor knew it had to rankle.

Now, however, Corm's efforts were being seen favourably, even if they were still accompanied by sour commentary about the fact that he would not need to be making up so much ground had he paid attention to his upcoming responsibilities when he was younger. Oddly, it was the Guard and Watch who had become his key supporters. Jalor was aware, unofficially, of at least one episode where Corm had been goaded by his former associates in the hope of causing further embarrassment only for members of the Guard to intervene and back up Corm.

So, positive steps were being taken, Jalor thought to himself as he watched Helt put some of the Guard with more advanced skills through their paces. There was another interesting one, he thought wryly. Almost without realising it, she had been improving her own formidable skills as Blaine worked through different forms with her and the Guard. From being a strong, formidable fighter whose tendency to hack and hew with that enormous sword was protected by the odd armour she wore - he was still trying to find out where that came from - she was becoming more adept at some of the finer points of sword-play. Jalor was not quite sure what those finer points could be when applied to that enormous blade, but Blaine assured him they existed.

And now the twins had re-appeared. Exactly where they had been was a mystery and they had mentioned nothing of it when they appeared at the door of the room that he occupied in the Citadel's administrative building. They were interested in getting started with Corm and were almost insistent that Jalor and Blaine both took part. That aligned with Jalor's wishes anyway, but the fact that they insisted he found interesting. The first session was about to begin, Jalor reminded himself, so he needed to stop day-dreaming and get on with it. He made his way off the training field and headed for the tavern. He was greeted companionably by various people as he walked through the streets and the main square, and returned the compliments.

By the time he made it to the tavern the twins were sharing a table with Corm and Blaine, all with the inevitable tankards in front of them. Another appeared for him as he sat and he smiled to Margo as she turned back to the counter. For a moment the thought that this was all becoming a little too comfortable passed through his mind, but then he dismissed the thought for later and turned his attention to the conversation at the table.

"Well, now that Jalor has joined us, I think we can begin," Raglin started. "First though, a message for Jalor from Varna. It's a little odd, and very short - just two words. 'Clay survived.'"

Jalor and Blaine exchanged glances, trying hard to show no overt reaction, and obviously failing.

"So that has significance, as I thought it might," said Raglin. "Is it something you can share with us?"

"Not just yet," Jalor said, with his outward calm restored even while his mind continued to race. "But yes, it is, or may be, significant and forms part of our mission to Ennaris."

"Mission to Ennaris?" Corm asked, confusion written on his face. "You mean to the Citadel?"

"No, I mean to Ennaris," said Jalor. "I'll explain once Raglin and Ragnor have done what they need to do. It is part of what you need to understand, and has a direct bearing on what Blaine, Varna and I are doing here."

"Well," Ragnor said, "we will come to that. For now, and because we have Jalor and Blaine here with us and you, Corm, probably have knowledge drawn from things such as childhood stories and the simplified popular tales that don't really tell you much, we will provide a basic summary of what we know. First, understand that the Guardians are real, although I understand Balgor has convinced you of that." Ragnor smiled at Corm's nod that was accompanied by a rueful smile. "Yes, I understand he can be quite forceful when he finds it necessary. I imagine they all are. What you also need to understand is that the Guardians are not all powerful, they are not gods, and they cannot read the future, despite the Prophecy ascribed to Halfgar and thought to have been influenced by the Guardians. They also have limitations on what they can do and how, which were imposed on them by some power we don't understand. It's humbling to realise that the most powerful beings we know are still subordinate to yet more powerful beings."

"The Guardians came to Ennaris before the time when the Ennarisi were primitive," Raglin continued, merging seamlessly with his brother's telling. "They assisted the Ennarisi to rise to civilisation, as the Ennarisi did with others later. In some cases, they used their own life forces to add to our own. In other cases, they encouraged our development in directions that may not have occurred to our primitive forebears. As a result of the additions made to our own physical beings, however, all Ennarisi carry to one extent or another the seeds of the Guardians. In some, those seeds come out more fully than in others."

Ragnor picked up the thread again. "So, the earliest civilisations were assisted by the Guardians, along different lines. The Guardians did not intervene when wars were fought, although they did seek to ensure that the wars over the many early lifetimes did not destroy Ennaris completely."

"But I thought the Guardians created Ennaris," Corm said, looking from one brother to the other. "And then created us."

"No," Raglin said in a tone that brooked no argument. "That is one of the stories that were put about by a very successful cult not long after the rebellion's end, in opposition to another that called the Guardians demons. It remains current in the form of a child's story. It's a convenient way for us to make the Guardians seem benign so we have persisted with it and encouraged it. But to return, the Guardians allowed the Ennarisi to make mistakes but they also decided that, if they could not intervene, then they needed to find some who could. Already there were people whose mental abilities surpassed others, and there were many with minor gifts who wanted to work for the betterment of their fellows. So, the Guardians established the Guides of Ennaris as a group well fitted to provide that help and, over time, the Mages became a separate group within the Guides."

"So where are the Guides now?" Corm was enthralled, almost spellbound at the story unfolding.

"There are no non-Mage Guides of Ennaris left," Ragnor said sadly. "They all died during the rebellion or in the cycles after. And the ones who may have become Guides were persecuted when they showed signs of their lesser gifts, because the Guides and especially the Mages were considered to be the cause of the destruction."

"And were they?" Jalor asked, knowing in part the answer already.

"We will get there," Raglin said calmly. "To return, the various Ennarisi civilisations continued to grow and extend. The planet of Ennaris went through many trials and tribulations, with the industrial output and the drive for profit over time producing a situation where the planet was threatened with extreme damage from pollution, the loss of many species and potentially the destruction of the Ennarisi should one of the wars unleash the extreme weapons that had been developed. The Guides, and especially the Mages, came to play a leading part in creating a single governing body, led by an elected leader drawn from the maze of governments that existed across the planet. This was the earliest Faero."

"Elected?" Corm queried, surprised. "I have always thought it was hereditary."

"No, it has always been elected, but the form of election has changed. The earliest Faero was an elected official. The detail of exactly how the forebears of your family made it a hereditary position is for another time, but you need only understand that it was during a period of extreme danger for Ennaris that the governments of the individual parts of Ennaris collapsed and the position of Faero was taken up by one of the most talented of individuals. Over his whole lifetime, and that of his daughter who succeeded him, the danger to Ennaris was overcome. Both lived long lives dedicated to the well-being of Ennaris and the Ennarisi. By the time that danger was passed Ennaris had a single planetary government and the role of Faero was established as both a hereditary leader but still one that relied on advisors and supporters. It was not in any way a dictatorship, although as always there were individuals who sought to make it so in the long history of Ennaris. That's why there remains the need to elect the Faero. It can be used to block individuals from succeeding to the role and allow a different branch of the Faero family to be elevated. It has been used, but rarely."

"What about the rebellion's damage?" Corm asked. "What do the stories not tell?"

Ragnor smiled.

"Patience," he said. "First you need to understand the role of Ennaris in the galaxy."

"Galaxy?" Corm was confused again.

"Yes, the galaxy. All of the stars that you see in the night sky, and many more, form the galaxy in which Ennaris exists. There are many galaxies in the universe, and the life force of the planets, stars, galaxies and universe are all bound together."

"I know what the galaxy is," Corm said with some slight indignation. "I didn't neglect all of my lessons."

"Of course," said Ragnor smoothly, "then you also know that Ennaris once claimed overlordship of almost one third of the galaxy."

Corm gaped at Ragnor. "One third?"

Jalor and Blaine exchanged astonished glances and Blaine echoed Corm. "One third?"

"Yes," Ragnor continued. "Ennaris' capabilities grew rapidly. The combination of highly gifted individuals in the Mages and highly intelligent people driving scientific endeavours resulted in Ennaris achieving space travel well in advance of others in the near vicinity. It also meant that they were able to establish colonies on uninhabited planets through the closer areas of space within a relatively short time. In fact, it was those colonies that brought Ennaris to the attention of a people who were slightly more advanced than us and who wished to extend their influence over Ennarisi space. It was that war that was the extreme danger we mentioned before. The war that followed was terrible and the destruction was enormous on both sides. Ultimately, Ennaris was able to defeat the Quorfus, who were thrown back to their own part of the galaxy and became less of a threat. At some stage the Quorfus civilisation ceased to exist. We don't really know why, although the Guardians may. It was speculated that they fought amongst themselves and destroyed their own civilisation following their defeat by the Ennarisi."

"So Ennaris was now supreme in its sector of the galaxy," Raglin broke in. "For many lifetimes, more than you can imagine, millennia after millennia, eon after eon, Ennaris grew and prospered. With the help of the Guides and Mages, many difficulties were overcome and, with the scientific achievements, great deeds were accomplished. The cities of Ennaris were beautiful and the arts were truly indescribable. At its peak, not long before the rebellion, Ennaris' standard of living that applied to all people was the highest known. Comforts were available to all. Almost no-one suffered short lives through illness. Many injuries from misadventure were able to be healed. It was truly a wonderful time to be alive."

Raglin exchanged with Ragnor a look of such pain that the others remained quiet.

Ragnor sighed and took up the story.

"Ennaris had been sending expeditions out to other worlds, to lift civilisations as the Guardians had lifted our own. Several successes were achieved over a very long time, with a small number of peoples achieving advanced forms of civilisation. Not all of them were of the sort Ennaris preferred but, in general, we honoured the principles of the Guardians and allowed them to make their mistakes or achieve their successes for themselves. Two of those civilisations destroyed themselves, unfortunately. Two others of which I am aware succeeded in achieving space capabilities, although both occurred after the rebellion. I'm not sure what happened to the other two in the intervening time. Because now Ennaris had problems of its own."

Raglin nodded.

"Goroth," he said shortly.

Corm looked from one brother to the other.

"Goroth? Balgor said he's not a myth!"

"Oh no," Raglin said quietly. "No myth. Goroth was one of the most gifted of the Mages. For many cycles, Goroth led missions to other worlds to monitor and adjust their rise to civilisation. For many cycles he observed the strictures and ensured the most careful observance without unduly influencing the peoples of those planets. We had always had individuals who transgressed and tried to use their gifts to enhance their own power on those planets, and they were dealt with by the mission leaders. Goroth had not shown those tendencies. Indeed, he was one of the mission leaders who tried to stamp out the practice. But something changed, and still we don't know what. Goroth was always an enquiring mind and perhaps he came across something that caused him to walk down the wrong path. What we do know is that he started to investigate the use of forbidden lore."

"What sort of forbidden lore?" Corm asked. "And why is this never discussed in the tales?"

"The forbidden lore is not discussed to hold back knowledge that it exists," Ragnor said. "That's why it's not in the tales. And Goroth was not the first to investigate and be seduced by the dark forces. But he was the most powerful of those who dabbled. The forbidden lore does not seek to enhance, protect or assist. Rather its purpose is to destroy, to take the life force from others and add it to that of the wielder, to reduce, to harm. It preys on those who are weaker. It's the reverse of the forces we Mages seek to harness and use to benefit others. Goroth and one of his lieutenants became very strong in the use of this forbidden lore and, because he was far from Ennaris, he used it to create a position of power on the planet of his mission."

"Earth," Jalor said bleakly.

"Your home planet?" Raglin smiled gently. "Yes and no. In fact, it was the planet of your enemy, those you call the Shadows. Your own planet temporarily had a group of Goroth's disciples who acted as demigods, but they did not over-run it as completely as Goroth and his minions did on Andoreth."

"So Goroth was not the Zeus figure, the all-powerful one of our home world?" Blaine was almost disappointed. "We only had the B team?"

"Indeed so," Raglin replied with mock sympathy. "Think yourself lucky. Andoreth yet groans under the rule of Goroth's lieutenant, Likud."

"So, we always thought there was something strange about the way the Empire leader seemed not to change. And the position was called the Likud, as far as we knew. I assume it is the same person?"

"I imagine so. Our knowledge of that world hasn't been maintained since the rebellion. But he was quite gifted and may still be alive. He was also vicious and utterly ruthless. He was not with Goroth when he was captured after the rebellion ended, nor was another senior Mage and possibly several other minor Mages. We cannot be sure of them."

"What happened with Goroth?" Corm asked, feeling a little forgotten, then gasped and turned to look at Jalor and Blaine. "Wait, did you say your home planet? You're not from Ennaris?"

"We're getting to that," Ragnor said. "Goroth was summoned home to answer for the actions of his mission, and those of his lieutenants on the world we know as Ordoreth, your home, Jalor. He only came, I believe, because he believed he was stronger than the Council members and would be able to assume control of Ennaris. I don't believe he considered the Faero's position in this. His arrogance had become such that he believed the Mages should rule, as they had power. The Council refused to countenance what he demanded, which would have amounted to turning power over to him. What was not known was that Goroth had a number of Mages and Guides who supported him, and after much dissension they formed a break-away Council."

"It was a terrible time," Raglin continued. "The Council was in disarray and it was Halfgar's counsel that brought it back to order. The Archmage declared Goroth to be cast out of the Council and decreed that he submit himself for judgement, which only served to tip Goroth over the edge."

"Who did that? Flin? Must have been a tough call," Blaine said, shaking his head.

"Oh no, Flin was not Archmage at that time," Raglin replied, with a shake of his head. "In fact, he is not officially Archmage even now, unfortunately. That was Hardus."

"Flin? You mean the storyteller who visited my father every few years was - is - the Archmage?"

Corm was struggling with the rapid telling of the story and the amount of information he needed to take in. So much of it contradicted what he knew.

"In almost all ways that matter, yes," Ragnor said. "But at the time of the rebellion Flin was a young Mage. One with great potential and enormous power, matched only by Marjory. Both of them were destined for greatness but at the time they were young and inexperienced and only just appointed to the Council against significant opposition. It was Hardus who led the Council, and who expelled Goroth from the Council and tried to bring him to heel. And it was Hardus who led the Mages through most of the years of the rebellion."

"There was a wider civil war?" Blaine asked quietly, taking a further sip of his brew.

"Yes," Ragnor said with a sigh. "It had started among a couple of cities where some of the rebel Guides had built a bit of a following. Initially it was just demonstrations and civil disobedience but a few heavy-handed actions from inexperienced city administrators was all it took for emotions to boil over. It was thought later that the rebel Guides had increased emotions and made the situation worse, probably just to add pressure. That was likely to be Grensor's work. Or his supporters. Over quite a short time it became a full-blown rebellion. The northern lands of Kebris were the first to try to break away, and the armed forces were asked to stop them. Ennaris never really had much in the way of planet-based military – it had not been required for a very long time – and they found that they had internal dissension also. Some of them refused to take part in actions against other Ennarisi and, when the commanders tried to force them, the military split. The problem was that they also took some of the most advanced weapons with them when, inevitably, they broke into factions. Those weapons were used in the north first and huge areas were laid waste. The Guides could not repair damage on that scale and so much of the north became a waste where little grew. Even today the damage remains in many areas, largely the lands of the twin kingdoms beyond the mountains."

"By that time the rebellion had become planet-wide," Raglin said, picking up the story's thread smoothly, "and even spread to the fleets that had been called back from the various explorations. We lost so much in such a short time." The Mage's young-seeming face was drawn as though he was reliving the disaster. "Finally, a special team of the best of the loyal militia was put together and managed to destroy the rebellion's cache of energy weapons. The rebel commanders fell back on their last card and fired every missile on the planet. They were designated for defence but one of the rebels had the command codes and reconfigured them to fall back onto targets on the surface. We think that was Likud."

The twin Mages stared into their tankards, wearing identical looks of despair, before Ragnor spoke again.

"The Guides, led by Marjory who had taken the role of battle leader, tried to establish a shield to destroy them. Many of the rebel Guides saw what was happening and abandoned the rebellion to join in but the effort was failing. The rumour grew at the time that the Guardians at the last moment joined with the Guides and boosted their strength such that every missile was destroyed, but the effect proved too much for many of the Guides. The stronger ones took the brunt of the back-lash and most of them died or were burnt out, and the weaker ones were decimated.

"So now there were few Guides left, the civilisation of Ennaris had been shattered by the effects of the warfare and none of the great cities had been spared. Worse, the rebel Guides were still there. They were reduced to a small number now but they were still there. And they had not given in. In fact, one of the problems was that they had tried to undermine the defensive effort and contributed to the backlash that battered the Guides when the missiles were destroyed." He looked into his tankard and, finding he still had a quantity of ale he drained it in one go.

"And then," Raglin said quietly, "Likud turned the primary weapon of the fleet flagship, *Scaliba*, on the planet, thinking to wipe out those of us who remained. Likud knows nothing of restraint. The primary weapon was an energy weapon of great strength, designed in days when Ennaris was threatened by a strong enemy, and never intended to be used in atmosphere. Marjory led the final defence against it, drawing on all those left. She even dragged most of the rebels who were left into the merge, whether they wanted to take part or not. I have no idea how she achieved it. Most of the Mages on both sides had been killed, including Archmage Hardus and almost all of the Council. Marjory and Drewflin were the strongest by far of those who remained. She managed to shield most of us from the energy beam but inevitably much of the power spilled into Ennaris before she could reflect it back to the ship. Of course, *Scaliba* then became a further part of the problem when it fell into the western ocean, causing a devastating wave.

"Ennaris was almost destroyed, many had died during the war. The vast majority of the remaining people were killed outright and the land changed irretrievably. I can't describe to you what it was like to walk the paths of the cities that we knew so well, that we had helped to create and recreate, only to find death and destruction everywhere. It fell to Flin and Marjory to battle Goroth at the end, after Halfgar had given his essence to create some sort of shield that ended the use of all advanced technology across most of Ennaris. Flin was the strongest of those of us left. In fact, he may be the strongest ever seen. We consider him to be the Archmage, although we were unable to perform the ceremony. And it was with the combined efforts of the remaining Council Mages that Goroth was sealed in stasis in a place where Halfgar's shield did not reach."

"How long did the rebellion last," Jalor wanted to know.

"Two cycles," Raglin said soberly. "City after city fell. The land itself rebelled. The Guides tried and failed to halt the spread of the destruction but could not. The glory that was Ennaris that had grown over such a long time was drowned out in only two cycles. The most advanced civilisation this galaxy had seen ever was reduced to barbarism."

"And why did the Guardians allow that to happen?" Corm asked, aghast. "I thought they were to protect and help us."

"And so we did," Balgor said from behind Corm, who spun in place to stare as though at an apparition. "And so we did. We absorbed as much of the damaging energy as we could, and in doing so three of us died, while the rest of us were able to do little to help Drewflin and his friends as a result of the severe injuries we received. So, you see Raglin, Ragnor, it was not Marjory and your Mages alone, fighting against the destruction. But the people were left to end it themselves, I'm afraid."

"Guardians died?" Corm whispered.

"I've told many people recently that we are not gods, nor are we all-powerful. Yes, three of us died. Appanu, Angor and Zang absorbed more of the deadly energies than they could manage and they died. The Guardians did not abandon Ennaris, but we could not save her from the destructive forces that remained. That was the rebellion's aftermath." Balgor stared at the table sadly. "Appanu and Angor were life-bonded and perished together. It was Appanu who did much work to protect Ennaris in the earliest days and he has been forgotten. Angor in legend has been defiled as a villain, but he also was a protector of this planet. Zang it was who created some of the most beautiful of Ennaris' forests and gardens, and her name likewise is forgotten."

"I will ensure their names are resurrected," Corm said softly, greatly affected by the story and by Balgor's evident distress. "But what happened after? And what of Jalor and Blaine?"

"I thank you, Guardian," Ragnor said formally. "You and your brethren. I was not aware that you took that part, although there were rumours of such. Nor was I aware of your losses. You have my deepest sympathy."

Silence reigned for several microns.

"After the rebellion's end, the world continued to change," Raglin said. "And the damage was enormous. All of the cities of Ennaris had been destroyed, either directly by those weapons whose power you, Corm, cannot imagine but that I feel Jalor and Blaine may well be able to do, or by the ground beneath them literally falling apart. Annareth, the home of the Faero and seat of government, was amongst the first to fall, destroyed by power weapons created in secret by Goroth. By the time the destruction had run its course over nine in ten Ennarisi had been killed. Over the next millennium that death toll rose ever higher, as diseases that were easily managed before the rebellion now took their toll. And we had wars such that Ennaris had not seen since the earliest days. Many people were killed, atrocities were committed by all sides, some in revenge for others."

"Nine out of ten were killed?" Corm asked, aghast at the loss of life.

"Yes, and many more, and Ennaris suffered accordingly. For the ones killed tended to be the ones who preferred not to fight but to work out solutions. A spirit of compromise was one of the earliest casualties, and it took many long cycles to bring that back."

"The Guides and Mages?" Corm asked resignedly.

Ragnor nodded.

"They were amongst the first to be killed. Because Goroth spoke as though he remained as a member of the Council, and because he had the backing of many Council Mages, although only very few Guides, all were brought into disrepute. The non-Mage Guides had only limited gifts, if they had any at all. They were dedicated to repair, to recovery, not to warfare and killing. But, because they were held to be responsible, they were killed and few tried to assist them. There were very few Mages left after Goroth was brought to heel, and we were unable to achieve anything much. We even considered using our own powers to force the people to follow our wishes but Flin and Marjory vetoed that, and rightly so. But I very much doubt any of us had the stomach for that anyway. As we now know from Balgor, even the Guardians were unable to assist.

"The result was devastation. For the last five thousand cycles we have tried to achieve some sort of recovery. The hatred for the Mages and Guides gradually fell away until they, we, became myths and legends. The Faero remained but he no longer played a role in a planet-wide government. In fact, when Annareth fell and the extent of the rebellion was known, the Citadel was built for the Faeronar. That was at Halfgar's behest. We built the Citadel as a refuge and protection. Later the Prophecy said the Faero would protect the Blood and together they would lead the people of Ennaris out of the darkness, aided by the Children of Ennaris and the Nine. The Faero therefore collected as many of the Blood who survived and held them close near the Citadel."

"And I was tasked with protecting the Faero and the Faeronar while my people retreated," Balgor interjected.

"But why did you have to leave?" Corm asked, bewildered. "Ennaris was your own home, and the Ennarisi your people."

Balgor nodded sadly. "I still don't know fully. The same Prophecy that told of the saving of the Ennarisi made it clear that the Guardians had to depart until the time was ready. We could leave only a token presence to ensure Ennaris' overall safety but little more. We were not even permitted to have contact with the remaining Mages until such time as the portents allowed. We did not feel that we could fight against that Prophecy, for the consequences would have been dire and would lead to the destruction of Ennaris as well as the client peoples. So we had to leave our homes."

"And Jalor and Blaine?"

"And Varna," said Balgor. "Don't ever forget Varna. For these three are the Children of Ennaris returned to us in our hour of greatest peril. They come to us from a planet they call Earth, but that was Ordoreth to the Ennarisi. For you, Corm," and Balgor glanced to the Faero-elect, who was looking wide-eyed from Jalor to Blaine and back, "they represent the best chance for Ennaris to resist the evil that is already in our midst. For Goroth's minions are returned and the ancient evil will be reborn if the Children of Ennaris fail."

"Fail at what?" Corm asked. "How can three people save the planet against whatever is happening?"

"Ah," Balgor said, while the twins nodded despondently, "that remains to be seen."

"You come from another planet?" Corm asked Jalor.

"We do," Jalor replied, "but don't say that too loud. We have no further idea about what should happen here than you, but we do know that part of our mission has been accomplished. The twins brought us word from Varna that Clay, the Champion of the Light, survived his landing some fifty cycles before us. We know no more than that, nor do we know about the other members of his party, but in knowing that we have hope that he may be alive still. He would be elderly now, of course, but if we can locate him then we must do so."

"This Clay is your champion?" Raglin asked, curious.

"It is a role and title given to only certain people. Clay is but the third or fourth I believe. They were and are the best of the best. All have been Warriors of the Light and all were used for the most difficult assignments, those that could only be handled by the best."

"And he was sent here?" Ragnor picked up from his brother.

"Yes. It had been discovered that there were signs of this planet being visited by Shadows - from the planet Andoreth, you called it - so Clay and a small team of three were inserted to find out what was happening. That was around fifty cycles ago, as I said."

"And yet the planetary shield remained functional at that time," Raglin said in a mild tone, causing Jalor to frown at him. "How did you even know this planet existed?"

"I'm unable to answer that," said Jalor. "All I know is that our Grand Admiral was behind it, as she was behind our mission to seek out Clay. And now that we know that Clay survived our mission remains alive."

"And yet you have your responsibility to the Ennarisi as the Children of Ennaris," Corm said.

"As we have been told without very much additional information. I need to consider what we do know," Jalor said to Corm. "Meanwhile, I have promised Flin that we would assist in your training, and so we will, at least until you have been confirmed as Faero."

Balgor smiled as he turned to walk away, saying, "You may find events move faster than you imagine, my friend. They always do."

12. Corm

Corm was confirmed as Faero fifteen days after his father's death. While there had been no challengers, there had been many people who were unsure of his preparedness for the role. Almin Bor had prevailed upon the members of the Citadel Guard and Watch to make people aware that Corm had their support, and to spread the stories about his training and education. It was notable that the physical sessions had more watchers than ever in the days leading to the vote, and many were the Faeronar who took note as Corm met with those who were teaching him, filling in the gaps.

Key among those teachers was Jalor, who taught the basics of strategy, at least as far as warfare went. Almin Bor became a major contributor to the strategy discussions, passing on details of battles of which he had heard and in which he had taken part. The twins continued to take Corm through the detailed history of the Faeronar and Ennaris, concentrating on the more recent events - the distant past was a long way away, and Corm had to deal with the situation as it was found today. They also spoke of the different cities and states that existed on present-day Ennaris, and described how the various priesthoods had built great power by preying on the cares and concerns of the people in many parts of both continents.

It was the twins who compiled the list of leaders who would be needed to support Corm in the event the Faero had to fight the battle that Prophecy said would result. And it was Jalor who assisted to draft missives to each of those leaders seeking their support, to be sent out after Corm was confirmed as Faero.

The change in public attitude towards Corm was cemented when he fought off two burly, well-armed men seeking to assault a young woman, holding both at bay while the watch was called. Standing in front of the woman, who cowered on the ground with her tunic torn, Corm presented a calm face and wielded his sword as though born to it. No-one, including Corm, was aware of Balgor's presence, and the Citadel watch arrested the two men with little trouble. It was noted and discussed how the watchmen seemed unsurprised at the new skill shown by Corm.

On the day of the election, Jalor and Blaine stood at the back of the crowd gathered in the main square, where a platform had been raised. Jalor was surprised to see that this was not a coronation but rather something different. Corm made his appearance on the platform dressed in little more than normal attire. The key change was a sword belt that was of much higher quality than the one he had been using. Hanging from the belt was a scabbard covered with odd markings but with no sword. Ragnor had appeared at the practice ground on the day prior to the ceremony, as training was ending, and with little fuss presented it to Corm. The belt was adjusted and Corm agreed to wear it the following day, slightly perplexed as to why Ragnor insisted on the point but seeing no reason to object. His father's plain sword belt and scabbard had been put into storage.

The ceremony itself was relatively brief. Several speakers spoke for or against Corm's election, using his recent behaviour for him or his past behaviour against him. The large crowd were largely silent, with some nodding with one speaker's comments, others with another's. But when Almin Bor, who Jalor had already realised held a place of honour amongst the Faeronar, spoke for Corm on behalf of the Old Blood the conclusion was foregone. The Old Blood still carried public opinion amongst the Faeronar, many of whom were traced from the same Old Blood anyway. Corm was confirmed as Faero by acclamation.

The first surprise came when Ragnor and Raglin both appeared, dressed in what Jalor and Blaine were later informed was the traditional garb of the Guide Mages. The shock amongst the crowd was palpable as the brothers walked unhurriedly down an aisle leading to the platform, mounted the few steps and approached Corm. Ragnor carried what obviously was a sword, wrapped in bright red cloth, while Raglin carried two staffs. A buzz ran through the assembled crowd as Ragnor unwrapped the sword, revealing a blade that shone with a cold light. Ragnor passed the cloth to Raglin, who laid the two staffs on the platform and walked calmly to a flagpole that no-one seemed to have noticed and without any hurry attached what was now seen as a flag, a standard. He waited until Ragnor nodded and then with a few rapid motions hoisted the flag to the top of the pole. The crowd watched curiously as the flag hung motionless in the still air with the standard's emblem hidden by folds in the fabric. Raglin walked back to where his brother waited and picked up both staffs. Ragnor lifted the sword above his head with both hands, one hand holding the hilt and the other holding the blade.

"This sword," Ragnor said in a tone that could be heard by all, "we hereby return to Corm Ramesa, today elected to be Faero. I am Ragnor and my brother is Raglin" - more rustles from the members of the crowd who recalled ancient tales - "and by the authority of the Council of Mages we acclaim Corm Ramesa as Faero of Ennaris."

He waited as astonished gasps ran through the crowd - the Mages were thought to be dead, the Faero had not been known by that title for long ages. Then, with a flourish he swung the sword in an arc so that the hilt lay along one arm as he offered it to Corm. The young man, open-mouthed and seemingly stunned by what was happening, hesitated and then reached out for the sword and grasped it by the hilt. Ragnor muttered a few words of instruction to Corm, and then walked to where his brother stood. He was handed one of the staffs and turned back to the crowd, who now watched proceedings avidly.

The brothers with one accord lifted their staffs and brought them down on the platform. A loud boom resounded through the citadel, scaring the birds roosting in the nooks and crannies and bring running many who had decided not to attend the ceremony. As the final rever-berations of the boom faded the brothers' staffs' heads burst into a bright light, and a breeze sprang up. Ragnor, waiting for the moment, gestured to Corm.

"The Sword of the Faero," Ragnor called out, his voice penetrating through the square and, in fact, through much of the Citadel.

As Corm raised the sword above his head a flame ran up the shaft and exploded from the point, after which it died away. At the same time, while the people gasped anew the flag fluttered into life and spread wide, showing the ancient symbol of the Faeros of Ennaris, a golden mythical figure, serpentine with four clawed legs and wings springing from its back. Its head faced outward and the eyes seemed to glow as it glared at those who watched. The attending people were on their feet shouting with one voice. Astonishment warred with shock and all was overlaid with unbounded joy at seeing the old symbols of the Faeronar unveiled.

Corm looked terrified.

The twins allowed the acclaim to continue, and after a long while they raised their staff and struck the platform again. Another long boom sounded, and the assembled people quieted, wondering what was to come. Corm lowered the sword and thrust it into his scabbard, unconsciously taking up the stance of a trained soldier at parade rest. Blaine held back a smile at the sight but several members of the as-sembled guard grinned - until Almin Bor glared at them. Ragnor and Raglin, in unison, bowed to Corm and stepped back, clearing the front of the platform. Self-consciously, Corm stepped forward, looking out over the crowd.

"I thank you for your vote of confidence," he started in a quiet voice that somehow was heard easily by all - Jalor was fairly sure he knew how. "And for those who voted against me I hope to earn your trust. For Ennaris will need the Faeronar as never before. Evil walks the land. The stories we have been told as children are shown not to be stories at all, but warnings and teachings. My father knew of this but was taken from us too soon. So, it falls to us. In this, the time of need," Corm continued, renewed confidence pushing him to stand straight as he addressed his people, "the Guide Mages have returned to advise and assist, as they did so long ago to my forebears and many others. As they did when they tried to heal the damage caused by renegades and criminals in rebellion, and in many cases died doing so."

The crowd was still, looking from Corm to the twins and back again, scarcely able to believe what they had heard before and were hearing now. And they looked at Corm, this youth who had been a source of trouble and amusement, who had eschewed responsibility for all of his life, standing tall and proud before them.

"Evil walks the land," Corm repeated. "The Faeronar will lead the forces to battle this evil and defeat it once and for all. To do so, we will need a war-leader and I ask our friend Vinca Jalor to accept the position of General of the Ennarisi, to bring together the forces of resistance and help us to defeat this evil. Our good and loyal friend Almin Bor has agreed to take the position of Captain-General of the Faero Guard." Corm gestured to where Jalor and Blaine were standing, and then to Almin Bor.

Jalor scowled as the people turned as one towards him and cheered. He turned to Blaine only to find him almost doubled over in laughter, tears streaming down his face, leaning against the wall behind him for support.

"Oh, that's good," Blaine managed to gasp out, "that's very good." And he dissolved in laughter again.

Jalor stared at Almin Bor, who regarded him with such an innocent look that Jalor knew who had put Corm up to the nomination. He briefly considered refusing but immediately realised that such a position, if it actually amounted to anything given the Faero had no actual power over Ennaris, may allow him to move around the whole planet readily. Not only could he search for Clay, and just maybe others of the landing party, but he might be able to halt the Shadows in their tracks. And to do so he would have to fight Likud and any others of

Goroth's followers who he might come across. That, he thought, probably aligned with his mission goals. The thought crossed his mind that the Grand Admiral probably would not object. It took a second or two for the sequence of thoughts to flash through his mind before he started to move towards the platform. At least there had been no mention of the Children of Ennaris.

Jalor reached Corm's side to be greeted by a lop-sided grin and a half shrug of apology. He merely nodded and, with a flourish bowed low to Corm before moving to stand behind and slightly to his right. He assumed a parade rest stance. A few moments later Almin Bor stepped up beside Jalor, a quirk of the lips the only indication of anything happening beneath the calm exterior.

The ceremony ended shortly thereafter, with Corm and his newly minted military leaders exiting the platform to renewed cheers. While the populace of the Citadel moved to partake of the feast that had been laid on in honour of the day, the three were joined by Blaine and the twins while they discussed strategy for bringing the forces of Ennaris together, despite the many fractured relationships that existed. The discussion went long into the evening, interrupted by well-wishers from time to time.

13. Women of Old Bastion

Flin led Varna and Dalresar through the countryside with unerring accuracy. After learning what he could from the Council Assistant, Flin had spent a tenday delving into the resources that usually were available to the Archmage as they started their time in office. He found the experience to be both interesting and frustrating. Varna had spent time exploring the facility end to end, and using the Council Assistant to learn more about Ennaris. A short length of time was spent with the twins when they appeared unexpectedly, but they left after only a day. As the time progressed, however, she became increasingly impatient. Dalresar sympathised with her but, in the absence of any ability to do anything about it, he also explored the chambers. Finally, Flin decided that he had gleaned all that he could in the time he had allowed himself. He had listened to what Varna had to tell about the fate of Clay, and thought long and hard about what it may mean. Finally, Flin decided that it was time for Varna to go to the Forest of the Guardians. Decision made, with little fuss the three left the Council Chamber and commenced their journey.

Varna walked in silence. The Council Chamber was more than three days behind them now, and she, Flin and Dalresar were heading for the Forest of the Guardians via as direct a path as they could. She was experiencing the return of the same sensations that she had battled for most of her time on this planet, but at least she now knew what it meant. She hoped that they would get to the Forest before the effects became severe, but she trusted Flin and Dalresar to look after her if not.

Meanwhile she continued to replay that last frame, trying and failing to read anything into the puzzle. She had told Flin about her discovery when he emerged from his own review of the Council records and, while he had expressed interest in the fact that Clay seemingly had survived, he had seemed to be distracted. He still was. The same questions went round and round in Varna's thoughts. What had happened to Clay? Could he be alive still? Was that possible on this world that was in so many ways hard and unyielding? And if he was, how could they find him? And what would happen if they did? Could it change anything? Was he the Champion referred to in the Prophecy of the Nine? How could that be, given his age?

Dalresar, meanwhile, had explored the Chambers as far as he was able. On the last day of their stay, he found a store of weapons and body armour that he had plundered. While Flin refused either, both Dalresar and Varna now wore close-fitting mail-like armour made from an extremely light-weight material that Varna had never seen before. Flin called it mittal and explained that it was developed in the time long before the rebellion. It was an advanced material woven through with the energy from smiths who had a special gift of binding. Designed for the off-world expeditions of Mages, it would also provide protection against most hand-wielded weapons. Both wore their new armour beneath their tunics.

Dalresar also had appropriated a sword, slightly longer than normal and shaped with a slight bulge towards the point. He claimed the balance was perfect and with some relief discarded the sword he had taken from the dead bandit. Dressed now in dark breeches, dark boots, a flowing cream-coloured shirt, a cloak of deep crimson and the sword sheathed in a belt and scabbard that had been similarly found in the weapons store, and paired with a long knife from the same stash, Dalresar looked more like one of the travelling mercenaries Varna had seen in the Citadel than a Mage's apprentice.

For his part Dalresar was disconcerted. He had watched as Varna replayed the scenes leading up to the battle and destruction in the small clearing without comment, and had also reviewed the findings of the Assistant that the two forces gathering around Ennaris were descendants of two of the peoples lifted by Ennaris' off-world expeditions. He had found and viewed footage of the battle where Goroth had been taken, and had repeated parts of it over and over, puzzling over oddities he had found. Goroth had drawn on the dark arts to drive home what he thought was an advantage, but at the end he had been thwarted by Flin and Marjory, aided by a small number of other Mages, who had been able to deflect Goroth's attacks and turn them back on him. How they managed to do that he was unable to discover. But it did look like Goroth had weaknesses in the use of those dark arts.

Dalresar knew that he had holes in his memories of the time before Flin had rescued him and partially healed him. But since being in the Council Chamber, he was experiencing odd flashes that seemed to be memories, of an older-seeming woman and a young child, a small dwelling that was more hovel than cottage, and he shied away from those memories instinctively. He knew Flin had found him in a slaver's camp, being mistreated along with many others, and had recognised some sort of spark of a gift, even though nothing had ever eventuated. He knew that Flin had caused the slavers to be apprehended and the slaves released, and he knew that Flin had arranged care for him with a farmer as he healed, before appearing one day to declare him as his apprentice and take him with him. He had never said what sort of apprentice, and Dalresar had never asked. But those images seemed to be from the time before Flin had found him, perhaps before he had been a slave. And while Dalresar tried to avoid thinking about them, the images resonated and returned, over and over, like a sore tooth.

Flin was puzzling through what he had found out in the briefing by the Chamber Assistant. Much of what he learned was what he already knew, he was relieved to find, and there were some information points that confirmed what he had guessed from time to time, but there were nuances and depths of information that gave him pause. The details included the existence of the Guides of the sea, including the potential for Mages among the leviathans and the wave-leapers, which he already had known. He had learned of, and been deeply shocked by, the deaths of three of the Guardians as they sought to deflect and absorb the enormous energies released by Goroth's lieutenants, and the damage caused to all of the others in the same effort. He doubted his fellow Mages knew of the Guardians' deaths, for the entry had been made by Halfgar just before he created the technology interdiction and died in so doing. Never had he realised how close Ennaris had come to complete destruction, believing that he and his remaining Mages had minimised the damage. He now knew that the decision to leave Ennaris was forced on them by the Prophecy. And he knew that a small number had remained to do what they could to help the devastated world and its people. He had delayed his return to Varna and Dalresar to allow himself time to recover equilibrium, to allow his rekindled rage at Goroth to subside. That a single man, a Guide and Mage, had wrought such death and destruction to further his own mean ends, was something that Flin could not understand, even though he had lived through it. That rage was merely banked though, like a fire was banked to carry it through a night. It was waiting, a coil of tight emotion deep inside, and Flin could feel it shifting and turning, gathering a sort of focus and intent. If anything, it now was deeper than before, carrying with it the deaths of Marjory and their son as well as the near death of Ennaris and its people.

He had also found that several of the systems had degraded. Not unexpected, he thought. But he was surprised to discover that the Assistant, a very advanced artificial intelligence, required his approval to effect repairs, and had been waiting for that approval for over five thousand cycles. He felt that he detected a tone of relief from the Assistant when it confirmed his directive to start repairs. When he queried why his approval was required, he was told that it was a fail-safe to make sure that the Assistant did not achieve full self-awareness. Another surprise - he had never considered that such could happen.

Finally, he had reviewed the condition of the planetary defences and was shocked at what he found. Goroth had plundered the advanced weaponry, as he knew, but had missed stores of weapons with shocking potential. Those stores, the Assistant had told him, were made known to the Battle Mage and Archmage alone, which meant Marjory probably knew of them. She, in turn, would have expected that he would know of them, and so the subject was never brought up. Had they been used by the Guide Mages in battle with the rebels then Ennaris would not have survived, no matter what the Guardians tried to do. It was a sobering thought. Hardus knew about them, as had Jorus, the chief Battle Mage of the time, and they had decided not to use them, understanding that in relying on their own enormous powers to defend Ennaris they were in all likelihood going to perish. Flin's respect for the leaders of the Council of that time grew enormously. Where he had thought them conservative and scared, he now knew they were wise - and scared, and now he understood the reasons.

So, as they walked through the countryside all three of the companions were distracted, tied up in their own thoughts and all, for one reason or another, were looking forward to reaching the Forest, still a journey of some days. But it was Dalresar, whose instincts were still awake even while deep in contemplation, who noticed the strange lights from deep in the woods. He warned the others to silence, removed his cloak and quietly entered the woods as Flin and Varna moved to the other side of the road and took cover. Dalresar returned quickly and, whispered to the others to leave their packs and come with him. The three moved into the woods, quietly, stealing between the trees.

They approached a clearing and stopped inside the tree line where they could see what was happening. Varna gasped even though she could not understand exactly what was transpiring. At her side she heard Flin growl softly, as though he did understand. Dalresar remained quiet, watching. A number of women were all roped to stakes set in a single line. Varna counted nine of them. All had been stripped naked and were being birched by short men dressed in long white robes with hoods. Bundles of twigs were being used to whip across their backs, causing welts to appear. As the three watched, one of the men stepped back, followed by the rest, leaving the women sobbing as they tried weakly to free themselves. The leader, the first man to step back, threw his hood back to reveal wild hair, and a haggard face, with his eyes wide and wild.

"Women are the bane of existence," he called out loudly, to be answered by incoherent cries from the others, "and they must be destroyed. I am the high priest of Likki and I say these women have been found guilty and must be sacrificed to the true goddess. Only then can the false Likki be defeated and we can take our place amongst the people of Likki once more."

The men cried out again, brandishing their bundles of twigs. All of them turned towards the self-proclaimed high priest. Two of them moved to the first woman in line and freed her hands from the stake, dragging her despite her weak struggles to what Varna had missed, a large rock at the back of the clearing where they bound her hand and foot to more stakes. They laid the woman over the rock as the high priest drew a wicked-looking knife from beneath his robes and advanced on the woman. And Flin erupted.

"No," he shouted as he emerged from the tree line, moving rapidly to the clearing. "You shall not defile the Guardian's name in this way. I know you, Urglith, and you have been warned before."

"You cannot stop me, I am the high priest of Likki," Urglith shrieked, jumping towards the bound woman and raising his knife high over her breast.

A bolt from Flin's staff pierced Urglith's body, and he dropped lifeless to the ground before the make-shift altar. Urglith's supporters stared for a moment and then surged towards Flin, drawing a range of weapons, shouting and screaming their rage and hatred. And then they encountered Dalresar, who had followed Flin and now stood between the Mage and the followers of the former high priest of Likki. Varna hurried forward to provide aid but no sooner had she grasped her staff than she stopped. Her jaw dropped open in astonishment. She had seen Blaine in action with a sword and believed no-one could possibly come close to his skill. She had seen Dalresar deal with the three bandits and was astonished. But now Dalresar did not dance through the attackers as Blaine had seemed to do. Nor did he merely exhibit superior skill as he had done with the bandits. Instead, he flowed, undulating and weaving through the attacking throng. His sword and knife seemed to be extensions of his body as it also waved and flicked. None of Urglith's followers were spared. Within moments all were merely lifeless bundles lying on the ground. Dalresar stood amid the carnage for a long moment, his face blank. When animation returned, he looked around himself as though surprised and yet resigned at what he found.

Flin walked to Dalresar and pressed one hand to his shoulder, as though in consolation, and then moved towards the women, all of whom were crying. Varna re-attached her staff and drew her knife as she hurried to the line of stakes. Between them, Flin and Varna slashed the ropes holding the women to the poles and helped them to move away from the bodies and closer to the tree line. By the time that was done Dalresar had cleaned his sword on the dirty white robe of one of the fallen and was gathering their bodies in a heap near the altar. Varna found a bundle that she assumed was the clothes of the women and brought them over, finding that she had to assist the women to dress themselves. They seemed to have been drugged in some way and their actions were listless, unfocused, even though the women appeared aware of what was happening.

Flin meanwhile had walked to the huge stone to examine it. With relief, he was unable to find traces of dried blood, so he assumed this was Urglith's first attempt, at least in these parts. He was musing about what it meant that Urglith was so far from the jungles, and replayed in his mind Urglith crying out about a fake Likki. It took only a moment for the significance to sink in. He was sure he knew why Urglith had been expelled. Dalresar finished the grisly task of piling the bodies of the slain against the altar, and moved to help Varna comfort and re-assure the women. Finally, they were ready to leave the clearing. Most of the women had recovered enough to travel unaided. As the last of the women left the clearing, clinging to another for support, Flin stopped and looked back. With a thought another bolt flew from his staff, striking the mound of bodies and causing them to burn, hot and bright. Within moments, there was nought but a charred space at the foot of the stone. Flin drew a deep breath, as the effort to use destructive energies was foreign to him and took much energy.

The women were found to be from a small village not too far away. The women told of being dragged from their homes by men in white robes, shouting about them being abominations and mothers of abominations and that they had to be purged. They had been dragged to the clearing and forced to drink drugged wine, and when they had re-awakened, they found themselves bound to the stakes. The three had intervened in time.

Flin nodded, and then was struck by something one of the women had said.

"Mothers of abominations, you said?" he asked.

"Yes, sir," the woman replied. "All of us have children who are different to the other children in some way. My Lim says he can hear what the birds say, and he does seem to know. Other children can make the grain crop grow faster and better just by talking to it, and Brea's Utha" - this with a nod to another woman - "can tell when it will storm."

"And all of your children can do these sorts of things?" Flin asked, excitement breaking through his normally calm demeanour.

"Aye, sir," was Brea's reply. "And it caused some trouble with some of the others. We were accused of all sorts of things, of causing hriths to die and crops to wither, even though there has not been a crop failure for many cycles."

"I understand," said Flin carefully. "Many people are worried about what they cannot understand. I would very much like to meet your children."

His latter statement caused many of the women to moan and start to cry again as they tried to hurry forward.

"My Utha was taken at the same time I was," Brea moaned, and all of the women cried their agreement.

Dalresar looked once to Flin, who nodded, and he left the group at a run towards the village. Varna remained with the women and Flin. When they reached the edge of the village, they were met by Dalresar, who drew Flin aside. After a brief discussion Dalresar departed again, moving away around the village.

"It seems the children are to be sacrificed also," Flin said grimly, as the women began to sob again.

"Not if I have anything to say about it," Varna growled.

Without looking to Flin for approval, she quickened her steps along the one road running through the village, reaching the small square where a small stage had been prepared with the inevitable altar. Several small children were being herded towards the stage, scared and uncertain. White-robed men were holding another group of men at bay, assisted by other men who obviously were villagers.

"Hold," she shouted loudly as she entered the square, unhooking her staff from her belt.

One white-robed man stepped between her and the children, while the others continued to move them to the altar. Why do the nut jobs always wear white, Varna thought, and then commit the vilest deeds?

"We are acolytes of Likki, the true goddess, and we will sacrifice these abominations when our high priest returns from sending the she-devils that spawned them to their hells," one of the men declaimed, his voice oddly distorted and yet penetrating.

"Then you'll be waiting a long time," Varna said coldly, continuing to move towards the speaker. "Your high priest is dead and the mothers of these children have been freed."

She pointed behind her to where the women stood in a group. As they gaped at the appearance of the women that they thought would be dead, Varna took the chance to thumb the button to release her staff's telescoping ends and with three swift strikes disabled the white-robed men guarding what she thought must be the group of fathers. The men surged at their remaining captors and over-powered them easily, as Varna continued towards the speaker.

"Stay back, or the children die," he shouted looking round wildly, only to find that the three who had been with the children were running from the village while Dalresar stood protectively with the children, his sword drawn.

The priest's hooded head turned back and forth, to the group of fathers, some of whom were advancing on him while others were running towards the women, and to Dalresar who stood perfectly still and stared at him, then back to Varna who advanced still, and finally to Flin, who had left the women and was striding forward, the stone at the tip of his staff now glowing a brilliant green. It was the latter that broke him, Varna thought, who was impressed herself at the sight. The acolyte of the false Likki pulled a short sword from the folds of his robes and with a shout of rage rushed at Varna, swinging the blade with energy but little skill. Almost contemptuously she brushed aside the sword with her staff, reversed it and pressed the stud to release the staff's blade. Dispassionately, she impaled her white-robed attacker. She withdrew the blade and he collapsed at her feet.

The villagers who had acted as guards were looking around uncertainly, blankly, standing in a small group. They had been disarmed and left alone by their fellow villagers. Mothers, fathers and children were re-united and were standing in a group, sobbing and crying, holding each other tightly. Flin joined Varna as she re-attached the staff to her belt. She noticed his staff's stone continued to glow.

Tentatively, other villagers appeared, entering the village square in ones and twos, women going towards the former captors where not a few angry comments could be heard, although the men did not respond. Curiously, Varna tried to turn her 'other' sight, as she thought of it, on the villagers who had acted as captors, and found they all exhibited a frame of black around what she thought of as normal colours. The black faded as she watched. She turned to look at the figure crumpled at her feet and reached down to fold back the hood, only to find a faint grey figure, almost vapour. She could hear it breathing heavily, stertorously. One of the women who also approached Varna let out a moan, pointing out to others what, clearly, was not an Ennarisi person. Clearly visible around what would be its neck was an amulet, a figure shaped like a bird with claws extended, made from a charcoal-hued material. Varna reached down to take hold of the amulet, but was blocked by Flin, with his staff's glowing stone throwing an eerie green shade over everything in the vicinity.

"You're not yet ready for that," he muttered to Varna as he grasped the amulet and with a single tug pulled it free, snapping the chain in doing so.

The Shadow sighed and died as the amulet was removed, and at the same time the men of the village who had been captors seemed to shake off their torpidity and looked around, seemingly unaware of what was happening. Flin nodded to himself, and smiled to Varna, while Dalresar joined them.

"Stop them from harming those men," Flin instructed Dalresar, pointing towards the former guards who were being confronted by angry villagers. "It was not their fault."

Dalresar nodded agreement and hurried across to the angry crowd, while Flin and Varna moved to stand on the small stage. The women who had been rescued were nearby, clutching their children, some with tears still flowing. Flin stood while the crowd finally listened to Dalresar and then turned towards him. The staff's stone had been extinguished, Varna realised, and Flin now stood straight and tall, a figure of authority, where usually he adopted a less emphatic pose in his guise as storyteller and conjurer. As the villagers came forward, he stood quietly, staff held in front of him by both hands. Finally, when he judged that the crowd was in a reasonable mood, he spoke.

"Do not condemn those men who stood as guards," he said clearly, "for they had no choice in what they did. They were under the control of creatures of Goroth."

"Goroth?" one of the fathers of the rescued children shouted. "Goroth is a child's tale. Don't try to use that on us. These men, who we thought were friends, were prepared to stand by and watch our women and children be killed. I say they should die."

"That would be a mistake," Flin said quietly after some murmurs of agreement quieted. "I tell you they were not acting of their own will. Tell me," he said to one of the former guards, "why did you follow that creature?"

"I, uh, well, we," the man stammered. "I don't know. I don't remember what happened. That one was talking to us about the strange happenings with the children and then ..." He spread his arms to indicate the current situation, and the others nodded.

"Tell me," Varna said, causing Flin to catch his next words and turn, surprised that she stepped forward. "Are you worried or afraid of the children who have been doing things that are not normal?"

The man addressed looked abashed. "Well, they're not normal, are they? I mean, some of them can talk to birds, or understand what a hrss is doing, or can tell when a storm will come. Some can make plants grow. For all I know they can make other plants die." He looked around at his fellow villagers, some of whom were nodding, others who regarded him with disgust. "Well, they're not normal."

Varna glanced to Flin as she stepped back, tacitly handing control back to him. He nodded, understanding why she had asked the question and pleased at the answer provided.

"And all of you who were chosen to be guards felt the same way, or at least had some concerns and fears," Flin said, a statement rather than a question, but eliciting rueful nods nevertheless. "Well, you are right in one sense. They are not normal children," and he raised his hands as a storm of protest arose, waiting until it quieted to continue, "but nor are they unwelcome. They are not any form of demon. The strange abilities you fear are those practised in days long gone by the Guides, some of whom were strong enough to become Mages."

"First Goroth and now Guides and Mages," the same father called out. "More myths and legends, stories for after the evening meal and around the fires. You might be able to make your shiny stone glow by some sort of trickery, and we thank you and honour you for your help in saving our families, but by peddling those old tales here you only make our children stand out more and make things more difficult."

Flin held still for a moment before looking to where Dalresar stood at the edge of the crowd. His apprentice returned a grin and a raised eyebrow, amusement flitting across his face before he assumed a bored expression again.

"I understand that you may find it difficult to believe, after all this time. You have been told the old stories, the old legends, of the Mages and Guides and Goroth and the rebellion. Those in the main are not just stories, but are our history. The Guides and Mages were real, they existed. Goroth is real and exists now and seeks to return. True evil seeks to return to Ennaris, as foretold in the Prophecy of the Children of Ennaris." Flin stopped, considering his next words. "You may not believe but you must be prepared. Your children who have gifts will be vital to Ennaris in the future, and those who do not have such gifts will need to understand and support them. In turn they will be assisted and supported by the new generation of Guides. Dark times are coming and the new Faero of Ennaris will require your support. But the Guardians have returned to Ennaris. The time is near."

"Who are you, old man, to tell us these things?" the father jeered, even as others tried to quiet him, impressed by Flin's demeanour and words. "All know that the Guides and Mages are no more, if they ever existed. And the Guardians, if they existed, deserted Ennaris."

"What proof do you require of me to show you that I speak truth?" Flin asked the truculent villager.

"Prove it by making the orchard bloom," the villager retorted, "like the stories tell of the Guides of old. Show us more than tricks with a crystal."

Varna felt a strange surge and she was startled when Dalresar suddenly straightened, evidently having felt something also.

"Like that?" Flin asked, pointing to where a row of apple trees stood, all with bare branches except for one, the one closest to the village, that was in full bloom, with fruit hanging from its boughs.

The villagers stared at the single tree and then back to Flin. The father making objections was standing with his mouth hanging open, staring still at the tree as Flin raised his staff. The stone at the top flared, dark green changing to a bright white that turned the developing twilight, that Varna had not noticed, into daylight again.

"I am Drewflin, Mage of Ennaris, and I tell you that the time of the Prophecy is at hand, the Children of Ennaris have returned to provide aid and succour, and the Guardians have returned. The ancient evil is alive once more and threatens us all. This," and he gestured around him and at the bundled robe that the Shadow had worn, "is but a small part of that evil. I bid you to send aid to the new Faero as he builds a force to defeat the armies of Goroth, even as the remaining Mages seek to defeat him and his evil followers, as we were unable to do completely so long ago."

With that, Flin extinguished the staff's light and the square was plunged into gloom.

The next morning dawned cloudy and with a light misty rain falling. It had been a night when the village was on edge. Relief of those who had been rescued warred with uncertainty and doubt felt by those who remained fearful of gifts that they did not understand. Many were utterly afraid to find one of those held responsible for the great destruction in their midst. Flin had found himself the centre of attention for those women and most of the fathers whose children exhibited gifts, answering question after question. The three had been offered food and drink, which they accepted gratefully. Dalresar found himself some sort of hero after several women described how he had decimated the white-robed acolytes, and several of the younger men queried him about joining the Faero's forces. To all of them he gave Almin Bor's name and suggested they make their way to the Citadel.

Now they prepared to depart. They shouldered their packs and said their thanks to the families who had provided accommodation, and turned onto the road out of the village, called Old Bastion after a fortress that once had existed nearby. They exited the town and had travelled only a short distance when they came across a woman, one of those rescued, and her young son, no more than eight cycles old. Varna recognised her as Granlin, the only rescued woman who did not have a husband to return to. He had been killed in an accident several years before. The son, Torden, had a gift of metal infusing, but with what effect no-one was sure.

"Please, Mage Drewflin," Granlin said when Flin stopped where she waited beside the road, "we would travel with you to the Citadel and take service with the young Faero."

Flin thought for a moment and then said, "We're not going to the Citadel immediately, and we have a long road to take yet. That's not something for you or Torden to bear. Several of the young men will go to the Citadel. I suggest that you join them. Look for Almin Bor and tell him that I sent you and Torden to help in preparations. Let him know of Torden's skills. I feel that Torden's skills may be of great help."

Granlin looked disappointed but nodded firmly.

"Then so we shall do, master Mage," she replied with an air of formality.

With a nod Flin led the way down the road.

14. Maf and Dharmoney

The field was quiet again. The birds started a tentative recital after the noise and clamour that had rung out only minims before. The light was waning and would be gone before too long. A few dark clouds scudded across the sky, joining forces to form a cloud front that promised rain on the morrow.

Maf sighed, as he looked over the field. This had been the largest group he had faced yet, and to do so he had had to bring with him some of the trainees. Most had acquitted themselves well. Several had seen fights before and so were better prepared for what they faced. For others this was their first taste of battle. But none had been involved in a battle against a force of forty. They were bandits, admittedly, and as so often with that type, they were poorly trained and armed. But still, it had been forty against only eight.

Maf and his trainees had overcome the bandits, using their combinations of fighting skills and gifts. Their fighting skills were courtesy of Maf and one other who knew the old ways and had dedicated a large part of his life to passing those skills onto the trainees. Maf still felt his loss keenly. The gifts were what they had fought to protect in the beginning, and what they still fought to protect wherever they could locate children exhibiting those old powers. Now they were part of the weaponry also. Maf, the strongest by a large margin, was a more than gifted fighter and healer, a very unusual blend, but he also had good control over air and water. Herik, the most experienced trainee of the group, was a fire specialist, and several scorched patches and burnt bodies told of his involvement. Lornas could make opponents' metal swords slag as though molten, but only in close proximity. Dresdin had reasonable air control and was improving - he could now move air currents in a defensive screen, which had helped this day.

The first-time trainees were just as mixed. Ursil had the skills to make him almost as good a fighter as Maf at some stage, and he could work with earth, but it took time and was of little use in the heat of battle. Trip could accelerate himself to twice or three times his usual speed, but only for short times, after which he was exhausted. He carried multiple wounds from today's fight because of that, and would learn. Jern had failed to bring her secondary skills of stone and air to bear, and was badly injured as she lost track of the fight in her efforts to make her skills work. Maf had done what he could for her for now and would have a second session with her later. Lexis also failed to bring his gift of earth to bear and had died, for the young man had fallen under sustained attack by three of the bandits after separating from the group.

All of the living would learn from this, including Maf. All would learn the grief of loss. All would learn the hard lessons that tactics were important and planning was vital, and also that a battle would reduce any such plan to a set of goals and intentions rather than defined paths, for such is the nature of battle. Being greatly outnumbered was less a problem for Maf and his charges than it may have been for many, but it still would be deadly if you did not pay attention to what was around you even while bringing other gifts into the fray, as what happened to Lexis and Jern could attest.

Maf was concerned, though. Against forty his band had emerged victorious and that would give them confidence. But the fact that they faced forty told him that the enemy of this region was organising. He was sure the northers were behind the growing number of bandits that infested this western area of Ennaris' northern continent. What did it mean? Were they building momentum for something greater? Was it an attempt to undermine the fragile civil structure in this region, where no warlord or petty king or confederation held the towns and villages together? They appeared to be bandits and nothing more, but for forty of them to come together was something very unusual. Had Maf not been informed of their existence as a fighting force he may have been under-resourced for this confrontation. Thinking back to the pieces of the battle that he could recall, he was pretty sure that he should have had another one or two fighters on his side.

Now he watched as Dresdin and Ursil used their gifts, although they were tired out, to drag the bandits into a ragged pile where Herik would incinerate them. Lexis was being removed from the field of battle far more respectfully. His body would be burned also, but with more ceremony. While the result was the same, Maf knew that the ceremony for their own loss was important. Maf's trainees all had beliefs that mirrored his own as to why this work was necessary, but they also had to believe that they were important, and ceremonies of this sort were part of that.

"It is a heavy burden," a voice said from behind Maf.

Startled, for he was always aware of his surroundings, Maf turned. An old woman, swathed in scarves and carrying something wrapped in nondescript cloth, stood behind him.

"Be not afraid," the old woman said with a smile. "I tend to be very quiet. Sometimes," she finished with a quirk of her lips, as though remembering times when she was not so quiet.

"I'm not afraid," Maf said. "This place may not be safe for some time, and it may be better for you to head for Teerman. The town is not far."

"I am safe where I am," the old woman said. "But I thank you for your suggestion. You must accelerate the training of your charges, however, for I fear you and they will be needed in the near future. The enemy stirs."

"What do you know of my charges?" Maf asked, trying to read the old woman but finding that he could not pierce something that obscured her aura.

"I know what I know, child of old Ennaris," the woman said seriously, but her eyes sparkled with mischief.

Maf suddenly realised that this old woman was toying with him. Ordinarily, he would have enjoyed the by-play, but he had one dead and another seriously wounded after a battle that had lasted longer than he would have liked.

"As do I," Maf replied. "And I also know that I have things to do here and little time in which to do them. Be wary as you go, grandmother, for I feel there are forces astir that you may not wish to meet."

"I am no grandmother," the woman said sharply, causing Maf to tighten his gaze again, "and I am more aware of the forces that stir than you." She paused, and continued in a softer tone. "Why do you patrol this region? Why do you protect the people of this region? They have done nothing to help you and your friends."

Maf was nonplussed. This old woman spoke as though she truly did know of Maf and those who worked with him. Something.... There was something about her. He could not work it through, but he was aware enough of what he did not know that he decided to respond with the real facts, not those that he usually told to those who asked.

"Initially, it was to protect and gather those with gifts who were hunted. Those of us who did that were able to gather dozens of gifted, some from under the noses of their persecutors. We found others where those who would have harmed them knew nothing of their gifts. That caused me to roam through this region and I came to know it well."

"And now you expand that to protecting the people of the region?" the woman asked.

She gazed at Maf as though reading deep inside him. Her eyes... Her eyes were not those of an old woman, Maf realised with a start. Every old woman he had spoken with suffered from some sort of eye degradation, but this woman's eyes were sharp and clear. Maf's sense of being in a presence grew stronger.

"I did," he replied carefully. "As chaos reigned, the people were less and less able to protect themselves. The strong ruled the weak and stripped them bare of anything they needed to live. Many died who did not need to die, especially after surviving the devastation caused by the rebellion. I was unable to stand by and watch the weak suffer, or the bullies take what they wanted. I used my training, and trained others to do the same, to protect the weak."

"And do you intend to continue to protect these people?" the old woman asked.

"I do," Maf said, watching the old woman intently.

"And if I asked that you extend your protection to other parts of Ennaris?"

"I fail to see how that is possible," Maf replied. "In the days long gone that may have been possible, but today I am limited to my own feet or those of a hrss. My range is limited as a result."

The woman nodded. "Nevertheless, were you able to do so, would you extend your protection beyond this region?"

"I feel it to be my duty, so yes, were I able to do so then I would," Maf replied.

The woman smiled as though in satisfaction and seemed to stand taller, although still only coming to Maf's shoulder.

"Will you protect the people of Ennaris, Maf?" she asked in a ringing voice, such that the trainees turned to observe Maf and the old woman.

"I will do so," Maf replied quietly, unable to stop a cold trail from running down his spine. What was happening?

"Will you protect the weak with your gifts and your skills?" the woman asked in the same ringing tone.

Maf recognised a ritual asking from his training so long ago and stood straighter himself. "I will do so," he replied.

"Will you protect Ennaris and her people from her enemies, from wherever they may come, and no matter the cost to yourself?" the woman asked, and her voice seemed to reverberate around the field.

"I will do so," Maf replied quietly.

"So be it," the old woman said as she held out the cloth covered item. "This is yours now by right, Marflin, Mage of the Hides."

Maf unwrapped the thin item to find himself holding a length of what appeared to be wood. Embedded in the top of the length was a stone, dark. Maf's mouth was dry as he beheld a staff of a Mage.

"But..."

"So be it," the woman said for a second time, and from a pocket in the folds of cloth drew forth a small stone, also dark, attached to a chain, which she reached up to drape on Maf's head. The chain arranged itself and the stone centred on Maf's forehead.

"So be it," the old woman said for the third time.

The Mage stone flared silver, shot through with green. At the same time, the stone on Maf's forehead flared with the same light.

Maf was bewildered at the sudden events.

"And you will need something more than a hrss, I feel," the woman said, gesturing above.

Maf looked up and his eyes popped. Dropping like a bolt from the darkening sky was a Roc. Maf had never met one and he watched with mouth agape as this one flared its wings in a spray of dust and settled to the ground, wings held wide apart, as it bowed to Maf.

"They do like to show off," the old woman said to Maf conversationally. "This is Hel-nor. He is a wing leader of the Rocs and is in need of a group of women and men to join his wing, as was done in the days long past."

Well met, Protector, Hel-nor projected to Maf formally, rising from the bow again. *I look forward to bringing you and your fellows into the Alnar-kun.*

"Protector?" Maf asked the old woman.

"Indeed, Maf. I name you Protector, one of the Nine to battle Goroth and his helpers in the time to come. I can think of few better suited to the name." The old woman smiled. "Your trainees, and others who you select, will join with Hel-nor and learn how to work together, as a team. You will extend your protection across this land."

Maf stared at Hel-nor, his mind reeling with the shocks he had experienced.

"Lady," he started to say, turning to the old woman again.
But she was nowhere to be seen.

15. Great Mirden

Jalor and Blaine sat in the small tavern, in a small town with the grand sounding name of Great Mirden. They were several days' travel by hrss from the Citadel, early in the morning ten days after Corm was proclaimed Faero. This was the third such town they had visited. Both had been shocked the previous evening to hear their exploits at the Citadel rendered into song. It was highly embellished and bearing, in some instances, only a passing resemblance to what actually occurred. But the story of the Children of Ennaris - and how was that known? - battling the evil army obviously was known already, for the singer was asked for repeat performances throughout the night. Blaine, who was always ready to find the absurd in any situation, was laughing at Jalor's expression at being referred to as the Hero of the Citadel, with a history of heroic deeds thrown in for good measure, and one of the most handsome of men on Ennaris. When he heard himself referred to as fearsome in battle but a plain and simple man, Blaine yelped in dismay, which caused Jalor to bury his face in his ale to stop from laughing aloud. The resultant minor commotion drew accusatory frowns from neighbouring tables.

After hearing of their own exploits five times, they decided that enough was enough and retired to the room they had reserved. Now they were deciding what they should do. Their intention was to get a better understanding of the people in the vicinity of the Citadel, and hopefully a better understanding of Ennaris as a whole, but it was obvious that the plan would not produce any better understanding of the position on Ennaris than the one they had received from the twins.

In fact, what they had found was that people knew very little of what transpired outside their own geographic area. They relied on travellers and storytellers for much of their information. Thus, during the previous evening, between hearing repeats of their own heroic behaviour, they heard tell of rumours of the return of the mythical Guardians, of the overthrow of the corrupt priesthood in several city states of both the north and the south continents, and of numerous attacks by the half-men, correctly identified by the teller as ghazrak created by the evil Mage Goroth.

As he was plied with ale, the teller became more expansive and the stories more lurid. The "evil from the far north" was described in greater detail, although Jalor doubted its accuracy. He recalled Flin talking about the kingdoms of the northern wastes and how they had caused problems for most of the time since the end of the rebellion, so this evil may be no more than that. By the time Jalor and Blaine retired the ghazrak were three times the height of a man and carried great scythes with which they killed twenty men at a stroke. Still, this Teller had known enough for the two Warriors to realise that he had been primed with sufficient real knowledge to make his stories resemble the facts. And that interested Jalor, for the twins remained at the Citadel and had not left, Helt was occupied in training Corm with several variations of swordplay, and few others would know enough to pass on the detail they were hearing. Jalor had found that the teller would be at the tavern again the next evening, and had determined that he would get some answers about the sources of the Teller's information.

Of interest to both men was the fact that the Guardians and Children of Ennaris, and Goroth and the Mages, were treated by most people listening to the teller as myth and fiction, but not by all. So, there were some believers already. Jalor knew that in a land of oral tradition, despite the surprisingly widespread ability to read and write somewhat, it would be important for the tales to be passed far and wide and to remain close enough to truth for them to be recognisable in the different parts of Ennaris. As he told Blaine, their strategy would be to get the right stories told across the planet, to revitalise the people's knowledge of their own past and of the potential future. The twins knew many of the storytellers and had provided their names to Jalor. The one at this tavern was not on that list. It seemed that someone else had a similar strategy. Of course, that was what the Mages had been doing for thousands of cycles.

They decided to remain in the near vicinity, to retain their room and to make sure that they stayed for the whole performance that evening. They intended to maintain a low profile while they tried to gauge the feelings of the people for the Faero and his intention to raise an army to deal with Goroth and the ghazrak, as they had done at the previous two towns. That intention lasted until they had finished a simple breakfast and walked from the tavern to the single street that ran through the town. The town blacksmith was already at work, with the sound of his hammer striking metal ringing out clear and bright, and the basket weaver had her goods spread out in front of her stall. A farmer's wagon was stalled in front of the town's one store, the single hrss standing patiently with head bowed. A mild buzz filled the air as townspeople spoke and called to each other, goods were stacked or moved, and the various noises of a small town's daily life filled the air.

From the western end of the road - Jalor and Blaine had entered via the eastern end - two men staggered into view, one supporting the other and both obviously badly hurt. Townspeople cried out and ran to help, and the orderly working of the town came to a halt as others ran to help or find out what had happened. Within moments, the two men had been taken from the road to the front porch of a small store. Bloody wounds were being exclaimed over by gathered watchers while a few worked to staunch bleeding. Many questions were asked, most being variants of what had happened. Jalor and Blaine joined the throng as the less injured man managed to speak, after gulping down a beaker of water handed to him by a quick-thinking helper.

"Some sort of beasts attacked our caravan," he gasped out. "They killed almost everyone and took the two women and children. We managed to get away."

"Where?" an older man asked.

"Back that way," the wounded man repeated. "Not far. It happened at sun-up."

Jalor and Blaine shared a single glance before turning to run back to their lodgings where they had left their swords. With a quick word of explanation to the proprietor, a normally jovial and quite rotund individual who had introduced himself as Big Sol, both men strapped on their weapons. Blaine also extracted his folding bow from his pack, along with the quiver of Starfire arrows. Within moments they had returned to the common room where Big Sol intercepted them on their way to the front door, pressing on them a stoppered flask of what he said was restorative in case of need. Jalor nodded his thanks and strapped the flask to his belt - the flask had loops for the purpose - and the two hurried from the tavern.

Returning to where the crowd still stood, Blaine nodded when he saw several other men also hurrying up with a variety of weapons, mostly old swords but one had a bow and quiver of arrows. He and Jalor had been impressed at what they saw as a no-nonsense attitude by the people they had met in this part of Ennaris, in the main descended from the Faeronar and their allies over the thousands of cycles since the rebellion, according to Raglin. The men were milling around, unsure about what to do next, as Jalor and Blaine arrived. The modern and obviously cared for weapons caused more than a few to stare, but also immediately impressed several, enough that when Jalor asked if there was any more news he was answered without hesitation.

"Right," Jalor said crisply, "let's get out and after them. There are women and children who will need help, if it's not too late already."

"Who are you to give us orders, stranger?" one man asked truculently, noticeably not carrying arms, even while the ones who were armed started to move forward.

Jalor considered briefly, glancing at Blaine who just nodded. Well, they had intended to try to sway people to Corm's cause if they could, but this was not part of the plan. Still, plans had to be modified as circumstances changed.

"We're from the Citadel," Jalor said quietly, causing more people to turn and listen. "I am Jalor, this is Blaine. And time is wasting. Are you joining us?"

Muttered comments broke out among the onlookers. The questioner backed away, ashen-faced at facing the storied heroes of the Citadel. Jalor merely watched him.

"I thought not," he said contemptuously, and looked around at the armed group. "Let's go."

The small group moved at a jog along the road, the men content to take the lead offered by Jalor. As they moved up the road, Blaine explained to them what they were facing.

"The beasts are called ghazrak and they are the creations of Goroth," he called out, breathing easily as he continued to jog, his words causing several to look askance. "They are armoured from neck to ankle and have natural bone helmets as skulls. They carry very poorly made swords and pikes, but they are good enough to kill you. They have no mercy and give no quarter. They fight with single-minded ferocity and keep fighting even if badly wounded."

"Goroth?" one of the men asked. "Are you serious?"

"Yes," Jalor replied. "These are what we fought against at the Citadel. Goroth is real and the ghazrak are very real. They may be accompanied by men, who will be just as desperate but without the armour and sheer animal ferocity of the ghazrak. When we catch them Blaine and I will tell you what to do, and you will have to do it exactly."

The group jogged for a short distance further and then Jalor called them to drop to a walk to catch their breaths. Several had started to blow hard and one had fallen out, whether because of the exertion or fear of facing the ghazrak he could not be sure. They could not have much further to go, though, as the attack had happened at sunrise and the two survivors had not been able to move fast. He was just about to start jogging again when they turned a corner and found the site of the attack, a small clearing at the side of the road. Several bodies lay around what had been a camp-fire, with two small tents at one side. Bed rolls were scattered where sleepers had spent the night.

With a gesture from Jalor, Blaine started to scout the edge of the clearing. Within a few moments he had found the trail leading away.

"Five," he called to Jalor. "I'd say they're carrying the women and children. There are only the boot treads."

"Half a troop," Jalor nodded. "Okay," he called out to the gathered men, "listen up. We're going after them. There are five of them, but they usually travel in troops of ten, so be watchful. I don't want the other half catching us unaware. Blaine will be on point. We go as quietly as we can."

He gestured again and Blaine slipped into the woods, following the trail made by the ghazrak. The trail went almost straight north. Blaine realised this was a game trail that the beast-men had used to make their way to the clearing, which probably meant there was a source of water close, also. With one quick stop for the men to get their breath again and have a quick drink from the variety of water flasks they all carried, the small group made good time. Jalor had no illusions about what they may find though, and he also knew the ghazrak would move quickly as well.

It was about the middle of the day when they came upon the ghazrak, five of them gathered around a camp fire. Blaine had been far enough ahead that he could return and stop the group before the ghazrak heard them approaching, or so he hoped.

"They're in a small clearing just ahead. Five of them. I can see two children tied up against a log at the back but no women. They have a camp fire going and are eating."

The latter was said with Blaine looking directly at Jalor, whose heart sank. He could guess what they were eating.

"Okay," Jalor said. "We're going to get the children back."

"What about the women?" one of the men asked, only to gulp as Jalor shook his head.

"We won't find the women alive," Jalor said, and the mood darkened as the import sank in. "Blaine and I will take most of them. You," and he pointed to the only other man with a bow, "take up a position where you can see if anyone else comes along this path. If you have to shoot, aim for the space between armour and helmet or under the armpit. Remember there may be five more of these creatures out there. The rest of you go for the children. Groups of three. Don't try to take them on alone if you need to fight one. Go for the joints or gaps in the armour or under the armpits."

The men nodded nervously. Jalor and Blaine moved to the front of the group and, with no small trepidation, the small band headed towards the clearing. Blaine drew two arrows from his quiver, held one between his teeth and fitted the other to the bowstring. He loosed the shaft as he reached the clearing, grasped the second, slotted it to the string and released in a single motion. Both arrows flew true, each taking one of the ghazrak through the head as they ate. With a single roar, the remaining three threw down what they were eating and jumped up with their swords. Blaine dropped his bow and drew his wicked broadsword from the sheath slung across his back, while Jalor drew forth his short sword. Both warriors moved to the left as they entered the clearing and continued to move left, drawing the ghazrak after them and away from the children.

The battle was short but ferocious. The three attacking ghazrak identified Blaine as the more dangerous and charged him, only to find that in leaving Jalor free they quickly became only two attackers. Jalor dealt with the first of the attackers by the simple expedient of running him through from behind. Blaine, on the other hand, found himself facing two ghazrak who seemed to be more adept in the use of swords, and, moreover, whose swords were of better quality and manufacture. He was forced to defend himself as Jalor dealt with the first and only when the two realised their error and one turned back to Jalor did he get some respite. With a quick wrist-flick, he pushed the ghazrak's attack wide, and then avoided a huge rebound swipe that left the ghazrak off balance, before bringing his own considerable strength to bear in a back-hand stroke that decapitated his opponent. Before the ghazrak's body even hit the ground, Blaine jumped forward and ran the remaining ghazrak through from the side while it was engaged with Jalor.

The Warriors looked around to see the two children being comforted by the townsmen, one of whom was looking bleakly at what the ghazrak had been feasting on. Jalor walked past him, clapping him on one shoulder and nodding to show he understood. With little fuss, Blaine extinguished the fire while the children were led away from the scene, traumatised at their experiences. Jalor knew they would have seen the women brutalised and then slaughtered and eaten. It was likely at least one of the women was mother to the children. In short order Blaine, assisted by two of the townsmen, gathered what remained of the women's bodies. With no digging implements all they could do was create a pyre and burn the remains, after which they followed the small party that trudged back to the town.

Great Mirden was a sombre town that night. None of the people of the caravan were known to the townspeople but, again, Jalor and Blaine were impressed by how these people rallied to assist the surviving men and children. It was found that each of the women was mother to one of the children and when the tale of what had been found was told the anger was palpable, but so was the fear of what may come next. Jalor and Blaine were feted not with excitement but gravely, their contribution to the expedition acknowledged and their advice sought.

The storyteller, having awoken from his drunken sleep during the afternoon, was spell-bound as the story was told by one of the rescuing townsmen, but found few people wanted to hear of the newer tales. Rather, Jalor asked him to tell a story of the rebellion and its aftermath, and with a suitable sense of the mood he toned down the exaggeration and told the story simply and, from what Jalor and Blaine could tell after listening to the twins tell the story from their perspective, with surprising accuracy. Only at the time when the storyteller came to how the Mages and Guardians abandoned Ennaris did Jalor step in.

"And after allowing such destruction to be visited on Ennaris the Mages and the Guardians left the Ennarisi to their own devices," Urdos the storyteller intoned gravely, "And so Ennaris fell into barbarism for long ages."

"No," Jalor said clearly, standing. "That is what has been believed by the people of Ennaris but it's not true. What is not remembered is that three of the Guardians gave their lives to protect Ennaris during the devastation of the rebellion, for Goroth unleashed such weapons that you cannot imagine and would have destroyed this world completely. Remember the names of Appanu, Angor and Zang, for they were the Guardians who died so that Ennaris may have the chance to live still. What is also not known is that the Guardians did not all leave Ennaris. Some remained to maintain a watch and do what little they could. The Guardians are not gods, despite what some would have you believe for their own ends, and they are forbidden to interfere in the normal lives of the Ennarisi. And the Guides and the Mages did not leave but continued to work with the Ennarisi despite suffering persecution by those who laid blame on them rather than on a band of rebels."

Jalor looked around the gathered people of Great Mirden, and especially looked at Urdos. All regarded him with wonder, some with scepticism, but all held their silence and waited for him to continue. Jalor thought back to why his team had been sent to Ennaris, and what they had found in this single part of the planet. He knew that he, Blaine and Varna had gained new perspectives and this was no longer a mission for the Union. He also knew that Ennaris needed more than the few Mages remaining and the three Warriors, whether they were called Children of Ennaris or not.

"Goroth was bound by the Mage Drewflin and the few remaining Mages after the rebellion, but those bindings are loosened by time. Goroth's underlings have started to grow strong again, and the ghazrak are one of the results. The new Faero of Ennaris has been named and

Corm Ramesa is preparing to do battle with these forces of evil." Jalor paused for effect, knowing he had to strike the right balance. "Tell the stories of the rebellion and the destruction, but do not neglect to tell of the evil of Goroth and the mighty efforts of the Guardians and the Guides and the Mages to save Ennaris from total destruction. And tell that the Faero of Ennaris will defend this world but needs your help and that of all people of Ennaris, no matter which land they hold dear. For as of old, the Faero does not wish for dominion over the land, but to guide and protect its people. Tell those stories. And tell of the Prophecy and that its words are coming to pass. The Guardians have returned to Ennaris, those who were forced to leave, to re-join those few who were able to remain. But the Mages are few."

Urdos roused. "The Prophecy tells of the return of the Children of Ennaris also and that one of them will lead the armies of light against the armies of the dark."

Jalor nodded, although the last bit was new to him. "Do you know the Prophecy well?"

Urdos inclined his head. "As well as most bards," he replied.

"Then tell also that the Children of Ennaris have returned," Jalor said quietly, and saw Blaine start at the statement. "The Children will assist Corm to fight this evil, as the Prophecy tells. But they cannot do it alone. The Faero will need the men and women of Ennaris to rally when he calls. The Prophecy of the Guardians is at hand and Ennaris must prepare."

Jalor took a last swig of his ale, looked around once more at the gathered crowd and walked from the silent tavern with Blaine tagging along. Without speaking they retrieved their packs from their room and, even though it was dark, they left Great Mirden. Neither wanted to have to deal with further questions at that time.

"So," Blaine said some time after they had moved past the edge of town and were approaching the site of their recent run-in with the ghazrak, "you've decided that we are the Children of Ennaris?"

"I guess so," Jalor replied. "Things are piling up a little too much. I'm not sure of exactly what is going on but I do know that we were placed here deliberately in the hope that we can assist."

"The divine Guardians?" Blaine asked wryly.

"Oh, I think probably someone a little less divine," Jalor said with a short laugh. "Our Grand Admiral knew more than she let on, I think. It will be interesting to find out just how much. But I think we can be sure that what we are up against here may well be bigger than any single mission we have seen. If what the twins told us is right then the Warriors have been battling against Goroth's forces for a long time. The Shadows are his people, ultimately, and we find them here."

Blaine merely nodded. "Well, we can only do what we can do. We need the people of this planet to come along for the ride also. I'm not too sure they will. From what I can understand, Ennaris has broken into smaller factions that are either jealous or afraid of each other. That doesn't augur well for a united front."

Jalor nodded glumly. "Agreed. But we'll stay the course. I wonder how Varna is getting on. She at least has found out about Clay, so there's some hope there, although after this time probably not much."

But word spread rapidly about what had happened at the Citadel and at Great Mirden, about the battles with the scouts of the evil army of ghazrak, of the appearance of the fabled saviours as foretold by the Prophecy, of the death of the Faero, Intika Ramesa, and his miraculous ascension to the Guardians. Urdos was to the fore of the telling as he roamed far and wide. And Jalor's words were repeated, woven into narratives that changed forever the stories of the rebellion, that celebrated the Guardians and their sacrifices for Ennaris, that recalled the great services done by the Mages and that reminded the people of Ennaris of the looming menace that was Goroth.

Many disbelieved. Many fights ensued as the Faeronar and others who had witnessed the events recounted them to groups who called them liars and tell-tales. But some believed and passed on the tales, and the bards wove the words into story and song, with embellishments as happens when such tales are told.

But central to the tales were Jalor's final words, repeated without alteration from teller to teller: "The Prophecy of the Guardians is at hand and Ennaris must prepare".

16. The Dead Village

It was four days after the encounter with the false priests of Likki. Varna, Flin and Dalresar had moved across the land, using roads when they took the direction required, or making their own paths through the woods when the roads diverged from the required direction.

Right now, they were walking along a narrow road. It was little more than a track in reality, although one that had once been broader and better maintained. Paving stones could be felt underfoot. Many of those stones were unstable so the travellers had to take care where they walked. At one stage, the road became bad enough that Dalresar stopped to cut a walking staff from a limb that had dropped from a tree near the road and Varna unlimbered her battle staff to use for the same purpose. Around them the country had changed slightly. The woods had become less dense. More scrubby bushes were evident as under-growth beneath the trees and the canopy was sparser than it had been. The bird life had dwindled to a few isolated calls, and then disappeared altogether, which caused Dalresar to be on guard. He and Flin shared a glance, and Dalresar discarded his rough walking staff and pulled his sword from its scabbard.

Varna was distracted, as she had become accustomed to, but now it was not so much disorientation but a sense of purpose that needed to be addressed. She was moving towards something that she knew was important, but she was unable to discern what that may be. She did not have the same sense of evil that she had felt when the ghazrak were in front of her, but evil nevertheless was ahead of her. Unconsciously, she started to walk faster and without thought she thumbed the second stud to extend the staff to its full length. Flin, watching closely, gestured to Dalresar to stay clear and the two men moved into formation behind her.

And so it was that they came upon a small village. Two rows of cottages spread along the road. Several others were scattered seemingly at random behind them. Narrow trails led to each of their front doors. The cottages were mostly built in the same way, with mud brick walls, thatched roofs, doors that were hung from sturdy leather straps and windows that showed shutters, mostly open. Small gardens grew around most cottages, with their bright colours adding splashes of life to the duller colour pallets of the cottages themselves. Several cottages had clothes attached to thin lines and they flapped in the light breeze. It was a peaceful and almost bucolic sight, except for one thing.

There were no people!

Varna could feel something calling her, a persistent pull at the back of her mind drawing her forward. She was unable to tell just what was calling her but she was sure it was a thing and not a person. If anyone asked her how she knew, she would have been unable to say. She just knew! Flin watched warily as Varna slowly moved along the short single street - more of a meandering path - that ran between the two staggered rows of cottages. Dalresar moved away from Flin, establishing separation in the event of danger. He could feel wrongness in this place.

Varna slowed before each cottage, peering into one every now and again. The silence was eerie, unnerving. Despite herself, Varna could feel her hackles rise. Her hair stood on end as she moved closer to whatever was calling her. She did not notice Flin grip his staff tighter, nor the stone clenched at its tip start to roil slowly. Varna stopped in front of one particularly decrepit cottage - a hovel, really - and close her eyes, although Flin had the impression that she was actually staring into the cottage.

Slowly, hesitantly, Varna stepped to the door that hung on frayed leather thongs and pushed it open. The door was constructed of branches rudely hacked to an approximate length and bound together by thick twine strips that were even more frayed than the leather that held the door to a post that formed part of the wall. It moved reluctantly, as though unwilling to allow trespassers. Varna took a deep breath and pushed harder. The door groaned as it moved back, coming to a stop against a bulwark of dirt that obviously was as far as it ever went. Cautiously, Varna moved through the entrance, trying to attune senses that she still knew nothing about to determine if danger was present.

Flin followed after Varna while Dalresar remained outside, watchful. A small ball of Mage light appeared and Flin swung it towards the ceiling of the small building, where it lodged against the rude timbers - which were more branches laid from wall to wall - and glowed steadily. Varna glanced back and nodded her thanks, then turned back and slowly examined the interior of the hovel, peering into each corner. Without volition she closed her eyes and could feel herself falling into a light trance.

Suddenly, she was watching events that she knew were from the near past, people panicking, running through the village and trying to gather belongings to flee. A small girl dropped her doll but her mother did not stop for it but ran on, one of a number of women and children who all sought escape. Many of them made it out of the village and ran along the road, but others she saw were herded like cattle into a small square by ghazrak. Most of them had lower torsos like a man, but all had barrel chests and small heads with odd protuberances extending from each side like immature antlers.

Varna gasped and groaned as the children were slaughtered without pause. She did not notice the tears running down her face as she saw the women thrown on the ground and defiled. She forced herself to watch the bestial faces and could almost hear the grunts as they had their way with the women and then casually killed them. Flin was startled to see Varna's pained expression turn to one of sheer ferocity and her hands, which had clenched tightly as she watched the scenes unfold, glow with a dim blue light.

Varna watched one old man creep from behind the village and enter the cottage where she and Flin stood. He moved to the back and in one corner scratched dirt away from a metal box. He opened the box and dropped into it an object, then closed the box and covered it with dirt again. He threw mounds of cloth and detritus on top of the disturbed ground and then crept back out of the cottage, until very deliberately he reached into a small barrel and drew forth a short sword, one that was finely wrought and gleamed as though in anticipation. The old man ran directly into the mass of attackers, swinging the sword lustily but with no skill, and with little strength. But the sword glowed and Varna could hear it sing as it sliced through two, three, four of the attackers. But the man was old and it was only a matter of time - he was run through from behind by a long spear. He dropped with a sob, the sword falling to the ground near his body.

One of the attackers, the leader Varna presumed, stepped forward and kicked the old man's body. It growled and bent to pick up the sword, only to yell in pain as the sword flared at its touch. Whimpering slightly and holding its burnt hand, the leader kicked the old man again and yelled at the remaining attackers. In short time, they had stacked their victims and their own slain in a pile in the middle of the square. Two of the attackers opened small packs that Varna had not noticed and drew forth small spheres that they threw into the heap of bodies. The spheres smashed and intense flames burst forth, consuming the bodies almost entirely. A few scorched bones and ashes were all that remained.

The leader made a gesture and the attackers separated to search the buildings, including the one in which Varna stood with Flin. She saw the creature enter and paw through the belongings left behind, moving across where the object had been buried but without finding it, before moving back out to join its fellows in the square. The leader growled when all of the searchers returned bare-handed. With a series of grunts the leader formed the remaining ghazrak into some sort of order and led the way out of the village.

Varna was sobbing as her vision faded and she slowly collapsed to the floor of the hovel, kneeling and keening with both hands tightly clenched as the full impact of what she saw took its toll. The blue glow died away. Flin, recognising that something was happening but not sure just what, knelt beside her and gently put his hand over hers. She gripped it tightly. After a few seconds Varna's sobs faded and she dashed away the tears, angrily.

"Many of the villagers were killed by ghazrak, after raping the women," Varna said to Flin, still holding his hand tightly. "All who did not escape, that is. There were no men in my vision, though, all except one old man who crept back into this hut and buried something at the back. Over there," she said, pointing to the back wall. "Then he went back out and deliberately attacked them with a sword that he had hidden in a barrel. He did that deliberately so he was killed himself. He could have escaped."

Flin nodded thoughtfully and slowly walked to the back corner. He pushed aside the bundle of clothing and rubbish that Varna had seen dumped in place, but the dirt floor appeared to be smooth to his view. "I can't see anything here," he told Varna.

She frowned and said, "I saw him scrape away the earth and bury some sort of object. It was wrapped and in a metal holder." She paused and softly said, "I can feel something coming from over there. Don't ask me how," she continued, "I just can."

Flin nodded again. "I'm not doubting you. There's too much happening here for me to do that. The floor appears to be undisturbed but," and he bent to touch the floor, "yes, it looks undisturbed but is soft to the touch. Odd."

Stepping back and looking around, Flin spied a small spade, with a handle that was split and warped. He carried it back to the cleared spot and gently scraped the earth away to a depth of about two hand-spans. The spade caught on something and Flin discarded the spade, knelt alongside the shallow hole and even more gently started to scrape the earth away with his hands. Within moments he had found the metal box. He opened the box to find a small parcel, wrapped in cloth. He lifted the parcel from the ground and with Varna in tow carried it out of the hovel into the light. Flin's Mage light sputtered out as they left.

"Oh my," Flin breathed as he placed the object on the ground, kneeling back on his heels as he regarded the object with something approaching awe.

"What is it?" Varna asked. "You haven't even unwrapped it and are treating it like royalty."

"Because in a way that's what it is," Flin replied. "The cloth - you can see the design even through the dirt - is very old, from before the rebellion. It's called hamtar, and was a special weave from a very special material, synthetic and very expensive. It was only used for the most important purposes. This cloth was once a banner from the Faero's hall."

"From the Citadel?" asked Varna.

"No," Flin replied, still regarding the bundle with fascination, "from the original hall in Arbogast, that has been gone for eons now."

"Are you going to unwrap it?"

"I think I may leave that to you. I have a feeling you were drawn to this for a reason, and I don't want to interfere more than I must." Flin glanced up at Varna, and smiled. "I'm starting to understand where you may fit into all of this, Varna. And I think this may be important."

Varna stood looking down at the bundle.

"Okay, then let's get all of the bits together before we do," she said, and Flin's eyebrows went up. "Can you bring that along with you?" she said, turning as she walked towards the centre of the small village.

Flin gathered the parcel reverently and cradled it like a small child as he followed Varna. Dalresar followed, bemused at Varna taking the lead and Flin following. She walked confidently, as though she knew where she was going. After a minute of steady walking, though, her pace faltered and she let out a small cry as she bent to pick up a small rag doll, lying in the churned-up path. Flin, bewildered, watched as she hugged the small doll to her breast for a moment, and then resolutely placed it in her pack, before straightening her back. With determination, she moved on again.

Shortly they came to the village centre. Here, the cottages were further from the road and a small tavern occupied one whole side. The open area was dominated by a large charred area. Flin saw Varna flinch as she looked on the sight, and then he saw the small fragments of bone scattered around the blackened ground. Varna's face was pinched as she stood, staring at the desolate sight, and Flin could see her gather her determination once again, her face hardening. She turned from the sight and looked around the clearing until, with a sigh, she walked to a spot just outside the charred area. Bending, she picked up the sword which had been wielded with such effect by the old man of her vision. The sword flared as Varna touched it, and Flin heard a pure note sound.

Varna, shaken by the sight and sound, stood looking at Flin. The sword was held in her right hand and unconsciously she adopted a guard position.

"What was that?" she asked softly.

"I think, my child, that was you." Flin walked over to where Varna stood. "May I have a look?" he asked.

Varna nodded and handed the sword to Flin. He was almost sorry that there was no flare of light as he touched it, but was not surprised.

"This," he said after turned it over a few times, "was the short sword of the last Faero before the destruction caused by the rebellion. It was, supposedly, ceremonial only." He shook his head in wonder - it was one thing after another lately, and this only the latest wonder. "But why was it here?"

Flin stood with a far-away look in his eyes as he remembered times past.

"Maybe that wrapped parcel will tell us," Varna said, drawing Flin back to the present.

"Indeed," he said, "but the sword gives me an inkling."

Gently, he peeled back the coloured cloth to reveal a further layer of cloth, this time a serviceable plain material which, to Varna, looked like muslin. Flin shook out the covering cloth to reveal a piece that Varna estimated was one metre long and almost the same wide, with the same design as flew on the flag above the citadel, only this one was picked out in what looked like gold. Flin nodded, confirming what he was already sure would be the case, and gently put the small banner to one side, before turning to the parcel once more. He unwrapped the last layer of cloth and laid it open, with the object exposed and resting in the centre. Flin sat back on his heels once more and stared.

"And?" Varna asked impatiently, understanding that Flin was deeply moved but wanting to know what it was.

"This," said Flin, his tone now matter-of-fact, as though no further wonders could affect him, "is the lost circlet of the Faero. The Faero was not so much a king as a sort of civil and spiritual leader. Oh, I think they were kind of kings very early in Ennaris' history, but for most of our history they were the heart and soul of the planet. The circlet was a symbol of that, with the stone in the shape of a sanfire, a mythical bird associated with the Guardians."

Varna bent to pick up the circlet but Flin blocked her.

"We really don't know what that may do, Varna. You activated the Faero's sword, after all, so I think we need to go carefully here."

"Okay," she nodded, agreeing. "But what is in that small pouch?"

Flin reached out and picked up a small pouch, also made of hamtar. He opened a drawstring and tipped into his hand a small pendant, comprising a milky white round stone seated in a finely wrought setting, with a simple metal chain.

"And this," said Flin softly, "was the Faero's mantarc." At Varna's quizzical look, Flin continued in explanation, "A mantarc is designed to rest on the person's forehead, with the chain draped around the crown of the head. There were very few of them and all were destined for individuals who play significant roles for Ennaris. I thought they had been made by Guides - Halfgar implied that once when I asked him. When the mantarc sits on the crown of its destined bearer, the stone glows and displays a sanfire in its heart. I have seen it several times and it is, um, impressive." He paused for a second. "Very impressive, in fact."

"So," Varna stood. "We have a poor and crumbling village whose inhabitants included one who had several very precious artefacts, attacked by a band of those creatures who seemed to be searching for something, and probably what we just found. What does it all mean?"

"I'm not sure," Flin said, "but I do know we need to protect them. I would return them to the Citadel if I could but I feel we must press on. Your summons to the Forest of the Guardians takes on new meaning, I am thinking. You seem to be central somehow, and we need to find out how."

In short order, Varna and Flin had done a quick search of the rest of the village while Dalresar remained on watch. They found nothing, and Varna sensed nothing else. They did find a tooled scabbard in the barrel where Varna had seen the old man extract the sword - sanfires on the scabbard said that it belonged with the sword - but Flin thought it had no special meaning, although it remained in good condition despite its age. They started to leave the village when Flin paused and turned back.

"No," he said as though to himself. "They cannot be left like that."

He stood in the road leading to the square and raised one hand. A swirling vortex took shape, reaching out to collect each of the bones remaining from the edges of the fire, before placing them in a small, pitiful pile in the centre of the charred area. Flin allowed the vortex to dissipate and turned to Varna.

"I am not a warrior," he said, sighing deeply. "Unlike Marjory, my talent is best used to celebrate life. I hope the villagers are able to return and that this will assist them."

Flin reached into his pack and drew forth a small packet, from which he drew forth a single seed. He walked over to the pile of bones and carefully dropped the seed into the middle, then returned to Varna's side. A glow arose within the small pile of bones. It grew in brightness and overflowed the bones to spread along the scarred and burnt earth, reaching ever higher, brighter, larger, brighter again. Varna, watching rapt, suddenly saw beyond normal sight, seeing the energies that Flin brought to bear swirling and turning. The bones were turned to dust and then merged into a new entity, a small tree that budded from the seed and grew to the beginning of what she could see would be a mid-size tree very quickly, fed by the power brought to bear by the Mage. But something was missing, something called to Varna and, unbidden, she pulled the Faero's sword from the bundle she and Flin had made only to see the hilt glowing, as were runes inscribed along the blade, running with golden fire in response to the energies being released.

Varna gripped the blade firmly and reached out to grasp Flin's hand. As they touched, the sword sang and the energies changed. Flin's creative energy was now mixed with a new energy that flowed from the blade itself, through Varna and into the swirling maelstrom. The tree was changing. Ribbons of light ran along the immature trunk and branches. Foliage took shape and emerged from the branches until, with a last flare and a pop, the energies ceased. Flin staggered a little, and Varna shook her head to get rid of the lingering buzz, which was different to the one that she usually suffered but was just as disorienting. All three stared at the tree now growing in the midst of a green sward in the centre of the square where the bones had been piled. The tree had bright white flowers, opening to display sword-like stamens of bright blue.

Flin turned to Varna and gasped, "What did you do? I have never experienced anything like that before. And the result was not exactly what I had planned."

"I, uh, didn't know what I was doing. Something just made me do that. The sword, I think. Your tree was going to be nice, but I think I like this one better." She smiled to Flin. "No offence, of course."

"None taken." He frowned. "You could tell what the tree was going to look like?"

"Yes, sort of. It was going to be about the same size but without flowers, and the foliage was going to be almost grey and spiky."

"Yes, I was using the seed of a ghost arbus."

"I could see the energies you were releasing and could tell what they would do, but I couldn't control what I was seeing, or what I was doing," said Varna.

"Then the sooner we get you to the Forest the better, I feel," Flin told her as he turned to pick up his pack. "You need to understand exactly what you can do and get control over it. There are too many aspects to this now, and I'm uncertain where that leads. But," he stood and looked at the tree with its white flowers shining in the sun-light, "I do prefer your version. Or the sword's version, perhaps. That itself is something to consider. I don't recall anything about the Faero's ceremonial sword having any form of power of its own."

Flin nodded decisively. "We need to get moving again. I think we have what we were brought here for."

Varna looked at Flin questioningly.

"Yes, I think we are being guided, and that is a little disquieting. We all like to feel that we're in charge, especially me who supposedly is the power around here." He smiled once more to take any sting from the words. "And the sooner we know what's going on the better."

The three turned as one and walked from the square. Varna turned her head as they left the village to see the tree standing guard over the site of the massacre. Or so it seemed to her, as the sword-like stamens shivered in the breeze, like so many swords being brandished.

Flin and Varna walked in silence. Both were reflecting on what they had experienced at the small village. Dalresar ranged ahead now, unsure what he was looking for but sure that there was something. For Varna, it was obvious that the events she had watched had taken place only a day or so prior to their arrival. That could mean the attackers were still in the vicinity, so she was trying to maintain a lookout, but once again she was experiencing the fluctuations of attention that she had suffered since arriving on Ennaris. Although, she considered, they were not quite as bad since she had been visiting Balgor's little oasis of calm at the Citadel.

Flin was occupied with other matters. He knew that they were being observed and was unsure by whom or what. He was not overly concerned by that and would almost have welcomed running into the same band of attackers that had decimated the village. He was sure that they had been after the artefacts that Varna had uncovered, but how did they know of them and, even more of a mystery, how did the objects come to be there?

Finally, after walking slightly apart for a couple of hours, Flin moved closer to Varna and said quietly, "We're being observed. There were only one or two before but now ..."

"... there are about six, four on one side of the road and two on the other." Varna gestured right and left as she spoke.

Flin smiled. "So, you are getting some control after all."

"No," she almost snorted. "They just aren't very good at hiding. I'm a Warrior of the Light, remember." She considered. "I think they probably are children, maybe the older ones who got away from the village. Which means the women and small children are close. Any ideas?" she asked Flin.

"There is a small clearing a short way further on, and in the forest somewhat. A cave opens onto the clearing. That's a likely hiding place. We can turn off just up ahead. It has been used as a stopping off point for a very long time."

As they reached the point that Flin indicated, both he and Varna made an abrupt right turn into the shrubbery and moved rapidly through the undergrowth. Dalresar now followed. On both sides they heard movement as the watchers tried to scamper ahead of them. Finally, they came to a stand of forest where the undergrowth had been cleared and could see an open clearing ahead. While not large, there was an expanse of open ground that would allow a determined rear-guard action to be staged to protect the cave that Varna could now see opening on the other side of the clearing and extending into a rocky hill.

As they emerged from the tree line Varna saw four children run into the cave. She and Flin exchanged glances - two children were still in the forest. They moved across the grassy clearing slowly, hands held out to their sides to show no weapons. Dalresar remained near the tree line, studying the edges of the clearing. Suddenly, from the cave stepped four women, each wielding spears. Two others emerged at the top of the cave with bows strung and shafts in place. Flin and Varna slowed further but kept walking until within easy speaking distance. They stopped as one.

"Far enough," said one of the women, who was younger than the others and held her spear as through she knew how to use it. Varna considered her carefully before deciding that it was the same woman who she saw with the young child who had dropped her doll.

"We mean you no harm," said Flin carefully. "Are you okay? Did any of you or the children take any hurt when you left the village? If so, we can help."

The woman regarded them suspiciously. "All are fine," she said, "and if we weren't we can look after ourselves."

"Not really," Varna said to the woman, pitching her voice so all could hear. "There are still some of those animal men, the ghazrak, in the vicinity." She paused as the women shared worried glances. "And the safest place for you all, believe it or not, may actually be back in your village. I know what happened there, and I know how scared you are, but this cave does not provide safety. If they find you here, you will all perish."

"We die if we go back to the village." said the woman. "We will await our men here."

"Where are they, your men?" Varna made no attempt to hide her puzzlement. "They would not have been able to do much against those creatures, but why were they not there to try?"

"They were called away, to track some bandits who attacked out-lying farms."

"Did all of those farms have young children?" Flin asked. "And were they all killed with nothing stolen?"

The woman looked at them suspiciously again, but with some un-certainty. "How would you know that? Unless you are part of them."

"The same thing happened to the south, near the Citadel. They appeared to be trying to kill those of the Old Blood." Flin paused as the women again looked one to the other. "Are you of the Old Blood also?"

The woman stood proudly, with the spear still held tightly. "We are of the Blood!" she declared.

Flin nodded. "And do you tell the old stories still? Do you remind yourselves of the legacy of the Blood? Do you recall the tales of the times yet to come?" A deeper timbre had come to Flin's voice, and Varna sensed a pulse coming from him, power being held back.

"We do," the woman stated defiantly, and the other women moved as a group to stand beside the speaker, each sharing the same determined mien. Varna was impressed by how they held themselves, after having been through so much.

"Then hear me well, daughters of the Blood! For I am Drewflin, Mage of the Council of the Guides, and the time has come for the Blood to stand together." Flin's voice boomed, and drew from the cave the rest of the women, as well as the children. "And I tell you this truly. Your village will not be ravaged by those creatures again, for the Guardians have placed a protection on it. It is safe for you to return there, and Varna and I will accompany you to ensure it."

"Mage? The Mages died thousands of years ago. Along with the rest of the Guides. Most of the tales are just stories anyway. Guardians? Pfffft," and she waved one hand in dismissal, "more stories. Just you and this woman to hold off those beasts? That is a jest for the ages."

Flin saw Varna look into the forest suddenly, frowning in concentration. She closed her eyes and stood perfectly still for a few moments, then sighed and opened her eyes to look at Flin.

"They're coming," she said. "And there are more of them, I think. I can't quite get it but they are being drawn here by something. I think there may be two or more bands together."

"The beasts are coming here, more than there were before. What they are is an old evil reborn and they are not going to be stopped by a cave. I ask you to trust me and come with me to your village. I can offer you protection there." Flin stopped short of entreating, but it was an appeal.

Varna spoke slowly. "They are getting closer. We need to move now."

The woman was torn, until Varna reached into her pack and drew forth the sword. Its blade gleamed brightly in the now waning light, and a lick of flame ran up its full length, flaring off the tip. The woman stared, recognising it.

"That's old Magyar's sword," she said. "I've seen him holding it and waving it around at times. He said it was from someone important in the past."

"Magyar died attacking the ghazrak who stormed your village. He killed three of them before himself dying." Varna paused, looking back to her vision. "This sword is what he used."

"Why does it burn?" another of the women asked.

"This is the sword of the last Faero before the fall," said Flin. "How Magyar came to have it and other artefacts is a mystery we will unravel at another time. It appears to have a power of its own that I did not suspect at the time. As to why it flames, it may be because the bearer is one of the Nine."

A gasp escaped the spokeswoman, staring at Varna and then Flin, who nodded mutely.

"Flin, we need to move," said Varna, reverting suddenly to a Warrior of the Light, watching the forest and missing the last exchange. "You need to come with us, right now," said Varna to the woman, crisply. "Right now!"

A moment passed and the woman turned to the others, decisive. "Okay, let's gather what we can and go with them."

"Leave anything you can afford to leave behind," Varna said, reaching into her pack again and pulling forth the doll, "but give this back to your daughter." And Varna handed the doll to the woman.

The woman stared anew at Varna, taking the doll. "How did you come by this? And how did you know it is Vanyar's?"

"I found it in the village where she dropped it. I saw you running with her, and I saw her drop her doll. It was in a vision," Varna finished, and shrugged. "I could not leave it behind."

The bustle in the cave became a small stream of women and children. The spokeswoman put two fingers to her mouth and produced a short, warbling whistle, and almost immediately two more children broke from the forest and ran to the group, past Dalresar who was still standing and watching intently. Flin nodded his approval and pointed into the forest in the direction of the village.

"There's a game trail through those bushes," he said. "I'm sure you know of it already. I think we head for the road via that path rather than the other way. We could meet them if we're not careful. But we need to move."

"We can go fast when we need to," the spokeswomen declared. "And we are not a burden. We are of the Blood!" she finished fiercely, to the accompanying nods of the other women, and strode off through the bush, daughter in hand. She was followed by the rest in good order.

Flin glanced to Varna and smiled. "Not quite what we expected, but sometimes you need to deal with what comes up."

She nodded. "This feels right. I'm not sure how, but this leads to something. I know it. I don't know how I know it, but I know it!"

The two of them followed the villagers into the trees. Dalresar took a final look around and followed, sword in hand.

17. Kingdom Armies

The Pass of Grentall filled with dust as the combined armies of Kresh and Ingten charged through the valley's opening. The charge was led by a squad of hrss-borne scouts, who were followed closely by the Red Legion, the elite of the conjoined military of the twin kingdoms of the north. They marched at double time, the military version of a distance eating jog. As they exited the Pass, the scouts separated and galloped towards their own target destinations. The Red Legion moved from eight abreast to a battle formation of twenty abreast and then increased their own separation to create the standard defensive battle formation. They maintained their pace for a further two hundred spans, and then slowed to a standard march, breathing heavily but holding formation.

The initial force was followed by a pike company, which was then followed by the rank and file. The army of the twin kingdoms flowed onto the steppe, the dry, grassy plain that stretched out in all directions ahead of them. Once safely out of the Pass, the army settled back into a standard march. They were fifty or more spans behind the Red Legion, which maintained their spread as the main army emerged from the Pass.

Five hundred spans further into the steppe the Red Legion slowed, spreading further and coming to a halt. The breakout had been timed for dark, a time when the commanders of the Red Legion were confident that there would be no witnesses. They had encountered no alarms, no opposition. Therefore, as planned, the commanders ordered the forces to enter camp where they remained close enough to seek the safety of the valley that had so recently disgorged them.

With the scouts out, General Morsen was satisfied that their security had been tight and that they had not been detected. After all, their scouts were the best that had ever been, and they reported no dangers. Five spies had been captured and all had died without revealing what their goals had been, but Morsen was assured that all spies had been captured. The force deployed their guards, had a cold meal and turned in with a standard night guard deployed.

On the eastern peak above the Pass, Murk watched the twin kingdoms' armies as they sped from the safety of the dusty valley onto the grasslands. The scouts of Tanga had been aware that the northern kingdoms were preparing for something for some time, and had kept a watch through the only way south. One of their spies, at enormous risk, had spent two tendays travelling through that benighted land, and had reported that the armies were mobilising. She had been the only one of six to return. Now Murk watched as the force slowed, milled around for a while and then settled for the night. Murk turned to the man crouched alongside him and nodded, a gesture not seen by his companion but, nevertheless, understood. The second man rose to a stoop and moved away to where his hrss awaited him. The deep of night held no fear for the Clans of the grasslands who knew their lands intimately, and the sentry flowed onto his mount and moved away, his mount's hoofs muffled to reduce the sound.

Someone seeing the enormous grassland of Ennaris' northern continent would believe that they were seeing a completely flat expanse. The short grass was no higher than an average man's waist, so around a quarter of a span, and was sustained by just enough precipitation, but not enough for the grass to grow substantially longer. Once this area had been the main growing area for grain and other crops on Ennaris, so legend said. The changes to weather systems following the rebellion meant that over time those crops failed more than they succeeded, and then just failed. The soils became parched as the nutrients leached away and were not maintained. In many ways, a stranger would see a wasteland.

And yet, that was not how these men and women from the northern kingdoms saw this land, those whose own land was hard and desolate, dusty and unforgiving. These lands had always held an allure for those of the hermit kingdoms, whose people were kept under firm control and whose contact with the outside world was strictly restricted. Merely seeing the ocean of grass stretching out in a single expanse to their front and both sides made their hearts soar. They had been assured that this land was ripe for the taking, and so it seemed. They had exited the valley, travelling via a path that had been dug out painstakingly over the last three generations in preparation for this moment. Their Old One had decreed that it must be done, and so it had been. General Morsen took one more satisfied look before retiring to his tent for the night.

Some who lived in these massive grassed plains had a different perspective. Dry as they were, moisture was available if you knew where, but there were few such locations and they were all hidden to preserve that most critical of resources. Stretching from the eastern edge of the land claimed by Escar to the western edge of the mist-shrouded mountain range that cut vertically through the continent, the extent of the grass range was such that a healthy person walking from one side to another would require half a cycle or more, if he or she did not get lost. That was assuming those widely separated water sources were known, and the types of available food were understood.

A little south of the centre of the great grasslands was one of only two structures in the grass plain, standing over the millennia since the rebellion's end. Where all of the other structures had been destroyed during the fighting, or had been collapsed and looted for available materials during the lawless and desperate period after that catastrophe, this strange building, like its companion that was located near the north-east edge of the plains, could not be entered and nor could its walls be damaged or dismantled. Many had tried over the cycles, and all had failed. It was built of strange stone, strange because one could not discover where the stones fitted together. It was surrounded by a low wall, with a sort of courtyard stretching away from what was obviously a set of doors - the only doors that many who made the grasslands their homes ever saw. This structure was the most prominent landmark for the plains dwellers.

It was in the general direction of this landmark that Borlak pointed his hrss after leaving the Tang scouts. Borlak was one who knew this land. He understood that it was not a single flat expanse and he would make his way through the dips and mounds, along the small gullies that occasionally held water but usually were dry, around the small obstacles that created big problems for those unaccustomed to them. He paused after a while to remove the wads of soft material that had been tied to his mount's hoofs to make it easier going, for the hrss would use its own senses to pick a way through the more uneven grassed areas.

Borlak skirted the wide edge of the bowl that spilled from the valley and that was now occupied by the twin kingdoms' armies, all the while remaining vigilant for the scouts that had sped in all directions. The northern fighters were poor by all accounts, but their scouts were reputed to be much better. Of course, those scouts still were northers, and Borlak was a Clansman, and the two were worlds apart in skill. Still, safer rather than sorry, as his old father would say. Once he felt that he should have made it past the extent of the norther scouts' range, he touched his heels to the flanks of the hrss, and the animal extended into the distance-eating lope that it could keep up for long periods. Borlak needed to make his report to the Clan, and he was heading towards the Gather that was to be held in the traditional location near the building. While the scouts' estimates were that the invading force represented only a quarter, or perhaps less than that, of the combined armies' resources, it was close to five thousand strong. The northern kingdoms had populations that were quite large given that they were reputed to be completely barren in the most part. Moreover, most of those populations were trained for war, poorly so in the eye of the few who made reports of such, but sometimes numbers outweighed skill, and the kingdoms had much greater numbers than the Clans, the Tang and Escar combined.

This was what Lak had talked to the Clans about on her return, of the impending battle for the future of Ennaris. She had told them of the Children, and of the Mages of old and the raising of a new Faero. It was myths come to life for most of the Clans. But the Clans had held to the faith, to the lessons taught by their own traditional tellers, as tradition said were passed to them by Lak of old before she had left. They had built their skills and they maintained them. They lived their lives on the grass as they wished, by and large, but they also held themselves ready to be called, for that is what their traditions told them, that the Clans would be vital to the final battle. Lak had told them that they probably would be fighting against the numerous northers, while warning them against complacency for these armies were not just men and women. There were rumours of strange beast-like men being seen around Ennaris, sightings that Lak confirmed. None of the Clans liked the idea of Goroth returning, myth or not. They would stand up as their traditions dictated, and defend Ennaris as the ancient stories told that their forebears had done.

Borlak grinned tightly as he rode. It looked like the Clans would be going to war.

El-bren was bored. She had been leading her flight in a series of sweeps high, very high, above the grassy plains. From up here the expanse could be seen for large distances. She could see the edges of the northern mountains to her right and she steered her flight slightly south-west to criss-cross the plain. Kunas' arrival had stirred the blood of the Rocs as nothing had for a very long time. Even the oldest of the great birds could recall nothing of the like, and Rocs could live for a very long time relative to their old land-bound allies. Their skills training had been strengthened, with Kunas helping to re-establish some forms of training that had been lost.

And the patrols had been re-established fully. The Rocs had never stopped their patrols but, over the long cycles, they had become a matter of form. Patrols had become short in duration and distance covered. In reality, El-bren thought with shame, the Rocs had lost their way. They had lost faith. They were going through the motions. Now, however, those patrols were stretching longer and further than had been done for longer than the oldest could recall. Rocs could stay aloft for a day or more if necessary. Their huge wingspan held them high above the land with minimal effort. Training served to make them stronger still, so they could carry partial load-outs of the weaponry for which the Rocs had been known. Some of them were being outfitted to carry the riders as of old. Kunas was helping with that, too. Already some had been trained. El-bren hoped she would be doing the same soon.

Meanwhile, while every Roc loved to soar above the landscape of Ennaris, the patrol of the grasslands was boring. This was not because the Rocs thought of that great expanse as being a single level plain, for the Rocs' eyesight was such that they could see the small rises and dips, the tiny rips and breaks in the land that told of gullies and dry watercourses. They could see some of the small animals that lived amid the grass and often dug their way into the sides of the small gullies. There was enough variation in the grasslands for a Roc to stay somewhat interested. It was just that nothing happened! At least the patrols to the east of the mountains showed an ever-changing array of things happening, not always things the Rocs thought were right, but things to hold one's attention. The patrols over the jungles that dominated the thin space between north and south also drifted over the great bight below the eastern lands where the huge maelstroms twisted the water into such dangerous funnels that no-one could navigate them. But they were always interesting to watch. Even the patrols over the southern deserts were interesting in their own way.

To the north was the ice where hardy souls made a difficult life, and where the Rocs must spend less time in the more frigid air. And below the ice was the blasted lands that were occupied by the two kingdoms. That brown and bleak land was relieved by three large swathes of brilliant green where the basic crops that the people lived on were grown, rising up the terraced sides of several small mountains. Fed by springs that gushed from the top of the peaks, in a way that El-bren could not fathom, and the patches of green stood out from far away. El-bren enjoyed seeing that surprising sight on the occasions that her patrol had covered the region.

And, of course, every Roc wanted to be part of the patrols that watched over the land east and south of the grass, the area above the great body of water that separated north and south and reached west to the ocean and north to the ice. More importantly, though, this was the land of the Faero and the Citadel. Each and every Roc wanted to be the one to fly to the aid of the Faero, as the old stories told of aid that had been rendered in the past.

Twisting her head left and right, and extending her senses to touch her flight members and make sure they were in formation, El-bren held back the sigh that threatened to tell all just how bored she was. Of course they were in formation. They were Rocs.

El-bren, look to the valley to the right at forty-five degrees, came the call from Ar-kin, the furthest member of the flight to the north on this path.

El-bren sharpened her vision and twisted her head to look where directed. There was movement at the mouth of the valley. With a thought El-bren shifted the patrol's flight path. Boredom was replaced by tight attention. Patrols had reported activity further up this valley for a time now. It seemed that a natural blockage in the valley was being removed. Now this. The flight soared across the land towards the mountain range that ran east to west. From the mouth of the valley had come a small number of figures on hrss, but from their height the patrol was able to see along the valley and the army could be clearly sighted.

The point above the pass, came the call from Ka-bed, El-bren's patrol second.

El-bren looked and passed a virtual nod of approval to her second. Hunkered down atop the point where the pass opened to the plain was a small group of men watching the army emerge from the valley.

El-bren and her flight watched as the army exited onto the plain, spread out in a defensive formation and settled down for the night. They also watched as one of the watching group broke away and began what would obviously be a circuitous path around the scouts that had spread wide. El-bren detached Ka-bed and Ar-kin to follow the path of the rider, obviously a Clansman, and to provide protection, as reward for their sharp-eyed work. The message he would carry had to get to the right people safely, and the Rocs would do what they could to provide cover.

She started to compose her report. Her patrol would be completed shortly and she needed to brief the incoming patrol leader as well as the Roc battle council.

Borlak relaxed in his saddle. He was sure that he was past the furthest extent that those scouts would have travelled, so he started to curve back in a long arc that would see him heading west again. He knew where the Clan would be about now. It would take him another whole day, he thought, to join the Clan's caravan, so he would keep moving for a bit longer.

Only a short way further on in his journey he realised that his over-confidence had played him false. He had little warning, merely the light twang of a bow string that allowed him time to shift his position, but not enough time to avoid the shaft entirely. The shaft took a deep slice from his upper arm, luckily his left. In itself that was not such a problem, but the shaft had come from in front, which meant at least one of the scouts was ahead of him, and was probably stalking him.

He wasted a moment in berating himself, even while he was searching out the slightest sound by which to tell where his foe might be. He ducked low over the heavy neck of his hrss and spoke gently, quietly.

"Come, Nightrider, we must make haste quietly," Borlak said, stifling a moan as his arm flared with pain.

Man and hrss had been together for many cycles. Nightrider, war-trained as he was, smelt the blood. Instinct kicked in and the hrss lifted his head and sniffed the air. His sense of smell was superior to his rider's, and he easily detected the strange odour. He unerringly pointed his nose towards it even while continuing to move in a direction guided by his rider. Borlak noted the pointer given and patted Nightrider on the side of the neck in thanks. Carefully, Borlak slowed Nightrider. Relying on the deepening dark he found a small gully, little more than a light slash in the land and guided Nightrider into it. Nightrider moved quietly, unerringly, along the sandy base of the gully, stopping when he felt pressure applied by Borlak on the loose reins.

The two stood silently, still as statues. Borlak listened intently, as did Nightrider. Once again, the hrss' hearing proved to be better for he turned his head to the right. Borlak nodded, then cursed inwardly as Nightrider followed that movement with a second turn of the head to the left, followed by a slight toss of his head. Three of them, to right, left and behind! This just became harder than he had expected. What to do? If there had been two, he would have sought to take them one after the other. Inevitably there would be some noise though and with three he was almost certain to lose, even against northers. The thoughts took but a moment.

Borlak rested one hand on Nightrider's neck and tapped a peculiar rhythm. The hrss almost glided forward, unnaturally quiet. Borlak could hear faint sounds of the enemy scouts closing in, but he thought they were almost past the one closest to their direction of travel, when Nightrider's unshod hoof struck a rock, skittering it into another. Borlak immediately tapped heels to Nightrider's flank and the hrss surged forward. Atop the edge of the gully appeared not one but two scouts to the right and another to the left. Behind him Borlak could hear the other coming faster. Four!

The two on the right were ahead of him slightly. Borlak's heart sank as he realised one was wielding a cross-bow. Still, one fought until one could fight no longer. Nightrider charged out of the gully directly towards the two to the right. Borlak's right arm swept back and forward again and his throwing knife leapt across the space between rider and cross-bow wielder, knowing as he did so that he would miss getting a good strike. Sure enough, the knife struck the opposing scout little more than a glancing blow, but it was enough to spoil his aim and the bolt went wide. Borlak now had his sword in hand, his injured left hand holding the reins but, in reality, it was Nightrider who had control of direction. The hrss jinked to the left, as he had been trained, and Borlak struck out, avoiding the scout's own blade and feeling the satisfying *thunk* of his own blade hitting true. Borlak's blade was razor sharp and made to much higher quality standards that the norther blades that Borlak had seen. The scout dropped lifeless.

Borlak did not stop to make sure but, using knees only, he instructed Nightrider to spin and charge back towards the crossbowman. He saw the other two coming at a dead run, the second stopping to wind his own crossbow. Blast! But Borlak could only do the best that he could do. He reached the first crossbowman as he was raising the crossbow to fire and ran him through in a classic Clan tactic, gritting his teeth against the pain of his wound to slide down the side of Nightrider so he could drive his sword into the torso, wrenching it free as Nightrider thundered past. Hrss and rider were in sync as they turned to the last two. The crossbowman was inserting his bolt and preparing to lift it as Nightrider straightened and charged. Hrss and rider would reach the first of them, Borlak thought, but not the second.

Borlak cast all thought of quiet aside.

"Undular Lak! For the glory of Lak!" he cried, holding his sword in classic charge position as he awaited the cross-bow bolt that would end his charge.

But his cry was answered! From the left flank came a pair of harsh cries, loud and ringing with challenge. Then, with a rush of wind two enormous shapes materialised in front of Borlak and swept the two scouts off their feet and into the dark sky. Astounded at the sudden event, Borlak stopped Nightrider's charge and listened. At a distance away to his right he distinctly heard two thuds, which he assumed were the two scouts returning to the grassland. He stood and waited, straining his eyes to see if his strange rescuers would return. Nightrider trembled beneath him.

Far above, Ka-bed and Ar-kin wheeled after disposing of their loads, diving back towards the mounted Clansman. The Rocs swept past at a distance that ensured Borlak would see them for what they were but not so close as to overly spook the hrss. As one they shouted the Roc battle cry one more time before flapping their powerful wings and racing back to the heights. The Clansman faced no further foes and it was past time for them to return to their eyrie.

Far below, Borlak wondered. His final glimpse told him that he had been delivered by an Ennarisi legend, one that he, and all those who he knew, thought had been lost in the dreadful upheavals of the past. He silently lifted his sword in salute before nudging Nightrider into motion. He was injured and hurting. Still, he had a message to deliver, and a story to tell.

18. Anhard Spring

The journey back to the village passed without incident, much to the surprise of both Flin and Varna, who continued to get impressions of the half-men following them and gaining. But the women kept up the pace and the children, in hand or held by one or another of the women as they walked, remained quiet and stayed with them.

At one stage, when one of the women was struggling to keep up while holding a small boy, Varna took the child from her and continued, not noticing her new blade change to a faint blue glow. Flin followed, intrigued and reflecting that he really did not understand what was happening. Not only had his long-held beliefs been shattered recently - and he was honest enough with himself to realise that those beliefs were caused by despair in the past as he was unable to affect a restoration of what had been lost - but now he had three off-worlders who seemed destined to play key roles in what was to come. He was not sure that he was best suited to the part he seemed to have to play - he really was not a warrior, he thought wryly - and of a sudden was beset by a desperate sense of loss as he thought of Marjory. She, he thought through a thin film that briefly obscured his vision, would know what to do. She would grasp hold of the tasks and carry them forward boldly.

Finally, they reached the village and the women exclaimed as they saw the tree in the middle of the square. Varna led them to the square and told them to settle around the tree. Flin watched her take charge and help the women settle their children. He watched one upset child who was being held by her mother reach up to grasp one of the flowers, which broke away from the tree easily. The child, on the verge of tears, relaxed immediately. Flin watched as other children, who were all fretting from their ordeal and aware that it was not yet over, also slowly settled, forming a ring around the trunk of the tree on the newly grown grass.

The day's light was waning rapidly and Flin was wondering what they would do to protect the group during the dark when he noticed that the flowers were glowing. He saw Varna glance up as she noticed it and then turn in his direction and smile, confidently. She had discarded the pack and shed her cloak. Somehow, and Flin did not know how, she had assumed leadership of the group and moved around the women, comforting them and reassuring them. Dalresar was called by Varna into the centre of the village square, and he came without demur, watching Varna intently.

Always in the back of Varna's awareness was the knowledge that the ghazrak were closing on the village, approaching it from multiple directions to ensure that no-one escaped. She now realised the awareness came from the tree itself, and she knew when the beasts started to enter the village. The tree burst into light, illuminating the entire square and part of the road on each side. Several of the women moaned as they realised what was happening, but Varna rose quietly from where she had crouched alongside one woman and her child and moved to a position where she faced the north road. She sensed the beasts move towards the square but stop, confused by the tree and the light. Varna saw Flin move to face the south road, while Dalresar moved to face the east side, as she drew forth the Faero's sword once again. She almost chuckled as she thought of what Blaine would think if he could see her now.

A growl heralded the approach of the half-men, but it was the leader who made its way into the light, squinting at the glare. It seemed surprised to see the women and children around the tree, but continued to advance. It stopped half way to the tree and stared as it noticed the sword wielded by Varna, held confidently and with no fear showing. Varna stared back. She maintained awareness of what was happening around the square, but stared directly into the half-man's eyes.

"Give power things," it grunted at Varna. "You live, we go."

Varna held her voice for a moment, watching as the half-man grimaced, with jaws slackening and fangs showing as it watched her.

Then she said, "No. I saw what you did here. You shall not do so again." She stood straighter than she thought she could and said clearly and coldly, "And you will not have the objects of power."

The beast-man grunted again and, watching Varna still, gestured with one arm, the other gripping a wicked-looking spear. The rest of the half-men, more than twenty of them, emerged from the shadows, some hesitantly, some aggressively, and encircled the party around the tree. Flin stood easily, one hand holding his staff with the stone quiescent and the other empty and held at his side, waiting for he knew not what, but aware that this was in Varna's hands. He could feel the tree's power but could not determine its source or what it could do.

As the entire party of half-men loosened their weapons, Varna held out her sword. Blue flame ran along the length of the blade and the beasts halted, mesmerised.

Varna said quietly, "You have no place here."

She pointed the blade at the leader and a shaft of blue flame blazed from the tip of the sword and pierced it through, burning it to ash as it stood, and then the ash itself burnt away to nothing. The beast-men moaned and turned to run but shafts of blue flame burst from the tree's branches, one for each of the attackers. Within moments none were left. Even their blades, spears and axes became molten puddles.

Varna staggered slightly, but then straightened and turned back to the women.

"You will be safe now, with the tree to make sure of that. And I need to rest a bit," she finished as she walked slowly to the trunk of the tree and sat with her back to it. Her sword was rested on the grassy sward alongside her. She leaned back and closed her eyes.

Flin, watching with eyes the women did not possess, could have sworn he saw two ghostly arms reach out to cradle her as she rested. He shook his head against such fanciful nonsense but then reflected that he had already seen a lot of what he would have considered as nonsense around Varna so far. Dalresar also was shaking his head at what had happened and moved up to stand with Flin.

"Who is she?" the lead woman asked Flin quietly, having approached unaware. "She seems so uncertain at times, and yet so forceful at others. And the Guardians do appear to have chosen her, for which we are ever grateful."

"She is one of the Nine," Flin said, turning to face the woman. "You recall the legend of the Nine?" He nodded as she did likewise. "Varna is one of the Children returned. Remember her when times are hard, for she will be striving for your good, and the good of Ennaris. She is seeking to understand who she is and what she must do."

The woman nodded, wondering.

"Well, her name will live here for ever."

Flin nodded as he turned to go.

"We must leave in the morning," he said, "but will stay for a short while longer if you wish."

"No," the woman said after a moment. "We have a lot to do here. It doesn't look like much here, but we are of the Blood, and I think we must prepare for what is to come, whatever that is. I am thinking that we should make a refuge here, with the Tree of Swords as the centre." She looked to the tree, now with all of the children snuggled around it, and Varna still reclining against its trunk. "And we cannot keep you or her from your responsibilities, Mage Drewflin."

Flin smiled to her, stepping carefully to where he also could lean against the tree. He could use some rest!

Dalresar remained standing, struggling with internal conflict of his own. For a short moment, the veil obscuring his memories had been torn aside as the tree destroyed the ghazrak. He clearly saw his family, now long gone, and the path that he had taken afterwards until Flin had found him and taken him away from the toil and filth of the slaver's camp. And he saw further back to a time when he had known himself, but the memory fog returned anew before he could get a grip on the memory. So Dalresar stood on the edge of the green sward under the silver tree of refuge, with its sword-flowers jingling lightly, with Varna and Flin, along with the women and children sleeping away their exhaustion, and tears crept from eyes that had not known such for a long time, tears of loss and tears of fleeting remembrance. Only after a long time did Dalresar, with a haunted expression on his face, move to a place under the tree and close his eyes. He never noticed the third protective arm that extended as a shadowy appendage from the tree to rest gently on his head. Finally, he slept.

The next morning, as Flin, Varna and Dalresar prepared to leave the village, a large group of men trudged into the village leading several families with carts drawn by hrss. Amazement showed on their faces as they beheld the tree and the women and children gathered around it. Explanations took some time and the three left later than planned, leaving behind the grief of men who had lost loved ones and determination of those left behind that this village, Anhard Spring, would stand with the Faero to protect Ennaris.

19. Frelor

Blaine drew rein on his hrss and waited for Jalor. They were five days of easy riding out of the Citadel after reporting back to Corm on the events of Great Mirden and were approaching the first of what Corm's map told them were the Free Cities of Algol. Almin Bor had suggested that these cities may provide assistance to Corm. They were a loose confederation of three, sometimes four, cities that were dotted along the northern coast of the inland sea, which in these parts was referred to still as the New Sea.

In Ennaris terms, I guess five thousand years - cycles - is still very new, Blaine thought as he watched Jalor struggle to control his hrss.

"We're about to reach Frelor. According to the map we're already in the area claimed by the Free Cities." He pointed ahead of them. "It should be over that hill and around a few bends."

"Right!" Jalor was quiet as he reviewed the plan. "I don't think we change anything from the plan, at least not yet. Ragnor thought this city was one of two likely to provide assistance, where the other three may hold back."

Blaine nodded. He deftly turned his hrss back into the direction of Frelor and gave a single gentle tap with a booted foot to the hrss' midsection. The animal stepped up to a steady walk immediately.

It was not much longer when Frelor came into sight. The smells assailed Blaine first. The outskirts of the city, usually, were where the less pleasant industries tended to cluster. In this case, there were a number of tanners. The unmistakable smells of the animal hides, the cleaning and tanning spirits and the residues of the processes permeated the place. Blaine's hrss stepped up the pace without being prompted, snorting and staying as far from the tanners as he could. Blaine could only agree with the sentiment, especially as he was sure that many of the skins were from hrss.

There was a small space before the rest of the city outskirts started. What looked like a permanent shanty town grew alongside the road, with everything from shacks and lean-tos to quite solid-looking timber-clad buildings. The inhabitants, likewise, spanned the gamut of wealth and style. Down-and-outs and beggars with outstretched hands watched the Warriors as they passed them by. Dirty bare-footed children with ragged clothes and neatly dressed men and women walked along the dusty street. Alleys ran at varying angles from the main road into Frelor, leading to what promised to be a warren. A beggar held out a hand as they went by, with a patch across one eye and a single leg emerging below a voluminous robe and cloak. Blaine took note of the men slouched outside one of the more substantial buildings, with hands hitched in belts from which were hung a variety of edged weapons. They all watched the newcomers ride by with varying amounts of disinterest. Like town bullies everywhere, he thought. He wondered who the crime lords were that ruled this shanty town.

Jalor was also taking note. The shanty town was the first signs of real poverty that they had seen on Ennaris. So far they had seen the Citadel, which had poorer people but not significant outright poverty to Jalor's knowledge - he had not seen the areas that Varna had walked - and small villages or towns where the people helped each other. This was something new.

The shanty town ended against the city wall, which proved to be a tall, stone rampart that was pierced by a broad opening. Guards stood on each side of the opening with the iron gates stretching out behind them, watching those who entered but not impeding anyone. Blaine took note of their stance and the state of their uniforms and weapons. They were relaxed but not sloppy, neat and tidy but not overly ostentatious. However, the guards appeared to lack any form of body armour. Perhaps this city did not see a lot of violence.

The two Warriors made their slow way into the city, following the stream of people who had entered ahead of them. They were scanning the signs hung outside the buildings strung along the road, looking for the inn. Almin Bor had recommended the Sleeping Log, an odd name for an Inn to Blaine's thinking, but he had seen stranger ones. It would be located between the gate and the central square. Jalor nudged him and gestured with his head towards a sign of a bed with what appeared to be a log lying in it. Blaine shrugged as they turned their hrss down a side street to where Almin Bor told them would be the entry to the stable.

The innkeeper, who told them his name was Gertag, was a bluff, hearty man. He was past middle age but was wearing his age well, even if his belt had extended a notch or two - or four. His greeting was hearty. His laugh when he made what he thought was a funny joke was hearty. Even his instruction to his staff to check which rooms were available was hearty. However, when Jalor mentioned Almin Bor's name it was as though a switch was flicked. He guided Jalor and Blaine to a table away from both door and bar and bade them sit.

"How is the Captain?" Gertag asked more soberly.

"He's well," Jalor replied. "He was forced off his farm by the ghazrak raiders."

"Ghazrak? There are ghazrak raiding?" The innkeeper paused, thinking. "Did the Captain give you anything for me?"

"Yes," Jalor replied, eyeing the man carefully before handing over a small packet.

Gertag examined the packet with a critical eye, taking particular note of the knots used to tie it together. The two Union warriors watched. Finally, the innkeeper pulled a belt knife and with a quick and deft motion cut the strings.

"The knot?" Blaine asked?

"Both knots," Gertag replied. "If there are two, they must the right two."

Quickly, the innkeeper opened the packet and extracted two sheets of rough paper, a commodity that was quite rare from what Jalor and Blaine had seen of Ennaris to date. A quick scan was accompanied by raised eyebrows and an in-breath. It was followed by a more careful reading of the missive. Finally, Gertag stood and bowed to Jalor.

"General," he said, before re-seating himself. "Gerhal Tag at your service."

Things fell into place for Jalor.

"You are of the Blood?" Jalor asked quietly.

"Aye," Gerhal Tag replied. "I am the Post Sergeant for Frelor. We maintain posts in many of the cities near to the plateau. From time to time we undertake small commissions but for the most part we listen and support those who may pass through. The Captain asks that I assist you in your mission. What do you require?"

Blaine nodded to himself. The Blood maintained a network of agents. It made sense. A closely knit community of people sharing a past, but also a culture of mutual defence and a paranoia that was built on centuries of persecution after the rebellion, would rely on themselves to ensure that their members were as safe as could be, and that threats were identified before they became threats. In this medieval-like civilisation, where threats formed over days or tendays or longer, a well-run network of agents could be effective.

"I'm seeking allies for the Faero. Almin Bor thought the cities may be one such source. I want to meet the leaders of the cities and ask for their support."

"I can get you introductions but I'm not sure of the level of support you'll find here. The Free Cities of Algol are not as their name suggests. They are anything but free, just not under the rule of a single person. Frelor is run by a cabal of merchants who seek profit over all else. Telsith is the same although they may be more amenable. Histhel has been taken over by a company of mercenaries who decided that owning a city was a more lucrative occupation than warfare, especially when there are few wars. Probably healthier, too.”

“How did they take over a city?” Blaine asked.

“They bought up a few of the key businesses. The usual thing. Some sold willingly, others not so willingly. Some died and their estates passed into certain hands who then sold. Within a reasonably short period the Red Shields - that’s what the mercenaries call their company - held sway over most of the businesses. It took a little longer but they now own most of the largest concerns. That gives them control. They’ve been smart enough to leave the smaller ones in the hands of private citizens and even protected them as you would expect a city council to do. The normal run of the mill people, the labourers and servants and such, haven’t really seen any great change. If anything, crime has diminished. One thing mercenaries don’t want is competition.” Gerhal Tag smiled grimly. “The old masters of the city took a cut from the criminal sector also. I understand there has been something of an exodus of the under-world element from Histhel.”

“Into the other two?” Jalor asked.

“Not really,” Gerhal Tag replied. “Some were welcomed into the two cities, but for the most part Histhel was populated by the lesser criminals and they’ve not been made welcome. The few who tried were dealt with by the Summary Court.”

“Summary Court?” Blaine had an inkling where this was going but wanted to get it clear,

“You need to understand the Free Cities,” Gerhal Tag said, glancing from Blaine to Jalor and back again. “They were originally termed ‘free’ around three hundred cycles back when they broke free from the rule of Kortus. He was a local warlord with a base in Kortus, around a day by foot north of the three cities.”

“He named his city after himself? Inventive,” Blaine said with a quirk of his lips. “But what is this city called now. Almin Bor mentioned no city named Kortus.”

"There is no city any more," Gerhal Tag replied. "There never was, really. It was a mountain redoubt in a tiny range that only goes up about a thousand paces, but the paths up there were very defensible. The redoubt was built inside a little ring of mountain peaks. Anyway, Kortus got old and he lost control of the cities. They were only largish port towns at the time, of course, but they were the only safe anchorages for a large distance. He used his garrisons in the three towns to extract revenue from merchants bringing their goods in at the ports. When Kortus died, he only had a handful of retainers with him. Frelor was the third city to break free and the merchants essentially continued his policy of extracting fees to land cargo, and then extended that to anyone using the city for any purpose. They set up the Council, but in reality Frelor is dominated by three families, and anything they want is what goes."

"Is that so bad?" Jalor asked.

"Well, for the last thirty cycles those three families appear to have decided to extract every last coin from as many people as they can. Smaller merchants have been leaving for some time. The farmers around the outskirts are looking for new ways to ship their goods, or they just go north and then west or east instead."

"What about all those people living in that shanty town?" Blaine asked. "How do they live?"

"Usually by day labour for the remaining merchants or the shipping companies. Some of the shipping agents maintain their own labour force, but many just hire day by day at the docks. They pay a pittance, of course."

"Which leaves crime as the only way for them to survive," Blaine guessed. "And who manages that?"

Gerhal Tag smiled and nodded to Blaine in acknowledgement. Guess confirmed.

"The Summary Court was set up to regulate the underworld. It's not all crime, though. In reality, the original Sergeant of the Court, as the head of the Summary Court is called, was a soldier who became disgusted at the way crime was not being dealt with. He knocked a few heads together to make sure the poor were not being preyed on too heavily and established the Court. It took a few cycles and quite a few examples had to be made, but he managed to get a system going. That was around seventy cycles back. His successors have come from varied backgrounds, including the criminal side, but the traditions have held."

"All this time?" Blaine asked, surprised.

"Indeed. There have been a few missteps, but yes. Most people recognise the authority of the Court, because it's been as impartial as it could be. Crime exists and anyone who doesn't take adequate precautions is fair game, but there are some who are under the Court's protection. The larger merchant families are not included in that number," Gerhal Tag concluded dryly.

"So, who do we speak with?" Jalor asked quietly after absorbing what the Post Sergeant had told them.

"I would approach the Merchant Council, if only because it makes the request official. Do you have any sort of formal clothing?"

"I have a uniform of an officer of the Faero's military," Jalor replied. "Is it necessary?"

"It's like this," Gerhal Tag replied with a shrug. "The merchants all want to be seen as being independent and free of any form of allegiance to anyone else. As a result, however, one of the things the merchants lack is any sort of pomp and ceremony. But the people love it, and you'll have to get the people on side. Even though the Council will act as though public opinion doesn't count, it actually has an effect. Especially at the moment when the Council is losing business and bleeding revenue. They can't afford to lose more of the tax-paying citizens."

"I'm not sure it's anything special, that uniform," Jalor said, scratching his left ear. "Certainly, with just the two of us the pomp won't be all that great. But I'm not a great pomp sort of person."

"You will have to become one in Frelor. We can help there," Gerhal Tag replied with a sly smile.

Three days later a very uncomfortable Vinca Jalor was presented to the Merchant Council of the Free City of Frelor. He was wearing a stylised military-inspired jacket, in a deep red that was almost the right shade for the Faero's banner. Gold braid and tassels hung off the shoulders, sleeves and hems of a tight-fitting waist-length jacket, which was accompanied by jet black breeches that clung tightly to waist and hips and then flared wide before they reached black boots that had been polished to a mirror sheen. He felt, he said to Blaine and Gerhal Tag, as though he was a cross between a flamenco dancer and a New Toledo cattle herder. Blaine snorted with laughter while Gerhal Tag had no idea what he spoke of, but smiled at the obvious discomfort. He had realised on first meeting Jalor that this was not a man who did things for show. Accordingly, wrapped around Jalor's hips was a functional sword belt, with his equally functional sword.

Blaine was arrayed in lesser finery, as befitted one of lower rank. He, at least, wore his own boots. A rich doublet in a shade of red matched Jalor's jacket, and he wore a linen under-shirt of no particular colour. He wore looser breeches of the same nondescript colour as the under-shirt. His short sword was in a scabbard slung from his hips, matched with a long knife on the other hip, and the greatsword was slung across his back, seated so the sword hilt reared above Blaine's head. Gerhal Tag glanced uncertainly at the latter sword but Blaine refused to leave it behind, so it went with him.

Gerhal Tag had also provided an escort. The procession leader was introduced as Kenderl Nim, who was a slender man dressed top to toe in deep blue, wearing a similar doublet to Blaine's, carrying a furled banner. His long face had an everyman aspect to it. His features were hard to remember once one turned away, and he was of average height with average length brown hair. Blaine nodded at the greeting offered, and tried to recall where he had seen Kenderl Nim before.

There were two armed men ahead of Jalor and Blaine and another four behind. All were dressed in the same nondescript linen as Blaine, but with doublets of a paler red. All of them clearly knew their way around the weapons they carried. Short swords, short knives and spears were what Jalor thought may have only been the most visible ones.

"Where did you get these men," Jalor asked Gerhal Tag.

"Oh, we have people here and there that we can call on," was the response. "Sometimes it comes in useful to get them together and remind them why we're here. This was an opportunity for that, as much as serving the Faero."

"I'm guessing they are Faeronar, also?"

"All of the people who will be around you are sworn to the Faero from birth," Gerhal Tag replied. "You will be safer among these men than anywhere in this city. And we will have others in the crowd that will form along the way."

"There'll be a crowd? How do you know that?" Jalor asked, curious.

"We've been passing the story that the Faero's representatives will petition the Merchant Council for help against the old enemy. It's helped that we've had some Tellers in the city recently reminding people of Ennaris' fall and the legends of the return of Goroth." He glanced at Jalor. "That's not our doing, by the way. Was it you?"

"No," Jalor replied, wondering if the twins were behind it. "But the Tellers are being encouraged to spread the old tales wherever they go, so that may have been a happy coincidence."

"Don't believe in coincidences," Gerhal Tag growled. "But if it helps then we'll take advantage."

Gerhal Tag was not part of the procession, being far too well known in Frelor. He did not want his cover story to be questioned too closely, nor did he want his support for the Faero to be visible. As he told Blaine as an aside, part of his job was to identify threats to the Faeronar and being known to favour that cause would make him ineffectual in his primary task.

The small procession wound from the inn to the Council Hall, which was a two-storey stone building with grand pretensions that was located close to the centre of the city. It was also in the centre of a large open space, which was less like a town square and more like a large park. Vivid green grass waved in the gentle breeze as Kenderl Nim led the procession along the broad path that cut through the park after leaving the lesser commercial zone. Jalor could see two other similar paths approaching the central building from left and right, and he expected that if he were to go to the far side of the Hall there would be a fourth coming from that direction. The Council Hall was very deliberately placed in the centre of the city of Frelor and all roads led to it. It was an expression of the supreme importance of the Merchant Council for Frelor.

The path ended at broad steps that led up to a grand platform, or what had been intended to be one. As Gerhal Tag had explained when describing what the Warriors would see, the building had been planned to be much larger but when the Council members saw the cost, they decided to make the building smaller. True to form, while demanding less cost they also demanded that all of the features should be built, so what resulted was an awkwardly small porch that stood at the top of the sweeping stairs and led through what could have been grand doors but, to save cost, had been reduced to little more than a gap in the large wooden panel that stood in their place. The stone columns that held up the top level were crude, being shaped effectively but not finished off, so each carried the signs of chisel work where the stone had been carved into the columns' segments. The building had no decorations, no statuary and no surrounding gardens, all of which had been reduced to save cost. The upper floor was constructed of wood also, and appeared to be balanced precariously on the lower level. It too had no decoration, no flags, and no particular appearance of solidity. In fact, Jalor thought that he could see gaps in the walls. As a monument to the Council, Jalor thought, it was as much a monument to mediocrity.

The meeting with the Council would take place in a chamber that occupied all of the lower floor. The procession was met at the oddly small door by an elegantly attired functionary who, Gerhal Tag had informed Jalor, was the nephew of the Council Head, Kreban. It seemed the Council hired family members for as many of the jobs associated with Council activities as possible, mostly to save money. Over the several generations since Frelor had been brought under the control of the Merchant Council that policy had resulted in a bevy of untrained and largely uninterested relatives being paid poorly for jobs.

Jalor thought of all of that as the procession reached the base of the Council Hall. A young man met them. His tunic was poorly fitting, and showed sweat stains around the bunched material of the tightly fitting arm pits and the strained material that stretched across his ample stomach. Uncertainty oozed from him. Jalor did not hold out great hopes for success.

Jalor's pessimism was justified. Less than thirty minutes later Jalor and his retinue left the Council Hall. It was not too soon by Jalor's estimation. In his eyes nothing positive had been achieved, but there were questions to be answered. Jalor was sure he knew some of the answers. Kreban, the head of the Council, proved to be a particularly unpleasant individual who had no interest in supporting the Faero or his fellow Ennarisi. In fact, he was singularly disinterested in any form of commitment to anyone but his own fellow merchants. Instead, he made a vague offer to provide hrss and carts, weapons and tools at what Gerhal Tag later assured Jalor and Blaine were enormous markups. The attempt to make profit from the situation was not what caused Jalor disquiet, however. Sitting on a table alongside Kreban was a metal bowl, filled with red gold coins.

"You're sure of that?" Gerhal Tag asked Jalor as they debriefed shortly after the interview with the Merchant Council leader. "That's a pretty big accusation."

"There was a container full of red gold coins on a small table beside Kreban," Jalor explained, to a nod from Kenderl Nim who sat on one end of the table. "In my experience that means there's some influence being exercised by the twin kingdoms. And that means Goroth, or his supporters."

"It certainly explains why there would no help forthcoming to the Faero," Gerhal Tag said with a shrug. "No-one would ever accuse the Merchant Council of being either ethical or intelligent, but I still can't believe that they would advertise it like that. I mean, anyone who knows the history of red gold would recognise what it meant."

"But it also means that we get no help from Frelor," Blaine said with a frown, "and it may result in us having to defend against a second front. That would be a problem, no matter where the battle comes."

"Well," Gerhal Tag said pensively after a moment of thought. "There may be a way to salvage something from this after all. It may not result in the Faero getting troops but we should be able to get rid of a nest of norther supporters."

"What do you have in mind?" Jalor asked.

"We go to the other authority in Frelor," Gerhal Tag replied. "Only this one doesn't like to advertise anything about itself."

"The Summary Court?"

"Yes. I'll see if I can arrange a meeting with the Sergeant of the Court. The Sergeant's the true power, despite the title. The current Sergeant is known as Gentry and has been the Sergeant for the last seven cycles. I'm fairly sure you'll get some sort of support but it will be on the Sergeant's terms."

"'Known as'?", Jalor asked.

"It has become something of a tradition that the Sergeant of the Court takes a new name when taking the chair. As a name, Gentry will have some meaning, but likely only to the Sergeant."

"Do you know this Gentry at all?"

"Oh, we've met," Gerhal Tag replied with a grin. "We have an agreement, call it an accord. I won't get in their way and they don't get in mine."

"How far does his authority go?" Blaine asked.

"The Sergeant's fingers are in almost all forms of crime in Frelor and parts of its surroundings, except for the corruption of the large merchant themselves. If the Sergeant says that something will happen, then it will happen. But if not, then it won't. So, you'll need to be convincing."

Jalor thought for a moment. The idea of working with the criminal underworld was not new for him. The Warriors tended to use whatever resources were available. In many cases, of course, the members of the underworld were less corrupt than the leadership that was being investigated by the Warrior team, so working with them was a logical course of action. Often, they formed the resistance to a suborned government, although in this case that was unlikely. However, also in this case, self-interest may turn out to be a useful motive. There may be further problems in the future as a result, but he thought that would be acceptable as a trade-off for now.

"Very well. Can you set up a meeting for us?"

"I should be able to," Gerhal Tag replied with a decisive nod.

20. Trabor

Trabor brushed the dust away from his jacket and trousers. His travelling cloak had been rolled and attached to his saddle since leaving the grasslands and heading south in a roundabout way. He was moving through the foothills of the Eastern Range, the tall and forbidding range of mountains that divided the larger western bulk of the north continent from the smaller eastern segment, on his way towards the dense jungle and then the southern continent. The small town in which he found himself was struggling to keep itself going, but it had a tavern, was located where many people could congregate and was one of Trabor's usual stops. He usually had a full house here, and the tavern owner always provided him lodging and a stall for his hrss. As always, Trabor insisted on looking after the animal himself, which he was doing now as he thought about his current journey.

Plying his trade as an itinerant Teller, Trabor told his stories in taverns, in the community halls or around camp fires. It could take him two or more cycles to make his way around the two continents of Ennaris, and many communities looked forward to his return visits. Most people enjoyed hearing the romantic tales. For this circuit, however, he included tales of the rebellion and its aftermath, of the battle between the Council Mages headed by the legendary Drewflin and the great Battle Mage Marjory, and the forces of Goroth, the notorious rebel Mage. He received varying responses, as always was the case when he included tales involving Mages. Interestingly, though, there was greater acceptance of the role of the Council Mages than he was accustomed to hearing.

Briefly he wondered what was happening on the other side of the mountains, as he almost always did at this point. As far as he knew, the destructive energies unleashed at the rebellion's end had caused every means of travelling between west and east to be destroyed. He knew there had been expeditions to try to re-establish contact in the early days after those events, but they had all foundered because of continuing instability of the terrain. So many had died making the various attempts that the mountains were considered to be impenetrable. Trabor thought about making an attempt himself, as he had thought many times before, but dismissed the idea. Maybe if he had a Roc available to him then he could do it, but he had not seen a Roc for thousands of cycles, and the last ones he had seen were in the process of dying after suffering from the extreme energy impacts. For all he knew, the Rocs were no more, he thought sadly. Despite tales of the huge birds being seen from time to time, he had never been able to sight any proof of their continued existence.

Which was a shame. If the Prophecy was correct, as far as Drewflin and the remaining Mages had been able to decipher it so far, they would need all the help they could get. And things were starting to happen, Trabor mused as he rubbed down his hrss. He had started his usual circuit from the Council chambers and moved through the north-west and then up into the icy wilderness, taking care to avoid the northers, of course. He had crossed the northern icy wastes and then moved south through Tang and then across into the vast eastern grasslands, although in reality they spanned the centre of the northern continent.

All along the way he had been hearing rumours of strange events. Normally not one to chase legends over logic, as befitting the engineer that he was long ago, still he could not avoid being excited by what he had heard and seen. He kept thinking back to the Prophecy, trying to piece together the scattered hints he had received with what that strange document had revealed so far. He was unsure that he was best fitted to do so, and looked forward to when he could reconvene with Drewflin and the twins so they could discuss it.

In the north-west, he had heard persistent rumours of some sort of protector. The tales he heard had been far-fetched in some ways. A tall young man would arrive in an area experiencing strife and take a hand, resolving conflict or dealing with miscreants, of which there were quite a few in that wild, relatively lawless area, protecting the weak and then healing the sick. And then he would disappear without waiting for thanks, or seeking reward. It was the stuff of legend, and Trabor had been hearing similar tales for quite some time. All of the Mages had been awake for over fifty cycles this time around, but the legends appeared to have existed for hundreds of cycles if not longer.

Had there been more Mages in existence then Trabor would have put it down to a travelling Mage, perhaps one battle trained or skilled in healing, although they were traits that did not go together happily in his experience. You only had to look at Drewflin to see the result. The most powerful Mage Ennaris had had for a very long time, perhaps the most powerful ever, and yet ask him to exercise the battle skills that all Mages were trained in to some extent and he would exhaust his energies very quickly, and cause himself some pain in doing so. Like-wise, Trabor's memories of Marjory, Ennaris' greatest ever Battle Mage, were that she could deal with anything in terms of weaponry or conflict but was unable to affect the sorts of healing that Drewflin handled as a matter of course without similar exhaustion. But the two together had been such a force, Trabor thought with a sad smile, as he continued to rub down his hrss.

Trabor had looked for the existence of untrained gifts among the people of the north-west, of course, but could find nothing. Drewflin put it down to a series of events with different players, which certainly made some sense, but that failed to explain the healing. Trabor had a nagging sense of something else, though, and it was a puzzle that he thought about each time he made his meandering way through the region. That there were no minor gifts to be found or even heard of over the cycles was surprising. As though they had been gathered.

This time around though he found something else to take his attention. He had been travelling for some time. He knew Drewflin and the twins would be trying to deal with the growing predations against the Blood, and he was anxious to learn what was happening. Then, in the frigid surrounds of a northern communal centre he heard stories of the return of Tine and her appearance to a young Junda man. There were many sceptics but Trabor found just as many believers. His way across the north this trip would take him close to the location where this young man, Xymin, lived, so Trabor decided to detour through that small settlement.

When he arrived at the place where Xymin was said to live, he found no trace of the young man, nor of his family. In fact, there were very few left of what had been a small settlement. The old woman, who was one of only a handful of remaining Junda at the settlement, told Trabor that all of the people had moved to a larger settlement, one that Trabor had bypassed in order to get to Xymin's home. She had ridiculed the whole idea of a Guardian, echoing the sentiments that had grown up from not long after the rebellion until recent times when the Mages and travelling Tellers had started to revive the old and true stories of those bleak times.

So Trabor had moved on. If the Guardians had returned, and Trabor was unsure about whether to believe in their existence or not, then the Junda had been taken under the wing of Tine, and that could only be good. If they had not returned and this was a fantasy, then it could do little harm and may result in more people believing in something more than their own well-being. The Mages would need more people to consider the good of Ennaris as a whole, Trabor thought. In his darker moments, which had been coming more frequently of late, he thought back to when he had stood with Drewflin and Marjory against Goroth. It was only the enormous skill and power of Marjory, coupled with the even greater inherent power of Drewflin, that had allowed them to prevail. Without Marjory ... He could not see victory over Goroth without the intervention of something. But the Prophecy also made it clear that the people of Ennaris would have to oppose Goroth as well. This he also wove into his tales and lessons. He was not sure if he was succeeding or not.

With gentle skill, Trabor moved his hrss into the stall assigned to him and found the cask of grains. He scooped up what he felt was enough and deposited it in the trough within the stall. As the hrss started the noisy and somewhat messy process of transferring the contents of the trough to its stomach, Trabor threw his saddle over the bolster provided for the task, grabbed his travelling pack and rolled jacket and made his way from the stable. He tossed a coin to the young stable-hand sitting in the doorway and made his way into the tavern. It was about half full and Trabor was able to grab a smaller table against one wall, against which he leaned his pack and jacket. An enormous mug of ale appeared in front of him and Trabor grinned to Marnie, the wife of the tavern keeper. He had been coming this way for a long time and Marnie knew his likes and dislikes.

The first mouthful of the ale slid down his throat and Trabor was sure it sloughed off a couple of layers of grasslands dust as it went. With a sigh he leaned back against the wall and relaxed. His thoughts made their way back to the current journey.

After leaving the freezing land of the Junda Trabor had made his way south-east through Tang. In its own way Tang was as hard as the icy wastes, perhaps more so. The Junda had the sea as a source of food and the ice as a source of water if you knew what to do with both, and they did. The Tang relied on a land that had been blasted during and after the rebellion. Trabor always struggled to reconcile his memories of the lush, green land of rolling hills and abundant wildflowers with the hard, rocky terrain that was Tang now. The sense of helplessness and hopelessness that pervaded Tang cast a pall over Trabor each and every time he made his way through the few villages and small towns that remained. Of course, a hard land bred hard people, and none were harder than the Tang. As scouts, they were without peer. As fighters, they would hold their own against most others on Ennaris. For many lifetimes, they had hired their swords to the highest bidder. The morality of the sides in a war meant little to the Tang as a rule. They were cynical enough, and had seen enough of the people who hired them, to understand that usually neither side was innocent or blameless of the causes of strife. And so it was that most of the men and women of Tang tended to be away from their home land.

All of which explained why Trabor had been astonished at what he found in Tang. There, too, he found rumour of the return of a Guardian. Wondering if this was the same rumour as he had found in the Junda lands further north and west, Trabor had listened as much as he talked, peppering his Telling routines with information-gathering questions and queries. Here, the story was of Tanga returning and making himself known to Murk. In a land of hard men and women, Murk was known to be one of the hardest, and Trabor had heard of his exploits for some time now. When Murk joined a fight there usually was only one outcome, and it was Murk who came out of it alive. Astonishingly, it was Murk to whom Tanga revealed himself, and it was Murk who became Tanga's acolyte. This time Trabor found his heart start to beat faster. The Tang were not dreamers, nor were they romantics. All of that had been burned away long ago.

Trabor acquired a hrss - one did not take a hrss through the northern ice lands, so he had left his with a trusted stable-keeper on the western side of the icy wastes - and continued his way south through the length of Tang. Watching with new eyes he became aware that the gloom and perpetual sense of despair was lifting. More of the Tang were standing straight and tall. He saw signs of some sort of militia drilling and was astonished when told that they had been told to improve their skills. The taverns were now places of conversation where in the past they had been the refuge of the desperate. Trabor heard laughter where he was accustomed to muttered complaints and weary acceptance of hard fate. And then, as he moved through Tang, he noticed the numbers of Tang fighters. There were more of them than he usually saw, and the usual drunkenness was missing. These Tang were clear-eyed and sober, enjoying the company of their fellow Tang but with the watchfulness of the natural warrior.

"It's good to see so many here," Trabor had ventured at the end of one of his tales. "I don't recall seeing so many at a time in the past."

"Aye," one of the listeners had replied. "We've come home to prepare for the fight to come."

"What fight is that?" Trabor had asked.

"No idea," the listener had replied to general laughter from many in the tavern, "but we've been told it'll be a good'un, and there ain't none of us will miss a good fight."

"Especially with our Guardian backin' us," another had added, to assorted nods and growls of agreement amongst the assembled company.

So, the Tang were coming home in strength, for the first time in living memory. Not for sentiment or homesickness but because they had been summoned. Summoned by Murk, Trabor was told in another tavern at the southern end of Tang. Summoned by Tanga, he heard elsewhere. There were stories of the Vale of Tang coming back to life. Other stories told of Murk moving from community to community, gathering his people to him. Still others told of Tang's words to Murk. And then there were tales of strange men who had been encountered by some of the Tang as they made their careful way home, men that looked misshapen and who carried crude swords and spears. The stories were told by enough of the Tang that Trabor felt a shiver run down his back when these strange men were described to him.

Ghazrak!

What were ghazrak doing roaming the lands of Ennaris? Did that mean that Grensor survived still, after all this time, as the Mages had speculated? Did that presage Goroth's return?

Trabor had been considering these questions as he made his way from Tang into the eastern portion of the grasslands. His target was a point where one of the clans usually stopped when they occupied this part of the grasslands. Trabor had no idea if he would find anyone there, but this spot had good and reliable water burbling up from between a pile of rocks from a spring in the depths below. It was one of Trabor's favourite locations in the grasslands, for it had been he who had shifted the paths beneath the ground to release the water that was held under pressure there. That had been when the Mages realised that the changes to Ennaris were permanent and the people would need to readjust considerably to the new realities. In this part of what once had been the centre of food production of Ennaris, that now meant unreliable water. So Trabor had waited until he was sure there was no-one else around - Mages were held in very poor regard by that time - and using his engineering knowledge had shifted and re-aligned the rocks to form a channel for the now buried water to come to the surface. The newly formed clans of the grassland had found it the next season and it had been a standard stopping point ever since. Trabor made a point of swinging past each time he did his round. Sure enough, he found the usual arrangements of tents, corrals and carefully planned cooking pits set a short distance from the spring.

This time, though, the clan was in some sort of turmoil. Trabor took his time getting himself established. The clans always provided a welcome to him. Some of them had been seeing him for their entire lives.

The turmoil was subdued, but anything that disturbed the even tenor of the clans was of note. Trabor merely observed. Groups discussed something that caused disagreement although it never flared into conflict. Some of the disagreements grew heated though. He knew these people so Trabor waited, biding his time. It came after the evening meal when Trabor was asked for a story. Usually, the clans asked for stories about figures from the clan past, and Trabor knew most of them, from the tragic tale of Astelis and Fenda, who fell in love while their clans were at war with each other, to the heroic tale of Gratesh, who saved his clan from a wildfire and gave his own life in doing so. There were tales of conflict with other Ennarisi people, of war with Escar and the various petty kings or warlords that had sprung up and died away just as quickly. There were stories of valour, stories of humour, stories of love and loss. What there was not, in the many and varied requests, were tales from the rebellion and later cycles, from the times when the clans changed from being simple herders and farmers to what they had become.

Until now. The first request, from clan chief Hurfil no less, was to tell of the rebellion and the formation of the clans. Intrigued, Trabor agreed and told the traditional tale up to the point where the rebellion had caused the land to heave and break up, water channels to change direction or in some cases to move underground. Here the tale usually ended or became generalities about the clans and how they came together to preserve resources, gradually becoming the clans of the grasslands. Trabor decided to change that.

"In the normal tales, the story ends with the clans forming as a way to save the people by banding together to share food, water, and shelter. But perhaps it is time for you to have a deeper understanding of what occurred." Trabor paused his Telling while the clan chief looked around his inner circle and then nodded agreement. "There were many bandits at the time and the people who became the clans were not militaristic or war-like," Trabor began again. "They faced so many obstacles that they fell into despair. Crops that they had spent their lives growing failed, season after season. Instead of grains, fruit and vegetables that fed Ennaris in abundance there was little more than tough grass growing. The water disappeared. Once there were rivers that crossed this great plain, meandering past the cities that housed and supported those who grew the crops. The weather changed also, so that where there had been regular rains assisted by the great skill of the Ennarisi now there was little or none. The soil dried and the hardy grass took over. All of that happened over the course of several hundred cycles."

"And the clans came from that time?" asked one of the clan chief's inner circle, a lean woman with grey streaks in her tied back hair and sharp eyes that, Trabor knew from past visits, could pierce any attempt at lying or avoiding the truth.

"In part, yes they did," Trabor agreed. "At the time, the people who became the clans were the farmers. They were peaceful, as were most people of Ennaris. The rebellion devastated this area. The few cities in the area were destroyed entirely by the rebellion that caused the fall of civilisation. Millions of people died in the blink of an eye. Everyone in the area lost family. Everyone lost many friends." Trabor looked back through his memories of friends and others he had known and lost who lived in this area, engineers and farmers, young, old and everything in between. And the Guides, his own colleagues. "So many people lost. And then there were those who decided to prey on others. Instead of helping, these ones decided to take whatever they wanted. The old peace had been based on everyone having what they needed to live comfortably, to contribute to Ennaris. Now there were bandits taking the little that others had. Many of the farmers died defending the few crops they had. The stores of grains were raided and carried off. That meant there were no seeds for future crops. The remaining buildings were dismantled and carried away to be used for other buildings."

"Like Escar," someone in the listening crowd growled, for the enmity between the clans and Escar had been intense for a long time and the echoes of those time remained.

"No," Trabor laughed. "At this time there was no Escar. And if you visit Escar, you will see that it is made largely of huge stones that were re-covered from the city of Aberwin that had been all but destroyed. Escar stands on Aberwin's bones. No, the buildings of the farming communities were stolen by many different bands of brigands and used in many places. But the brigands also stole women and children, using them or selling them into slavery or both. It was a fraught time, a time of great peril. The farmers were not best placed to deal with the dangers."

"Then how did the clans come to be?" Hurfil asked.

"You had help," Trabor said. "Marjory, the greatest of the Battle Mages of Ennaris, who survived the devastation and captured and imprisoned Goroth, came to you and helped you to become what you have become. She taught those who would listen how to fight. She showed you how to make weapons and how to use them. She taught you how to divide into your clans. Drewflin, the leader of the remaining Mages, taught you how to use the land as it had become, how to locate the foods that can be found and how to prepare them. He showed you how to use some of the grasses to heal certain hurts and illnesses. Many did not listen and either fled the new grasslands or perished. But those who became the clans were those who listened. They were those who learned and who carried on to forge your traditions.

"Tell me, Hurfil, why are you interested in this now? None of the Clans have ever been interested in hearing of the true formation of the Clans. It has been something avoided, as though there was great shame in being something different to what you have become."

Hurfil considered before speaking. "We have been told by the runners that Lak has appeared to one of the Long Grass Clan. She has told us that we need to relearn our history. She has told us that we should be ready for the one to take us into battle against the evil that caused the destruction. It has been understood that the Mages caused the fall of Ennaris but Lak tells us that is not right. Horint, a colt of the Long Grass who spoke with Lak, says that some come to join with the Mages and lead the people of Ennaris against Goroth. That is a name used to scare children but Horint says he is real and will return. How say you, Trab?"

Trabor stared. Lak? Were the Guardians real after all? Were they coming to help?

"I'm unable to confirm what Horint has been saying," Trabor said. "I can confirm that Goroth is real and that the rebel Mages caused the damage to our land, as the story I have just told shows. The terrible weapons turned on their own people caused the destruction that resulted in what we have today. I know you know of the Prophecy, for I have told of that in the past. The Prophecy tells us that the Children of Ennaris will return to lead us against our old enemies and that we, the people of Ennaris, must be prepared to join the fight."

"Are you the one to ask us to fight, Trab?" Hurfil asked quietly, with the fire crackling and the light of the flames jumping to cast strange shadows over speakers and the closer listeners alike.

"I?" Trabor shook his head. "I'm a Teller who roams Ennaris. No, I'm not the one who will ask the clans to fight. But I am one who urges the clans to listen to the message, whether it was Lak who appeared to Horint or not. Because the Prophecy is coming to pass."

"You are a Teller who has been coming to entertain and instruct us for many cycles, Trab, as you did for my mother's brother when he was clan chief, and his father before him. And yet you are no older than my eldest son. We have other Tellers who do not know of the early history as you do. Nor do others speak as though they are seeing the events of which they speak. It is more than skill in the tale, Trab, is it not? Lak also told the clans to be ready to listen to those who witnessed the rebellion and not those who tell of hatred. You never tell of hatred, Trab, but only of the people and the lives they lived. Are you the one who witnessed those events, Trab?"

Trabor looked around the sea of faces as the firelight played across their visages. All looked at him, some with interest, some with scepticism, some with confusion, many with the usual impassive mien of the clans. He sighed to himself as he reached out and drew his small pack closer to him, pulled the opening aside and extracted the short length of what seemed to be wood from its contents. Trabor stood. As he did so the staff extended and the stone embedded in its top flared, bathing the scene in a cerulean wash.

"Aye, Hurfil, I witnessed the events. I am Trabor, Mage of the Council of Mages. I stood with Marjory and Drewflin against Goroth and will stand against him again in the time to come. That time is coming and the Clans do need to prepare."

Trabor had then stayed with the Clan for almost a tenday, telling them of the old times, of the rebellion and the hard, the terrible times that followed. He left to continue his rounds and sensed that these hard people had somehow grown harder. As he was leaving, Hurfil met him at the corral where Trabor was saddling his hrss.

"Tell whoever needs to know that we will listen to the one who comes to speak with us," Hurfil said. "He or she will be given the time to speak and may face hard questioning."

"But will the Clans join the fight with the rest of the people of Ennaris?" Trabor had asked.

Hurfil had stared at Trabor with the impassive face that he was sure the Clans people practised every day. For a space of five heartbeats the two were silent, each watching the other. Finally, Hurfil nodded, once.

"The Clans will fight, Trabor of the Council of Mages."

Trabor halted his reminiscing to partake of the meal placed in front of him by Marnie. He nodded thanks and passed over some coins in payment. The simple but hearty stew and generous portion of a fresh bread loaf was welcome and he tucked in with a will. The tavern was filling and he was sure he would be called upon to give a tale soon. Which would it be? There was a rising tide, rumours of Guardians appearing to followers that to his mind had not been the case in the past. The Guardians, were they real, had remained apart from the Ennarisi, at least as far as Trabor knew. The Junda, the Tang and the Clans had all been subject to some sort of visitation and no-one who knew any of them would suggest that they were easy to fool.

So, perhaps a tale or two of the Guardians, and then see what the reaction may be.

Trabor had just exchanged his used plate for a fresh tankard of ale when two women and a man approached his table.

"May we join you, master Teller?" the first woman asked.

Surprised, for he was accustomed to being left alone in most of the stopping places he frequented, Trabor inclined his head in assent and gestured to the table in general. The three nodded thanks, one of the women moving to share the bench on which Trabor sat while the man and other woman sat opposite.

"We would ask a favour of you, Trabor," the first woman said quietly.

"And what would that be?" Trabor asked, intrigued that she knew his name, for he usually travelled under the name of Trab.

"We know that you have visited the Deep Spring clan of the grass, and before that the Tang and the Junda. We ask that you continue your usually cycle of visits but that you also go to the lands in the south continent."

"I was planning to go to the desert. Do you mean that I should go further south than that?" Trabor asked, looking at all three in turn.

Something, he could not say what, but something was odd here. How could they know of his visits to the Junda or the Tang unless they had been there also, and not long after him? Why would they trail behind if so?

"The ninth shall come from far below," the second woman said softly.

Trabor started, recognising the reference. The woman had quoted a passage of the Prophecy that Trabor and the other Mages had puzzled over.

"We believe the reference to far below is the land south of the desert, along the coast of the southern continent," the man said.

"Hendis," Trabor replied. "That land is known as Hendis. There is little there but a line of fishing ports and a single small city, more a larger town, where the local warlord resides."

"Nevertheless, we believe that is where you must look. If it is the ninth then you must locate him or her as soon as possible." The first woman smiled warmly. "The Nine must all take part."

Carefully, Trabor placed his tankard on the table and stared at the woman.

"Who are you to speak of the Nine like that? To know the Prophecy as you appear to?"

"I'm Tine," the first woman said simply.

"I'm Lak," the second woman said, smiling at Trabor's stunned expression.

"And I'm Tanga," the man said. "And I could use a drink."

21. Summary Court

It was the night after their interview with the Merchant Council. Frelor's sky was overcast and a fine drizzle fell intermittently. Gerhal Tag led Jalor and Blaine through the back alleys of the city. They made their careful way past seedy shops and dark doorways that led to equally dark interiors. On two occasions, a well muffled individual - male or female could not be discerned - stepped out of a doorway as though to accost the trio, but stepped back quickly when Gerhal Tag growled a warning. Interesting, Blaine thought. It appeared that Gerhal Tag was not one to be trifled with.

Neither of the Warriors had a clear idea of where they were by the time Gerhal Tag stopped in front of a doorway that was no more or less dark than any others that they had passed.

"I apologise for the convoluted path," Gerhal Tag said without a hint of contrition, "but I'm sure you understand the need for security in matters such as these."

"Of course," Jalor replied, knowing that he would only find his way back to the inn with difficulty.

"How many times did we double back on our track?" Blaine asked with a sly smile. "I made it six times."

"Seven, actually," Gerhal Tag replied with a grin. "The seventh was more of a partial. We're not that far from the Log in a straight line, but there's no straight path from there to here."

Blaine nodded his understanding.

"Now," Gerhal Tag said seriously. "The Sergeant is no fool and is pretty much hooked into everything that happens in Frelor. Your mission will already be known and the outcome of your meeting with Kreban will also be known. I suggest you act accordingly. In many ways, the Sergeant has more sway in Frelor than the Merchant Council."

"But not over the military forces?" Jalor asked, curious.

"Not over all of the military forces," Gerhal Tag replied with a smile. "You never know how far the various merchants' private armies have been penetrated. Let's go in. I'll do the introductions and then leave it to you."

After Jalor and Blaine gave their nodding assent, Gerhal Tag rapped in a peculiar sequence on the door. The three waited for a slow count to ten before a slot opened high in the door and then closed again. The door was cracked open and held with enough room for one at a time to pass through. Once inside a small vestibule area the three were stopped and searched. Jalor's sword and belt knife were confiscated, as were Gerhal Tag's sword and a boot dagger. Blaine waited while his sword and belt knife were taken. As the searcher started to move away Blaine reached out to stop him and handed him a small dagger that he slipped from one sleeve, then took off his left boot and removed a tiny sheathed dagger. He reached behind his neck and drew forth a throwing knife on a neck cord, which was also handed to the searcher. Jalor stared at his fellow Warrior, astonished at the additional weaponry displayed of which he had no idea, while Gerhal Tag chuckled appreciatively and nudged the searcher.

"Got you there, Leodis," Gerhal Tag said.

Leodis smiled ruefully and nodded.

"I'll have to remember that," he replied. "The Sarge will never let me hear the end of this. I don't suppose you'll stay quiet about it?"

Gerhal Tag merely grinned broadly, and Leodis sighed, "I thought not. Ah well, if we're all done then follow me."

He turned and led the way along a short hallway. At the far end, Jalor could see a set of stairs heading up, but rather than climb the stairs Leodis stopped at the first step and pushed on a segment of the hand rail support. A click sounded and the centre section of the first four steps jerked up. Leodis grabbed the edge of the section and pulled it up, revealing a doorway and steps leading down to a dark room. Leodis retrieved a lighted lamp from a shelf inside the opening and gestured for Gerhal Tag to lead the way down the steps. Leodis stopped half-way down the staircase. Once Gerhal Tag, Jalor and Blaine reached the bottom Leodis pulled on a strap attached to the open section of staircase. The doorway closed into place smoothly with a second click. Leodis moved to the front of the group and led the way once more.

The room at the foot of the stairs became a broad hallway that stretched for a surprisingly long way. At the end of the hallway was a blank wall with a door on each side. Leodis opened the door on the right side and stood back, gesturing the three others through. He then closed the door, remaining on the outside. It seemed that his job was done.

Inside what proved to be a single large room there was a surprising tableau. A small dais had two chairs positioned to face the room. Around the room were a motley group of women and men, all standing around the walls. All turned to look at the newcomers. Their clothes ran the gamut from fashionable to rags. Swords, knives and staves were in hand, but all were re-sheathed or lowered when Gerhal Tag made a gesture. Blaine glanced around the room's inhabitants quickly, but Jalor knew that he had taken the measure of all of them. Gerhal Tag nodded companionably to the assembled group, individually or in their small groups. No words were spoken.

A door at the back of the room opened and a woman walked through, speaking to someone on the other side of the door. A short laugh sounded, which was cut off as the door was closed. The woman walked to the centre of the dais and stood, regarding the trio for several moments.

"Gerhal Tag," she said in a challenging tone. "Why do you bring strangers to the Court?"

"Good evening, Sergeant," Gerhal Tag said smoothly. "I thought you may be interested in a proposition that Jalor and Blaine here" - Gerhal

Tag gestured to the two Warriors - "have to offer. I believe it would be in your best interests to listen to them and then to offer help."

"You do, do you?" the Sergeant replied with an edge to her voice. "And what could the Faero's men possibly be able to offer me that I don't already have?"

Gerhal Tag smiled and opened his arms wide.

"Ah, and that is the question. I will allow General Jalor to explain."

"General?" the Sergeant asked. "General of what?"

"Well, for my sins I have agreed to lead the Faero's army," Jalor replied. "My mission here is to raise that army from the peoples of Ennaris."

"To fight against who?"

"Goroth," Jalor replied, and waited for the inevitable scorn.

Instead, the Sergeant stared at Jalor and then at Gerhal Tag. Gerhal Tag smiled smugly in return. Around the room the ragtag group also straightened from their various relaxed positions.

"Goroth?" the Sergeant breathed. "The evil one is freed?"

"You know of Goroth," Jalor said evenly, although surprised at the reaction. "And more to the point, you seem to believe he is real which is unusual. Why is that?"

"Not all people are brought up believing the ancient evil to be myths and lies," the Sergeant said. "In several parts of Ennaris the old tales are told and retold."

Jalor nodded pensively. That was possible but there was something else here. He glanced to Blaine who gave an enigmatic shrug of a shoulder. Did Blaine suspect something? What was he missing? Jalor decided to continue.

"Well, Goroth is not yet freed, at least as far as we know. However, according to those who know such things the Prophecy is pointing to that happening shortly. There are strange creatures called ghazrak that are preying on the gifted children, seeking to kill those with gifts. Several of the portents have been seen. It is enough for Corm, the new Faero, to start his preparations."

"And how can the Summary Court of Frelor be of assistance to the Faero?" the Sergeant asked. "We are not the legitimate rulers of this city, no matter how much sway we have in certain matters. I am aware that you sought help from the Council and failed."

"Yes, we did fail to get that help. Unfortunately, I think we were beaten to the punch," Jalor said with a frown. "The Merchants' Council has been suborned by supporters of Goroth, I believe." He held up a hand as the Sergeant started to laugh, as did the others in the room. "Oh, they probably don't believe in Goroth and would not believe that they're helping him. However, during our discussions we noticed that the Council room has a pot full of red gold coins. It looked like quite a sizeable amount. From what we can ascertain, red gold only comes from the north where Goroth's supporters have sway."

The mirth died.

"I repeat, what can the Court do to assist the Faero?" the Sergeant asked with an edge to her voice.

"I don't want to leave a potential enemy behind," Jalor replied evenly. "While I am aware that Frelor is unlikely to provide any additions to the Faero's force, I want the likely threat of the Merchant Council opening a front in our rear to disappear."

"And?" the Sergeant prompted Jalor to continue.

Jalor glanced to Blaine who gave a shrug. Blaine could guess where Jalor was taking this conversation. It was not an unusual situation for the Warriors, although here Jalor was speaking for Corm and he had no idea if the latter would be happy or not. Still, that was a minor problem compared to the likely battle to come.

"The Faero will support your claim to overthrow the Merchant Council, should you decide to do so," Jalor said calmly. "Blaine and I will observe your actions to make sure that they do not exceed the boundaries of what is required. I expect you to ensure the safety of the common citizens of Frelor and even the merchants once you have assumed control."

"And if we don't?"

"Then there will be some very upset Mages and Guardians that you will have to deal with," Jalor said with confidence, despite having no idea if he could back up the threat in his statement.

"Mages and Guardians?"

"Mages and Guardians," Jalor repeated.

"Well, we wouldn't want to have Mages or Guardians upset with us, now would we?" the Sergeant said in a serious tone that was belied by the twinkle in her eye. "What says the Court?"

She glanced around the various leaning, slouching and reclining figures. These, Jalor realised, were the members of this Court of the criminal underworld. None demurred, none nodded. All merely stared back at the Sergeant when she met them eye to eye. The Sergeant paused after the last shared glance and pursed her lips.

"The Faero will give a charter for Frelor to be a free city, with the government elected by its citizens," the Sergeant stated.

"Agreed," Jalor replied. "Those citizens are to include men and women of a suitable age to be agreed, and not only the property holders."

"Agreed," the Sergeant said nodding, with a smile. "The Faero will station a garrison in Frelor for a period of ten cycles once Goroth is defeated."

"Agreed," Jalor said with an eyebrow raised in surprise. "That's not something I would have thought you would want. The garrison will reinforce the civil authority in fighting crime as much as providing security for Frelor."

"Agreed," the Sergeant replied promptly. "But those accused of a crime must be proven to be guilty rather than have summary judgement applied. Appeals against convictions will be to the Faero's court with the Faero or a senior member of the court sitting in judgement."

"Agreed," Jalor smiled.

"And any of those who are subject to this Court may choose to join the Faero's army without any stain on their record," the Sergeant continued.

Jalor smiled again. The Sergeant had just ensured that her followers would not be victimised or treated unfairly, provided Jalor could be taken at his word.

"Agreed."

"Well then," the Sergeant said with something approaching relief, to Jalor's further surprise. "You have a deal, General Jalor of the Faero's army. Should you or anyone go against the deal then you risk a significant civil disturbance. Do you still agree?"

"Yes," Jalor replied simply.

"And the Faero will supply armour and arms for any Frelor citizens who choose to join his army?"

"If they do not have their own, or if it is not of sufficient quality," Jalor agreed. "But I am trusting you that this will not just be a means of building an arsenal for Frelor's underground. If that is the case, then, you know, angry Mages."

"And Guardians," the Sergeant said with a grin.

"I think the Mages will be sufficient in this case," Jalor replied wryly.

"And who is the leader of the Mages that we should fear," the Sergeant asked, in a voice that was more curious than angry or challenging.

"Drewflin," Jalor said quietly.

The assembled Court had been listening attentively to the exchange, but now each and every one straightened once again. Several stood from where they had been sitting or reclining. Their expressions reflected shock, sheer and absolute shock. Absolute quiet reigned. Jalor and Blaine glanced to each other, mystified. Their attention was drawn to the Sergeant as she drew a shuddering breath.

"Drewflin!" she exclaimed. "The Drewflin?"

"As far as I know there has only been one," Jalor replied. "In any event, this one stood against Goroth and is preparing to do so again."

"The Prophecy tells of the return of the Children before the battle against Goroth takes place," Gerhal Tag said into the renewed quiet that followed Jalor's statement.

"The Children have returned," Blaine replied.

The Sergeant took another deep breath. She turned to each of the members of her Court in turn, looking each in the eye. Each returned a short nod. After surveying her Court, the Sergeant turned to Gerhal Tag.

"What is the position of the Blood of the Faeronar?"

"The Blood will support the Faero," Gerhal Tag replied. "I have received no information about the Children or the Mages, but if the Mages truly have returned then the Blood will support them, too."

"The Mages never left," Jalor stated. "They went underground but never let go of their role to help to rebuild Ennaris."

Jalor's statement was met with stares.

"We must consider this," the Sergeant said. "The Court will do as you ask, General. Exactly how and by how much is what we will need to consider. I will ensure Gerhal Tag knows of our decision."

Jalor nodded. "That is all we ask at this stage," he said. "We merely wish to make sure that we don't have an enemy at our backs."

The Sergeant gestured to Gerhal Tag, who nodded.

"We will leave," Gerhal Tag said to Jalor and Blaine. "I'll let you know what the Court decides."

The two Warriors nodded and turned to leave via the door through which they entered. Gerhal Tag held out a hand to stop them.

"We'll go out this way," he said, as he stepped onto the podium and pulled open the door that the Sergeant had used to enter the meeting room.

Jalor and Blaine walked through the door and found themselves in a well-lit cellar. Gerhal Tag pulled the door closed behind him and led the way to a set of stairs. At the top of the stairs, he opened a door and stood aside. Jalor and Blaine walked through the door to find themselves, surprisingly, in the bar of the Sleeping Log. On a table near the door was a pile of their weapons. They stopped short and turned to Gerhal Tag.

"The Sergeant uses your premises?" Jalor asked quietly with an edge to his voice. "Answer carefully Gerhal Tag. Blaine is the most lethal person I know and neither of us like being lied to. And I can guarantee that Almin Bor will make sure the Blood takes a dim view also."

"Almin Bor?"

"He is my second in the Faero's army," Jalor replied.

Gerhal Tag closed his eyes and took a deep breath, as though to calm himself.

"I was not aware of that," he said carefully. "In any case there is no need to worry about the Sergeant. You see she ..."

"Is of the Blood," Blaine finished for him. "As are the members of her Court, if I have a make a guess."

Gerhal Tag nodded with a rueful grin. "And she is my heart," he said, spreading his arms wide as if surrendering to the two Warriors.

"The Court is a Faeronar invention?" Jalor asked.

"Oh no, the Court was established to oversee the criminal element of Frelor. We have co-opted it. The various guilds don't know about that. As far as they're concerned the Court oversees their activities just like it always did. But, over time, we're creating a base away from the plateau. But do not be mistaken here. This is not intended to be an offering to the Faero or anything like that. The Blood will run this city once we take over, and we will defend our interests here."

Jalor nodded thoughtfully. Whether it was the Blood or other criminal elements made little difference beyond the fact that the Blood seemed to have a tradition of service for the Faero and preparation for the fight against Goroth. Outside of that, they were people who were hard and self-interested when dealing with those not of the Blood.

"What are the guilds?" Blaine asked.

"Each of the major forms of criminal have a guild that regulates their own activities. So, the pickpockets have a guild, the burglars have a guild, and so on. They make sure territory boundaries are assigned and honoured, deal with conflicts, and so on. Anything that they can't deal with or conflicts between guilds are brought to the Court."

"And are the Blood infiltrating other cities, too? We're going to Telsith after Frelor, but we plan to bring as many of the Ennarisi together as we can. If the Blood has other bases, then we may be better placed going directly to them."

"None others that I know of yet," Gerhal Tag replied, with a shrug. "There may be others, of course, that I'm not aware of any. I think it's unlikely, though. Frelor is the first attempt. Now, I think a drink is in order."

22. Jungle Cities

Bordering the western side of the dense jungle that occupied the narrow neck of land that joined the northern and southern continents were the twin cities of Port Killnar and Killfor. As the name suggested, Port Killnar was a port city on the huge inland sea and occupied a prime position. It was moderately wealthy as Ennarisi cities went. It provided merchant vessels to carry goods and people from north to south, with landing rights in smaller towns dotted along the shores of the sea on both continents. It also had a monopoly on shipping the produce from Killfor, its twin city.

Killfor was a slightly larger city located a short distance away from Port Killnar and was the centre for production of gums, resins and spices harvested from trees and shrubs that grew close to the edge of the forest. Both cities were built on the ruins of the former, much larger, city of Waslir, which had been destroyed during the rebellion. Its inhabitants had fled the destruction into the swamps and jungle and formed the basis of the Waslit, which was what the inhabitants of Waslir had termed themselves in the days of glory. As stability returned to the area, some of the people from the nearer edge of the jungle returned to the old city and rebuilt, using materials harvested from it. Over the cycles the two small settlements grew into the two small cities.

Both cities had been ruled by the Lord of the Eastern Sea who, at one time, had claimed the area occupied by them as well as extents of land along the sea's edges to north and south. His current descendant continued to occupy an honoured position in the cities but the family no longer ruled supreme. In Killfor, a seven-person Assembly of Ministers oversaw the city's existence, usually drawn from the small number of old, wealthy families. Port Killnar maintained a hereditary oligarchic ruling Council. In effect, both cities were ruled by the wealthy class.

Killfor prided itself on having broken away from the rule of the Lord of the Eastern Sea before the family lost its extensive holdings. Those of a pedantic nature pointed to documents from far in the past that showed that the merchants of Killfor had, in fact, bought the city's freedom for a large sum of money and an annual payment to the Lord. That payment continued to be made without any fanfare but, as was the case in those matters, now was worth much less in real terms than it once was.

The people of Killfor accepted with equanimity that they shared common ancestry with the Waslit, but contended that they were not at all like the jungle savages of legend. The people of Port Killnar refused to accept that kinship publicly, although most did so privately, including the Lord. That simple difference had caused many fights between those of opposing views and at least two wars between the cities were attributed to the disagreement. Now, the cities were independent but were closely linked by trade and long-standing family ties. Still, old arguments and enmities were remembered even while common interests forged closer ties. Both cities had established standing armies during their troubled period. These had been merged, after long negotiation, to form a joint militia.

It was a seven-day trek for Emdur, Ester and Maxnil to make their way to Killfor from the Waslit camp. They did so because Likki had decided that all of her people, and she included the inhabitants of the twin cities, should provide support for the Faero when the time came. Credar was charged with taking Likki's message to the Waslit camps in the depths of the jungle, and it fell to the three men to take the same message to the cities.

Killfor was their first destination, being closer to the jungle. It also was where Emdur hailed from. Although he had not been home for a considerable time, he was confident that he could convince the members of the Assembly to provide military aid.

The three men walked up to the city gate. They were far from being strangers to Killfor but still they paused to take in the city wall that gleamed in patches where the suns' light was reflected by the amazingly smooth stone harvested long ago from the old city. These huge rectangular stones had been dragged laboriously from their far-flung resting places to be carefully stacked and held in place by their own weight. It was rumoured that assistance was provided by two of the legendary Mages at the time, but that was agreed by most to be a fanciful notion. If one took the time, however, one could see where some of the huge stones - those closer to the top, oddly - were tightly fitted together without any gap, while others below showed far less precision.

"Assembly House?" Emdur asked of his companions as they admired the walls.

"May as well," Ester replied. "I really don't know what sort of reception we'll find. Not too many believe in the Guardians but the religions have some true believers now. And Likki has a pretty poor reputation here."

"Only way to find out is to try," Maxnil said.

The three walked through the gate, nodding a greeting to the gate guards. They turned up the short road to the main square, returning occasional greetings with nods and waves. Across the square they strode, commenting on the minor changes that had occurred in the time since they had last been in Killfor. The changes were few, of course, for change came slowly to Killfor.

The Assembly was convened in a building close to the city's centre, on a small square that was also faced by the main guard barracks and the temple to Gel, currently one of the main deities in Killfor. While the Assembly building, called Assembly House by most of the populace, and the guard barracks had been used for the same purpose for generations, Gel was the latest in a string of religious deities to occupy the temple. It had even housed the cult of Likki at one stage, until the particularly obnoxious period when members of the cult resorted to cannibalism and torture of women, apparently at the urging of Likki herself. The cult was driven out of Killfor and the temple was dedicated instead to Merta, one of the ever-changing pantheon of gods that acquired a priesthood for a while before fading to insignificance and being replaced. The Gel priests had occupied the temple for almost fifty cycles now.

Emdur walked confidently through the entrance door of Assembly House and down the short hall to the large reception desk, trailed by his friends.

"Good day," he said cheerfully to the attendant, who he failed to recognise. "Is Gilman around? I have a message for the Assembly."

"Master Gilman has retired," the attendant replied shortly. "What is the message?"

"Ah, and you are?" Emdur asked.

"I am Master Junsin," was the sour reply. "What is the message?"

"Well met, Master Junsin!" Emdur exclaimed. "You must be new to Killfor. I thought I knew everyone working for the Assembly. My name is Emdur, and these are Ester and Maxnil. We've just come from the deep jungle and have been tasked with seeking assistance from the Assembly for military aid for the Faero against Goroth and his supporters from the northern kingdoms."

"I see," Master Junsin replied in a flat tone, frowning. "Goroth, eh? And who is behind this request?"

"You may find this hard to believe, but it comes from Likki herself," Emdur replied with a smile.

"Likki? And she wants to help the Faero? Why? Does she want to eat him?" Master Junsin snorted. "Be away with you or I'll call the guard."

"It's true," Emdur objected. "Likki has returned, as have the other Guardians, and Goroth has been freed or will soon be. The Children have returned to aid us in the fight. Likki wants all of the people of old Waslir to join with the other forces to fight alongside the Children."

"Guard!" Master Junsin called as he gave three sharp raps of a gavel on the desk.

Four armed guards walked from a door in the entrance passage. Ester and Maxnil glanced to each other. Ester shrugged and grimaced.

"Get these three trouble-makers out of here," Master Junsin ordered, before glaring at Emdur. "And no more stories like that. Riots have been started with less. If I hear of you causing more trouble, you'll find yourself in the cells."

"But this is the truth," Emdur objected as one guard clamped a hand on his shoulder. "We really have been sent..."

"Enough!" Master Junsin shouted. "Out!"

The guards hustled the three acolytes back down the short hall and out the front door. When Emdur stepped back toward the door, the lead guard put a hand on his sheathed sword while the other three blocked the door entry. Maxnil grabbed Emdur's arm and pulled it to stop him.

"Come Emdur," Maxnil said quietly.

Emdur stopped. He glared at the guards for a moment before throwing his hands in the air with an exclamation of disgust and turning away. Ester and Maxnil flanked him as the trio walked away.

"What now?" Ester asked.

"We'll get to speak to the Assembly. If we can't speak to them directly then we speak to them indirectly." Emdur slowed as he looked around, taking his bearings. "We'll start at the Sleeping Crawler."

So began a whole tenday of the three young men visiting every tavern in Killfor and telling their tale of being rescued by Likki, of spending time with the Waslit people and being charged by the Guardian with bringing the twin cities of the jungle into the coalition led by the Faero. They were met with derision and laughter, or scepticism and anger but occasionally with a pensive mien and questions about the Waslit, the jungle and Likki herself. Emdur was rescued by Ester and Maxnil on several occasions when he or his audience became overheated in their exchanges. On at least one occasion, they were forced to beat a hasty retreat and evade pursuers. By the end of the tenday, they were not welcomed in several of the taverns that they once had known well.

The eleventh day dawned with overcast skies and high humidity. They had tried to reach the Assembly or even individual members several times, and each time they had been rebuffed. The guards now turned them away without bothering to check, and the personal guards of the Assembly members had threatened them with violence on several occasions. Their inability to convince the people of Killfor to support their cause added to their sense of failure. In their hearts, they knew that they had done the best that they could do, but they also knew that Likki would be disappointed. On this morning, all three awoke with heavy heads and uncertain stomachs, having used some of their dwindling coin to drown their sorrows the night before.

As a result, they were not prepared to be arrested as they stepped from the small inn. The waiting contingent of Assembly guards grasped them roughly as the under-officer leading the group mumbled that they were under arrest. They were hustled along the streets, being prodded hard with staves at the slightest indication of slowing or speaking, or just when the guards felt like inflicting pain, which was often. As they were pushed and prodded along the street a crowd formed in their wake. Laughter and jeers followed them on the short journey to Assembly House. Into Assembly House they were dragged and along the short corridor, past the reception desk and through the large doors of the Assembly chamber. They were followed by many of the following crowd.

The chamber was large enough to hold almost two hundred observers, and the available seats filled up quickly. Arrayed in a raised bench across the front of the chamber were the Assembly members, the five men and two women who had been elected to represent the wealthy citizens of the city. All stared stony-faced at the three men as they were dragged to a square marked on the floor.

"Well, I guess we managed to meet the Assembly," Emdur said as a aside to Ester.

"Quiet!" rapped out the under-officer, hitting Emdur a hard blow to his stomach.

Emdur responded by vomiting prodigiously all over the under-officer's tunic, trousers and boots. A round of laughter among the onlookers was met by a glare from the thoroughly soiled under-officer, who raised his stave to strike Emdur again.

"Hold!" the Assembly member at the right-most end of the line called out, halting the under-officer in mid-swing. "I suggest that you don't repeat that. You!" he said pointing to one of the guards, "go and arrange for that to be cleaned up. Under-officer Clegg, I suggest that you get a change of uniform and then return. Maybe a wash, too. I suggest a short break while that happens."

The suggestion was accepted readily by the other Assembly members, several of whom were looking unwell themselves. The three acolytes were marched into an ante-room where they were held by two of the guards while the chamber was cleaned. A short time later they were marched back into the chamber. The floor sported a large wet patch and the room was ringed with smoking sweet-sticks in an attempt to mask any remaining smells. Clegg had returned wearing a fresh uniform that looked a size too small for him. The glare he directed at the trio promised nothing good if they were left in his care.

"Now, let's begin," the Assembly member who had spoken previously said once all was settled again. "I am Klors. You are Emdur? An adventurer and treasure hunter, I believe? A citizen of Killfor?" He waited while Emdur nodded shortly. "Excellent. And Ester, a guide and equipment bearer, from Port Killnar?" Another wait for the nod. "And Maxnil, also a guide and equipment bearer from Port Killnar?" He waited until the third nod was received. "I believe you usually travel with Credar, daughter of the former Assembly member Crindis, and also an adventurer. Where is you travel companion?"

"She is with Likki and the Waslit people," Emdur replied, staring at Klors eye to eye. "Preparing to lead the Waslit to join the Faero's coalition."

"Is she?" Klors nodded calmly as laughter rippled across the chamber. "How convenient for her. But not for you. You are charged with treason and sedition. You are charged with promoting the false god Likki rather than the approved deities of Killfor. How do you plead?"

"Likki is not a god," Emdur replied. "The Guardians are not gods and have never claimed to be. And we have never claimed her to be a god."

Mocking laughter rose again, as though on cue, Maxnil thought. He turned to look over the Assembly chamber. There were very few who he recognised, and while Killfor was a reasonably sized city he thought he would at least recognise more than he did. Oddly, rather than looking at the three accused many of the audience were watching Klors intently. Another ripple of what now seemed to Maxnil like forced laughter started and stopped abruptly. Intrigued, Maxnil turned back to see an irritated frown get smoothed from Klors' forehead.

"Many see Likki as one of the false gods," Klors stated as though that proved the case. "And you claim to have spoken to her."

"We have," Emdur said.

More laughter rang out but died away quickly. Maxnil was sure that Klors had given a peculiar twist of his wrist just before the laughter began and again just before it petered out.

"And you claim she ordered you to come to Killfor and for you to order us to provide an army for the Faero?"

"She bid us to come here to seek assistance for the Faero and the Children of Ennaris in the battle against Goroth, as the Prophecy says will happen."

Another wrist twist resulted in more laughter, which Klors allowed to run a little longer before he ended it with the second twist. So, Maxnil thought. This is staged. To what end? They were in custody already, so why the charade? Could it be because Credar was the daughter of a still very influential father? Possibly so, which meant that Klors needed to have a pretext for whatever he was planning on doing. What about the other assembly members, though? Two of them Maxnil recognised but Klors and four others were new to him.

"The Prophecy?" Klors asked, oozing scepticism. "The Prophecy made by the mad Mage Drewflin? I suppose you spoke to him, too?"

"Drewflin?" Emdur asked, confused, to more ritual laughter. "The Prophecy was written by Halfgar, not Drewflin. All know that. And no, we did not meet with either of them."

Klors looked embarrassed momentarily at his gaff.

"But be aware Klors," Emdur said clearly, "that Drewflin and the Mages live still and will be at the final battle against the old evil. As will be the Children who have returned to Ennaris."

Ah, Maxnil thought. So Emdur had picked up on what was happening and decided to fight back. Ester looked unsure of what was happening, but he could be caught up later. Strangely, there was no laughter this time. Klors, it appeared, had frozen in place for a moment. Maxnil had not stopped watching the other Assembly members and now he saw two of them frown at Klors. Perhaps to hurry him along?

"Old tales with no meaning," Klors scoffed finally. "So, you claim to have spoken with the false god Likki and have said that it was the false god Likki who sent you to lure the army of Killfor away. Was that intended to ensure that we were defenceless? Was that so that Port Killnar could take over Killfor? You are traitors and spies!"

Klors made the last statement with what he probably intended to be a flourish, but unfortunately his raised hand caused some in the audience to mistake it for the laugh signal. Incensed, Klors stared at the audience and the untimely laughter died away again.

"This is not a laughing matter," Klors shouted angrily. "This is about the safety of Killfor." He looked over the audience and then turned back to his fellow Assembly members. "I name these three and Credar to be traitors and spies for Port Killnar. I say they are guilty of sedition against the true gods. I say they are guilty of heresy in claiming to have spoken with and acted at the bidding of the false god Likki. I demand that these three should be executed and that Credar is declared outlaw."

Cheers rang out in the chamber. Ester turned to Maxnil, appalled, while Emdur shook his head. For his part Maxnil was not surprised and, oddly, he felt no real emotion. He was surprised at that but he realised that he trusted Likki and accepted that his new role came with risks. This appeared to be one of them.

"Do we get to speak?" Emdur asked as the cheering diminished in volume.

"No," Klors stated flatly but with a triumphant glint in his eye. "You have condemned yourself when you stated that you spoke with the false god."

"Likki is not a god," Ester shouted. "She is a Guardian, our Guardian, all of us from the old land of Waslir. We must heed her request to aid the Faero against Goroth."

Ester was almost in tears, such was his passion. Maxnil knew it would avail little, but perhaps some in the audience would heed Ester's words.

"How votes the Assembly?" Klors demanded.

The trio were found guilty of treason and sedition by four votes to three. Oddly, while the two who had frowned at Klors agreed with the guilty finding with alacrity, one of the members hesitated before agreeing with it. Some sort of signal had passed between her and Klors, after which she found them guilty. Perhaps a threat? Maxnil found himself intrigued again. Why was this matter so important that a sham trial was required with an Assembly member being coerced into taking a position?

"You are found guilty," Klors stated triumphantly. "You are sentenced to death for treason and sedition. Your sentence is to be carried out within ten days. Take them away."

Under-Officer Clegg swaggered forward wearing an evil grin, joined by two other court guards who appeared to be less enthusiastic at performing their duty. Clegg snarled at the three.

"Move along. I'm goin' to enjoy this."

Emdur stood for a moment, regarding Clegg closely before nodding, apparently in acquiescence.

"Where are you from Clegg? Somewhere up north, I expect? Far to the north?" Emdur asked loudly.

Maxnil glanced from Emdur to Clegg in time to see a fleeting look of panic be replaced by Clegg's usual sneer.

"Same as Klors, I imagine," Emdur continued at just the moment when total quiet settled on the chamber. "The same as other new members of the Assembly."

Several of the audience looked around, startled. Klors stared as though frozen, but only for a moment as a murmur started.

"All members of the Assembly are from families who have lived in Killfor for at least two generations," Klors shouted. "Clegg, get them out of here!"

Clegg wielded his truncheon with vigour as he shepherded the trio out of the chamber and down to the basement cells. All three took welts and Ester was cradling an arm when they finally made it to the single large cell. Maxnil guided Ester to the bench that occupied one wall while Emdur brought up the rear, grunting at the strikes from Clegg's stave. Maxnil turned back for Emdur as Clegg raised his stave high, intending to bring it down on Emdur's unprotected head. Instead, he found his swing was blocked by Maxnil, who demonstrated his unexpected strength in plucking the stave from Clegg's hand easily and delivering a single hard poke to the Under-Officer's chest. Clegg collapsed to the floor in agony while Maxnil tossed the stave to one of the guards and gestured to Clegg.

"Take this one with you when you go," Maxnil said calmly, turning back to his friends.

Maxnil ignored them. The two guards glanced to each other uncertainly before grabbing one of Clegg's arms each and dragging the portly Under-Officer from the cell. The door was closed and locked.

23. Waslit Society

Two days later Clegg re-appeared at the cell door. He walked carefully and held himself quite stiffly. Maxnil noticed him first and nudged Emdur with a foot to alert him. Ester was sleeping fitfully. The two acolytes ignored Clegg. Emdur bore a range of black and blue bruises over his body, as did Maxnil. Ester had fewer bruises but his arm, which thankfully appeared not to be broken, was swollen and very painful. Emdur and Maxnil had assisted Ester to eat the thin stew that was their morning and evening meals, and the three had discussed what had transpired and why. Emdur was convinced that Killfor had been infiltrated by northers, as Likki told them had occurred elsewhere, too. Maxnil was not so sure but all three agreed that the sham trial had been a strange affair. However, none could see a reason for it. If the Assembly had been taken over by the northers, then they only had to decline to assist the Faero. Perhaps they were not in charge after all?

Clegg satisfied himself with glaring at the three acolytes while reflexively gripping his truncheon before he departed. Maxnil could hear him wheezing his way up the narrow steps that led to the floor above. What, he wondered, came next.

The next six days followed a pattern. Each morning, Clegg accompanied the guard who delivered the morning stew and waited outside the cell, glaring at them almost as though daring them to try to escape. He maintained a firm grip on his truncheon as though it was his most valuable possession. The three prisoners ignored him every day, while thanking the guard who delivered their food. He did not return for the evening meal, which was also when the refuse bucket was emptied.

On the seventh day, the ninth of their confinement, the pattern changed. Clegg was walking more easily now but, still, he gripped his truncheon in a tight clasp. This day, however, his eye gleamed as he regarded the three prisoners. This day he chose to speak, even while they continued to ignore him.

"Tomorrer's the day," he said with grim satisfaction. "Tomorrer's the day you three die. And I get to throw the handle. I like to do it slow, so the floor opens slow and you take longer to go. Gonna be quite the spectacle, it will."

The stew was delivered and the guard withdrew. Clegg smiled evilly.

"They won't let me treat you how you should be treated," he said as he turned to go. "But tomorrer you get what's comin' to ya."

Clegg almost managed his usual swagger as he walked from the cell. Emdur and Maxnil shared a glance and a shrug. Maxnil wondered just what Likki would do when the time of their execution came. He could not believe that they would be allowed to be executed after all the trouble she went through to save them from the butcher priests. Then again, Guardians had a different view of time to the normal Ennarisi, so who knew?

The day stretched out. All three found the tension to be nearly unbearable. Ester stared at the floor and shook his head periodically, as though negating the situation. The other two adopted a more stoic mien but Maxnil noted that Emdur's foot started to tap occasionally before being brought under control and he had to force down the urge to display his growing anger.

Meal time saw the usual guard return, along with two others. It seemed there was heightened concern that they may seek to escape the day before their sentence of death was carried out. All three were watchful, with staves in hand and knives in their belts. With the stew delivered, the guards turned to leave. Maxnil heard the three blowpipes expel their darts and a moment later all three guards collapsed. From the narrow steps emerged three men. They wore the usual garb of working Killfor men, but the blowguns they were tucking away were pure Waslit. Like most of the city-based descendants of Waslir, these men were taller than the Waslit of the jungles and their skin colour was lighter. However, they did have the high cheekbones and aquiline nose that were common traits among the jungle dwellers.

The first of the rescuers relieved the guard holding the cell key of his burden and unlocked the cell. He gestured to the three men.

"Come," he said. "We have a safe place for you."

"Why?" Emdur asked.

"It was a request made of us," the first rescuer replied, his eyes going slightly wild. "We were in our meeting place and a woman appeared from nowhere. She was very beautiful. She said that she was Likki and that we were to help you to escape." He stared at all three in turn. "Was she truly Likki?"

"Yes, I would say that she was," Emdur said. "She did leave it a bit late, though."

"Enough talk," another of the rescuers hissed. "Let's go!"

The trio followed the first rescuer from the cell and up the steps. Above was the hall leading from the Assembly chamber, which was empty. The guard room was not, however. Eight guards were slumped in various forms of collapse. One of the Waslit darted into the room and carefully extracted the blowgun darts from each neck. The three were led from the Assembly House by a back door and into the gathering gloom.

"We are of the Waslit Society," the first rescuer told them as they sat around a wooden table in the safe house. "We are descendants of the Waslit of the jungles and we practice the old skills. I am Nersli, and these are Krellis and Perslil."

The other two Waslit nodded companionably as they kept a watch out the front windows of the small cottage.

"How many of you are there?" Maxnil asked. "I've lived in Killfor or Port Killnar all my life and never knew any sort of Waslit Society existed."

Emdur and Ester nodded agreement. Emdur realised that, to his knowledge, none of the four acolytes had old Waslir blood, although Credar had mentioned a family rumour of some form of admixture. Each of them came from families from some distance away, drawn to the region several generations ago for various reasons. This, then, was something kept very close to the Waslit descendants, and probably the slowly shrinking number of full blood descendants, which supposition was confirmed.

"We are not many and our numbers decline with each generation. In my father's day there were two thousand initiates but today we are only around seven hundred. Of course, there are many more Waslit descendants in the cities, but most do not follow the old traditions."

So, Emdur thought ruefully, it was likely that some of the Waslit descendants with whom he was acquainted had been members of this secret society. He felt a momentary twinge of anger that he was excluded from such knowledge, but stamped it down. Instead, he turned to Nersli.

"Are you prepared to assist the Faero in the battle with Goroth?"

"Was everything you said truth?" Nersli asked seriously.

"It was, as far as we know," Emdur replied. "It was told to us by Likki, and we have had no reason to doubt her."

"Then we will see what can be done to assist you," Nersli nodded. "I am unable to guarantee any numbers but I'm sure many will want to play a part. The traditions are important to us and one tradition is that Likki would return and ask us to play our part. It appears the time has come."

Nersli looked to each of his companions. An unspoken question was greeted with nods.

"There is someone for you to meet," Nersli said. "But we must wait for any search for you to die down."

The search was intense but fruitless, and the Assembly members expressed both anger and concern at the escape. Rumour grew that Waslit sorcerers had spirited the three away. Given that there was no mention that any guards had been incapacitated, and that no-one had seen any sign of an escape, that was presented as the most logical outcome, at least by Clegg and several of his fellow guards. That rumour was given little credence but spawned many jokes about other things that went missing.

A second rumour told of Likki rescuing her acolytes and leaving the guards asleep, which grew rapidly when one of the guards told of waking to find them gone. The Waslit people had always maintained an undercurrent of belief in Likki and the Guardians, despite the oft-spoken denials in some quarters. That belief now was re-awakened in many.

Then there was a third rumour of a Waslit team seeking retribution for the capture and ill treatment of Emdur, Maxnil and Ester. This rumour caused some consternation among the guards, most of whom were of long-standing Killfor families. This rumour took on new dimensions when a member of the guard, one of the new group who had been hired by the new Assembly headed by Klors, was found dead with a very Waslit-looking dart sticking from his throat. When Nersli told the group of this event on the morning of their fourth day in the safe house, he declared that it would not have been done by any of the Society initiates, for they would have retrieved the dart. Maxnil was not so sure. The Waslit, he had been told in the jungle, practised psychological warfare when they felt the need to do so, and the very unsettling effect of this one act may have been exactly what was wanted. Could it have been the jungle Waslit playing a role?

They whiled away their time and were itching for something, anything to break the tedium. Maxnil fared best as he had decided to learn more about the Waslit traditions as practised by the city dwellers. Blessed with excellent coordination and unexpected strength, while in the jungle he had toyed with the blowguns and darts of the Waslit, and had even been presented with his own blowgun, which had been left behind. Now he spent a lot of time with the three Waslit when they were at the house, which was increasingly intermittent, as they had their own lives to lead. In doing so, he found that he had an aptitude for the short javelin that some of the urban Waslit carried when they trained as part of their Society, and he could often be found practising with it.

There was a steady stream of Waslit Society members who wanted to meet the three. Some were purely for curiosity's sake, while others wanted to see for themselves the men who claimed to speak for Likki, and to gauge for themselves whether they spoke truly or not. Others still wanted to understand what was known about the Faero and his battle with the legendary Goroth. All left feeling satisfied that the trio were genuine.

It was a further tenday before Nersli brought a visitor to meet the three former prisoners. Maxnil had just returned from a practice session with both javelin and blowgun with Perslil when Nersli entered the house, followed by three others, all of whom were wearing nondescript clothes but who carried themselves with unmistakably military bearing and that indefinable air of command.

"This is Commander Joplin of the militia, along with Captain Derslin and Captain Kreslin," Nersli said by way of introduction. "Commander, this is Emdur, Maxnil and Ester."

The three stood when the Commander was introduced and bowed a greeting as they were named. They knew of the militia, of course. It was, in fact, why they were in Killfor, to get the militia to join with the Faero. The militia was the dominant military force of the region and it was shared between the twin cities, a collaborative effort that had survived recent disagreements between the city leaders. The Commander was expected to play no favourites between the cities, and he was reputed to be scrupulous in being even-handed. There were around five hundred full time soldiers but more than four thousand citizen soldiers who could be called on when circumstances dictated.

"Commander," Emdur said once introductions were complete. "We are very pleased to meet you, at last."

"I have been told of your, er, difficulties," Joplin replied easily as he took the offered chair. "I was sceptical of your story when first told it, but I have been assured that you tell the truth. I am here to judge that for myself."

"I can only offer assurance that what we have said is true," Emdur said ruefully. "Some parts will seem fanciful to those who do not believe in the Guardians. Some will be discounted because of prejudice against the Waslit of the jungle. Some will not want to assist the Faero or may try to impede him. We hope there are enough who will believe to provide some assistance, as Likki requested."

"There are those who believe in the Guardians and the ancient duty to come when called, but who don't wish to be taken in by someone who makes that call for the wrong reason," Joplin said mildly. "I am one such person."

"Then you agree that the people of old Waslir must offer assistance?"

"If it is offered to the right ones at the right time. But if we provide our services to anyone who demands them then we risk much. This could be a ruse to call the militia away from the cities, for example, and leave them defenceless. That's been done before."

Emdur thought for a moment before nodding.

"I can't force you to believe. Likki came to Nersli and his Society and asked for them to assist. If you believe Nersli then you believe us. One follows the other. If you don't believe him, then you don't believe us. All I can tell you is that we will be with the jungle Waslit when they march to support the Faero. We would like the other half of the Waslit to join us."

"We may have to go against the Killfor Assembly's directive," Joplin said in a carefully neutral tone. "How do you advise us to proceed with that?"

"I can't advise you on that," Emdur replied with a smile. "We ask for the support. The Assembly appears to be dominated by those who oppose such a path. Our trial was a show trial, that much was clear, but to what end we're not sure. I suspect that there is a norther influence, however, which Likki told us has been tried in other cities and kingdoms. In the Faero's own Citadel, in fact."

"Not norther, no," Joplin said with a firm head shake. "But there is an easterner influence. They believe it is hidden but three of the Assembly are from an eastern family. A forebear made it through the jungle several generations ago and two others a little after. They established a sort of cell of easterners. It's possible that they're trying to make sure that we don't provide support. We have been watching them for some time."

"We believe that Clegg is a norther," Maxnil said. "It's possible that he brought the message from the north to trigger this opposition."

"Ah, Clegg," Joplin frowned and nodded. "Yes, I can see that being a possibility, and his fellow new guards. You think Klors, Mantis and Prentis are agents that have been made active?"

"It fits a pattern," Maxnil said, nodding. "But not only Clegg. There were many in the Assembly court room who were assisting Klors. While some of them may have been paid dupes, there would have to be some others who organised the charade. I doubt it would have been the Assembly members themselves. Oh, and you have another Assembly member who has been compromised somehow. She was forced into voting against us."

"That would be Bresniv," Joplin mused. "I'll look into that."

"You said that we have been watching the easterners," Ester said for the first time. "Is that just you in recent times or others from the past?"

Joplin smiled at the question and said, "They have been watched for several generations, by members of the Society."

"And you are a member of the Society," Ester guessed.

"As have been most of my family for many, many cycles," the Commander replied, standing. "You've given me a lot to think about and a few tasks to have done. So, I'll take my leave now. It has been an honour meeting the acolytes of Likki."

"So you will support us?" Emdur asked as he, too, stood.

"We will, both the Society and the militia. I will have to make sure that's not known too soon or it may be blocked or at least challenged, which would cause problems. And we will step up our training. It has been a little lax in recent times of peace. But," he paused as though struck with a sudden thought, "how will we know when the Waslit are marching?"

"Stay ready, for we are not sure when it will be," Emdur replied with a slow smile. "But from what we have been told you will know when it happens."

24. Attack at Frelor

"We're being followed," Blaine cautioned Jalor.

It was the day after the meeting with the Sergeant. Jalor and Blaine had broken their fast in the Sleeping Log before deciding to take a look around the city. Blaine was interested in getting an understanding of the opposition that may be encountered when the Court took over the city, while Jalor wanted to make sure that the innocents of the city would be protected and thus was looking for safe locations should any fighting prove to endanger civilians. Blaine was without his greatsword but both carried swords and knives.

"How many?" Jalor asked without breaking stride or looking around.

"Six," Blaine answered. "Too many if they know what they're doing."

"Can we turn back to the Log?"

"We can try. If they're experienced, they'll be onto that straight away. But at least we'll know."

"Okay, then let's try," Jalor replied. "Ideas as to who?"

"May be the Sergeant," Blaine said, "in which case we'll be fine. That's unlikely though. I would expect Gerhal Tag to let us know if we were to be shadowed. It's also unlikely to be one of the guild gangs, because the Sergeant probably put us under some sort of protection."

"The only other one would be the merchants. They may know we met with the Sergeant."

"Which means she has a security leak," Blaine agreed. "We'll know soon. They're closing in. We'll stop in the next intersection."

The two Warriors stepped into the centre of the road as they reached the intersection. Standing back-to-back, they watched the six pursuers take positions to surround them. All six held knives and staves steady in hands, ignoring any onlookers as though they had no concern about them.

"Merchant Council," Blaine said quietly. "I recognise that one with the crooked nose."

"Yes," Jalor agreed. "So, the Sergeant has a leak. But how do we get out of this? They don't seem to be worried about being seen to do whatever they plan on doing."

One of the attackers made a curt gesture, at which all rushed the Warriors. Jalor met two, parrying the first and stepping away from the line of attack of the second. Blaine stepped into the trio attacking him, accepting a knife graze across one arm to allow him to grasp the arm of one attacker, who he threw into the path of another's stabbing thrust. The two went down together with the knife of the second buried to its hilt in the side of the first. That, however, was the extent of the two Warriors' success. Jalor was rendered senseless by a sharp rap to his head by a stave as he avoided another swipe by one of his attackers, and suddenly Blaine found himself fighting against five assailants. He managed to hold off two, collecting cuts on both arms in doing so, before the same stave rapped him over the head. He collapsed beside Jalor.

Blaine woke first. He found himself lying on a bed of straw. His arms had been roughly bound with dirty rags, but blood had seeped through the rags and run down his arms. The blood was dry, which told him that he had been out for some time. He could feel that his sword and knives had been taken. He tried to sit but found that he was attached to a dead weight. He twisted his head enough to find that the weight was Jalor.

"Jalor," Blaine whispered urgently. "Jalor, wake up."

Jalor remained stubbornly unconscious. At least, Blaine hoped Jalor was only unconscious. He shook his head to try to clear it. The fog that wrapped around his thoughts told him that he had suffered a concussion, but he had to see if Jalor breathed still. After several attempts he managed to twist so that he could see the rise and fall of Jalor's chest, which released some of the tension that he felt. If he could rouse Jalor, they would have a chance. Two Warriors could take on whole armies and win, but with Jalor they could do so with a plan!

"Jalor, wake up," Blaine repeated, shifting so that Jalor was jostled back and forth.

Blaine was rewarded by a moan. Jalor's eyes fluttered for a few seconds before opening to slits, the usual method of awakening of a Warrior. So, he was aware at least.

"Jalor, it's me, Blaine," Blaine whispered. "Stay still for a moment. We're in some sort of barn or outbuilding or something. We're bound together. Can you understand me?"

Jalor muttered something but Blaine could see that he nodded. Blaine forced the pain away.

"Okay, so I want to try to sit up. I need you to push against the floor and try to sit up. I think we can sit back-to-back, but I'm not sure. Are you able to try that?"

Jalor muttered something again that Blaine could not make out, but he tried to work himself into a sitting position with his back to Blaine. Slowly, the two Warriors worked themselves into a position where they were back-to-back. As one, both took a deep breath.

"Are you okay?" Jalor asked quietly.

"Not really," Blaine replied as quietly. "I have a concussion, I think. We need to do something soon or I may drift off."

Their attention was taken by a commotion somewhere beyond the door. Various thuds, thumps and grunts could be heard, then quiet. The two Warriors held themselves still, making no noise.

"General!" came an urgent whisper.

Jalor relaxed and, before Blaine could caution him, called out, "In here."

A gasp sounded outside the room and there was a rattle, obviously from a bolt being loosened and drawn. The door was flung open and Gerhal Tag stormed into the room, sword drawn. He looked around quickly, saw there was no-one else in the room, and sheathed his sword. A second man entered after him, but ducked back out after a quick glance around. Gerhal Tag drew his belt knife and approached the two Warriors.

"Are you both okay?" Gerhal Tag asked.

"Cuts and headaches, but otherwise okay," Jalor replied.

"What happened?"

"Tell the Sergeant that she has a leak," Blaine said as his bindings were cut and he stretched arms and legs.

"No need," the Sergeant said as she walked through the door. "I've handled it. The guards have been dealt with," she said to Gerhal Tag, "so if they're okay it's time to go."

Jalor shook his head and nodded. After a concerned glance to Gerhal Tag he followed the Sergeant from the former cell, with Blaine and Gerhal Tag following after. Blaine leaned against Gerhal Tag as he staggered forward. In a corridor outside the room two men lay, one with his head tilted at an odd angle and the other with his throat slit open. Blood pooled on the floor, so that the four had to step carefully to avoid it. The Sergeant led the way along the passageway, past door after door. The small party came to a junction and turned left. A short distance further and the Sergeant led them into a room. A woman stood, protected by five sword-wielding men. All relaxed as the four entered the room.

"We have injured," the Sergeant said.

The woman nodded and gestured to Jalor and Blaine to approach. She examined each, Blaine first, followed by Jalor, before turning and muttering to one of the men who had been standing guard. He turned and ran from the room. No-one spoke, although the woman ran her hands across Blaine's wounds and then placed one hand on each of Jalor and Blaine's heads. The two Warriors exchanged surprised glances, as they felt the pain recede. The man returned a short time later with a bucket of steaming water and some cloth that looked like a sheet. The woman nodded her thanks and turned to Blaine.

"This may hurt," she said.

She dipped a cloth in the steaming water and then washed down the now filthy bandages, gently releasing them from the various wounds.

As she removed the bandages the knife cuts were revealed. The guards muttered to each other at the number and severity of the cuts, while the woman frowned. She glanced to Blaine, who smiled back to her. Gently, she washed the cuts that were now bleeding again. Then, without ceremony, she held her hand over the worst of the cuts and concentrated. A green glow formed around her hand and Blaine's wounds closed. Blaine stared and looked to Jalor, who nodded tiredly. Returning gifts indeed!

A short time later, both Blaine's and Jalor's wounds and concussions had been treated. The woman, who had belatedly been introduced as Belanis, leaned back tiredly. Jalor looked from Gerhal Tag to Belanis.

"Thank you, Belanis. I feel that I need to introduce you to someone. He will, I am sure, value you even more than those of the Blood do."

Belanis looked up and smiled.

"Thank you, general. Who would value my gifts more than those of the Blood?" she asked. "My fellow Faeronar are among the few who readily accept the gifts, even today."

"I'm thinking of one who values those gifts more than most," Jalor replied. "Drewflin."

"D - D - Drewflin?" Belanis gasped. "The Mage Drewflin? The greatest of the Mages? He lives?"

"He would dispute the title of greatest, but yes, he lives. I think healers will be in short supply in the near future, and your skills would be valued more than I think you can imagine. Who taught you?"

"No-one taught me, General," Belanis replied, looking down at her clasped hands. "There has not been anyone to teach me."

"That will change," Jalor replied. "Gerhal Tag, as general of the forces of the Faeronar I charge you to get Belanis to the Citadel. This is of the utmost importance. She is to seek out the Teller Flin. Belanis, tell Flin that I sent you to him."

"It shall be done, General," Gerhal Tag replied. "Meanwhile, we have started our operation to remove the Council from Frelor. Do you wish to take part?"

Jalor looked to Blaine, who responded with a 'what the hell' grin. So be it, Jalor thought. This was part of their main mission, after all, or so he could argue.

"Lead the way, Gerhal Tag," Jalor answered.

"But we need weapons first," Blaine replied. "Our weapons were taken from us."

"We found their weapons store," Gerhal Tag replied. "Your weapons probably are there, but if not, then there will be many other to choose from. Follow me."

The Warriors followed the Blood agent along another corridor to a large room. They were trailed by four other men and Belanis. The room contained barrels of swords and spears, buckets of knives, weapons like maces lying against the wall. Scattered around the room were piles of leather armour. On a small table were the weapons that had been taken from Jalor but not Blaine's. While Jalor reclaimed his sword and belt knife, Blaine started to look through the accumulated weaponry. A few moments later he gave a triumphant cry. From a barrel full of assorted swords and spears he drew forth an enormous greatsword, sheathed in a leather scabbard for a back mount.

"Are you sure, Blaine?" Gerhal Tag asked. "That's a heavy sword."

"It's fine for some of the work we'll be doing," Blaine replied as he worked the scabbard into position. "Fighting ghazrak needs heavy weapons. For close work I have the short sword."

"Ghazrak? What is that?" Belanis asked.

"Ghazrak are monsters created by Grensor," Jalor replied as he settled his own sword and belt knife into place. "They have horned heads, hooves for feet and a very strong bony armour that covers shoulders, chest and back. The thighs are also protected by heavy, thick muscles. They're very hard to disable and harder to kill. Normal arrows bounce off their armour. If you find yourself fighting them, make sure there are two or three of you to one ghazrak and go for gaps in the armour plates or under the arms."

"And don't think that they tire," Blaine continued as he started to strap several knives and a short sword into place. "Because they don't. Their weapons are rough and ready but they make up for that and lack of skill with brute force and they're pure berserker. According to Flin … er Drewflin … Grensor made ghazrak for the rebellion. These seem to be similar."

Gerhal Tag shook his head.

"Grensor, Goroth, Drewflin, the Children returned," he muttered. "We must be close to the prophesied time. How can we tell if ghazrak are near?"

"Well for one, they eat most people that they capture," Jalor said, and looked around at the sudden quiet. "What?"

"There have been reports of missing people, more than usual," Belanis replied. "And also reports of remains of bodies, many bodies, as though wild animals had torn them apart and eaten of them. Could this be these ghazrak?"

"Where was this?" Blaine demanded as he searched through the remaining weapons for anything of value.

"In several parts of Frelor," Gerhal Tag replied. "They are near places where the Merchant Council have their forces gathered. Our attacks will target these places."

"What attacks? When?" Jalor asked tersely.

"Any time now," Gerhal Tag replied. "There are three targets. General, we may have made a grave mistake."

"You, you and you," Jalor said, pointing to three of the men who had followed them into the room. "Get to those areas as fast as you can and stop them. Move!"

The three men stole a quick glance to Gerhal Tag, received a short nod in return, and dashed from the room.

"Right. Gerhal Tag, get us to the closest of those places," Jalor continued. "It's time we took a hand."

He turned to Blaine to receive a nod to indicate that he was ready, or that he agreed with Jalor, or both. Given the nearly feral grin that the Warrior gave with the nod, it was likely the latter.

25. Threat Removed

"The Council's hideout is in the next block," Gerhal Tag said.

The Blood's agent was leading the two Warriors, Belanis and Malin Kar, the remaining Court soldier whose name gave away his Blood heritage, in a rapid trot through the streets of Frelor. The citizens of the city who saw them pass moved out of the way. Not only did all wear forbidding expressions on their faces, but Gerhal Tag and Malin Kar also carried naked swords in hand. The cobbles under foot were uneven and smooth but such was the intent of the five that little notice was taken.

Half way along the next block, however, was a scene of carnage. Lifeless bodies of men and women were strewn along the street. Many had horrific wounds to heads, arms, legs and torsos. Several were missing limbs. Many others were running along the street in panic. Screams could be heard coming from a large building, in front of which was gathered a knot of people. Gerhal Tag breathed a sigh of relief when he spied the Sergeant amongst the group. The rescuer who had served as messenger looked at Jalor with relief as they drew near.

"General," he panted, still recovering from his run to stop the attack, "I tried to explain what you said but…"

"Monsters?" the Sergeant growled, rounding on Jalor. "You claim there are monsters now?"

Jalor opened his mouth to reply when Blaine interrupted him.

"Jalor, look."

Blaine pointed to a pile of black material. He jogged over and lifted it to reveal a hooded cloak.

"What happened here?" Jalor demanded. "What happened to the Shadow, the one who was wearing those robes?"

"There's a rent in the fabric," Blaine said. "I expect somehow this one was killed with a knife or sword. Probably a knife."

"Which means the ghazrak have no controller," Jalor replied. "They've gone wild."

"What do we do?" Gerhal Tag asked, watching the front door of the building.

"I want someone at every exit to the building," Jalor ordered. "Do not try to fight them. I want to know how many get out and where they go. If any do," he amended.

"And what do we do?" the Sergeant demanded. "Just stand around and wait? Those people in there are not all the Council's people. Some are just people who sound like they're being killed."

"And eaten," Gerhal Tag said with a shudder.

"Eaten?" the Sergeant gasped. "They eat people?"

"Blaine, how good is that sword you found?" Jalor asked, ignoring the Sergeant.

"It's good," Blaine replied. "I can use it against them as long as I have the space. Not as good as our usual weapons but it'll do."

"Where's the city guard?" the Sergeant demanded of one of her men.

"Hiding," was the sneering response.

"Do you have any archers?" Jalor asked.

"No, why would we have archers in the city?" the Sergeant demanded. "Distances are too close."

"Shame," Jalor said, turning to Blaine. "I guess we do this the hard way. Okay," he said as Blaine nodded, "we go in. You'll know the ghazrak when you see them. They're like nothing you've ever seen before, I hope. Two or three together. Go for under the arm or between the bony plates."

"General..." the Sergeant began, then sighed. "The command is yours."

"Thank you, Sergeant," Jalor said. "Detail some of your force to cover the exits, please. Blaine and I will take point. Follow as you can."

It was as bad as Jalor thought it would be. Bloody drag marks were scrawled along the walls and floor of the entrance and blood sprays crawled up the walls and stained the ceiling. The building had two levels above the ground but the screams were coming from the rear of the ground floor, so that was where Jalor and Blaine headed. Behind them came the Sergeant's men, with Gerhal Tag and the Sergeant at the rear. The hallway ended at a door that was being held ajar by a foot that had been thrust into place to stop it from closing. Just the foot, as far as Jalor could see from his angle. The screaming stopped.

Jalor stopped several paces from the door and gestured to Blaine to proceed. Blaine moved past Jalor with his booted feet barely making a whisper on the hard wooden surface. Jalor held up a hand to stop the rest of the party. Blaine stopped at the door and glanced down, grimacing as he saw what was holding the door open. Carefully, he edged one eye so he could see into the room. He stayed perfectly still for several moments, taking in as much of the scenario as he could before carefully leaning away from the door and then picking his way slowly back to Jalor.

"There are all ten of them in the rear room," Blaine said at little more than a faint whisper. "Not sure how many people have been killed but there are none alive now. They're eating," he finished bleakly.

Jalor nodded, considering. He turned to where the Sergeant waited impatiently and gestured back towards the door.

"Who are your best men at being quiet?" he asked in a whisper.

"Malin Kar, Belanis and me," the Sergeant replied.

Jalor smiled briefly and nodded, acknowledging his gaff.

"I want the three of you to go up to the top two floors and see if there are any survivors. If there are, then see if you can get them to come down, very quietly. I'm not so worried about the Council's men, but give them the chance. Is there a basement to this building?"

"Yes, of course there is," she answered. "But the door was locked when I tested it as we came down the hall, so probably there's no-one there. The Council's men occupied this level and the next one up. The top floor is where some families live. Lived," she concluded with a frown."

"See what you can do. If we can get any survivors out, we may be able to burn the building."

"That will burn much of this district," the Sergeant objected. "Are these things truly so hard to kill?"

"Yes, but see for yourself," Jalor replied, gesturing to the door. "Very quietly."

The Sergeant sniffed and moved past Jalor without making a sound. She was wearing something like moccasins, Jalor saw, and was lifting and placing her feet very carefully. She reached Blaine, who was staring at the door and listening intently for any change in the sounds coming from the room. The Sergeant, when she realised what she could hear, paled but still she touched Blaine gently on one arm. The Warrior glanced to her, then to Jalor who nodded. Blaine pointed to the point alongside the door opening and then pantomimed sliding a single eye around to see the scene. She nodded and proceeded with exaggerated care. A glance down at the foot that was holding the door open made her clench her jaw, but she edged around the jaw opening, stayed like that for a few moments and then retreated again. She was trembling when she reached Blaine but met his gaze and nodded before proceeding past him to where Jalor waited.

"I agree," she replied tersely. "I will look for survivors and get them out, then we burn the place."

She turned back to where the stairs started, tapping Malin Kar and Belanis on their shoulders as she passed. The two followed her, adopting the same exaggeratedly careful stepping style. At the foot of the stairs the Sergeant gave them terse instructions and the three of them moved onto the staircase, testing each step before putting their weight on it.

Meanwhile Jalor moved back to join Blaine.

"We may not have much more time," Blaine whispered. "They're eating pretty fast. We have no real idea what they'll do when they get through this lot. They may just settle in for a nap or they may go looking for more food, or just go on a killing spree."

"We'll just hope the Sergeant can get anyone from the top floor down and out," Jalor replied in a similar low tone. "If we do have to take them on then we may have to bottle up the doorway. We don't want to be fighting all ten at once. If we can get survivors out then we'll just torch the building and see if we can get them that way."

A slight noise behind caused Blaine to stiffen and Jalor to turn. Belanis had crept back down the stairs and now stood by the front door, preparatory to pulling it open. Behind her came several others. All were shocked and terrified, with wide staring eyes and trembling limbs. They were trying to be quiet but they failed. Belanis gently pulled the door open and the escapees started to leave, when one gave a desperate sob as she made it to the door. Immediately all sound ceased in the back room. Jalor and Blaine shared a despairing glance before Jalor gestured for everyone to pull back to the door leading to the street. Blaine took a stance in the centre of the hallway with the greatsword in both hands. Jalor positioned himself to one side, almost out of reach of the huge sword. Grunts came from the back room.

People continued to stream down the stairs, encouraged by the Court members, as the door to the back room was wrenched open and the first of the ghazrak appeared framed in the doorway. It took a single look at Blaine standing in the hallway and roared in challenge. That elicited screams and panic from those still to exit the building. A final moment of respite was gained when the ghazrak's crude sword was caught on the door jamb, but it was wrenched free and the ghazrak stormed into the hallway.

Blaine stepped forward and swiped the greatsword from right to left. The leading ghazrak's neck was shattered. With an effort Blaine drew his sword back as the ghazrak slumped, dead. The following ghazrak stumbled and received Blaine's second slash, which sliced through its right arm completely. The arm fell to the floor and dark blood pumped from the wound but the ghazrak tried to clamber over its fallen companion, before stumbling and allowing Jalor to step in and drive his sword through the gap between the armour plates behind its neck. But Jalor could not withdraw the sword, leaving him weaponless.

A brief glance was shared between Blaine and Jalor and they began a withdrawal with a single mind. Jalor hoped that everyone that was left upstairs had been brought down, because they were heading for the door. He also hoped that the Sergeant had her forces outside, because there was no way Blaine and Jalor could handle an entire troop of ghazrak. The remaining ghazrak boiled through the door, tripping over the fallen two and blocking the hallway in their zeal to reach the two Warriors. Jalor took a quick glance behind to see that the hallway was empty. The Sergeant stood at the door and gave a "come on" gesture. Jalor tapped Blaine on the shoulder and turned to run from the building. Blaine followed on his heels.

The street was surprisingly quiet. Jalor glanced in both directions to find the street nearly deserted. A knot of people who had been removed from the target building was being shepherded away by a few women. He could see others with fearful expressions peering out from windows of buildings along the street. Otherwise, the only people left were those that formed a loose ring around the doorway, standing thirty paces away. There may have been a dozen of them, to Jalor's very quick estimate. All were armed with sword and knife, several carried wicked-looking battle axes. In the centre of them was Gerhal Tag with the Sergeant by his side. A few paces behind them was a young man standing empty handed, calmly watching proceedings.

The two warriors took in this tableau as they darted from the doorway and leapt the three steps to the street. Even as they joined the ring of Court members, all of whom Jalor expected to be of the Blood, the remaining ghazrak charged from the building. Jalor heard a sharp intake of breath from several of those waiting, but none fell back.

"Three to each one, target the plate joins," Jalor shouted as Blaine handed him his short sword, even as Blaine stepped forward again.

The first ghazrak charged directly at Gerhal Tag with its sword raised high. Unseen to Jalor, from behind Gerhal Tag and the Sergeant the young man's hands blurred. The ghazrak suddenly sported a knife sticking out from its left eye and another from its neck. The roar of challenge became a gurgle and the ghazrak stumbled forward to collapse, lifeless.

Behind it the others made their charges in different directions. At the far left end of the line three men converged on one ghazrak. The ghazrak roared and swung its sword while the three tried to find an opening. One of the three stumbled and the ghazrak brought its sword down on his unprotected head with a shattering blow, killing the Court member immediately. In doing so it left an opening and one of the remaining two men ran his sword through the unprotected armpit, while the other found a gap between the bone plates at the ghazrak's back and plunged his sword through the opening. The ghazrak fell on top of its victim, twitched and lay still. The two men managed to extract their swords with an effort and turned to help others.

Blaine had taken care of a second ghazrak and was engaged with a third. Nearby Jalor battled with the fourth, which was largely a case of holding it off until someone else could come to assist. Two groups of three men were involved in desperate battles with the fifth and sixth ghazrak. Two other men lay motionless. Belanis was turning away from them with slumped shoulders. The final ghazrak was engaged with Gerhal Tag and the Sergeant. The two Court members separated to assist the two groups of three.

Gerhal Tag sought to draw the monster away from the Sergeant but was failing. The ghazrak seemingly had zeroed in on her and would not be dissuaded. It continued to charge at her as she and Gerhal Tag fended off its frenzied attacks. Both moved backward slowly and the ghazrak followed. Behind the Sergeant the young man kept pace. Strike after strike was blocked by Gerhal Tag, while the Sergeant tried to find an opening. Neither were prepared for the ferocity with which the ghazrak drove its attack, and both were tiring quickly. Finally, Gerhal Tag took a savage blow from the ghazrak that slipped off his sword and plunged through his leg, digging deep and shattering the bone. Gerhal Tag cried out and fell, casting a despairing look to the Sergeant. The ghazrak ignored Gerhal Tag and turned back to the Sergeant. A great swipe of its crude sword just missed her as she staggered backward. The ghazrak roared in triumph and followed, swinging its sword in swift arcs.

Blaine had dispatched his opponent and then, despite several wounds, made quick work of Jalor's. That allowed Jalor to swing around - stagger really, as he also had taken cuts, at least one of which was deep - in time to see Gerhal Tag fall and the Sergeant become the focus of the ghazrak's rage. Even as he started to move across the short distance separating them, however, the young man leapt from behind the Sergeant. At the top of his leap, he twisted so that he faced the Sergeant and knives appeared in each hand. He landed astride the ghazrak's shoulders and immediately stabbed both knives into its neck, one on each side. The ghazrak staggered. With a shouted "Blood of Ennaris", the Sergeant knelt and drove her sword up through the small gap in the bone armour that existed in the lower torso. Black blood gushed over her hands as she held her grip on the sword. The ghazrak tottered and fell sideways. The young man lithely jumped from the falling creature and landed beside the Sergeant.

Jalor heard another fall and turned to see the final ghazrak tumble to the ground with a sword and knife wedged between the bone chest plates. Two of the three men who had been battling it stepped back wearily, one of whom had no sword. The third of the group, who Jalor saw was Malin Kar, was slumped over, holding his side. The other group of three were also turning away from their ghazrak opponent, which was lying spread-eagled on its back.

Belanis ran forward to Gerhal Tag, even as the Sergeant gave a cry and ran to the Blood agent. Belanis arrived first and immediately tore his trouser leg away from the wound. Blood ran free. Gerhal Tag was unconscious so Belanis swiftly laid him flat on his back and held both hands over the wound. The green glow appeared with much greater intensity than it had when Jalor first saw her use her gift. The wound closed swiftly and Belanis pushed away and ran to Malin Kar, where she repeated the effort. He gasped and shuddered and turned pale but his wounds closed quickly. She turned to Blaine and Jalor, both of whom waved her back to Gerhal Tag.

"Have you finished with Gerhal Tag?" Jalor asked, standing with a lean.

"No, there remains much to do with him," Belanis replied. "I've healed the wound to stop the blood loss but the deep wounds remains and the bone is badly damaged."

"Well, we can wait," Blaine replied. "You will be losing energy that you'll need for him if you treat us. If we can get some water and bandages then we'll be okay for a while."

Belanis looked uncertainly to Jalor but Blaine merely nodded and gestured to Gerhal Tag with a tired smile.

"We've had worse and survived," Blaine said. "Come back to us when you have a chance."

"Very well," Belanis said, before reaching over and placing one hand on the worst wound of each.

The green glow appeared on each hand for a short time before either Warrior could object and the wounds closed. Then, with a brief smile, she scurried back to Gerhal Tag's side. Without ceremony, she pushed the Sergeant away and knelt beside him. Both hands were extended over the wounds and glowing a deep green within moments.

The Sergeant walked up to Jalor, wiping tears from her eyes. The young man accompanied her.

"General, I thank you for your help. We heeded your warning but these creatures were like nothing any of us have ever encountered. I doubt we would have survived had we come upon them without you being here." The Sergeant looked across the intersection where the encounter had occurred, her eyes misting as she looked on the casualties. "Are these what the Faero will face?"

"These and norther men and women, and possibly other creatures spawned in the mind of Grensor," Jalor replied.

"And you believe this battle will take place in the grasslands?"

"So Drewflin believes, and he's been right about most things," Jalor replied. "It makes sense, given the twin kingdoms would have to go through that area to cause damage. If we can meet them there, then we hold back the majority of the enemy."

"We will do what we can to hold the rear," the Sergeant replied firmly. "I will see what we can to do provide additional support."

"What of your other teams?" Jalor asked. "This was one of three locations, as I recall."

"The other teams faced little true opposition. We were able to prevail without serious casualty."

"Check for the presence of red gold," Jalor advised. "That seems to be a pointer to any subversion. Why it would be held onto I don't know, but they seem to do so."

"And so we shall," the Sergeant replied. "We now go to eject the Merchant Council. Do you wish to be part of that?"

"No," said Jalor. "I think it may be best if we are not seen to be part of it. We'll return to the Sleeping Log and await the outcome."

The outcome was a foregone conclusion, Most of the Merchant Council's defensive forces were housed at the three locations targeted by the Court, and so were not able to be used. The few mercenaries who were stationed at the Council building fled at the approach of the Court members, which now included many of the underworld, and many of the populace. Red gold had been found at each of the three locations and in the homes of four of the larger merchants. That news had spread far and wide very quickly. Outrage drew many to join the march on the Merchant Council.

Kreban, he who had denied any aid to the Faero, was apprehended by part of the growing mob as he and his son tried to flee with pails of red gold. The crowd's outrage boiled over and both were hanged where they were found. The news spread through the city and the other members of the Merchant Council fled. The mob rampaged through the streets. Every one of the Merchant Councillors' houses and places of business were destroyed. The Court exerted its influence to control the mob before many innocents suffered, although there were the inevitable incidents. In the days to follow the Sergeant would lead a heavy crack down on those who looted innocents or committed various acts of violence.

The two Warriors were visited on the following day by the Sergeant and a very sore Gerhal Tag, accompanied by Belanis. While the healer, who had bags under both eyes to demonstrate her exhaustion, ministered to Jalor and Blaine, the Sergeant filled them in on the events of the previous day and night.

"So, we now have control of the city," the Sergeant concluded. "There is much to do, of course, and a lot of damage to repair from both last night and the decades of Merchant Council misrule, but we're up to the task."

Jalor nodded.

"That's a good outcome. I think Corm would be happy with that. By the way, who was that young man with the knives?"

"That is Lespis Kor," Gerhal Tag replied. "He seems to have a gift for battle but is proficient with knives the most."

"A gift?"

"Indeed, general. It seems we are seeing some of the old gifts return."

"As they are elsewhere," Jalor nodded. "I will mention him to Drewflin. He may have some ideas. Should Lespis Kor wish to join the Faero's army then tell him to ask for Blaine or me at the Citadel. There will be a place among the Blood."

"Thank you, general. We will tell him. And you will honour your pledges for the other members of the Court?" the Sergeant asked.

"We will. If you wish we can provide you with a written confirmation," Jalor said.

"I believe your word is sufficient for me, General," the Sergeant replied with a tired smile. "I admit, it would be something to join with the Faero and the Children. Even just to meet them. The wait for the Blood has been long and many have despaired. It would be good for the Children to know that we stand still."

Jalor smiled gently. "The Children are well aware of the sacrifices of the Blood. You need have no fear of that. I will make sure your actions are known."

"I thank you, General," the Sergeant replied. "If you will forgive me, I believe we will take our leave of you. Frankly, I'm exhausted and Gerhal Tag is yet to recover his strength."

"And I have done all I can for you," Belanis chimed in.

"As I said once before," Jalor said. "I believe it would be good for Belanis to meet with Drewflin. No matter what else happens. To his knowledge, he is the only one with the healing gift left on Ennaris."

"I will think on it, general," Belanis replied. "I would play my part when the time comes."

Jalor nodded. "We can speak more when you have rested. Blaine and I will spend a few more days here as we recover, if that is not too much of a burden."

"Indeed not, general. Where do you go after this?"

"Telsith," Jalor replied. "What sort of welcome will we receive there?"

"Uncertain," the Sergeant replied. "Telsith is much wealthier that Frelor but appears to have been on the verge of civil war for some time. Reports are that the Merchant Council there has been bleeding the city for many cycles and our information is that the situation is grim. You may find yourself in a dangerous situation."

"Wonderful," Blaine replied with an exaggerated sigh, having sat quietly and let Jalor carry the discussion. "I may stay here and let Jalor go alone."

"Well," Blaine said as they stood on the deck of a merchant sailing ship three days later watching Frelor diminish behind them. "That was interesting."

"Interesting," Jalor asked without looking at Blaine. "We've probably broken just about every rule in the Warrior handbook since we've been on Ennaris, most of them in the last tenday or so. And you call that interesting?"

"Those rules are written by people who sit in nice big towers and have no real idea of the world we face as Warriors, and especially of the worlds that we have to deal with." Blaine quirked his lips as he spoke.

"Even so, they have a point. We need to maintain our principles or we become what we're fighting," Jalor said quietly.

"I know," Blaine replied, "but at the same time we're after results. On this mission those lines are closer together than we've seen before. In fact, if Flin is right then it's the most important mission any Warrior has seen. The lines may well be redrawn."

"Maybe," Jalor replied, "but I doubt it. Our procedures were codified some three or four hundred years ago by a very clever general, as we were picking ourselves up after the first encounters with the Shadows. The rules of engagement were defined precisely to help us to make these decisions. The key is that, even if we feel the need to bend or break some of them, the underlying drivers remain intact and we need to keep that in mind."

"Well, at least we have Frelor on side, for now," Blaine mused. "Who knows what that may lead to? Next stop Telsith."

26. Goroth

The bonds held still.

Goroth had a moment of clarity, which was unusual. Something had changed. Here, in his prison, he knew. He remembered! He was Goroth, a Mage of great strength, who had been brought down by the only ones who could have challenged him successfully. His bonds held still, but they were not as strong as they had been.

He had no idea as to how much time had passed. It felt like it was only a short time since he had been imprisoned. He ran through the events that had seen him imprisoned in this odd stasis chamber, one that seemed to be comprised of pure energy. He felt the skeins of energy that held the chamber together. They throbbed. The power flowing through them gave Goroth pause. He would not have been able to create this chamber, and yet Marjory and Drewflin had done so. That was something to consider, for the two of them had survived the final battle along with a small number of other Mages. Goroth shuddered as realisation struck. If he had to face them again the same result would occur.

The solution? Don't face them both again. That was easier said than done, of course. He assumed that the Fleets would have been rebuilt, probably stronger than before. Goroth's supporters had been destroyed as the Fleets fought against each other, but to his knowledge most of the opposition was destroyed also. That would leave Marjory with a hard task, but he did not doubt that she was capable of rebuilding the defensive force, and populating it with those who would oppose Goroth. It was something else to consider.

The bonds resisted any attempt to touch them mentally, or even to find any gaps in the binding ribbons of power. And yet, he was aware. He even had a vague memory of contacting Grensor, although that may have been a hallucination. So be it. He would use the time available to plan, then. Did Grensor actually survive? Did Likud? He had no way to know. Assume one of them did, for they both had significant power. Likud had not stood with him at the end, which may have allowed him to escape. Perhaps he would be able to reach Likud via the links that they had established between themselves. Grensor, likewise, had not stood with him, but that was planned. Grensor was trying to rebuild the ghazrak army while Goroth and Likud held off the Council Mages. So, Grensor may have been able to survive also. He would see if that link remained also, when it was possible to do so.

Assume only one did. What did that mean? If it was Likud then they would need to build a suitable force to assault the non-gifted forces that would have been rebuilt, leaving Goroth and Likud to battle the Mages. Likud was a blunt instrument, however. He was vicious and single-minded, as lacking in imagination as he was lacking in scruples. He was not Goroth's choice of companion, but choices were lacking.

Using the dark gifts that Goroth and Grensor had stumbled upon it should be possible to subvert individuals or groups. By targeting the right individuals and groups they would be able to take control of a Fleet, perhaps more than one, and parts of the defensive forces. They had done so before and Goroth expected that he could do so again, even if Grensor had not survived.

What if Grensor did survive? Then there may be ghazrak. Goroth still may have to use his dark arts to subvert the Ennarisi forces, and Grensor would help him there, but a full army of ghazrak would turn many battles. He would use them, like he would use Likud if possible. He would make sure that he did not fail again. He was sure of his right-ness in fighting against the Council, no matter the cost. He, Goroth, alone had the vision to know how to make Ennaris the brightest light of the galaxy. None could stand against Ennaris. No other powers in the galaxy had been able to stand against Ennaris for ages past and those that tried had perished. It was the Council who lacked both imagination and a backbone so that any who wanted to propel Ennaris to its correct role in the galaxy were demonised, removed, restrained. Fools! Ennaris was the power. And it was right for Ennaris to take the clear lead over the emerging peoples of the galaxy.

Who would stop them? No-one, except the Council Mages. Marjory had spoken of the Guardians and their ethos of protecting emergent peoples, which was absurd. The Guardians did not exist, as everyone knew. Goroth knew that Drewflin had lost faith in the Guardians, if he ever had believed, no matter that he spoke of them in the same way as the rest of the Council fools. He would never gather Drewflin to his cause, though. Marjory would see to that even if Drewflin were susceptible to being influenced which, Goroth conceded to himself, he was not. So, they would have to be dealt with, somehow. Maybe he could take some of the lesser Mages or the young trainees away from the Council. Ah, he thought, of course the trainees had all been killed, so there would not be many young gifted, at least with sufficient strength. He gave a mental shrug. They would have supported the Council anyway, most of them so, in reality, all Likud did was remove opponents when he destroyed Resgalar and the other learning centres. Yes, many others died as well, but the cause was right. Goroth was not stupid enough to believe that innocents would not suffer when he launched his fight against the Council fools, but their deaths would help to bring a brighter future for Ennaris.

Now, what if both Likud and Grensor survived? That would take much more consideration. Far greater possibilities opened up for both ghazrak and whatever forces Likud could provide! For now Goroth had nowhere else to be so he could plan. How could that scenario play out?

27. Telsith

Telsith proved to be quite a different proposition to Frelor. Where the latter city based its commerce on its location as a strategic cross-road for the northern continent and the site of a deep-water port that allowed larger ships to arrive and depart at will, Telsith's wealth was derived from its near monopoly on fine cloths and woven goods.

Not only did Telsith have access to the finest thread produced by the fine fleeces of the sanbor, it also had access to deposits of ochres, plants and minerals that could be used for colouring the cloth that was made from the thread. Telsith's fine fibres attracted most of the best weavers who, over time, developed a distinctive style. In turn, they attracted many of the best cloth dyers who developed distinctive colours and patterns. They, also in turn, attracted the better clothing designers and makers. Over more time, the various skills were subject to consolidation which meant that, where there had been many independent weavers, dyers, designers and clothing makers, now there were a handful of vertically integrated producers. Usually, these were centred on the owners of the flocks from which the finest fleeces were drawn.

However, starting around five hundred cycles before the Warriors' arrival it was discovered, or re-discovered, that a specific type of grub, the selth worm, that lived in a specific type of shrub and ate very specific leaves, spun a thread so impossibly fine as to beggar belief. Thus, a new industry was born to sit alongside the sanbor wool, with even higher margins for the producers.

The owners of the flocks and the owners of the grub-laced groves became the employers of the other skills and grew very rich on the proceeds. Dockyards grew larger at the port and huge warehouses were built to service the growing trade in fine cloths and weaves. With greater trade came greater wealth and the problems that greater wealth caused.

Here, however, Telsith also diverged from its relatively near neighbour Frelor. Perhaps the divergence was caused by observations of the state of Frelor, or perhaps the cloth merchants were merely of a different mindset. In any case, rather than striving mightily to gather the riches of Telsith to themselves, the cloth merchants shared what was generally agreed to be a reasonable share of the wealth generated. The city thrived with a largely content citizen body. Crime was present, of course, but was not a significant problem, for Telsith's Council also spent its tax money wisely on the largest and best armed defensive force of the Free Cities of Algol, the better to discourage any jealous neighbours, as well as an efficient and well-funded city guard. Telsith, therefore, appeared to be the most stable of the three trade hubs. Appearances were deceptive, however.

Jalor had hopes that Telsith would contribute a significant part of its defence force to Corm's army. The Sergeant of the Court of Frelor told him that Telsith was wealthy and had been ruled wisely and so was optimistic that some resources could be provided, but she warned repeatedly that there were rumoured to be rumblings of discontent among some of the influential citizens of the city, and mutterings about civil war. She had no details and Gerhal Tag added that the Blood had no resources of note in the city beyond a couple of low-level watchers whose reports about the veracity of those rumours were uncertain. Still, contact names and locations were provided, as were names of trusted allies of the Blood.

Jalor and Blaine disembarked after a quiet and uneventful three-day journey sailing along the northern coast of the great body of water that separated the northern and southern continents. The sailors expected nothing less. There had been no piracy in the region for generations, for Telsith also maintained a maritime defence squadron that took its responsibilities seriously. The two Warriors spent their time discussing tactics and reviewing the current position. When the time for disembarkation came their plan was put into action immediately.

The Warp Inn was their destination. The innkeeper was a friend to the Blood, although not of the Blood himself, and he was trusted and well-regarded. Gerhal Tag had sent a fast runner to reserve a suite for them, with instructions to play up their reputations as the Heroes of the Citadel and the Battle for Frelor. The suite was reserved for General Jalor of the Faero's Army while Blaine was given the rank of Captain, much to his chagrin and Jalor's amusement. They also were identified as the personal representative of the Faero and the most skilled warrior on Ennaris, respectively, which Gerhal Tag warned may make them targets as much as it gave them prestige of sorts. Gerhal Tag made sure that their names and recent exploits were described in the Telsith taverns and wherever crowds gathered to gossip, so there would be no anonymity for them in Telsith.

They arrived at the Warp Inn in a hrss-drawn carriage hired at the docks. Jalor wore his deep red uniform from Frelor, while Blaine wore his usual nondescript garb. Jalor's sword hung from his belt and elicited little comment. Blaine's newly obtained greatsword - he had decided the one purloined from the Frelor Council guards was better than the other - was strapped to his back and was of much greater interest. A small crowd awaited them at the inn, comprising a representative of the Council, several representatives of the city guard and a number of servants of various merchant houses.

Their arrival coincided with preparations for an annual city festival that celebrated the discovery of the selth worm, and the inn was a riot of activity. Bunting was hung from light posts and balconies. Large trestle tables were being put together in several of the main city squares, and fire pits were being prepared for the spits that would roast the different meats that would be offered. Their carriage even had to wait for a small train of ale barrels that were being moved across their path. The inn was no different. They arrived to step onto freshly scrubbed paving stones in the inn's entrance courtyard. A mix of bunting and festive wreaths were being hung from several vantage points around the large building.

Their light-weight baggage was spirited away by a servant from the inn, as they were welcomed by a stout woman wearing a bright floral apron over a more sombre-hued dress. As Jalor and Blaine entered the inn, they were trailed by a group of men who, Jalor realised, had been waiting for their arrival. Perhaps Gerhal Tag's tactics had worked.

There was little fuss made over the Warriors, although the welcome provided was genuinely warm and respectful. The woman introduced herself as Elstha and informed them that she was the sworn companion of the innkeeper, Janthil. The Warriors were shown to a spacious room with one large bed and a small table with four chairs spaced around it. A wash-basin and jug stood on a shelf beneath an open window. The noises of the large square on which the inn was placed drifted into the room to form a background hum with, occasionally, louder shouts or laughs.

"Is all to your liking, good sirs?" Elstha asked as Jalor and Blaine dropped their packs against a wall.

"It is," Jalor assured her. "In fact, this is more than we expected."

"This is the best room we have," she replied. "It would not do for the Faero's representatives to be poorly roomed."

"Ah, you have our thanks nonetheless," Jalor said with a smile. "I understand there is a festival taking place?"

"'Tis the Selth Festival," Elstha nodded. "This year marks five hundred and twelve cycles since the selth was rediscovered." She gave a conspiratorial smile before continuing. "Telsith makes great profit from the selth. Some have more reason to celebrate than others, but 'tis also the chance for everyone to eat and drink too much, make a fool of themselves and get ready for the main harvest. 'Tis harmless fun and no-one gets hurt beyond a few fist fights and sore heads."

Elstha bustled around the room making sure all was perfect and that her guests were settled.

"Should I send up the first of your guests?" Elstha asked when she was satisfied.

"Certainly," Jalor replied. "Who would you recommend to take priority over the others?"

"I would suggest Junstil, who represents the Council, followed by the Guard and then the merchants in whatever order they work out between themselves." She gave a twist of her lips. "The Guard carries almost as much authority as the Council these days, so they should be treated accordingly. The merchants probably want to be seen to associate with the Faero's people."

"You don't like the Guard having that level of authority?" Blaine asked, sensing an undercurrent of unease in their hostess.

"The Guard has grown in authority since Krevil took charge. That was two cycles ago. He put his own people into positions of authority and shut out those who had been there. There are some in the Guard who think themselves above the people of Telsith." She smiled to take the sting out of her comments. "But that is a small number. The Telsith Guard remains one of Algol's jewels and has kept us safe and free for many cycles."

She took her leave and Jalor and Blaine shared a wry smile.

"Politics raises its head everywhere," Jalor commented, to which Blaine merely nodded.

Junstil proved to be a tall, lean individual, with a perpetually mournful expression. His long face was seamed and weathered almost grey and his grey hair was hung in a simple tail, extending about half way down his back. He was dressed in clothes of sober hues, greys mostly. The contrast to the colourful clothes exhibited by people in the street was marked. Where Junstil would not stand out at the Citadel or in Frelor, in Telsith he did.

"I bring greetings from the Council of Telsith," Junstil intoned in a flat, funereal drone. "Alas, the Council members are unable to offer greetings themselves as they all are preparing for their roles in tonight's celebrations. However, I am bid to invite you to the Premptor's gathering after the formalities are complete. Premptor Heristis would like to understand the reason for your visit to Telsith ahead of greeting you formally with the full Council."

"Please offer our thanks to Premptor Heristis, and inform him that we would be honoured to accept his invitation," Jalor replied. "What duties do the Council members undertake during the festivities?"

"Oh, they are ceremonial responsibilities in the main," Junstil explained in his mournful voice. "Premptor Heristis will initiate the selth ceremony at his orchard and then he will lead the procession to the main square where the feast will be held. Other Council members will perform similar rites in different parts of Telsith and then join the procession before branching off to their own feasting locations." He gave a wintry smile. "It is very impressive," he said tonelessly, "and quite exciting."

"We will look forward to observing the ceremony," Jalor said with a smile.

"I will have one of the Council officials meet you here at dusk. She will escort you to the Premptor's orchard. I hope you enjoy the festivities and wish you farewell for now."

Junstil gave a small bow that was made more solemn by his unchanged expression and took his leave. Within moments he was replaced by four members of the Telsith Guard. Three of the men, who Blaine thought of as squaddies, wore the same deep blue breeches and shirt with thick boiled leather armour plates covering shoulders, chest and back. The chest plates had a simple device of a bare tree etched on them and were died a pale blue. Helmets were of deep-blue-coloured leather that almost matched the clothes, and each sported a tuft of bright red plumage from the top. Short swords and knives were hung from belts of the same deep-blue-coloured leather. Tough, unpolished leather boots rounded off the outfits. Each of the men looked experienced and competent.

The fourth Guard member wore a blue shirt and breeches of finer weave than the three squaddies. His chest and back armour were made of gleaming metal, shaped to have wider shoulders but then narrow to the waist. On each shoulder was an epaulette denoting a rank that neither of the Warriors recognised, although they had received a briefing on the ranks of the Telsith military. His helmet was a plain metal skull cap with what looked like a bronze ridge piece riveted to run from front to back. His sword and knife pommels were decorated with square cut, coloured stones that struck a memory chord for Blaine, but he could not place it. The fine leather boots were polished to a gleam.

The four men came to attention and saluted Jalor, fists striking chest with audible thumps. Jalor returned the gesture with a Warrior salute, his right hand held flat and raised to almost touch his forehead. The Telsith Guardsmen relaxed into a similar parade stance. Blaine stood at parade rest behind and to the left of Jalor, holding back a grin as the four Guardsmen glanced to his greatsword, belt sword, belt knife and the hilts of other knives that poked above the belt line from behind.

"General, I have the great honour to welcome you to Telsith on behalf of Guard Commander Krevil. I am Machim Junil," he said with a slight bow. "Guard Commander Krevil apologises for not being here to greet you himself but he is preparing for tonight's event. He did order me to offer his hospitality for this evening, however."

"Thank you Machim Junil," Jalor replied, unsure if the name included a title or just first and last name. "I understand that the leadership of Telsith all have parts to play in the evening's festivities, and so look forward to meeting with Guard Commander Krevil tomorrow. However, we have already accepted Premptor Heristis' invitation for tonight and so must decline the Guard Commander's generous offer with regret."

Junil's face tightened at the reply. Blaine was sure he saw at least one of the Guardsmen smother an involuntary smile.

"But Guard Commander Krevil's estate will be the safest place in Telsith for you. He does not wish any harm to come to the Faero's delegation."

Jalor was surprised, for Elstha had said that there was no danger beyond high spirits and excess revelry.

"What harm does the Guard Commander expect?" Jalor asked. "I am given to understand that there is little danger during the selth festival."

"There have been threats to the stability of Telsith," Junil replied. "The Guard will be on high alert tonight and it would not do for the Faero's general to be endangered."

"Ah, I see," Jalor said. "However, our mission here requires that we meet with the Council leadership, and we have accepted the Premptor's invitation already. I believe we should be safe at his orchard. Please convey my thanks to the Guard Commander for his kind thought."

"The Council will not..." Junil started to speak and then thought better of it, stopping abruptly. "I will so inform Guard Commander Krevil," he said.

Junil gave a peremptory bow, turned and stalked from the room, followed by the three squaddies.

"There's something odd happening here," Blaine said when he was sure Junil had departed. "I expect that Junil is one of those who Krevil imported, but I think his rank may be quite junior. And did you see his sword and knife? I'm sure I've seen those sorts of stones before but I can't remember when. I'm sure it's significant, though."

"Well, let me know when you remember," Jalor replied. "The other three didn't seem all that upset that we declined Krevil's invitation. And I'm sure that Elstha would have said something if she thought there was real danger during the festival. Yes, I do believe something is happening. Question is, what?"

Their discussion was cut short by the first of the merchants' servants. A series of invitations to the merchants' homes were received for the evening, all of which Jalor declined while suggesting that he would be happy to meet them once he had met with the Council. The servants departed with a variety of expressions ranging from mildly unhappy to neutral. None of them suggested that Jalor and Blaine were in any danger at attending the Premptor's function, merely regret that they would not be able to meet with their mistresses and masters early in the festivities.

The afternoon had worn away with the number of meetings that they had stood or sat through, so they repaired to the inn's taproom to try the ale ahead of preparing to meet the Premptor's representative and discuss the confusing situation that they appeared to have walked into.

"Good evening, good sirs," the young woman said once Blaine had opened the door of their room. "I am to escort you to the Premptor's orchard farm for the festival opening. My name is Lilli."

"We're ready to go, I think," Blaine replied. "I'm Blaine and that one over there taking his time is Jalor."

"Er, Captain Blaine and General Jalor?" Lilli asked hesitantly.

"Yes, that's us," Blaine responded with a sigh.

"Don't worry, you'll get used to it, captain," Jalor said with a hearty clap on Blaine's shoulder as he walked past. "Lilli, lead the way. I trust we are dressed appropriately. I'm afraid we travel with a limited wardrobe."

"Well, your military uniforms will stand out," Lilli said, glancing to Jalor as they headed down the single flight of stairs. "And I don't believe you will have any need of your weapons. The Guard makes sure there's no trouble during the festival and most people prefer to wear their festival clothes without weapons. It destroys the effect, you know."

"Ah, yes," Jalor replied, nodding. "However, as our military outfits are all we have the lack of weapons would look just as odd."

"Um, I guess so," Lilli said as they exited the main door of the inn. "We have the carriage for the short journey to the Premptor's estate. It will be far more comfortable than walking."

"So are citizens usually averse to wearing weapons in Telsith?" Blaine asked once the carriage was moving. "In the Citadel, and certainly in Frelor, most people wear swords and knives as a matter of course."

"Here, also, we carry defensive weapons, although with relatively little need compared to Frelor," Lilli said carefully. "However, during the festival very few do. It's a chance for the usual working garb to be replaced by the finery made possible by the selth and our designers, weavers, tailors and dressmakers. Almost everyone enters into the spirit of the festival."

"So only the Guard will be armed," Blaine said with a glance to Jalor. "In fact, we were also invited to observe the festival with Guard Commander Krevil. I assume that he has a similar responsibility during the festival to the members of the Council?"

"Oh no," Lilli replied with a shake of her head. "The Guard Commander usually attends the Premptor's ceremony. I'm sure there was a mistake. Who made the invitation?"

"Machim Junil. He seemed to feel there may be some danger involved with the festival."

"Oh, he may not be all that familiar with the festival," Lilli said with an easy smile. "Machim Junil and several other officers and their men only arrived in Telsith within the last cycle, so they have very little experience with Telsith traditions. Where they are from it may be different during festivals."

"Where are they from?"

"I'm not sure, really," Lilli replied, with a tilt of her head to indicate that she was considering. "Somewhere in the north, I believe. He once mentioned that he had skirted the grasslands to get here. And here we are," Lilli continued, dropping the thought and gesturing to her right. "This is the Premptor's estate. It has been in his family for many generations and is one of the older selth orchards in Telsith."

The estate was extensive. A long, low building of old, weathered stone, sporting red brick walls and a dark tiled roof, formed three sides of a u-shaped box, open at the front. Lanterns burned as the day's light diminished rapidly and Jalor fancied that he could see them take over lighting duties as he watched. A sparse garden of low shrubs extended across the opening of the U, with spaces to each side allowing for vehicles to enter and leave. The space inside the U was extensive, demonstrating how large the building was. The space was largely clear, with the exception of a small wooden platform that was flanked by flaming braziers.

Blaine had gone quiet. Jalor glanced at him to see a frown form. Blaine was, he knew, working through something. Jalor shrugged to himself as he climbed from the carriage. Blaine would let him know when he had it worked out.

"The Premptor will be available for a short time before the opening ceremony," Lilli said to Jalor. "I will take you to him and then to your viewing location."

The Premptor was a middle-aged man of middle height but with broad shoulders and a well-developed paunch. His hair was thinning and part way on its journey from dark brown to grey. Still, a slender tail draped a short distance down his back tied with a colourful ribbon. An ankle and wrist length robe carried a swirling pattern of bright reds, blues, greens and yellows of varying shades on a white background with the hems being jet black and laced with a shiny thread that glittered in the bright lantern lights. Sturdy boots of jet black peeped out from beneath the robe's lower hem.

"Premptor Heristis, may I introduce General Jalor and Captain Blaine?" Lilli said as the trio approached him.

"General, Captain," Heristis said jovially, giving a small bow that Jalor and Blaine returned. "Welcome to Telsith. I apologise for not being there to greet you, but you come on an important day for our city and I needed to prepare. Please be assured that we will discuss your mission, of which I have been apprised, once the festival opening is complete. The festival runs for three days, so we will have ample time."

"Thank you, Premptor," Jalor replied. "We're looking forward to seeing your opening ceremony and joining with your people in the festivities. I asked this of Lilli, but are we, er, under-dressed for the occasion?"

Jalor gestured to the brightly coloured robe that Heristis wore.

"Ah, this?" Heristis waved a hand to indicate his clothing. "This is the chance for the people of Telsith to celebrate the wealth brought by the selth and our other textiles. For those of us who produce the thread it's also an opportunity to demonstrate what can be achieved. Thus, you will see all manner of designs and hues on display. I, as you can see, tend to be more conservative than most."

Jalor nodded as he eyed the riot of colours in front of him.

"I look forward to seeing what the less conservative of your number have on display, Premptor."

"Indeed," Heristis replied with a wry smile. "Now, I must ask you to take your place in the viewing area and we will make a start."

28. Defence of Telsith

The ceremony was quick and to the point. There were no invocations of guiding spirits, although there were votes of thanks given to the Guardians, described in somewhat vague terms as god-like beings of tradition, for the bounty upon which the wealth of Telsith was based. Most of the ceremony, however, was devoted to reciting the history of the breeding of the sanbor to produce ever finer threads and then the discovery of the selth, which had been thought of as a pest and now was anything but. The ceremony was conducted in good spirits, with jokes and laughter at points in the story where certain historical individuals were held up to ridicule or humorous events were described. The stories and events described were well-known, obviously, to all except the two Warriors, and the mood of the crowd was light-hearted as most joined into the spirit of the ceremony.

Premptor Heristis departed the platform and made his slow way toward Jalor and Blaine. His path was diverted often to exchange greetings with various people, or to accept thanks for the ceremonial opening and, at one stage, to rescue a toddler who was about to slip from her perch on a garden wall.

"Well, that's the first part done," Heristis said as he reached Jalor and Blaine. "We'll allow people to have a drink or two and then we'll have the procession to Red Square. That's the main square of Telsith. Other members of the Council will have their own opening ceremonies and then join us there."

"I was under the impression that Guard Commander Krevil would be here," Jalor said.

"Oh, well, he's only been to one of these before, so maybe he attended a different Council member's opening," Heristis replied with a shrug. "It matters little which he attends, although it's usual for the Guard Commander to attend the Premptor's one."

"The Telsith Guard is well respected in the region," Jalor said as he accepted a mug of ale. "That is why we were asked to come here by the Faero. The Telsith Guard's reputation is widespread."

"Indeed," Heristis said expansively. "The Guard is the most effective deterrent force for a large area around. The free cities of Algol remain free largely because of the Telsith Guard, or did in the past, at any rate. We've always had good Commanders and the troops have always been the best trained. Telsith also is wealthy enough to ensure that they are armed well. As a result, we have few bandits in the area, and those who try to set up in the area are dealt with quickly. There are no pirates in the region either. Between Frelor and us we hold the New Sea open."

"New Sea?"

"You probably know it as the Bitter Sea," Heristis smiled. "For us we call it as our forebears did, even though it's thousands of cycles since the sea broke through what was the coastal barrier. We'll discuss how Telsith can assist the Faero in the coming days. We were informed recently that the Prophecy of Halfgar is upon us. Where the merchants in Frelor will bicker and do nothing, Telsith remembers our responsibility."

"Frelor has had a change of heart," Jalor said with a smile, "along with a change of government. I think you may see some changes in that city in coming cycles. But one thing you must understand is that there have been concerted efforts to undermine governments across the northern continent. Even at the Citadel. We found the Merchant Council of Frelor was taking payment from the northern kingdoms, probably to obstruct the Faero's efforts, and the Chancellor of the Citadel was compromised likewise."

"Jalor!" Blaine interrupted urgently. "Junil's sword. It's a norther sword. That's where I remember seeing similar decorations. The northers who Creely had imported. Most of them had similar stones in the pommels of their swords."

"Are you sure?" Jalor replied, swinging to stare at Blaine.

"Yes. I only had a glimpse of them, as we were getting through the gate to defend Intika, but I'm sure. That means ..."

"That the northern kingdoms have infiltrated Telsith, and the festival is the ideal time to take over," Jalor finished, turning to Heristis, who was watching the exchange with concern etched on his face. "Premptor, where did Krevil come from? We know Junil at least is from somewhere north, and probably others of his group."

"Why, I'm not sure. He was recommended by two of the newer members of the Council..." Heristis' voice trailed off. "Oh, by the Guardians! They could only get onto the Council because they had been able to purchase two of the estates. Council members must be significant landowners. They suddenly had the funds to do so." His face was ashen. "You think they may have..."

"I think they may have brought the enemy into your camp," Jalor replied tightly.

He was interrupted by shouts from the road. He gave a glance to Blaine and the latter set off at a jog to see what was happening.

"Do you have any of the Guard here?" Jalor asked.

"Yes, a troop always is with the Premptor for any ceremony. But they are in ceremonial dress."

"Do they have their weapons?"

"I believe so," Heristis replied hesitantly. "You would have to ask Troop Leader Neril to be sure."

Blaine returned at a jog. His short sword was in his hand, causing Heristis to gasp.

"It's Junil and a number of others. The Guards are holding off a larger force," he reported to Jalor. "But the Guards don't have their full protective clothing, so they will have to fall back. They need somewhere to stand."

"Premptor, do you have a defensible location?" Jalor asked, looking around at the ceremony's guests who had started to gather together. "We need to get these people to safety."

"There's a stone barn," Heristis said, pointing. "Over there. But, why..."

"Okay, let's get everyone who can't fight into the barn," Jalor interrupted the Premptor. "That includes you. This attack will be aimed at you. I expect there are similar attacks on other Council members. Hope that some of them survive."

Heristis shook himself out of his shock.

"Lilli," he called, waiting while the young woman trotted over. "Start getting everyone to the barn. Have Bensivel open the arms cupboard."

Lilli trotted away and started to cajole the now frightened guests to move in the direction of the barn. Shouting and clashes of arms could be heard, growing closer. Heristis looked around but seemed to be frozen, indecisive once again. Blaine glanced to Jalor and gestured with his head in the direction of the barn. Jalor nodded and grabbed Heristis' arm.

"Premptor, let's get you into the barn, too. You can do no good here and will only risk getting caught. Blaine will be a rear guard for us to get you and your people safe."

Thankfully, Heristis allowed himself to be guided after the others. He and Jalor reached the tail end of the group who Lilli was leading away and Jalor started to urge them on, too. He got their attention when he drew his own sword, after which they moved faster, several running the last few paces to reach the barn. It was made entirely of a smooth, almost polished stone, with stout wooden doors through which the now panicked people were guided. Jalor glanced inside and saw a small door at the far end. The inside of the barn was divided into hrss stalls that stretched down one wall and a variety of farm implements in a neat row down the opposite wall. The rest was open and was where the people were milling. A mezzanine level made from wood planks extended over the space where the implements were, but stopped short of the stalls. Jalor looked up and was relieved to see a tile roof. That would make it harder for them to burn the barn. Usually, he would have counselled against ushering all non-combatants into a potential trap but, in this case, it seemed to be the only way to protect them.

Heristis stopped in the centre of the barn. His gaze swept around the interior once, twice, a third time. Evidently, the Premptor was faced with a situation that he had not faced before, and he was lost. Lilli took charge of the refugees, settling them in groups around the centre of the barn. Jalor saw that a young man was struggling to open a timber closet and made his way to him.

"Bensivel?" Jalor asked.

"Aye ser," the young man replied distractedly.

"Is this the weapons cabinet?"

"Aye ser," Bensivel replied again, as he tried and failed to wrench the door open.

"Let me," Jalor said, reaching to the top and releasing a stout latch that was holding the door closed.

Bensivel looked abashed but Jalor just smiled and drew the door open. Inside was an assortment of weapons, most very old and in poor repair. However, Jalor did find two bows and a mouldy quiver of arrows. He drew them out and handed them to Bensivel.

"Take these to Captain Blaine outside the main doors," Jalor ordered. "Tell him General Jalor felt one of these may be of use."

"G - General?" Bensivel squeaked, eyes wide.

"Yes," Jalor replied evenly. "To Captain Blaine at the main doors. Go. And then shut the doors."

He gave Bensivel a gentle shove to start him off and then turned back to the weapons. Several short swords that had not seen a sharp edge for many a day could still cause some trouble, if necessary, while there were three pikes in similar condition. The hilts of the swords and the poles of the pikes were serviceable still, but the blades needed work. Jalor poked around for a while longer and, with a satisfied snort, pulled from a small bucket a well-used whetstone.

"Lilli," Jalor called, "is there a metalworker here?"

"I know my way around most things metal, sir," an old grey-haired man called out from the closest group of refugees. "Used to be a bit of a handyman around here."

"Do you know how to sharpen these blades?"

"I do, sir," was the reply.

"Good, then you're the weapons master. I need these swords and pikes sharpened as far as you can until they're needed," Jalor instructed the old man. "Quick is better than perfect."

"Understood, sir. I'll see if there are any more sharpening stones and get some of the others onto them, too."

"Good man," Jalor said, nodding his approval. "Get started."

Jalor turned to see Bensivel returning at a trot, carrying one of the bows and a handful of shafts.

"The Captain said this one will shoot left and low," he told Jalor. "And these arrers may not be straight. And he said to tell you that the one he kept may not last long and the string is old."

"Alright, then," Jalor nodded, knowing that Blaine would at least have some stand-off defensive capability. "Who here knows how to shoot a bow?"

Jalor's question was met with mute looks. That was not unexpected. He turned to watch the main door, which was when he realised that Bensivel had his hand in the air beside him.

"Bensivel, you do?"

"Aye ser," Bensivel nodded hesitantly. "But I never shot arrers at anyone. It were just sport."

"Good enough. You're the rear guard. I want you about ten paces from the rear door. Put whatever you can against it, wedge it shut, whatever you need to do. But if it gets opened then you shout and fire as many arrows as you can. Aim at their heads and a little to the right. If Captain Blaine is right then you'll do okay."

Bensivel gave an audible gulp, but nodded and gripped the bow with a shaky hand.

"Don't think too much about it," Jalor said. "Get someone to help you to block that door and then if you have to just do the best you can do. The main thing is to shout if anyone comes through. Okay?"

Bensivel nodded, unconvinced, but he turned away from Jalor and tapped another young man on the arm. The two of them headed for the rear door. Jalor watched them for a moment, shrugged to himself, and then turned his attention back to the centre of the barn.

Blaine stood easily in front of the barn. He had heard the barn doors being latched shut, followed by what he imagined was a hefty wooden beam being dropped in place to resist attempts to force the doors open. This, he thought, was unlikely to end well. Already he knew that the meagre guard detachment would have been overwhelmed by the infiltrators, who he assumed were from the northern twin kingdoms. With luck, one or two of them would make their way to the barn and join the defence there. If not, then it was him and Jalor, and whatever could be found in the barn. The bow he held was long past its best, but could do for a few shots. He had no idea how many soldiers were attacking, nor the direction from which they would attack, nor even if the barn had a rear entrance. He trusted Jalor to do something about that if it did, but it was frustrating.

He could hear the sounds of fighting coming closer. So, some of the guard remained alive and engaged. That was good. The fighting had provided a background noise for the short time that they had taken to round up the revellers and retreat to the barn. The screams and shouts, intersperse with clashes of metal weapons - he hoped only swords and knives - were clearer now, and he could orient better. They were coming from the direction of the courtyard where the ceremony had taken place, which indicated that the attackers knew the layout. One advantage to them.

From that direction came two men, dressed in the uniform of the city guard, staggering as they ran. Were these real guards or infiltrators? Blaine nocked an arrow and waited. As the two men came closer and into the fitful light given out by the torches that lit the barn entrance,

Blaine recognised both from the honour guard. Both sported bloody wounds but both held their swords in hand. They spied Blaine and straightened slightly as they approached.

"Hold," Blaine called, low but clear, lifting the bow.

The two men staggered to a stop, seeming to be nonplussed at being challenged. Both lifted their swords but stayed outside sword strike range.

"Captain Blaine?" one of the men ventured, blowing hard between words.

"I am Blaine," came the reply. "And you are?"

"Guardsman Kensy and Guardsman Pren."

"Why are you here?" Blaine asked.

"The Troop Leader sent us to act as final guard for the barn," Kensy panted. "He said this would be where the Premptor would retreat to."

"Where is the Troop Leader?"

"He stayed with the other three to give us time," Kensy said, getting his wind back.

"I see," Blaine nodded, lowering the bow, knowing the Troop Leader and three guardsmen would give their lives. "Come forward and take a position with me. How many are we facing?"

"There are twelve that I could count," Kensy replied as he and Pren separated to flank Blaine. "There were fifteen when they started."

"How many have you lost?"

"Eight so far," Kensy said bitterly. "They surprised us, they did. It was only because we were spread out that they didn't get more. That and the Troop Leader. He knew somethin' was up and gave us warnin'. I think Junil gave himself away somehow. Do you know what's goin' on?"

"The northern kingdoms have infiltrated the guard. This is an attempt to take over Telsith and deny the Faero the use of the guard," Blaine explained. "Junil is leading them, you say? He doesn't strike me as a very good leader, so we may have a chance. What weapons?"

"They all have swords but also at least one pike that I saw," Pren said, entering the conversation for the first time. He was winding a kerchief around his upper arm, trying to stop the flow of blood from a shallow slice. "They seem to know what they're doing. Junil gave us some time by wanting to talk, show how clever he was at taking us by surprise. That let the sergeant set up a bit."

Blaine nodded. There were no battle noises now, so he guessed the sergeant and his men had fallen. The two guardsmen glanced to each other, faces tight. Both turned to face the way they had come.

"I expect they'll be here soon," Blaine said calmly. "I'll see how well this old bow goes and then we'll engage them. I want you to give me room when we do."

The two guardsmen looked at him quizzically. Blaine reached back to lay a hand on his greatsword and the two realised what he meant. Neither wanted to be in the way when Blaine started to lay that thing around. Both nodded.

A few moments later the first of the attackers made his way up the broad path, followed by two others in a short skirmish line. Blaine lifted the bow, drew and fired. The first of the attackers spun and dropped, but Blaine knew he had not killed him. Still, he would be out of action for a while, if not for good. Meanwhile he fired a second arrow, allowing for the slight right drift that the first had taken. The arrows were not as straight as he would want but he had chosen the best of what Jalor had sent, and they would do. He scored on the second man, who stopped and then dropped to form a motionless mound, but the third turned and called something Before Blaine's third arrow took him through the back. That, however, would be the last shot, for the string broke as Blaine drew it for a fourth shot. He threw the bow behind himself in disgust and waited.

Into the pale light came the rest of the attacking force. There were eight, including Junil at their head. Several limped or had an arm hanging, but all carried swords in hand except one, who carried a long pike.

"So, Captain Blaine, we meet again," Junil called mockingly. "I had hoped to find you here. It will be my pleasure to rid Ennaris of your presence."

Blaine remained still, watching and appraising the eight who faced him and the two guardsmen. His opinion of Junil was low, but the seven men who accompanied him held their weapons like veterans, and Blaine did not discount them at all. He could not see what the quality of their weapons was like in the poor light, but he did not assume that they were as poor as the ghazrak weapons.

"Ready," Blaine muttered so only Kensy and Pren could hear him. "I'll take the pike."

"Nothing to say?" he gloated. "Too bad. I would have liked to repeat your last words to the Old One."

Junil gestured and his seven men moved forward. Blaine reached back and smoothly drew his greatsword, holding it by the large hilt with one hand in a demonstration of sheer strength.

"Stay back a step," Blaine said to the two guardsmen, and then advanced at an angle to put the pike wielder in the centre.

The guardsmen stayed with him as he moved, staying a pace back and offset to left and right at a distance they hoped was beyond the reach of the greatsword. The action left the barn door exposed but Blaine had to deal with the pike quickly. In any event, the door would not be breached quickly enough while the fight was in train.

The pikeman now found himself in the centre of the attack. He held the pike firmly. It had a large stabbing head, with a curved spike extending below it which could be used against hrss-mounted opponents or as a means to turn aside stabbing weapons used against its wielder. Blaine stepped toward the pikeman, now gripping the greatsword in two hands. The pikeman stabbed the pike forward and Blaine feigned a retreat. The pikeman grinned as he strode forward and stabbed again, and was still grinning as Blaine spun left, crashed his greatsword through the pike's shaft almost half way down its length before leaping forward and slashing the huge sword horizontally, slicing through the pikeman's throat. But Blaine did not stop there. He allowed the momentum of the sword to continue so that he cut through the right arm of the infiltrator next to the pikeman. Blaine continued the turn caused by the sword's momentum and pirouetted with the greatsword whistling as it cut through the air to slash through the waist of the next in line.

Kensy and Pren took their chances as the northers gaped at the carnage Blaine had caused. Two of the men at the left end of the line were injured, so the two guardsmen glanced once to each other and charged at that end. Junil shouted in alarm and the other two infiltrators leapt to intervene. Kensy and Pren now found themselves facing four and started to back track. They concentrated on the two who were uninjured while trying to avoid giving the injured ones an opening.

Junil, meanwhile, had become Blaine's target, which fact he almost realised too late. Turning from watching his remaining four men engage the two guardsmen, Junil started when he realised that Blaine was advancing on him, with the greatsword gripped in both hands. Blood dripped from the enormous blade. Blaine was watching Junil coldly, with implacable intent. Desperately, Junil raised his sword but Blaine swatted it aside without effort and drove the point of the sword through Junil's mid-section. The decorative metal armour gave little protection, such was the force with which Blaine delivered the thrust. The Warrior withdrew the blade and left Junil tottering. He had turned away to assist the two guardsmen before Junil fell.

Pren was hard pressed. He was a competent swordsman, as were all of the Telsith guard, but he was weary and already injured. He held his own while the two northers managed to get in each other's way in their zeal to be the ones to kill him, but when they finally separated Pren knew his time was done. He turned to one and then the other, finally deciding he may as well take down at least one of them and chose the already injured one. He took two quick steps to the side in an attempt to give himself time and managed to come at his target from his injured side. Pren took advantage and swung his sword wide to make the norther defend his uninjured side before halting the stroke and slashing the injured side. His sword bit deep and stuck, lodged amid muscle, bone and leather armour. Pren tugged once and gave up. He started to turn back, empty handed, when he heard the whistle of a sword through the air. He tensed but, rather than feeling the sword strike some part of his body he heard the unmistakable crunch of Blaine's greatsword as it stove in the side of the norther.

Pren looked to be sure and sighed deeply before recalling Kensy. He tried to release his sword again but failed. Once again, he heard Blaine's sword deal death but turned in time to see Kensy fall with the last norther's blade thrust through his side before Blaine dealt a final strike, almost decapitating the remaining norther. Pren rushed to Kensy, kneeling by his side but knew immediately that his comrade, the last of his troop but himself, was dead.

Blaine leaned on his huge sword, breathing deeply. He was spattered with blood and gore and had acquired some minor cuts and nicks, but was unharmed otherwise. Pren knelt back from Kensy's body utterly spent. He hung his head.

"I'm sorry I could not save your friend," Blaine said quietly after a time while both caught their breath.

Pren looked up at Blaine and shook his head.

"You did more than we could have done, Captain," Pren replied. "Without you there would have been no way to save the Premptor from those men."

Blaine nodded.

"That's true, but I still am sorry."

He walked over to Junil's body, wiping both sides of the blade of his greatsword on a finely crafted sleeve. Then he reversed the sword and thrust it into the scabbard strapped to his back. Finally, he gripped Junil by his legs and dragged the body to one side. Dropping the legs, he turned back to where Pren still knelt beside Kensy's body. Several trips later Blaine had piled the norther attackers into an untidy heap.

"Come," he told Pren. "We need to let the others know it's over."

Jalor was waiting, standing in the centre of the barn near the main doors. He had listened intently to the sounds of battle but had no idea what had occurred. He turned to look at the gathered crowd of revellers, most of whom stared at him bleakly. Several were weeping quietly. His gaze travelled to the rear door, the front of which had been piled high with an assortment of tools, some buckets that Bensivel had found and odds and ends from the stalls. Bensivel stood with an arrow nocked, nervously stretching and untensioning the bow string. The second young man now held one of the old swords, which had been sharpened as much as could be done in the short time allowed the newly minted weapons master. It was obvious to Jalor that he had no training in its use at all. Several other men carried other swords. The steady *swip, swip* of a sharpening stone on metal told Jalor that the old handyman was staying to his task.

But what had happened to Blaine?

A thudding sounded on the large barn door. Several people jumped and one man dropped his sword, while small moans and squeals could be heard. The thudding restarted. Three thuds, a pause, then two more, another pause then four thuds. Jalor relaxed. He walked to the door and started to lift the wooden bar. He was joined by Lilli and together they lifted the heavy beam, dropping it with a crash. Jalor swung the door open and stared.

Blaine stood in the centre of the door, with a single guardsman by his side. Both were covered in blood, gore and dirt. Blaine's utilitarian garb showed the scratches that he had suffered while the guardsman had a bandage around an arm and favoured one leg.

"It's done," Blaine said wearily. "The attackers were led by Junil. Pren here is the only survivor of the Guard detachment. I am assuming the rest of the Guard is dead but we have yet to check."

"Come in and sit," Jalor said softly, gesturing generally to the inside of the barn. "Lilli, can you scare up some water for washing and drinking, please?"

Lilli nodded mutely and moved away. Two of the women who had been sitting with the group stood and guided Blaine and Pren to a place where they could sit. Jalor looked over the gathered group once more, knowing that he would get no help for Corm from Telsith.

Two days later Jalor and Blaine visited Premptor Heristis again. Both had been appalled at what they found when they had returned to the city the previous day, after helping the Premptor's staff to clear the estate. As Blaine had thought, the Premptor's Guard detachment was dead to a man other than Pren, with the Troop Leader lying in a deadly embrace with one of the northers. The city had suffered greatly. The Guard had managed to defeat the infiltrators but with great loss of life and huge damage. The Telsith Guard was almost obliterated. Most of the Council had been killed by sneak attacks like that on the Premptor's estate. The city had lost its leadership at a critical time, for it had suffered great damage, too.

Fires had been started in several sections of the city, including the warehouses and docks. Not only had buildings been lost but so had a stockpile of precious selth thread and cloth of all types. Many buildings were partially damaged and would have to be pulled down and rebuilt. The number of homeless was huge, and the dead and injured would stretch the city's resources.

They met Heristis in a temporary Council chamber, for the grand, old chamber had been burned enough to be unusable. It came as no surprise when Heristis could offer them no military support.

"I'm sorry, General," the Premptor said, brushing a hand across his thinning hair. "But we have almost no military left, and they will be hard pressed to defend Telsith should it be needed. In fact, we are in need of assistance ourselves."

Jalor could only nod his agreement.

"I understand completely. Perhaps we can assist you, however," he said before raising his voice. "Balgor!"

"Balgor?" Heristis repeated, perplexed.

"Yes, Jalor?" Balgor's voice asked from a point behind Heristis.

The Premptor swung around. His mouth gaped as Balgor appeared, seemingly from nowhere. The sandy haired Guardian glanced from Jalor to Blaine and then to Heristis.

"Well met, Premptor," Balgor said with a smile.

"Balgor, the people of Telsith need help," Jalor said with a grimace. "You can see the destruction. Many have been killed and many more are homeless."

"You know we don't directly interfere in the doings of the people of Ennaris," Balgor reminded Jalor.

"And I'm not asking you to. In this case I'm asking for you to carry a message to Corm for me, please? Ask him for aid for Telsith. I'm sure Drewflin and the twins can help him come up with something."

"That I can do," Balgor nodded. "In fact, I can go one better. I've mentioned it to Eresh and she'll get her Guides to provide aid also. They're across the inland sea but should be here fairly quickly." He smiled. "I'm almost certain they'll have a fair wind behind them."

"Thank you," Jalor replied, turning back to a bewildered Heristis.

"Premptor, I would like you to meet Balgor, one of the Guardians."

"B-B-Balgor?" Heristis stammered.

"Just Balgor," the Guardian replied. "Jalor, I'll be getting back. So should you, I think. Events are moving. The twin kingdom's armies are preparing to march."

"So, it's started already? We're not ready."

"Goroth is not yet free, but yes, it's started. Perhaps prematurely. Grensor is not a good tactician."

He turned to Heristis and bowed, before disappearing from sight.

"Well, I guess we're leaving too," Jalor said to Blaine. "Premptor, you will have assistance for Telsith and her people. I regret that we could not do more."

"More?" Heristis said, still struggling to take in what he had heard. "You saved my life and those of my family and many of my staff. And you have arranged for aid to be delivered. By a Guardian!" he said the last breathlessly. "I have always thought the Guardians were childhood stories. And he said Goroth? And Grensor?"

"They made a mistake letting that belief take root," Blaine cut in. "As did the Mages. But we have what we have."

"Mages? There are Mages?"

"There are, indeed, Premptor," Jalor said with a nod. "But not many and not enough. However, Goroth and Grensor are real and remain the threat to be countered. And that's what we must do. I hope to meet you again in fairer times, Heristis. For now, though, farewell."

The two Warriors nodded to the Premptor and strode from the room.

29. Old One

The crowd quietened. The large square was well lit by stakes wrapped in rags that were then coated with a waxy substance that burned brightly for a long time before consuming the stake itself. There were enough of them to cast sufficient light so that the square's crowd could see clearly, those whose eye-sight needed the light. For some, the light was too bright and they wrapped their heads in cloth to reduce impact. All waited impatiently, for tonight the Old One would tell of the Creation. It was a favourite story of all who gathered to hear it.

Out of the darkness shuffled the Old One, one of the Great Ones who had been at the rebellion and had gained glory in fighting against the enemy. He had taken severe injuries and his gifts had suffered, but he had survived to be one of the authors of the stories told around the square at night, passing on tales of the old, better times, and giving those of the now times instruction by means of story, myth and examples.

The Old One moved to a seat placed in the centre of the square. He leaned a chipped staff against his chair and accepted a tankard of ale. He took a deep draught, smacking his lips and making a sound like deep sigh of satisfaction that caused those assembled to hoot with approbation. In reality, he hated ale and longed for a glass of the white wine of the slopes of Astorgan, lost now beneath the seas for thousands of cycles. Still, one can't have everything. The common people of the Kingdoms loved the local potent ale, and so he played up to them when he addressed gatherings. He waited until the commotion died away before lifting his old walking staff and striking its heel three times on the hard-packed ground. At each strike, a dull thud reverberated through the crowd and anticipation grew.

"Listen well," the Old One said in a guttural tongue, "listen well and take heed. For this is the story of the making of Ennaris and the casting out of Goroth.

"At the beginning was the All God, and the All God created the universe and the Guardians. The Guardians were placed under the rule of Odruf, the favoured one of the All God and the most powerful of the Guardians. Of the Guardians there were 24 and each took a powerful talisman, all except Odruf who assumed the form of the sun. Thus, Odruf sees all parts of the world every day.

"And the All God looked over the universe and found it was empty, so he created the stars. And for a long time, the All God enjoyed looking on the stars with the Guardians. But after a long time, the All God decided that the stars were not enough, and he wanted more for his dominion. So, he commanded the Guardians to create a world.

"For five ages the Guardians laboured to create the world of Ennaris, building mountains, oceans, rivers, forests and all manner of plants, rocks and grasses, from the largest rock to the smallest grain of sand. They placed the two moons of Ennaris in the sky and caused them to move around the planet at different times.

"And after five ages they stopped and looked at the world they created and most believed that it was good and fit. And so, for a further five ages the Guardians devoted themselves to other pursuits and Odruf placed parts of himself in the sky to maintain a watch over the land, and Odruf lit the land for half of each day as his spirit moved around the world continuously.

"And after another five ages the Guardians stopped again and looked at the world and the sky and most believed it was good and fit. And they rested for five further ages.

"But after five further ages the Guardians decided that the All God did not just want Ennaris and the sky, with the stars and the moons, but also wanted a greater universe. So, the Guardians left Ennaris for a time and created other worlds. And when they had created other worlds, they rested again and looked at the universe and most believed it was good and fit.

"And after resting the Guardians decided that Ennaris needed animals and people to live in the world. And Odruf assigned Guardians to create the animals of the land and the animals of the seas and oceans and rivers and the birds of the air. And finally, the Guardians laboured long and created the Ennarisi, both women and men, of great variety of physical forms, using parts of themselves and using their own images.

"And the Guardians allowed the Ennarisi to have authority over the animals of the land and the seas and the air where they were able to exercise it. But Goroth, who had laboured mightily to create many of the animals was not pleased and allowed the animals of the land and the seas and the air to defend themselves and escape the bonds and thus was strife born between the people and the animals. And thus was strife born between the Guardians. And Goroth caused the animals to grow horns and sharp teeth and claws to better defend themselves, and some began to kill and eat the Ennarisi who they encountered.

"And Odruf was angered and called Goroth unworthy to be a Guardian. But Goroth replied that Guardians were not only for the Ennarisi but for all creatures they created, and he would not allow them to be destroyed at will by the Ennarisi.

"Then Odruf, rising from his place amid the skies, did cause Goroth to be cast from Ennaris into the depths of the universe, and a great barrier was placed around the place to which he was banished. At the last, however, three others of the Guardians accompanied Goroth into banishment, in opposition to Odruf, and thus were the Guardians on Ennaris reduced to 20.

"But Odruf counted not the growing power of Goroth and his supporters, who had discovered the arts of the deepest parts of the universe and gained the additional strength to be gleaned from their use. And so it was that after many eons Goroth escaped his bonds and returned to Ennaris to confront his betrayers.

"Now during the eons of time since his banishment the people of Ennaris had flourished, and they had spread throughout the stars created by the Guardians and had assisted many and varied types of creatures to attain intelligence, leaving them to live their lives without guidance after having done so. Seeing this Goroth provided his wisdom and aid to such peoples as he could assist and, in doing so, he attracted many worshippers, for Goroth was as a god to the creatures he helped.

"Finally, Goroth returned to Ennaris where he gathered about him many Ennarisi, including a host of Guides, who believed Goroth had been wronged and that Odruf had falsely banished him from Ennaris. Bravely, Goroth called on Odruf to meet him in single battle to decide the issue, but Odruf refused and caused his Ennarisi supporters, including the Guides who he had subjugated to his ill purposes, to attack the supporters of Goroth and vilely and falsely accuse him and his supporters of all manner of ill deeds. War ensued and great deeds were performed by Goroth and his army.

"Yet at the end, after much destruction caused by Odruf and his ilk, and by force of numbers Goroth was brought low and vanquished. Goroth and his supporters were destroyed, and the victorious Odruf danced on his grave!

"But lo! The cream of the Guides was also destroyed and the lickspittle Mage Drewflin was left almost alone to rule over the remnants of the once-great people of Ennaris, to make them subservient to the Guardians who survived when so many others fell.

"And the world was changed forever by the forces unleashed by Odruf and the Mages. And many Ennarisi perished, as did many other creatures of the world. And the Guardians were well satisfied and left Ennaris to pursue interests on other worlds, forgetting the suffering of the people of Ennaris. And the Guides withdrew from the people who perished and those who suffered so they could preserve themselves.

"And the people of Ennaris were reduced to beggars. Almost all learning was lost in the damage caused to Ennaris, and the people were forced to live like those of far antiquity and were little better than animals themselves. The people of Ennaris in their woe called upon the Guardians to help them, but the Guardians refused. And so, the people of Ennaris broke apart into small groups and founded their own nations where they could find suitable land amid the destruction. And so they have existed for long cycles.

"But not all is lost! The spirit of Goroth persists and will return in glory. Survivors of the great host remained and returned, to great rejoicing by all people of good heart and they became the brave and stout people of Kresh and Ingten.

"And the prophecy was born that the cause would be taken up again when the Children of Ennaris took their rightful place among the Ennarisi, and a Champion would arise to win back the world from the perfidious Guardians and their lackeys, the Guides.

"The time is coming when all right-thinking Ennarisi must choose. Choose well!"

The final words were delivered in a rising crescendo, and at the last the Old One struck his walking staff on the hard-packed ground again. The reverberations were lost in the raucous cheering, stamping of feet and bashing of tankards on rough board tables.

The cheering subsided as the crowd realised that, this time, the Old One had more to say. As the last sounds died away, he stood and looked around the gathered throng. He gestured widely with one hand.

"I give you the Children of Ennaris," he shouted in a strong voice that could be heard clearly in the deepest places.

At his words three black-shrouded figures glided forward to stand before the Old One, each deeply hooded.

"And the Champion!" the Old One shouted once more.

This time a huge figure emerged from the dark. Its deep barrel chest easily was greater than any present. It carried a huge sword and a great spear. Legs like tree trunks supported the great body, and its snout had great tusks emerging and curving upwards. Dark, beady eyes regarded the crowd with barely subdued ferocity.

The gathered ghazrak and their Ennarisi allies broke into cheers such that had not been heard in that part of the Kingdoms of the northlands, while the three hooded and shrouded figures of the Children of Ennaris stood motionless. The Champion of the ghazrak swung its head back and forth as it drank in the applause and adulation, eyes glittering.

The noise abated as the crowd realised the Old One had yet more to say. He waited until the sound had dropped to a murmur.

"Soon we ride to attack the old enemy. We will strike at their heart and tear it out," the Old One shouted, and the crowd roared again. "Goroth!" he shouted, holding his staff high.

"Goroth! Goroth! Goroth!" the crowd shouted back, their acclaim rising into the night sky.

And Grensor, the Old One, he who had been a Council Mage and had stood with Goroth during the rebellion until near the end, smiled a wintry smile. What he had just declaimed was confused rubbish, of course, but it served a purpose in reinforcing that Drewflin and his allies were the enemy.

Long ago, he had fled before the wrath of the Battle Mage, Marjory, and so had avoided being confined in stasis with his master after the rebellion. He and Goroth had agreed that he should be working on new ghazrak rather than fighting, but in truth he had feared facing Marjory in combat.

Once Goroth was defeated and confined, he had used his great skills, even without properly working technology, to restart his work to create a race of Ennarisi more suited to conquest and annihilation, and then had watched over these, his and his master's creations. He had tried to alter many types of animals and birds, but with repeated failures. In some cases, like the carrion birds, he could exert no control and they went wild. Now, however, his long work was coming to an end. The portents were occurring as the Prophecy had said they would.

Likud would be coming to join him shortly, Grensor was sure, after making some of his subject race available for more than the last fifty cycles.

More importantly, Goroth would be freed to take up the fight again. And this time, they would not have Marjory to fight. Victory would be sweet.

It was time to start the softening up process. His ghazrak, controlled by the Andorethi adepts, had been sent out to remove as many of the gifts as could be identified by his spies. Already, the army that he had spent much time building in what were merely thought to be two reclusive kingdoms had taken the field and would create fear and mayhem. He had already dispatched his embassy to the eastern lands, through a path that they had only been opened recently, with great effort. He would join them soon.

He thought Goroth would be pleased. His army would force Drewflin and the remaining Council Mages into the open, and his spies and the fear invoked by the army's actions would undermine any efforts to form a united front. Without Marjory, Drewflin would not be able to stand against Goroth and Likud. He had more ghazrak growing, and a few surprises on that front also. His plans, that had been laid and re-laid over the last five thousand cycles, were coming to fruition at last.

Jalor and Blaine made their way through the outskirts of a small town, more a large village really, seeking the inevitable tavern. They had opted to return to the Citadel by land rather than by sea, in part because they had the chance to see more of the country between Telsith and the plateau, but also because there were a limited number of vessels available and none were heading back that way for some time. Telsith had commandeered as many ships as possible to bring in aid and assistance, and Jalor was not about to try to use influence to take one of them. They did accept the gift of two hrss, however, and set off on the trip immediately after they farewelled the Premptor.

Blaine found that he liked this land. It had a natural grandeur, an unspoiled wildness that called to him deeply. He and Jalor had become increasingly familiar with some of the main trails and parts of the lands in the territory around the Citadel and now they were experiencing some of the more distant reaches of the northern continent.

Since leaving Telsith they had moved quickly, swinging through the green and verdant land of the lower northern continent. They would be several days on the journey and events were moving ahead without them. Still, they had removed genuine threats that could have opened a southern front, and had proven that the agents of Grensor had a much greater reach then had been thought. It was something for Drewflin to consider, but also for Almin Bor and the network of Blood agents.

In villages and towns, they located a tavern or the equivalent and met the people, listened to the stories being told and spoke of the recent happenings at the Citadel. They found that all those with whom they spoke had heard something of their own exploits and, as they had found previously, those exploits were exaggerated. The events at Frelor were known in part but those in Telsith were too recent to be included in the tales told. All wanted to know about the new Faero. Some had heard of Corm and were surprised at the positive comments made by Jalor, while others were dismissive of the Faero and all that he stood for. They also came across stories of ghazrak attacks, of individual travellers being killed and of isolated families being wiped out. The people of that part of Ennaris were drawing closer for protection. Local militias were forming where none had been deemed to be necessary for a long time. Jalor took every opportunity offered to remind them that the Faero was one who they could look to for help.

The current town was similar to others they had visited, although perhaps a touch larger. There were the neat rows of cottages with, in this case, several cross-streets as well as the main road running through the town, with the usual town square fronted by shops, stables and the tavern. However, here they came across a man declaiming loudly about the Prophecy and the return of the ancient Guardians, how the Three would return in the time of Ennaris' greatest need and lead the people at the final battle. He was subject to good-natured heckling by watchers who laughed and questioned why now was the hour of need – crops were good, taxes were kept low by the local lord, the weather was good.

"Final battle?" said Blaine with a raised eye, as they paused to listen. "Flin never said anything about a final battle, did he?"

"Probably an embellishment, although he did say that there would be some type of battle against Goroth," said Jalor after a moment's thought.

Blaine nodded. "I really like this land, but at times I find myself wishing we were back on the ship. There's still too much here that we don't know or understand."

"Yes. I think we need to understand this Prophecy better and from someone other than the Mages," said Jalor, and made his way to the man, inviting him to take a drink with them and explain this Prophecy.

The man agreed readily and the three sat down at a table in the tavern, nodding to a waitress who delivered a huge tankard at the same time. He drank deeply and sat back, licking his lips and sighing contentedly.

Jalor was amused.

"You seem to be well known here," he said accepting his own tankard from the waitress. He took a tentative sip and nodded appreciatively before taking a deeper draught.

The man nodded. "Yes, I've been here for some time now trying to convince these people that they need to prepare themselves for the coming battles. The Prophecy is at hand and all need to stand ready to help the Three."

"'The Prophecy is at hand'," said Jalor thoughtfully. "I've heard that before, using exactly those words. Why describe it that way?"

"Why, I'm not sure. That just is the way I tell it. I've not thought about it deeply."

He took another long drink, draining the tankard and beckoning to the waitress for another as he placed it carefully on the table.

"Well, before you get too many of them into you," said Blaine, his own tankard almost untouched, "how about you tell us of the Prophecy. What is it about and what do you think it means? Not many seem to know of it, at least with the sort of detail you seem to have."

"Ah, the Prophecy of the Guardians!" said the man reverently. "The Prophecy is attributed to one of the Guides from long ago, just after the days of glory ended. At that time the world was broken and the people were terrified. Most of the Guides had been killed in their battle with those who opposed the traditions of Ennaris, and those who survived were unable to stop the breakdown of our civilisation. We had wonderful machines then, able to do fantastic things, and people with magical power, the Guides among them, and there were many who could perform feats that today seem wondrous. And in a few short days it was all gone, all gone." He stopped to take a drink, sighing at what was lost, before starting again in a deeper voice.

"And it came to pass that the greatest Guide of them all, Drewflin, the last true Mage, on the brink of death from his exertions for the people, had a vision of the future and in his delirium repeated the Prophecy over and over until someone thought to write it down with some of the last of the magical writing materials, after which Drewflin died. It was as though he was waiting only to make sure his words were recorded. But the Prophecy was passed down through the long ages since, and it's given to some few of us to watch for the portents and inform the people when it's time to do so. That time is now."

Jalor could feel his spirit flag. Given that they knew that Drewflin was alive, this version was flawed immediately. Still, there may be some truths in this version of the tale.

"What portents?" asked Blaine quietly, aware that they had an audience now.

"The portents go back to the time of my grand-dam," the man said, "but they have continued to this time. Bright lights in the sky during the middle of the day, as my grand-dam told me about, and as many of these good people have been told by their forefathers." He looked for confirmation and many in the now attentive crowd nodded. "And then the dead-eyes were seen," he continued with a shudder, "and they truly send a shiver up one's back. They appeared without warning at some towns in the far north and wiped out the people without mercy, and then just disappeared again." Another drink, longer, as he looked into the distance but saw the past. "My ma and da were among those killed and I escaped by just running away and they didn't follow. I was just a boy but that's stayed with me and will for ever. Nothing stopped them. Our arrows just bounced off or broke against their chests."

Jalor and Blaine noted a few others nodding again with shared despair reflected in their eyes and expressions.

"How long ago was that?" Jalor asked softly.

"Thirty-five cycles," said the man, and he shook himself out of his reverie. "And then there were the black birds swarming through the north lands and attacking all other birds, driving them away from their nesting sites until there were none left. Only black birds up there now, so they say. And vicious they are, I'm told, but I never saw that for myself. One man told me he saw a swarm of them kill a horned hangar, which is as big as a full grown hrss and twice as fierce, and feast on it. Usually, the black birds avoided contact with live beasts, only eating those already dead." He shook his head, as in disbelief, or perhaps to negate memories. "That started about the same time as the dead-eyes started to be seen. Then the few rivers still flowing from the north dried up. Just a trickle was left for some, nothing for most. People depending on that water had to leave and the crops all failed. There was not much rain for most of the places just below the north land, so if the rivers don't give you water then there's no choice but to leave. So many did just that. Others tried to stay and died as a result."

He sighed heavily. "My childhood places are all gone, for that was my home land. Harsh and rugged it was, no forgiveness in it at all for those who were not careful, but there was beauty in odd places," he smiled wistfully, "perhaps made more so in my memory of long ago. But there were valleys that bloomed after the rare rains – red, blue, gold, lilac – and waterfalls along several of the rivers that caught the sunlight of a morning. All gone now!"

Again, he seemed to shake himself away from personal memory.

"But the portents continued to be seen. There were cattle born with abnormal features – cloven hoofs, two heads, extra legs, no eyes, just to name a few. That was just as the rivers were drying up and people blamed the lack of proper water supply at the time. But the Prophecy predicted that the beasts would sicken and die in torment, as the land would sicken, dry up and fail. And then came the storms, great dust storms sweeping from the north and destroying the remaining crops, turning the last available drinking water to poison. They were storms such as were never seen when the land was alive, and they continue still, blowing the dust from the north across the new border lands, such that they are already showing signs of the sickening. 'The sickness will spread,' said the Prophecy, 'on the winds of evil.' And so it has."

The man took a drink, surprised to find that his tankard was empty, but it was replaced at a gesture by Blaine to the waitress, who had joined with the others in a hushed audience. He nodded and drank.

"And the portents have continued, as the Prophecy said. The dead-eyes left the north lands and came into this land to destroy the Faeronar, which the Prophecy calls 'the people of Light' but were driven back with the help of strangers who appeared with the old soothsayer. Actually, the Prophecy says they are the Three returned."

He nodded sagely, although Blaine suspected that, after imbibing three huge tankards of the potent ale in quick succession, he may have been falling asleep.

"The Three?" said Jalor, anxious to keep the man talking and learn as much as possible. "We have heard that term before."

"Nothing but children's stories," one of the audience members called out.

"Not so," said the storyteller, "but it's hard to believe they are returned. Still, the Prophecy says they would so maybe that is who they are. The Three were ancient heroes, imbued with ancient powers, who it is said have saved Ennaris from total destruction on several occasions."

"Who can destroy a whole planet?" scoffed the same sceptical voice from the crowd.

Any number of people, Blaine thought, including me with the right gear. But he waited to see what the response was.

"Ah well, I don't know about that, just reciting what the old tales say. The Three came from the Old Blood, and were of legend that is now seen as tales for children. They sided with the Guides and Mages during the battles past, and will be seen again in the battle to come." The man shook his head once again, possibly clearing his thoughts from the fog of drink. "They no doubt had real names but were called The Defender, The Dreadlord and The Seeker. The Defender was a fabled warrior, able to master any weapon, never defeated. It is said time slowed for him and the old images showed him with a golden glow, as of an inner light as he wielded his sword *Genardil*. The Dreadlord was reputed to be able to speak to the dead. His prowess as a warrior was spoken of highly but he was the supreme battle leader also. It's said that he could win any battle by strategy."

"They sound formidable," Jalor said into the silence, "but it's a little hard to believe."

"Nay, sir, for they were reputed to have fought against the dead-eyes only a few ten-days past, saving the Faeronar from destruction and allowing the Faero to die in his citadel. It's said the Dreadlord also interceded to give the old Faero a proper send-off."

"And the Seeker?" Blaine asked softly.

"Reputed to be the most beautiful woman of the age, and able to communicate with all manner of creatures. It was said that she could speak with the Guardians themselves. The Seeker had the power to locate any item when there was sufficient need."

"A load of old rubbish," said the sceptic, who stomped out of the tavern after slamming his tankard onto the bar. A few others nodded, although others seemed uncertain. The crowd broke up as the story telling seemed to be at an end.

Jalor caught Blaine's eye and then nodded to the now thoroughly inebriated man. Blaine nodded and went to arrange a room, while Jalor stayed with the story teller and pondered. Then, between the two of them they carried him up to their room and deposited him on one of the four pallets the room held.

"That seemed to be thoroughly confused," Jalor said. "But there are a few things we may be able to find out tomorrow and then we can ask Flin to confirm or deny them. I want to know more about this final battle, and I still want to find a copy of the Prophecy if possible. We need to learn to read the local script, by the way."

Jalor settled himself on another pallet, grimacing as their guest started to snore loudly.

"Only those two? There are dozens of things I want to understand and I doubt the Prophecy will tell us in detail. Where did the 'dead-eyes' come from? I assume they are the ghazrak, although I would have thought the eyes would be the last thing anyone noticed with them. Or is that another kind of creature we'll have to face? What's happening in the north that would cause those problems? How come these stories are rolling up now, and with such full detail, given how old they must be?"

Blaine settled himself against the door and took his sword out to take first watch.

"The stories are being spread by the twins, as we already know. But some of the detail here is different and, from what we know, wrong. For our friend here, it was Flin who delivered the Prophecy, for example, and I can't see either of the twins allowing that to be believed. So, there's something more here that we need to understand. It's possible that some of the old tales were brushed off by real storytellers, and the traditions are incorrect. That's likely, in fact."

"The lights in the sky? His grand-dam may have seen something of the blitz mine going off if that happened during the day but the timing seems off. Varna will know what time of day that would have been, I think, if she was able to locate more detail than that Clay lived." Blaine shook his head. "Clay lived," he said in wonder. "He survived a blitz mine! How is that even possible?"

"More questions," Jalor said, nodding. "We may get some of the answers in the morning from our friend here, and we will have to see if we can find out anything about Clay. And we need to get back to the Citadel. I need to speak with the twins about all of this."

31. Fredas Falls

The army of the twin kingdoms of Kresh and Ingten had been marching for seven days. General Morsen consulted his maps almost continuously. This was the furthest a norther army had been outside the confines of the twin kingdoms, at least to his knowledge. It was the first foray out of the confines of the kingdoms in many generations, at least in force. The Old One had decreed that they should march west to the sea and then south, attacking everything they came across. And so they had. Numerous farms were laid waste. The farmers and their families were killed mercilessly.

The opposition they had met so far told him that there was no organised armed forces of note in the areas through which he was marching. He knew that would change as they approached Escar, but his force would change character before reaching that city. He was not destined to field his full army this time around. This expedition was to spread fear through the land, with the intention of causing the various armies to hold back and protect their own homes.

How Morsen did that while killing everyone they came across was a question. Someone would have to be allowed to escape to raise the alarm, surely, or others would not know that they even existed. Of course, once that happened the possibility was that the armies would join together to form a united opposition. Morsen thought that was unlikely given what he had been told about the highly fractured political situation, but he had to be aware of the possibility.

His ruminations were interrupted by the return of a scout. He had only a few of these, and had lost track of some immediately they broke out of the valley. Whether they had deserted or been killed he did not know, but it reduced his abilities to find out what they faced. The scout reported to the march captain, who directed him to Morsen. Morsen held his hrss still as the scout approached and knuckled his forehead in respect.

"You have a report?" Morsen asked.

"Yes, General. There is a town less than a day's march south and a little east. The direction of march is quite open for the most part, but the forest closes in on the town to the south and east." The scout half-turned and pointed back the way he had come. "If we continue in this direction the army will miss the town, so we must move a few points to the east."

"How many defenders?"

"No more than two hundred I would guess, General," the scout replied. "It's a small town. There's a town wall made of logs but it's not been well maintained. A few farmers live in the surrounding area."

"Very well, get some rest and then head out again. Avoid the town and see what is beyond," Morsen ordered. "But first, give Captain Grilter as much information as you can about this town."

Morsen sat his hrss as the scout nodded, saluted once again and then turned to find Grilter. Only two hundred defenders and a poorly constructed town wall gave Morsen the chance to split his force and test one of his sub-commanders. He would like to direct the attack himself but it was important that others were given some experience, even if he also lacked that experience. He considered and then called for a messenger.

Two hurs later Morsen was sitting his hrss watching almost a thousand of his troops, including a ghazrak troop of ten, march away from his lines towards the town. Fredas Falls, as he had been informed it was named, would soon cease to exist. Morsen admitted to a little envy as Grilter led the column away followed by the Grensor Brigade, named after the Old One. Still, Grilter was his second in command and this would enhance his credentials. Morsen turned his thoughts to the march ahead as the last of the column moved away. He had no doubt as to the outcome.

Fredas Falls' nondescript existence ended shortly before nightfall. It had been established by a merchant who found himself lost one day more than two hundred cycles earlier. The land around was not settled because of the extreme population loss following the rebellion, and even millennia later there was no settlement. But the merchant - Fredas - realised that he had found a patch of singularly rich land. He laid claim to the land, passed the word around that good land was available at a reasonable price and then sold parcels of land to the first comers. Rich beyond his dreams as a result, he decided to leave the new town of Fredas, bought a hrss, although he had never ridden a hrss in his life, mounted the animal and almost immediately fell off, breaking his neck as he landed. The townspeople decided to commemorate the event by changing the town's name to Fredas Falls. This mostly confused visitors as the small river nearby was calm and smooth of surface almost all the time.

Grilter followed doctrine to the letter. Advancing in good order, he sent one quarter of his force in a wide circuit of the town, to make sure that there were no escapees. When the agreed time had elapsed, he ordered his troops to charge in a skirmish formation that doctrine said was best suited to attacks on small towns. The town dwellers were taken by surprise. The ghazrak charged through the town gate before anyone had the chance to close it, for there were no full-time guards. Immediately they started killing people. The bulk of Grilter's army followed them into the town, while a small contingent was held back as a defensive formation. The townspeople were bottled up in the town with Grilter's forces at each of the two gates.

Grilter made his way into the town shortly after, walking his hrss along the small main street. Bodies were strewn along the road sides, men and women with a few children mixed in. None were to be spared, and none were. Grilter had no sympathy. These people were under the thrall of the evil Council Mages and they did not even know that they were damned as a result, so death was a mercy for them.

Grilter called his senior lieutenant to him and ordered him to make sure everyone was dead, after which he was to form up the troops and then he was to fire the town. That done, he sat his hrss in the wider space that he thought probably was a small town square, and waited. In short order the men of the troop were formed up, with minimal losses and only a few injuries, and Grilter started them moving out of town by the opposite gate to the one by which they had entered. The troop of ghazrak were waiting just outside town with a small fire going. After throwing into the flames bones that Grilter decided he did not want to look at too closely, they grunted and shambled into their places with their black-robed controller gliding just ahead.

The column had wended its way for around thirty minims when Grilter turned back to see columns of smoke drifting up from the town. Satisfied, he turned to the front once more. A short time later his lieutenant made his way past the marching men and women, skirted the ghazrak slightly and finally reached Grilter at the front of the column. Grilter raised an eyebrow in question, to which he received an affirmative nod. Grilter turned to the front again. They had a short march to reach the rendezvous point with General Morsen.

General Morsen received Captain Grilter in his tent, taking his report while eating a modest evening meal. So far, they had achieved what the Old One had asked for, with everyone who was encountered being killed. Morsen thought once again about the goal of this march. He had almost reached the western extent of the expedition and would turn back to the east shortly, at which point he would divide his force. His maps had not been too wrong so far, which was a little surprising given how little contact the twin kingdoms had with outside parties. He knew that Grensor had a reasonable spy network in these southern realms, so maybe the maps came from one of them. Certainly, the material on which the map was drawn, and the fine detail, exceeded any he had seen from the twin kingdoms.

So, he decided it was time to let people know that they were here, and that meant letting at least one person live. Probably two or three, just to be sure.

The opportunity came two days later when the scouts reported that a caravan of travelling actors were camped just off the army's line of march. Morsen considered the various angles and decided that the direct approach was best. This time he left Grilter in camp and put the small attack force under the command of his junior captain, Grensil, named in part after the Old One. Morsen thought long and hard about this but it made sense, politically. Grensil was favoured by the Old One, the obsequious gesture of his name having variously been interpreted as being an attempt to curry favour or the sign of an actual blood relationship. That he was not truly skilled enough to have his current position favoured the latter interpretation. Either way, Morsen decided to allow the young captain to show what he could do.

"The goal," Morsen said to Grensil, "is to ensure that enough people escape so that the people here in the south and west fear us. We want them to stay in their own cities and allow us to attack them one after the other as the Old One commanded. Do you understand?"

"You want me to let some of the enemy go," Grensil replied shortly, respect for his commanding officer barely in evidence. "Our orders are to kill them all."

"I know what our orders are," Morsen said evenly and with a barely perceptible sigh, "and this ruse is the way that we make sure we can do exactly that. The people that you allow to escape will be included when we reach them again."

Grensil stared at Morsen for a long moment. The General could almost see the thoughts chasing through Grensil's mind, slowly, and he considered reversing his decision about this command.

"I understand," Grensil said at last. "We kill all but three of them and allow them to escape."

"Yes," Morsen said. "Three would be a good number. If it ends up being four or five that will be okay, too. The most important thing is that they understand we have a large enough army and that we are coming."

Grensil nodded to show his understanding, which would have been more comfort to Morsen if he had not also frowned hard in concentration, muttering as though to remind himself what the message was to be.

"Scouts say there are no more than thirty people. Take one hundred of the Goroth Brigade, but no ghazrak," Morsen cautioned. "They would not stop until everyone was dead, which would defeat the purpose. No-one else lives, just the ones you choose to let escape."

Grensil turned away to select his troops, allowing Morsen to exchange a rueful look with Grilter. The latter shrugged and then turned back to the maps that he and Morsen had been studying. The army's sweep west and slightly south had been done. Now they would start to follow a sinuous path east and then south again. Their target would be Escar, the fortified city on the edge of the grasslands. After victory there, they would move north across the grasslands to meet more of the norther forces when they emerged from the pass at a time still to be determined. Then the combined army would march straight through the grassy plain to the rich lands around the Bight, which was what the map called the large inland sea.

The attacking party descended on the carnival caravan like a hammer. Grensil's sergeant suggested the main tactic and the captain agreed, surprising everyone, and the tactic worked flawlessly. More than twenty men and women were killed and the remaining seven herded to where Grensil sat his mount. As the wagons were fired, Grensil inspected the captives, four women and three men. Two of the men and one of the women glared at him, either not being cowed by the overwhelming numbers or acting like they were not. These Grensil pointed out and all three were stabbed to death by the guards. The remaining four captives' terror escalated. The remaining man, a sickly-looking person, wet himself without appearing to notice, while the three women were shaking with fear. Grensil found that he enjoyed the effect.

"You," he said to them in a haughty voice, "have been selected to escape and tell everyone of the glorious forces of the Old One that are coming to destroy you all. We are an army three thousand strong and have already destroyed everything in our march. We will march to destroy Escar and then we will re-join our main army before we march south to destroy all."

Grensil was pleased with his speech, and so missed the incredulous look of his sergeant. The four captives looked at each other and then back to Grensil, but remained quiet, shaking still.

"Well, go," Grensil said with a shooing motion. "Escape!"

"Captain, sir," the sergeant said quietly, "they may be able to spread the message faster if they had mounts to ride."

Grensil considered that and found he agreed.

"Let them have their mounts, then," Grensil declaimed grandly.

With a gesture, the sergeant sent a squad to round up mounts. They returned a short time later with four hrss that had been found picketed in the trees near the camp, each with reins and a blanket on their back but no saddles.

"Do you understand the message?" Grensil asked as the four scrambled onto the hrss.

"Yes, sir," the scrawny man said. "You have an army and are coming to attack Escar. But, sir," the man continued, becoming slightly bolder, "which army are you and who is the Old One?"

Grensil was shocked. These people did not know which army they were? Well, they had killed everyone they came across, so that made sense. But not to know the Old One? These people truly were barbaric.

"We are the army of the Kingdoms of Kresh and Ingten, marching on the orders of the Old One, Grensor." Grensil looked at the selected escapees and snorted at their lack of understanding. "We await the coming of Goroth and then we will sweep all unbelievers from this land."

The four stared at Grensil, astounded at this man spouting such nonsense about mythical figures. But he did have soldiers and, perhaps, they were an army from the norther kingdoms.

The sergeant growled an order and the four were led to the edge of the camp, past the pile of bodies that were being placed on a rough pyre of wood made from the wagons. Crying openly at what they had experienced and seen, the four were released and sent on their way. They needed little further urging and kicked the hrss into motion down the road. There were villages and towns on the way to Escar, but for now their only thought was to get away.

Satisfied that he had done what he needed to do, Grensil ordered the bodies and wagons to be burned and prepared to return to the army.

32. Legends

The morning found Jalor and Blaine awake and ready to start the day while the storyteller remained asleep. Jalor tried to stir him with a foot, then kicked harder. Blaine grinned, opened the door and went to a pitcher standing on a stand along the hall outside the door. He returned and poured the content of the pitcher over the story teller's head. The man sat up spluttering, gulping air as water streamed from his hair and face.

"Wha, where, huh?" he managed to get out as he looked from Jalor to Blaine and back again.

"Not quite as well-spoken as last night," observed Blaine.

"You're the two from last night." He squinted as he took in the room. "What am I doing here?"

"You had a little too much to drink and we thought it safer if you stayed with us. And we wanted to ask you a few more questions about these legends." Jalor spoke offhandedly, but the man regarded him suspiciously.

"Why are you so interested?" he demanded.

"We collect old stories," Jalor replied blandly. "You know, like legends, fables, prophesies and such."

The story teller sighed.

"Really?" he said dryly. "Well, you haven't killed me so I guess that counts. You can stake me to a morning meal and ask me your questions. If I can answer them I will. But then I go my own way." He looked from Jalor to Blaine and back to Jalor. "Okay?"

Jalor nodded. "Fair enough."

The three men made their way to the common room and found a table near the front window. The storyteller ordered bread, cheese and meat. Jalor made it the same for three. Three tankards were clunked in front of them and the teller grabbed his and took a deep swallow, sighing deeply afterwards. Jalor and Blaine took smaller drinks, then Jalor took the man's tankard and placed it closer to Blaine.

"We don't need you getting into the same state as last night. Not yet anyway. I have a couple of questions and would prefer that you could answer. Such as, who are the Guardians and who were the Guides. Not too many people really seem to understand, although all seem to have heard of them."

The story teller nodded, grimacing.

"Aye, you're right there," he said. "Not too many lands kept their old tales intact, and in many cases they became tall tales. The truth was fabulous enough but, even then, people kept adding to the stories until it became hard to separate fact from invention." He eyed the tankard wistfully, but continued. "The Guardians were the creators of the universe, and Ennaris became one of the places where they stayed. They created us, the Ennarisi, and then stayed on to provide guidance and protection – thus they were called the Guardians. How much of that is truth or not, I don't know. There are many stories about how they created the universe and Ennaris in a tenday, then rested from their labours for an Age before creating the birds, fishes, animals and, finally, us. One legend says that each of the Guardians had a speciality – some for the birds, some for the fish and other beasts, the trees and such - and that multiple Guardians were involved in creating the Ennarisi, which is why we have different skin colours, hair colours, eyes, and so on. It was said that we were made in their own images."

"I guess that would mean some of the Guardians looked like trees," said Blaine. Jalor shot him a pained look to which Blaine returned a wide-eyed innocent appearance before saying, "and rocks."

The man was startled.

"Why, I never thought of that," he said. "That would certainly end that argument."

"Or make everyone very careful about which tree they cut down," Blaine said as the food arrived, ignoring the withering glance directed at him by Jalor.

"Um, yes," said the man uncertainly.

He turned his attention to piling cuts of meat on his plate, breaking a hunk of bread from the loaf that had been deposited on the table, and starting to eat using a belt knife he suddenly produced.

Jalor and Blaine followed his example, but more sedately. Each of them partook of the vegetables that had been included with the meat, taking smaller serves of the latter.

After a short while the storyteller paused and started to speak again.

"No-one that I know of has ever seen a Guardian, but there were tales of the Old Blood being able to speak with them. That sounds like a tall tale though. It was said that they could take any form, too. But again, that sounds like a tall tale." He went back to eating, starting to mop up meat juices with his bread.

"And the Guides?" Blaine prompted him.

"Well, the old story is that they were the Ennarisi that the Guardians chose to rule on their behalf. But I don't think that's right, because the stories also tell of the Guides choosing to be subject to the Faero. In any event, they were said to have great supernatural power, able to perform feats that normal people could only dream of. And they could live for very long times. In fact, I can't recall a tale of a Guide dying because of age. And I know a lot of the stories."

He nodded in affirmation that he knew a lot of the stories.

"But we keep hearing of the glorious past of the Ennarisi and how they went to other worlds before the rebellion. What part did the Guides play there?" Jalor said as he gave the tankard back to the man.

He nodded thanks.

"Well, the stories are vague there, probably because they are inventions. I mean, going to other worlds? How could you do that? Even in the glory days? For some reason, the Guides are always spoken of as though they were the ones who led the Ennarisi in those glory days but there's very little detail in the stories. Or maybe they were lost and the only ones to come to us are of the Guides helping to keep Ennaris safe." The man paused, considering. Then he shook his head. "No, can't think of anything much in the stories about what was done on those journeys. But the rebellion, we know that it was caused by some of the Guides who wanted to become rulers of Ennaris but who were stopped by the loyal Guides led by Drewflin. The names change according to who tells the story, but all agree that the rebel Guides tried to force the Faero to hand over power and were thwarted by Drewflin. It seems they decided to stage a coup and take power by force, which took the Council of Guides by surprise but still they opposed the rebels. Some of the tales tell of loyal Guides being conflicted because they didn't want to fight other Guides.

"The choice was taken away from them when the rebels attacked one of the great cities. The cities of that time were wondrous things, with buildings many times the height of our own. They destroyed it completely using terrible weapons, but the tales say they also used the powers of the rebel Guides. The legends say that 'evil entered into their hearts', but whatever the case it seems that they were thwarted and tipped over the edge into some sort of madness. Up to that time, the loyal Guides had not really taken sides but held to just helping people to recover from wounds, or to repair things, crops and such. Now the Faero asked them to take a part against the other Guides." The teller shook his head sadly. "He knew what he was doing. Hardus was Faero then and he was close to the Guides, so he knew what he was asking. The Council of Guides was convened and after quite a short debate it was agreed that the loyal Guides would combat the rebel Guides, but would not take part in the rebellion that was now occurring otherwise.

"They were unable to halt the destruction though. In a short time, the great weapons wielded by both sides destroyed much of what had been great about Ennaris. They were weapons such as we cannot understand."

"What happened after that?" asked Blaine, who could see in his mind's eye the destruction a large quantity of advanced weapons could produce on a single planet. "I assume the rebels were all caught and killed?"

The storyteller looked at Blaine, his face still haunted. Then he looked at Jalor.

"Why are you interested in all of this?"

"You said the Prophecy was being fulfilled. We want to understand that and it seems the place to start was with what caused that destruction of the Ennarisi civilisation in the first place. Where we are from has no memory of this."

"Oh, and where are you from then? These stories are known across Ennaris, although they are not told to the level of detail I know." He squinted at Jalor. "So, where?"

Jalor paused to recall the geography of the continent on which they landed. "A long way south, on the islands below the southern shore. The people are fairly self-contained there, with few of the traditions passed down. That's why they send some of us out from time to time, to collect stories for the people to tell."

"Oh. Why, that makes sense," said the man, nodding.

Blaine stared at him before catching himself. That made sense?

"So," Jalor continued smoothly, "about the remaining rebels."

"Well, they were all caught, right enough." The teller shrugged. "But they put up a fight. The last of the Council Guides traced them to one of the Guides' meeting places, not terribly far from here, as a matter of fact. There was quite a battle of magics and at the end of it all Goroth, the rebel leader, was taken captive but his two main followers disappeared. The rest, and there were more than twenty according to the old tales, perished. On the Council side, all but seven of the Guides also perished. Goroth was sealed away from this world in a magic cage. And wards were placed around the cage so that he couldn't awaken without the Council being aware."

"So where does the Prophecy come in then?" Blaine was unsure how to align what Flin had said with what this storyteller said.

"Drewflin, the last Archmage, had taken terrible wounds during the battle and he was rendered insensible by the effort to wall away the rebels. And it was while he was feverish and failing that he had his visions and raved about the evil that would arise again, and how the champions of old would return to succour Ennaris in our hour of need. And it was Marjory, his lady who had been the battle leader, who realised after the third repetition - or maybe the fourth or fifth, for the stories are uncertain about that – anyway, she realised what was happening and recorded what Drewflin said, using the tools of the time. And after the recording was done Drewflin, who was the greatest of the Archmages, died." The story teller halted, looking from one to the other. "So say the stories that have been handed down though the long years since."

"And the Council Guides? What happened with them?" Blaine gestured to the serving woman, the same one as the night before, for more drinks.

"Ah, well. Some say that the Guides roamed the land trying to recover as much of the glories as they could, but too much damage had been done. And over time they gradually faded away until, finally, there were none left. Others say they did what they could and then just went to sleep until they were needed to protect Ennaris again. Others still don't believe any of them survived the battle. The Prophecy tells of the Guides leading the Ennarisi to greatness again, so I want to believe that they are asleep, still. But we may not know until the day of the Prophecy finally arrives. But the portents have started, and it can't be far off."

The serving woman placed three tankards on the table and removed the detritus of their breakfast.

"So where is the original copy of the Prophecy now? If these materials were so special it may have survived," asked Jalor.

"It's unknown if it survived or not. The tradition is an oral one, passing from parent to child, occasionally skipping a generation or jumping to another line to be continued. At one time the Tellers were honoured but we've lost that also as Ennaris slipped into barbarity. In fact, I am one who was not of the line, and was trained by the last of the Great Tellers. There are very few tellers left, and most do not know the complete stories."

He took another drink, draining his tankard and stood uncertainly.

"And now I must be away, for my life is one of wandering and recounting the stories. For the people must be ready. Thank you for your interest and your assistance last night. And for the meal and drinks. It's rare that someone remains interested in the morning."

He weaved from the table to the door and out into the daylight. Jalor and Blaine sat where they were, sipping their ale.

After a short time, Jalor dropped a few coins on the table and the two men left the tavern to continue their journey to the citadel.

33. Trees

Conversation had been kept to a bare minimum. None of them felt like talking. For five days, Flin led the small party via a meandering set of roads and trails. The country slowly changed from lush green trees and shrubs to tall evergreen trees similar to Varna's memory of pines. Spiky needles and broad leaves now provided a spongy carpet which gave back no sound as they strode between the majestic giants. The forest was almost devoid of undergrowth, and the light which filtered through the canopy of needle-encrusted or leafy branches was wan and pale. Varna felt as though she was walking along an aisle of sentries who watched her, who were stolidly standing guard over who knew what. When she tentatively reached out with her senses as Flin was teaching her to do, she encountered a feeling of ancient, immense patience, awaiting some event but content to slumber until it occurred. As she withdrew her sensory probe, she became aware of a warmth, a welcoming psychic embrace, from all around her, and a faint rustle moved through the forest. She gasped, eyes wide.

Flin stared at the trees. This felt so familiar, but now he looked around with different eyes. He had always felt at home here, while not understanding why. Now, knowing that the Guardians, especially Fernis, existed, he understood better. That Fernis had remained on Ennaris but had not made contact hurt, but he had to move on from that and he forced that wound back down. He smiled.

"You are honoured, Varna," he said quietly as they resumed their trek. "The Forest of the Guardians is the most ancient left on Ennaris. It was the most ancient before the rebellion, but most of the other old forests were destroyed. I always felt that these trees have almost a sentience about them. According to Balgor, that may be the case. I spent much time here when I was a young Guide Mage, learning my craft, and after the rebellion's end, but I never realised why they are like this. I have always felt welcome in this Forest, but I have never felt such a welcome. You need fear no harm under these trees."

With that, he moved to the lead and picked up the pace, his powers of endurance and the speed at which he walked belying his appearance of great age.

The party had been walking through the Forest of the Guardians for most of the afternoon, when all sound died. Startled, Varna slipped into what she now thought of as her sixth sense. She sent out tendrils of mental enquiry that she envisaged to be like sonar and hoped to make sense of what returned. She was able to "see" Flin and Dalresar, the former oddly showing much less shielding and allowing bright flickers to show through his aura, while the latter's light golden halo almost caused Varna to slip out of the partial trance. She caught herself and made a mental note to come back to that. She could sense the trees that bordered their path. All of them were massive, and all sheltered myriad life forms, from worms and insects to birds that were perched quietly, abnormally quietly, in the heights.

She went further, into the surrounding Forest. Peace. Tranquillity. Welcome. And then some of the trees seemed to come to meet her. She found individual differences, almost personalities, among these giants. They gathered her into themselves. She felt relief, it seemed, that she had finally arrived. They had awaited her coming for such a long time but, now, anticipation rustled through them.

Varna stopped walking, standing quite still, tense. Flin, who had been expecting something without knowing what that may be, watched in astonishment as the massive trees that were so still, so tall, so upright, seemed to bend towards them. He had the amazing impression that they were listening, discussing. He watched, spell-bound, as a wave rippled through the treetops from that spot, a circle that spread through the Forest.

Flin and Dalresar saw Varna relax and smile, relief and contentment evident. Her eyes were closed but the eyelids twitched like she was still seeing. Occasionally her mouth quirked. Flin stood impassively by Varna's side. His eyes narrowed in concentration, seeking to identify what Varna was seeing, and he experienced a little frustration that he could not do so. Only a careful observer would have noted how intently he watched Varna from behind those half-closed eyelids. Dalresar was such a careful observer, and in turn he gave extra attention to the Forest. He could almost feel something, but was not sure what that may be.

Varna was oblivious to it all. She was talking to the Forest, passing through the trees, being directed by them toward she knew not what. She was greeted by each tree with a term that she gradually discerned as "Dharmoney", the name Balgor had given her. She still did not know what that meant, so she merely returned the greeting and floated in the direction indicated by a pointing bough. At one point a vagrant thought interrupted her progression – I'm talking with trees, she thought, but we never had Tree as one of the language packs! - and was met with tree-ish laughter and merriment. In which she joined. Another ripple passed through the tree tops.

As she moved further into the Forest, Varna became aware that only a relatively small - in fact, a tiny - percentage of the trees were sentient to any degree. The rest were ... well ... trees, but only by observing their auras could she discern a difference. The normal trees were brown and green, steady and dull. The sentient trees glowed fitfully to her sight. They were still brown and green but they pulsed with bright specks that appeared and disappeared. Varna compared it to a skin of lucidite that she had picked up in a planet in the Tamm system, that could be filled to bursting and that repaired any rents in its skin caused by overfilling immediately they appeared, allowing occasional glimpses of its contents. Her observation – to herself, she had thought – was greeted with satisfaction and an even higher degree of delight in her presence by the Forest entities.

Finally, she found herself looking at a massive tree. An immense trunk supported huge boughs and an enormous crown. It was like the sentinel tree which protected her and the children from the ghazrak, but so much larger and with a presence that left the sentinel tree almost mute. The King of the Trees, she thought before she could stop herself, and was again greeted with more merriment, not least by the tree she faced. The trees stilled. Varna found herself waiting breathlessly – did one breath psychically? (suppressed titters from some trees) – for the huge tree to address her. Its aura was golden brown, glowing as the brilliant specks appeared and disappeared rapidly.

Varna, you are now and will always be welcome in our midst, the tree sent in a formal tone, after which it relaxed – Varna stifled the query about how does a tree relax – and 'spoke' to her more normally. My child, we have long awaited your coming, and that of your companions. We hope you will prove to be the instruments of repair for Ennaris, joining with our chosen Champion and remaining Magi to overthrow the evil sown in our midst. We offer our support when it is needed. Our guiding principle has always been that the affairs of ordinary men and women cannot be our affairs directly, so our involvement has been advisory. Rarely have we involved ourselves directly. But we feel the time is coming when this unnatural evil will reveal its true nature.

Varna was astounded at this. Thank you. But, we are here to find someone who arrived long ago. We are not meant to become involved in local problems, even though we have done so.

Varna, the tree said patiently, you will find your Champion when you find ours. And your help is not just for our planet, but for the whole galaxy, for the evil seeks to use the ancient strength of Ennaris to conquer it all.

Clay is alive still? Varna seized on the point most relevant to her. Where is he? Can we reach him?

Your Champion will be found at the site of the final battle with Goroth and his minions. You must face the evil for your Champion to return.

As Varna frowned psychically (and physically, observed by the two men watching her) the old tree continued. The battle you fought and won before the gates of the Citadel was but the precursor, as you well know. Goroth is determined to destroy the Faeronar, the true hope for Ennaris to regain a place in the galaxy. We will help you to control your gifts, and we will help you to make sense of what you do not yet understand. And please tell the Mage Drewflin that Hollow Branch offers greetings and that I look forward to meeting him. Tell him that his time is at hand and his sacrifices have not been for nought.

Varna shook herself as her senses returned to her body. She found her two companions ready to ask questions but forestalled them as she turned to Flin.

"Hollow Branch says to say hello. He's looking forward to meeting you."

Flin nodded, smiling at Hollow Branch's name, a name of legend and children's stories that he had thought to be little more than that not very long ago.

"And Hollow Branch said something about my companions being revealed and that your time is at hand and your sacrifices have not been for nought. He's going to help me to control my gifts. And the only way for us to find Clay is to fight Goroth. I'm not sure exactly what that meant, but hopefully we'll find out more."

Flin once again nodded without question.

Dalresar asked, "And who told you all this?"

"Hollow Branch," Varna replied.

"And who is Hollow Branch?"

"Um, a tree."

"A tree?"

"A tree," said Varna defiantly. She continued with a quirk of her lips, "They're quite friendly once they relax."

"How," Dalresar asked of Varna as they started to walk again, "does a tree relax?"

Evening had fallen when Varna, who had tried to keep the trees in the background as she walked along the path through their midst, sensed the strong presence of Hollow Branch. As their path rounded a bend a large space opened before them, with the ancient and massive tree dominating its centre. The huge girth of its trunk was even larger than she expected and the enormous branches reached out on all sides to the edge of the clearing. Taller than even the tallest of the giants of the Forest, the presence overwhelmed Varna's senses momentarily until she felt Hollow Branch dampen his own aura and allow her to recover, even as her companions experienced their own reactions.

Flin, walking beside Varna, stopped in his place and stared, mouth agape, at the sight. How much time had he spent in this Forest and yet he never knew that this existed? The tree was glowing, shedding light on the clearing even as darkness dropped. Unbidden tears came to his eyes as he recognised the tree and sudden insight caused him to gasp. He dropped to one knee and his staff flared to life, the milky green stone embedded at the top glowing brightly.

Dalresar, meanwhile, just stood and stared. His own perturbations, which had been experienced continually since the night at Great Mirden, melted away and he felt as though he was being welcomed, absorbed into the tree's embrace. His growing fear, that grew more each time part of his past was revealed, subsided and his habitually tense expression softened to calm.

Varna looked from one to the other as she regained control. Dalresar's change was interesting enough, but Flin's reaction was not expected.

"Flin, are you okay?" she asked tentatively.

"The Mage is well," a familiar voice said. "I imagine he is a little overwhelmed."

Varna turned back to the tree, or rather to the figure that was materialising in front of them where they stood. He was tall, with long straight black hair that extended past his shoulders, a kindly mien and dressed in a green robe, the newcomer smiled in welcome.

"I am Fernis, who you know as Hollow Branch," he said. "And once again I welcome you to Ennaris and to the Forest of the Guardians. Rise Mage Drewflin, for you of all people have no need to bow before the Guardians."

"You are a Guardian?" Varna asked. "Not just a tree then?" Which she realised was a stupid question as soon as she asked it.

"Not just a tree," Fernis confirmed with a smile, humour resonating in his voice, before turning to Flin who was standing deferentially. "Well met, Drewflin. I'm aware that you have had your doubts, and of your troubles at assuming a difficult office while unprepared. For that I take responsibility and I offer you my apology. I did not foresee the likelihood of the leadership of the Council being removed in such a short time frame, and then the Prophecy gave us little opportunity to put anything in place. Know that your efforts and those of your fellow Mages have been watched and where possible supported, although that support has been too little I fear."

"Master," Flin said, quietly, "I've been informed of your difficulties and while I don't understand fully I do accept that there was the need to be circumspect. I wish there had been another way," he continued with some chagrin, "and we may have been able to effect some better outcomes. But what is done is done, and we must deal with what we have."

"Indeed we do. We have some explanations to make, and some work to do to help Varna and Dalresar deal with their blockages."

Flin raised an eyebrow. With his equilibrium regained he showed only mild surprise at mention of his apprentice's name.

"Dalresar too? I'm aware that he has gifts of some sort, and the Council Chamber Assistant made that clear also, but I've been unable to establish what sort."

"Well, let's see if we can do something about that, shall we?" Fernis said with another smile, before turning and gesturing towards the enormous tree. "We have supper ready and then you need a good night's sleep. The morning is an appropriate time to commence our efforts. I shall have some help in that," Fernis said, eyes twinkling as he smiled again. "There are some who wish to be part of this effort."

So saying, Fernis led the way to the tree and then inside it, through a doorway that Varna was sure did not exist until they reached it. Inside was a single large room, with a large wooden table spread with a variety of simple and wholesome foods, leafy greens, fruits of all shapes and sizes, breads and vegetables. Reclining on cushions scattered around the room were three people.

"Balgor!" Varna exclaimed, her face lighting up as the sandy-haired Guardian rose from where he had lounged and moved to greet her, seemingly oblivious to the others as he took her hands and greeted her with a chaste kiss on each cheek.

"It seems one of us has met his match, at last," said a woman dryly as she also stood. "I am Eresh. Mage Drewflin, I wish to thank you for your efforts to save my people after the rebellion. You may not be aware of it fully but your efforts and those of the Guides and Mages of that time were instrumental in allowing them to survive and develop. I am in your debt. And I, too, welcome the Children. Varna, I look forward to helping you to unlock your gifts."

"Nicely said," the third said, stepping forward. "I am Ogun, and I welcome you also. It will be my task to help you to understand yourself," this to Dalresar, "and to explain your place, as far as we know it. We are a little in the dark, of course, and so we're making the best guesses that we can based on our reading of the Prophecy."

"Ogun? Then Dalresar's gifts involve...?" Flin paused, looking from Ogun to Dalresar.

"Battle!" Ogun said with some relish. "I will help you to make the most of your gifts, and I expect you will play a significant role in the times to come."

"I can think of someone who will be just a little envious of that," Varna said with a laugh, one hand still claimed by Balgor, not that she seemed to mind.

"Blaine has his own role to play," Ogun said. "He will have other guidance when the time is right."

"So, introductions are done for now. You have come a long way and I know you are weary. Varna has had a difficult time, notwithstanding what Balgor has been able to do to help her, and we have a lot to do in only a short time. Let us eat and then rest, if Balgor feels ready to let Varna have the use of both hands, that is," Fernis quipped.

Balgor actually blushed as he released Varna's hand, causing the other Guardians to laugh at his discomfiture.

"Oh, I've been waiting for this," Eresh said with a crafty smile. "The prankster has been caught at last."

She led the way to the table with a wink to Varna.

The three travellers were made to feel very comfortable, and the meal was enjoyed by all. Eresh and Ogun, two of the Guardians who had left Ennaris in response to the strictures placed on them by the Prophecy, told tales of their travels through the galaxy, including stories of their efforts to lift several races to the early stages of higher civilisation that left Varna spell-bound. Flin brought the company back to the present with his own stories of the rebellion's aftermath and the attempts to help the people of Ennaris survive. Those stories were given a completely new perspective by Fernis and Balgor, who imparted their own views, including information that Flin had never known.

He recalled trying to help the people north of what became known as the Gulf of Ennaris when the cities of Wentogar and Fellanor were destroyed by Goroth's forces. The effects caused a rift to form such that the great valley holding several small lakes was opened to the sea. The Mages and remaining Guides had sought to lead the people away from the now unstable area and, using their gifts to help plants grow, had provided short-term relief from hunger in a small valley where they caused gardens to grow. That garden valley was long gone now, Flin said regretfully, as one of the failures they had been forced to endure. Fernis shook his head, long locks flowing back and forth.

"Not so, Drewflin, not so at all. In fact, Lak has started to regenerate the gardens. Yes, they need a lot of work but the valley remains. Know that those gardens helped the people to survive for two generations, sufficient that they learned to survive in what have become the sandy steppes. Those gardens are part of the legends of those people, and they honour still the memory of the Guides involved."

"Similarly, your work to save those in the frozen wilderness was effective. It was the same for those of the south who were forced to endure the rapid march of desert. They survived and have thrived in what became a truly harsh part of Ennaris." Eresh took up the story. "As I found when I returned. Your interventions were timely and critical."

"But millions, billions, died," Flin said in a low voice, with anguish threaded through every word, and a deep rage simmering below the anguish. "And so did the Guides, and we, I, could not halt it. All I could do was watch it happen."

"No, you were unable to stop global catastrophe," Balgor chimed in. "Nor were we able to do so, and believe me when I say that we had more power between us than you have ever had as the Magi. And like you, we have suffered accordingly, and lost our friends and family. But we also recognised that we would not be able to save Ennaris entirely, which is why we lent you support where we could. But do not hold yourself responsible for what happened. Goroth and his ilk caused the loss and destruction. A few ruthless and selfish people caused much subsequent loss of life and damage to Ennaris and its inhabitants."

"What you and the remaining Mages did do, though," Fernis said, "was despair and this led you to remove yourselves from the Ennarisi for long periods. We were unable to help you. For that, we share accountability, no matter that we were responding to dire predictions of destruction should our reduced presence be known."

"We did," Flin said quietly, dropping his head. "We realised that we would be unable to return Ennaris to any semblance of what it had been, and we drew away from the rampant greed and self-interest that grew rapidly. I made the decision to go into stasis and only return periodically."

"One aspect of that is that the presence of the Magi was forgotten," Balgor said. "And perhaps as a result of that so were the Guardians. Luckily, we don't need people to believe in us, and we certainly don't need them to worship us."

"Indeed we don't," Eresh said between gritted teeth. "Remind me to tell you what idiocy I found when I returned. It's going to take me a while to get it right."

"Others have found the same or similar," Fernis said with a wry smile tugging at his lips. "You can't expect to be gone for millennia and find things just as you left them."

"Likki found cannibalism in her name! Blood offerings!" Eresh was mortified. "How could our people have fallen so far?"

"That would have been in Waslir, I expect," Flin said. "We often had to spend time there each time we came out of stasis to stamp out new forms of blood worship. For some reason the priesthood had a real hold over the people there and it kept recurring. I thought we stamped it out but we found some of the supposed Waslit priests trying to sacrifice women and children not so long ago." He shook his head. "We managed to stop it but they were a long way from the jungles."

"Likki drove them away," Balgor said with a grimace. "It looks like we'll have to be wary of things like that."

"I expect if we went back far enough, we would find Goroth's hand in there somewhere, or more likely Grensor's. It's a way to unbalance society and that was what Goroth would have wanted, but the method is pure Grensor." Flin rubbed a hand across his face. "Forgive me, but I feel the need for sleep, and I expect Varna and Dalresar do likewise. We have come here as a result of a summons for Varna, but I feel some urgency in understanding what is happening through the various lands. So, I plan to head back to the Council Chamber shortly."

"Of course, Drewflin," Fernis replied. "We have chambers readied for you and your companions. After a good rest we will start to train both Varna and Dalresar. And you and I have several things to discuss before you depart. For now, rest."

Balgor took charge of showing them to rooms that had been carved out of the tree somehow. They seemed to walk a long way, through corridors with chambers leading off them, all showing unmistakable signs of being tunnelled through wood but it was seemingly impossible for them to be within the confines of the tree trunk. Flin and Dalresar were left in their chambers, and Varna was taken slightly further to a room that seemed to overlook the Forest through a window.

"Is this real," she asked Balgor, standing at the window and looking over the Forest.

"Yes and no," Balgor said, moving to stand close behind her, one hand resting lightly on her waist. "Yes, in that we are high in Fernis' tree and can see over the Forest as a result. No, in that this is a sort of viewscreen rather than a window in the tree itself. And don't even ask about how all of this fits in. Just accept that it does, okay?"

"Okay," Varna said with a smile, leaning back into Balgor. "Is Fernis the only Guardian here? Some of the trees are sentient also."

"Oh, that's because of Fernis. He has lived inside this tree, been part of this tree, for so long that the surrounding Forest has, well, inherited some of the overflow of his presence. Some of these trees are many tens of thousands of cycles old and they have become sort of aware." Balgor shrugged. "They really were quite excited to have you here. Like us, they have been waiting for this time for long ages."

"Does that mean your wall is also aware?" Varna asked, half-turning to watch Balgor's expression.

"No. The trees are organic and so can have those sorts of impressions made on them. The wall is not. Oh, it may be stronger than when it was made, but it can never be self-aware in any way."

"Hmmm, so Fernis has created a new race of beings? I can feel them when I open my perceptions. They do seem to be watching me fairly closely." Varna felt a little discomforted by that.

"A new race? Why, that may be the case," Balgor said, considering. "You know, I don't think we have considered that. We just accepted that Fernis has had a sort of influence. With Pio back that may be stronger. I'll have to discuss that with him. As to their interest, well, I can shield that for you until such time as you can do so yourself. Done. They're disappointed!"

"And why are you here rather than at the Citadel? Not that I mind. I've missed having you around," Varna said lightly.

"Well, I wanted to see you again and this was a good opportunity, so here I am."

"You could have seen me any time, I'm guessing. Why now?"

Balgor hesitated and Varna was astonished to recognise a sort of shyness in him. He looked out the "window" as he sought for words.

"Balgor? What is it?"

"I, um, have found that I wanted to be with you," he said. "I mean, that I, um, have felt, ah, less for you being away. In fact, I, ah, was hoping that you might have, well, felt ..."

"The same?" Varna smiled at Balgor's awkwardness.

"Um, well yes," Balgor said, making eye contact with Varna, and sighed. "I'm not very good at this. I have never sought any form of intimacy with any of the Ennarisi, although others have."

"Is that even possible?" Varna turned her back to the view and looked up into Balgor's eyes. "Are you taller?" she asked accusingly.

"Maybe a little," Balgor replied, visibly losing height to be back to the same height as Varna.

"Well don't do that again. It's bad enough that you're this great god-like creature - yes, I know, you're not a god, but it's near enough. What I don't need is for you to change who you are with me. So, is it even possible?"

Balgor smiled sheepishly. "Yes, more than possible. You see, the Ennarisi were seeded by the same force that seeded us, the Guardians. And the same that seeded your planet, Earth. We were corporeal, just like you, until we evolved to be able to control energy with our minds. It was always one of the things we could do to some extent, but some of us became so good at it that we sort of outgrew our own planet. That was in another galaxy. But this is the real me, when I choose to take my own form. Just as Fernis tonight showed you his real form, and Eresh showed her own. We usually do take our own physical form when we, um, solidify. And the rest of us is pretty much compatible with the Ennarisi and with you. Most of the Guardians have had partners from time to time among the Ennarisi people. And, of course, the Ennarisi cross-bred with the people of Earth also, so elements of our physiology intermixed with yours."

"That's where the gifts come from?" Varna asked shrewdly.

"Yes, most likely," Balgor nodded. "Perhaps not completely, though. I expect there was some sort of transference from the base stock seeded such a long time ago. But the bloodlines would have spread the gifts among the population."

"So, you never felt the need to have an Ennarisi partner?"

"No. Up to the time of the rebellion's end I actually led a fairly self-absorbed existence and didn't take too much notice of the people of the planet. I spent a lot of time with the moons and other satellites. It was one reason I was selected to remain, because I had fewer ties that might get in the way." He grimaced and then shrugged. "I didn't realise how lonely that could be, and how alone I probably was, until meeting you. Of course, I'm not supposed to have any ties still, but ..."

"But you can't help Mother Nature?" Varna smiled.

"Oh, but we can," Balgor said with a wicked grin. "We can indeed."

"Three thousand?" King Ensert asked of his guard captain, Sir Linset.

"Aye, my king," Linset replied. "This army has been marching around in the northern reaches of Hensert laying waste to all they could find. I've sent some scouts out to see what that might actually mean. Apparently, this army means to attack Escar and then return to join the main norther army. The woman who brought the message told a garbled tale about ancient myths come back to life and coming to destroy us all. She was part of a travelling troupe and they were overrun by a group of soldiers. Most were killed and their captain, or someone who was called a captain, selected four to escape and inform us that they were coming."

"Why would you do that?" Ensert asked, mystified.

Linset shrugged and shook his head. He had no idea why someone would do that either. Selecting a group to escape and to inform the people who could stand against you that you were coming was a strange action. Telling of your army's strength and planned route was not something they would have done either.

Ensert turned to the two who sat at ease by the king's side, travelling Tellers who had been coming to Escar quite frequently of late.

"Have you heard anything of this?" Ensert asked of the Tellers.

"No," the first Teller replied. "But we came from the south-west this trip, so if they truly were killing everyone and everything up there, we wouldn't necessarily hear about it. And, in reality, there isn't much up there anyway. A few towns and scattered farms. If this is a norther army, they won't really have too many ideas about life outside the twin kingdoms."

"It's still strange, though," Ensert said. "Why give away your strategic advantage like that?"

"The norther people are held firmly under control," the Teller said. "The Tang have had people go into the norther kingdoms and see what they're doing from time to time. Apart from breeding they don't seem to do much. It's a very hard land and lacks almost every amenity. Education is severely lacking except for the elite, and even they have little understanding of Ennaris. The whole place is kept in a sort of siege mentality. I wonder," the Teller looked to the ceiling in thought and turned to his fellow, who merely quirked an eyebrow in query.

"Wonder what?"

"Well," the Teller made a slight gesture to indicate that he was only stating a possibility, "it may be that this captain thought he was being quite smart. If I was trying to scare everyone into falling apart, I would make sure they knew of this army's approach. If I was living far enough in the past, when this whole part of Escar was ruled by petty warlords who didn't cooperate with each other, that tactic could cause them to fall back on their own defences and leave the rest to make their own arrangements."

"But the last time this area had those warlords was over three hundred cycles ago," Linset objected. "No-one could believe that was the case still."

"And it was Ensert's ancestor who ended that time, although he started as one of those warlords," the Teller said.

"Yes, that's true," Ensert replied. "But Linset's right in that it was a long time ago."

"Not so long for some," the Teller replied with a smile. "What ancient myths did you refer to?"

"That's stranger still," Linset scowled. "She said that the army marched under the instruction of the Old One, who this captain said was Grensor. And that they awaited Goroth's coming to destroy us all. Madness!"

"Not so mad, perhaps," the Teller said. "Grensor was never found after the rebellion. The Prophecy tells us that Goroth will return. In fact, we have seen the portents already, which is what we came to discuss with you."

"Well, it will have to hold for a while. I have something else to deal with now," Ensert replied. "Stay here, please, both of you. This concerns the news you brought and the stories you have been repeating in the taverns."

Ensert gave a signal to a hovering guard, who marched to the heavy, iron-bound double doors and pulled one open. He nodded to someone outside and stood back. Through the door walked a man of average height, with thinning dark hair. He wore robes of exquisite quality and a haughty expression of supreme arrogance. He was followed by a guard who went straight to Linset and spoke to him in low tones.

"My liege," the newcomer said in an oily tone, with a faint nod of the head.

"Krytfor, what's this I'm hearing about Guardians returning, Mages coming back to life and strange and unworldly beast-men?" King Ensert asked of his chief advisor bluntly. "Why is it I heard about these events from passing Tellers and not from my advisor?"

Krytfor's arrogance slipped. He looked uncomfortable and did not meet his sovereign's eyes, so Ensert was ready for the lie.

"Why, I have heard nothing at all, my liege," the advisor replied, striving to make his tone light. "I doubt that myths can come to life, anyway, so I would not take to heart what a wandering Teller says."

"I would have thought that also, had it not been for the master merchant and the caravan master who both gave the same information to my guard captain. It seems the lands around have been seething with the news, and the fact that the Faero has passed over and been replaced by his son. Last I knew Corm was a blundering fool more interested in wine and women, but it seems he has become something more. Know you any of this also?"

Krytfor smiled a sickly smile, probably believing it was one of confidence.

"Nay, my lord, and as you know my cousin, Creely, formerly Chamberlain of the Citadel of the Faero, has been staying with me for the last three ten-days and has mentioned nought of these things. Again, I am inclined to believe they are fabrications."

"Indeed?" Ensert responded, brushing back long moustaches with one hand. "Why don't we find out for sure, then? I have asked your cousin Creely to attend this morning. These men are the Tellers who have been recounting those stories and myths, and who have brought us disquieting news." He made a signal to one of the guards in the throne room. "Bring in Creely."

Krytfor started and stared at the Tellers, now standing with Linset and obviously having been in discussion with Ensert. Dressed in long brown robes hemmed with blue-grey coloured material along the edges, black boots and breeches and pale blue shirts, the Tellers' sense of calm and air of confidence shook Krytfor. The huge wooden beam doors were pulled open to admit Creely, looking nervous, scared and quite unwell. The Tellers' confident mien made Creely's unease even more evident. Krytfor licked his lips as the Tellers bowed as one to Ensert and smiled.

"My lord Ensert, we have been honoured to be asked to attend your presence," one Teller said smoothly as he rose from the bow. "We have passed our news as requested. How may we assist you further?"

"Do you have any idea why I asked for you to attend me this day?" Ensert asked.

"As you have said, because of the news we have been spreading. Although from the appearance of friend Creely here I assume it has to do with events in the Citadel of the Faero. It's my understanding that Creely had to depart somewhat rapidly." The Teller paused to smile knowingly. "It was a life and death decision, as I heard it."

"Oh?"

"I would not listen too much to these Tellers, my lord," Krytfor broke in hurriedly, sweat beading on his upper lip. "They are known for inventing stories, as you well know."

The Teller nodded.

"Indeed, we are known for inventions, my lord," he said, noting Krytfor's relieved smile. "But our primary task is to pass the news of the land to all who wish to hear. And in that role, we deal in facts only."

"And the tales you were telling in the Blue Roc tavern last evening?" Ensert asked. "Of the events at the Citadel?"

"All true, my lord," the Teller nodded. "As told to us by someone of good repute who was there at the time and took note of all that occurred. In fact, she took part in the defence of the city."

"She?" Ensert's expression changed to one of concern, with a brooding anger not far away.

"Indeed, my lord. 'She'." The Teller smiled broadly. "Do you wish to guess who that may be?"

"I was not made aware of this," Ensert said through gritted teeth, "even in her own missives."

Krytfor's lips were trembling, and Creely looked like he wanted to sink through the enormous stones of the floor to the chamber.

"In fact, it is our understanding that the Princess has sent many such missives, my lord, without reply." The Teller smiled wryly. "Which is why she asked us to deliver her latest one."

"So, tell me, Krytfor, why did my daughter's letters not make their way to me?" Ensert's anger was clear for all to see now.

"Y - y - you said you did not want to hear what the Princess Anhelter had to say, my lord," the advisor stammered. "So, I, I merely acceded to your wishes."

"And you read those letters and yet did not see fit to let me know what they said?" Ensert held up a bundle for all to see. "These letters?"

Krytfor stared at the king's hand, holding a parcel of letters aloft, feeling sick to the depths of his stomach, wondering why he had kept them. He made no comment.

"And these letters accuse Creely of being in league with Goroth's minions, of accepting red gold in payment and attempting to subvert the Faero. Your cousin, Krytfor. What say you to that, Creely?"

The king turned to stare at the former Chamberlain.

Creely stared at Ensert with undisguised hatred. His fear was overwhelmed by the depth of his feelings and he snarled, even as one of the guards clapped a gauntleted hand on his shoulder and held him in place.

"You have no idea what you do, kingling," he said in disgust, waving one arm wide. "None of you do. The power of Goroth rises and you will have no answer for it when it comes for you. My master awakens and will continue the fight for this land."

"So, you admit to being in the pay of Goroth? I had always thought he was just a tale to frighten children." Ensert looked to the Tellers.

"No tale, fool," Creely spat. "I serve Grensor, who is Goroth's right hand. Goroth will be your master if you even survive what is to come."

"Indeed, my lord," the first Teller said, "Goroth is not a tale, as we have just discussed. That is one of the truths we tell, even though people have forgotten that such is the case. And Goroth is stirring from his captivity, as the Prophecy says."

Ensert twisted his mouth as though tasting something foul.

"Take these two away," he instructed his guard chief.

"And do what with them, my lord?" that worthy asked.

"I care not. Use them for target practice for all I care. They are condemned as traitors and worse and I sentence them to die for their crimes. Make it happen."

The chief of the guard bowed and made a signal. The two men were marched out forcefully at the hands of guardsmen.

"What am I to make of this?" Ensert asked of the Tellers.

"Why, my lord, you have been given advice for quite a long time designed to ensure that you did not take part in any joined actions. The time for those actions is at hand, so it was time to bring events to light." The first Teller smiled gently to the king. "The Faero will have need of the knights, my lord."

"Even more, my liege, we may have that need closer to hand," the chief of guards said carefully.

"Why is that?" Ensert asked warily.

"News has arrived via the Clans telling of an army of the twin kingdoms emerging on the grass plain, my liege. They are said to be three thousand strong. This must be the army we have just talked about," Linset replied. "But it is also reported that they have been joined by some sort of monsters, my liege."

"Monsters? What sort of fanciful notion is that?" Ensert responded, an element of disdain in his voice.

"If those monsters are what I think they are, King Ensert, they are ghazrak," the second Teller said. "Goroth had ghazrak to serve as his shock troops during the rebellion, created by himself and Grensor."

"Goroth and Grensor? Names of myth and legend, but you say they are real?"

"Aye, my lord, very real."

Silence fell as King Ensert turned to place the packet of his daughter's letters on the heavy table behind him.

"It seems we face an enemy of great power, if Goroth it is. How do we stand against him, even with the Faero and others from Ennaris?" Ensert muttered, as he scrubbed his face tiredly.

"We must prepare to defend against the norther army, my liege," Linset said carefully. "We have warned that they will come against Escar. That may be no more than two tendays."

"Aye, you will have to take up that fight," the first Teller nodded. "But you should also know that the norther kingdoms have been Grensor's for most of the time since the rebellion. So, you will be taking the fight to Goroth's minion. When the time comes for you to join with the others under the Faero's banner, will you do so?"

The Tellers looked at Ensert closely.

"We are but men, not Mages," Ensert said in a tone that was almost one of despair.

"Events move forward. The time of the Prophecy is at hand, my lord, and you must recall what that says. The Children of Ennaris have returned and walk the land, and the remaining Mages will take up the fight. The Guardians have indeed returned, my lord."

"More tales and myths. How can I be sure of that? Tales are no substitute for proof, and I have been hearing nought but tales, it would seem, from all and sundry." Ensert's anger rose again. "Tell me Teller, how can you be sure of this? I need to be sure now."

The Tellers glanced to each other and nodded shortly. Both reached beneath their robe, causing Linset to react by unsheathing his sword. But the Tellers only revealed short lengths of old wood, gnarled and dark with age and with darkened stones embedded at their top. The king and his guard watched in awe as the short lengths extended in unison to become full length staffs and the stones flared to life. Blue-grey light flooded the chamber. The Tellers' eyes glinted, reflecting the colour emanating from the stone.

"I am Raglin, Mage of the Council of Guides, and this is my brother Ragnor, and I tell you truly Ensert, King of Escar, that the time of the Prophecy is at hand. Hear me well! Your Faero has need of your service to protect this land from the ancient forces that seek to destroy it utterly. It is your duty!"

The king stared at the men in front of him, simple Tellers no more but two of the mythical Mages, and in his astonishment, he said nothing. As the light faded from the staffs in front of him the chief of the guard looked from king to Mages, wonder in his eyes.

"It's also about the only way you're going to survive," Ragnor said in a more reasonable tone with a shrug. "We haven't seen them, but if that norther army is three thousand strong then it's only a small part of the total forces Grensor has available, from what we've been told by the Tang scouts."

Ensert stared at the twins, nodding as though to himself.

"My king, do I call out the Gathering?" Linset asked.

Ensert roused himself after a lengthy period of thought and looked from the Mage to his chief of guards who had just asked the question. He nodded.

"Aye, sound the Gathering. Get all preparations under way to defend against this army. Escar rides!"

Morsen watched as the army divided. Most of the regular army would move back to the safe confines of the twin kingdoms. Only the red Legion would remain to act as protection for Morsen and a few of his command staff. The regular army had been deemed to be too important to the final battle to risk it in the second phase of the plan. In place of the more than two thousand of the regular army that had returned to the twin kingdoms was a mass of irregulars, partly trained men and women armed with whatever weaponry could be made available. Morsen had about five thousand of them which, he thought, should make them a viable force to create damage. What they lacked in discipline they made up for in enthusiasm and numbers.

The small number of ghazrak that Morsen had in his army for the first phase had been difficult to control, and at least two of them had to be executed when they attacked and killed their own norther patrol, feasting on the flesh of the patrol's first and second before the black one could exert control. Now he had many more, although by no means the full number that the Old One had available. The ghazrak were a force to be careful of. Far be it for one such as Morsen to criticise the Old One or the great Goroth, but there was something very wrong about the ghazrak. These creatures that were made rather than born were terrible to watch in action, and worse when not fighting.

And the winged ones! They made his blood freeze in his veins. They exuded malevolence. All ghazrak existed to kill and destroy but the winged ones were even more efficient at killing than the land-bound ones. Morsen would use them, of course, for they gave his army an edge that could not be denied, and they could not be defeated from what he had seen so far. There were only a few of the winged ones, but the Old One had promised that more would be coming soon, as there would be many more of the normal ghazrak.

Then there were the black ones. Morsen was sure that they could read his very thoughts, but there was no way for him to gain any sort of understanding of them. Once he had been in the Old One's presence when he demanded that one of the black ones removed his hood. He saw nothing but a faint grey haze where a person's head would be. To say that Morsen was astounded would be true, but that simple word could not convey the shock and fear that coursed through him. That these could then be revealed to be the Children of Ennaris, as had been reported to Morsen, was a second blow. The Children of Ennaris were meant to be the Ennarisi who would lead them to victory over the hated Mages who had enslaved the races of Ennaris. These shapeless creatures of mist most certainly were not Ennarisi. The story of them being from another world was fanciful. Nothing in Morsen's education, or that of any other norther, spoke of other worlds with people. There was only Ennaris with the Ennarisi.

Still, the black ones did seem to be able to exert some control over the ghazrak, so for now he would use them also. As a soldier, he looked for advantage, and he would need any he could find. As a soldier of the twin kingdoms, he followed his orders to the letter. The Old One may be ancient but he retained his power, and Morsen had seen what happened when his orders were questioned, let alone disobeyed. In common with most norther men and women, Morsen had long ago learned to school his expression and behaviour to suit the occasion, and no occasion allowed for dissent or the possibility of dissent.

The plan called for Escar to be rendered incapable of fielding a force to support the Faero in the near future. Neither Morsen nor his commanders expected to be able to defeat the fortress city, although they would try to do so. Rather, the goal was to reduce the army to relative impotence and to stay at home. The ghazrak would have the most impact in that goal, Morsen admitted. The irregular force would cause problems but were meant to wear down the defenders. It was callous but such was the plan. Morsen held his scepticism at bay as his army marched away.

35. Oracle of Manis Reach

Trees, trees and more trees. Blaine, while maintaining a careful watch as they rode their hrss along a poorly kept road, bemoaned the fact that they continued to travel through heavily wooded areas. He knew from the scans ahead of the mission that the planet had desert and grassy steppes, as well as mountains and rocky coasts, but where they had landed was all trees.

Blaine could feel himself changing, and it was uncomfortable. He had been on many missions on many planets in his time with the Warriors and during his earlier military career. It was rare to find a planet in the Union where some form of higher industrialisation had not occurred. Of course, he reflected, Ennaris had been the pre-eminent civilisation in times past, and the current position was the result of the rebellion and its aftermath, so he was being unfair. But when he considered that there was only a tiny population relative to what Ennaris had before, he could feel nothing but horror at the scale of the loss of life that had ensued.

No matter that it was thousands of Earth years ago, the fact was that fellow beings had died in the billions as the result of the actions of a single man and his followers. Blaine was a Warrior in every sense of the word, and death was nothing new to him in its many forms, but the scale of that loss was staggering.

He was musing on what Earth would have been like had all but the smallest part of its population been destroyed when he noticed that the sounds of the woods had diminished. Bird-life remained but only smaller birds were in evidence. The occasional sounds of larger animals moving through the undergrowth were no longer evident. And the road was showing signs of more intensive use. He knew what that meant.

"Town coming up," Blaine said to Jalor.

Jalor just nodded. He was not as attuned to the wood noises as Blaine quickly had become, but he had noted the road's condition. As they continued the sounds of the town could be heard, at first faintly and then growing clearer. Inevitably the first sound was of a blacksmith's hammer. Only when very close could other sounds be distinguished - people calling, animals calling - but the hammer of metal on metal was distinctive. Jalor now knew that it told him that the town was larger than the small villages that they had passed through not long before, which usually were too small to have a blacksmith, but the fact that he could only hear one indicated that it would be a small town. Larger towns tended to have more than a single blacksmith.

This town had two streets running parallel, with myriad alleys running between them. The road Jalor and Blaine followed ran through the town, and the second was carved from the wood to run beside it. They walked past small thatched cottages of a type they now knew well, nodded politely to townspeople who regarded them with wary suspicion, and correctly so in Blaine's estimation. He noted that many of the men had swords strapped to their belts and all carried belt knives, including the women. They had not seen that since their dealings with the Blood, and they were a people within a people. This town was on guard, but the people did not seem to be panicked. Just careful.

As they started to move further into the town Blaine noted that most of the alleys had been blocked where they formed a boundary to the town, acting as a defensive barrier. The ones that remained open had materials stacked ready to be thrown into place to close the gaps also. The internal alleys were clear of refuse and Blaine could see a large barrel, and at times two of them, placed near each and every building. He made a wager with himself that the barrels held water. He revised his thinking - this town was not on guard; it was ready for a fight. He glanced to Jalor who just nodded, having come to the same conclusion.

At about the midpoint of the path through the town a larger passage, a cross-road in reality, led to the second street and that was where the town square was located. Stopping at the cross-road while Jalor made the turn and headed towards the square, Blaine could make out fields beyond the other exit, stretching into the distance. They were neatly laid out. Furrowed soil was in those close to the town and some sort of crop was carried by those further along. People were working in the fields. It was a peaceful scene, Blaine thought, except for the preparations for defence. He nudged his hrss into motion again to catch up to Jalor.

As they reached the square the smith's hammer stopped, as did many of the minor sounds of the township. People stopped what they were doing to look at the newcomers. Stare was too strong a word, but there was definitely a close scrutiny of them. Looking around, they spied what looked like the only tavern in town and headed toward it without any conversation. As always, the tavern was the most likely place to meet people and find out what was happening. The two hrss were tied to posts in front of the tavern, and they moved inside.

"Mornin'," Blaine greeted the waitress as he and Jalor took a seat at a table closest to the square. Here they could see what was happening but also give some assurance that they were not doing anything untoward. In a town that seemed to be on edge that was a consideration that both automatically took into account. "Two o' ya best ales, if'n ya please," he continued in a drawl.

"Coming right up," she replied, moving behind the simple counter to pour the drinks into two somewhat battered but obviously clean tankards.

Blaine nodded thanks and handed over two coins, waving away change. Both sampled the drinks, finding them acceptable and settled back. They had worked their way through no more than a third of their drinks when the waitress returned.

"Don't recall seeing either of you gents before," she said. "Name's Edmas, by the way."

"Blaine and Jalor," said Blaine, pointing to each in turn and adopting a slower drawl. "Nope, we've not been this way before. Been travellin' roun' the region a bit. Headin' fer the Citadel. Seems like a nice town, although you do seem to be settin' up fer a fight."

Jalor's lips quirked as Blaine fell into a passable imitation of the Ecturian horse-herders they had spent time with on a former mission.

"We've been havin' problems with strange people attackin' people, breakin' into places and such," Edmas replied. "Looks like a band of bandits have taken up a place in the region and they are thinkin' Manis Reach - that's this town, by the way - is ripe for them to use when they feel like it."

"How many?" Jalor asked.

"Not too sure. Last time they come they was about twenty, but we can't be sure that was all of 'em."

"Likely not to be. There would'a bin lookouts an' such," Blaine chimed in. "Prob'ly another four, mebbe five, of 'em out thar."

Jalor grimaced. Blaine's Ecturian horse-herders were blending into Triellic freighters. The combination was not good on the ear!

"What we thought," Edmas agreed. "That's a fair number for us to defend against. Not had to worry about that before this, so we're not really all that well prepared. But the Oracle told us what we should do. And it's worked so far."

"Oracle?" Jalor asked. "Someone is advising you?"

"Not someone," Edmas responded, smiling and shaking her head. "Senasarra was first found by Mannat, Grannad's gramp, oh, would be forty cycles gone now. He was out huntin' and got himself chased by a grintas. Ended up fallin' down a small gap in rocks and gettin' trapped. The grintas couldn't get to him so he laid there a while unconscious. When he woke up he asked out loud where he was, talkin' to himself, you know, and got the shock of his life when the voice came out of the cave and told him he was caught in a small crevice four hundred fifty spans from Manis Reach."

"A voice from a cave, ye say?" Blaine asked, his accent straying even more into Triellic. "Sounds a bit far-fetched, innit?"

"Well, the people thought so when old Mannat made his way back to town. But, next day he took some o' them back and showed them where he fell. And some of them climbed down and took a look in and sure enough there was somethin' in there. So they said hello and it said hello right back to them and asked how it could be o' service." Edmas laughed. "The way the story goes none o' them knew what to make of it so they just asked who it was and the voice said it's Senasarra and asked again how it can assist."

"Senasarra? That's an odd name," Jalor mused. "What happened after that?"

"Yep, odd enough name. But finally, someone got around to askin' an actual question. Just for the heck of it Unthat, him who was black-smith before Hunder, asked what the weather would be like next day. Well, Senasarra told him the weather would be clear in the mornin' but a storm would blow up before night. Well, they didn't know what to make o' that so after a little while askin' questions and not under-standin' much of the answers they went home and waited. Sure enough, next day was bright and clear but clouded over fast and by night it was a cold rain."

"So this Senasarra can tell the weather?" Blaine asked, losing bits of his accent. "Ya just need to look at the sky and read some o' the animal and bird actions to tell that usually."

"Sure," agreed Edmas, "but after that they started to ask more questions and got good answers. Things like how to make the fields yield better, and what was eatin' the melons, and stuff like that. Unthat asked about how to make his ploughs better and got a whole lot of stuff about mixin' different ores and how to temper the metal. His ploughs are better than any others and most o' them are still going'. Hunder inherited all o' that and is tryin' to make 'em better still."

"I think I'd like to speak with Senasarra, if that can be arranged?" Jalor said thoughtfully.

"You prob'ly should ask Hunder about that. We don't make a lot of noise about it but we don't hide it away neither. Hunder will be comin' in soon for his supper and I know he was plannin' on goin' out tomorrow." Edmas nodded to herself in affirmation.

"Can we arrange a room and some food, then?" Jalor asked. "We may as well stay here for the night, if that's possible. And a repeat of these," he added, gesturing to the tankards.

"Sure, we have rooms at the back. Standard fare good enough for you? It's just bread and stew but we make a good one."

"Standard fare will be fine," Jalor agreed.

As Edmas headed off to the kitchen, Jalor and Blaine shared a glance and a shrug. Neither knew what to make of the discussion, but they also knew that discussing it would not help.

The next morning was partly overcast and a breeze was blowing but rain did not seem likely. Patchy clouds scudded across the blue sky as Jalor and Blaine made their way to Hunder's forge. They had spent considerable time with the smith the previous evening and were impressed at his efforts to improve his metal-working techniques. Senasarra had been giving him instruction in how to smelt different alloys, a term that he had not known but was developing the techniques anyway. So far, he said, he had been able to make ploughshares that resisted rust but he was having trouble getting the metal strong enough. It still picked up nicks from rocks and he was hoping Senasarra would be able to give him some advice.

The smith was waiting, his massive chest and shoulders making it clear what his trade was. He greeted them in his deep voice and with few additional words led the way. The three men exited the town through a path that ran behind the tavern and up the slope, into a rocky and densely wooded area. The trail was well defined, and Hunder told them that the townspeople ensured that it was accessible. It was not far to walk, and within a short while they arrived at what had once been a cliff-face but was now a jumble of rock and scree. The path to the cave had been improved over the time since Senasarra had been discovered and now wended through the large rocks, ending at a dark opening. Here Hunder stopped and pointed. A short way into the tunnel two huge boulders had come to rest, leaving a small opening.

"Senasarra is behind these rocks," Hunder said. "We've tried to make the opening larger but so far we've not been able to make much impression on it. It's a type of rock that is very hard."

So saying, he moved to the gap while Blaine examined the boulders, running one hand across the roughened surface. His expression was one of surprise as he felt the rock's texture. Jalor glanced to him and then moved to stand near Hunder.

"Senasarra," Hunder called.

A voice from within the cave responded immediately.

"Greetings Hunder," it said. "Greetings also to Jalor and Blaine. How may I be of assistance."

Hunder laughed at Blaine's expression of surprise when Senasarra acknowledged the two Warriors. Jalor merely nodded, as though it was expected and merely confirmed a suspicion he had formed. Hunder turned back to the oracle.

"Senasarra, I need to know more about how to make my ploughshares stronger. I tried what you said and it doesn't seem to have worked."

"Did you obtain the correct wood to form the charcoal and then use the coal from the deposit I mentioned to you?" Senasarra asked in an even tone.

"I managed to get the wood alright," Hunder confirmed, "but haven't been able to locate the coal so I used the same stuff I usually use."

"You need the alternative coal, what is called thermal coal. It burns hotter than the less dense type that you have used to date, and the additional heat is necessary for you to blend the metals correctly. With the extra heat you will also get a better tempered steel alloy and thus a stronger outcome."

"Ah, okay." Hunder scratched behind one ear. "Guess I better go find that thermy coal."

"Do you recall the location I gave you?"

"Yep. I can get a couple of the men to give me a hand. It's not very deep you said?"

"My ... understanding ... is that it is close to the surface in that location and may even be exposed."

"Right. Well, Jalor here wants to ask you a question or two also. Is that okay?"

"Indeed, it is. Welcome Jalor, how may I be of assistance?"

"Thanks, Hunder. We can take if from here. I think we can find our way back to town. Meet us at the tavern later and we might be able to help you with the new coal also." Jalor nodded confidently as Hunder looked uncertain.

"Well, I have plenty to do," the blacksmith said. "I'll see you tonight, then."

As Hunder made his way back out of the tight space, Jalor turned to Blaine and gestured. With a nod Blaine followed Hunder to make sure that he had departed and checked the surrounding area quickly but carefully.

"Clear," he reported when he returned. "Hunder is well on his way back and there is no-one around."

"Okay. Then let's see what we have here." Jalor turned to the hole in the rocks, thought a moment and then addressed the patiently waiting oracle. "Senasarra, please state your designation and status."

"Sensor Array 413," Senasarra replied without hesitation. "Status active, ninety-five percent of function available."

"What happened to the other five percent?"

"Several sensor nodes were damaged by ground-quakes slightly more than four thousand cycles ago. I have been unable to restore them. All other sensors are functional."

"How far do your sensors extend in this region? Do they cover the town of Manis Reach?"

"Sensor coverage is limited at this time. Damage has been detected to the targeting antenna and so I am unable to contact the imaging satellites."

"Where is the antenna?" Jalor asked, looking around at what remained of the entrance to some sort of passage.

"The antenna array is within the sensor pod, located in a cavern at the end of this access passage."

"Are you the primary node of the array?"

"I am the array," came the reply. "You address one of the access portals to the array."

"Understood," Jalor said, thoughtfully. "Are you linked into the entire planetary system?"

"I am," Sensor Array 413 replied. "My connection to the main array was repaired sixteen days ago."

"Can I make a request of the system?"

There was a short moment which Jalor fancifully thought of as the sensor array sucking its lip as it thought. He exchanged glances with Blaine, who was listening intently. A different voice issued from the array's speaker.

"Council Assistant Five recognises Flight-Colonel Vinca Jalor and Weapons Sergeant Argus Blaine. On authority of Mage Drewflin, Vinca Jalor and Argus Blaine are members of the Council of Mages. Please step closer to the scanner for DNA comparison."

Jalor and Blaine exchanged a surprised look before Jalor turned back to the hole. "We are unable to get further than we are. A rock fall has blocked the entrance to the sensor array's scanner. We only have a small opening in the rock through which we can converse."

"Please extend one arm through the opening," The Council Assistant requested.

Jalor shrugged and complied, after removing his jacket and rolling up his sleeve. There was a short cheep, which he took to mean whatever was happening was finished, and Blaine took his place and followed suit. Another cheep issued forth from the hole.

"Thank you. Genetic match confirmed. Membership of the Council of Mages is confirmed. System access is open."

Jalor whistled quietly while he thought further. There were so many things he could use this portal to tell him, but his immediate consideration over-rode all others.

"Can you open a channel to the fleet orbiting Ennaris?"

"Which of the two fleets do you wish to contact?" came the reply, causing both Warriors to pause.

"Can you identify the Union vessel *Starfire*?"

"Yes, based on communication traffic being monitored *Starfire* has been identified."

"You can decrypt the communication traffic?" Jalor asked, his voice laced with surprise.

"Yes. It is an advanced method of encryption that required significant system effort to decrypt."

"How long did it take you?" Blaine chimed in, fascinated.

"Fourteen point seven microns," the Council Assistant replied.

"That long, eh?" Jalor muttered, thinking of the legions of cryptologists who would have laboured to develop that secure interface.

"Have you cracked the code for the other fleet also?" asked Blaine.

"Yes. That took three point one microns."

"Well, at least we held out longer," Blaine quipped to Jalor, who nodded with a wry smile.

"Okay, please open a channel to *Starfire*," Jalor directed, nodding to Blaine to do another sweep of the area.

Jalor thought about what was happening here, standing at a hole in the rock interacting with an artificial intelligence system that probably was older than Earth's history of civilisation. And, he thought with a start, on a planet where technology should not work! His thoughts were interrupted by the Council Assistant.

"Contact with *Starfire* has been established. Grand Admiral Serra requested secure mode Alpha-7 which has been established."

Jalor's eyebrows rose in astonishment. That was the highest security protocol the Union had, and this system just invoked it without discernible effort.

"Thank you," Jalor said after a moment. "Admiral, do you read?"

"Jalor, indeed I do. How are you able to make contact? Admiral Bard is with me, by the way."

"Acknowledged. We have located a working advanced AI system from the prior civilisation of this planet, Admiral. There is some sort of interdict on advanced technology functioning but there appear to be holes in the coverage." Jalor took a deep breath before continuing. "But you knew that already, did you not Admiral?"

"Something of the sort," Serra replied, and Jalor could hear humour in her voice. "The current link will remain active for three minutes only, so please make your report."

"Affirmative. We have made contact with the remnants of the former civilisation. The planet was once a unified civilisation but now is fragmented into many small states, after some sort of disaster caused by civil war thousands of years ago. We are working with members of some form of leadership group called Guides, and there seem to be advanced beings called Guardians, whose full role I am yet to understand. We have encountered multiple Shadows, who appear to be working with, or have been coerced to work with some form of enemy force that is preparing to take over this planet." Jalor stopped for a moment.

"How effective is this enemy force?" Serra's voice was tight with tension.

"Not sure at the moment. There seem to be some sort of supernatural capabilities in place, at least, supernatural to us. I think you can expect the same to be coming at you, by the way. The enemy here is related to Likud of the Shadows and I expect that this planet, Ennaris, will be the focus of his efforts."

"Likud?" Serra sounded unsurprised. "Are you sure?"

Jalor's lips quirked. "Sure, Admiral. And it is the original Likud, not a set of hereditary descendants sharing a name. At this stage we are providing support to the titular planetary leader, who actually has almost no power. What we are hoping to do is establish an adequate force capable of withstanding the attack that we expect in the relatively near future."

"Understood. Anything else."

"Yes Admiral. One more thing." Jalor took a deep breath. "Clay survived his landing and some sort of attack for which he used a blitz mine. I repeat, the Champion survived. We have not located him nor do we have any further information."

He waited a moment. "Admiral? Did you get that?"

"Yes, I did," Serra replied, her voice betraying strong emotion.

"My three minutes will be up, Admiral. Do you have any further instructions for me? Any extra intelligence that I should be aware of? You know, from your sources?" He kept his voice steady but knew some of the sarcasm leaked through.

"Nothing specific," she replied serenely. "I do think you can trust these Guides, though. They seem to be working for the same thing as us."

"Affirmative, Admiral. Oh," he continued in an off-hand tone, "you may be interested to know that Blaine and I are now members of something called the Council of Mages."

"What?" Serra responded, shocked. "That, um, sounds interesting?"

Jalor laughed aloud. "Indeed, Admiral."

"This link will close," came the voice of Sensor Array 413.

"Gotta go, Admiral. If I can get in touch again I will. All three of us are intact and we will continue the mission. Note that the parameters have changed, though. Look after yourselves up there."

"Thank you, Jalor." Serra took a deep breath which was audible over the crystal-clear link and said, "Go in the Light of the Guardians, child."

Jalor stared at the hole in the wall.

"Communication link closed," said the sensor array.

"Thank you," Jalor said, distracted, before rousing himself once more. "Are there further sensor arrays nearby?"

"There are sensor arrays across Ennaris," was the reply, "although many have sustained damage and are less functional."

"Is there one at or near the Citadel of the Faero?"

"Yes, within the lower levels of the Citadel there is a portal that was re-activated at the same time I was."

That got Jalor's attention. "How long have you been active?"

"Fifty-two point four cycles," was the reply.

Jalor nodded. About the time of the original mission, if he was not mistaken. Interesting.

The mood in Serra's cabin on *Starfire* was pensive. Admiral Denton Bard looked to the woman who he had trusted with his life all those years ago, who had been lost for such a long time and who, just months ago, had returned to his life. He knew there were secrets being held close, and he knew that Serra would not betray him. But he also knew that he was responsible for the safety of the women and men on the ships of the Fleet and, just perhaps, of much of the galaxy. That thought scared him like no other.

"Admiral," Bard said, breaking the spell. "To echo Jalor's thoughts, are there things I need to know? I take it we can expect Likud to show up and with him, I'm betting, will be most of the Empire ships."

"You will know everything you need to know very shortly, Denton. And yes, I am expecting Likud to be here at some stage."

"The original Likud, Jalor said." Bard looked anxiously at Serra. "We have always assumed Likud was a hereditary name. Jalor implies that is not the case."

"I know," Serra said, nodding.

"So I gather," said Bard. "Admiral, I never thought I would say this, but just who are you, really?"

Serra smiled. "It has taken you a while to ask that question, has it not my friend? Do not fear. I am no enemy to the Union. I ask for your trust for a short while longer. Events are coming to a climax, as they must."

Bard nodded and stood to leave but turned back to bow formally to the Grand Admiral.

"You will ever have my trust, Mavin Serra," he said, "and whatever assistance you need, when you need it."

Bard turned and walked through the door that silently opened ahead of him and closed behind him, leaving Serra alone with her thoughts.

36. Goroth Stirs

The bonds had weakened, loosened, further. The stasis remained in place, but Goroth's reviving strength was such that he could push past and feel the weaves that sustained the virtual chains by which he was bound. He was unable to break those bindings, not yet, but that time was coming. The chamber was going to collapse in the near future.

He still had no idea how much time had passed, nor did he know what he would find when the stasis collapsed. He expected to find some changes, especially if he had been bound for any reasonable length of time. The damage caused by the rebellion and the response by the Council was unfortunate. Goroth did not regret it, however. His cause was the right one, and he would prevail.

The time was coming when he would take control of Ennaris. The rebellion had destroyed most of the Mages and Guides, and he knew that damage had been caused to the land. How much damage was done remained to be seen. His forces had decimated city after city and they would have had to be rebuilt. That probably was under way already. The key problem that he had was that his main supporters were Grensor and Likud, if they survived. Both were believers, although for differing reasons. Neither had stood with him at the end when Marjory proved to be too strong for him.

Goroth quailed anew when he recalled the strength Marjory had shown. Never had he expected her to be able to best him, but she had. Never had he expected her to be able to turn back the attack by the primary weapon of the Scaliba, the main ship of Goroth's fleet, but she had done exactly that. He knew that she had drained several Mages to do so, but he could not truly fathom just how. That she was powerful he already knew. How powerful she was had proved to be a shock. Goroth needed a plan to deal with Marjory, and he was confident that, should they live, then either Grensor or Likud would be thinking likewise.

Despite everything else, Ennaris was the power of this and several adjacent sectors of the galaxy. The damage unleashed during the rebellion would not have changed that. The remnants of the fleet could still be in orbit. Goroth knew where there was a sufficient cache of weapons in nearby asteroids to continue the fight against whoever Drewflin and Marjory had left.

Drewflin, Goroth mused. There was another surprise packet. Goroth remembered him as a young Mage and yet he had been able to rally the Council forces when Hardus fell. Goroth had not considered Drewflin to be a potential leader, and that under-estimation had proved to be fatal to the rebellion. That Marjory deferred to him was a bigger surprise, but it was also a weakness that he thought could be exploited. Perhaps he could separate the two somehow? Yes, maybe.

First, though, was getting free and finding his way to the hidden base in Kelgris. That was where Grensor had his laboratory, and that was where they would rebuild. The space-borne sensors had been destroyed once, and they could be destroyed again if necessary. Goroth considered moving his base to another world. Likud had always wanted Andoreth to be their home base, although Goroth favoured Ordoreth, but there were other possibilities. The populations of both worlds were ripe to be subjugated properly. Goroth gave a mental shake of his head as he thought of the many cycles when he had upheld the strategies of the old fools of the Council to leave the indigenous populations that they lifted from the dirt to fend for themselves. For such a long time he had shied away from exercising the power that he held in his own hands, and only towards the end, taking counsel from the Kindred called Groks, had he realised what he had given up for so long.

Groks had revealed much to him, not the least of which was the existence of universes other than their own. Goroth had heard theories expounded about such for tens of thousands of cycles, of course, but the means by which experiments could be undertaken were some of the arts the Council had forbidden. Logically, the Council knew about those alternate universes and were keeping the knowledge for themselves, for what reason Goroth was unable to determine. Once Grensor had made his discovery, however, and the gateway to the universe of the Kindred was opened, Goroth's eyes were also opened.

Groks had reached out through the fire and shown Goroth and Grensor the vision of greatness. To them Groks had given a glimpse of the power available to them through the dark arts. But Groks had gone further, performing a sort of meld that passed information directly from the Kindred to them showing how the vision could be achieved. Goroth's eyes were opened wider. The scales that had been bound over them by the Council were ripped apart. The glory that he could achieve for himself and Ennaris was close to limitless. That vision had provided the impetus for the ghazrak, who were modelled on the foot soldiers of the Kindred that Groks had shown them. Grensor had laboured long to create those first examples, expressing doubts even as he did so. Many had died to further their goals, but Grensor had achieved the basic aim of creating their own army of terrible ferocity. Marjory and Drewflin had destroyed that army, of course, along with Groks after the Kindred had come through the fire, but they would rebuild. If he lived, Grensor would have continued to work to remove the flaws, Goroth was confident in that. He also was confident that no-one knew where Grensor's laboratory was located.

That only left the block on advanced technology that the fool Halfgar had somehow created before he died. But if this stasis cell was deteriorating then perhaps that meant that Halfgar's block was also failing. It could not have lasted overly long, anyway. The amount of power needed would have been overwhelming. Perhaps a Guardian could do it, but Goroth doubted it, if the Guardians even existed. Halfgar had always contended that they did. Fool he might be, but Goroth could not recall Halfgar ever being caught out in a lie, and nor could he recall

Halfgar being wrong. But if they did exist then they were forbidden to interfere in the working of the planet, anyway. All they could do was watch. Which is all that the Council wanted the colony teams to do - watch and not take action unless there was a threat to destroy the world. So, the block probably was failing, and the Guardians - give Halfgar the benefit of the doubt there - were impotent.

Goroth ticked off point after point in his now seething mind. With the weapons that remained, the fleet in orbit, Grensor's ghazrak created anew and the non-gifted army rebuilt, he would also be able to gather a new generation of the gifted who wanted to share the power with him. And then he could take his battle to the Council once again. Oh, it may take some time, maybe a few dozen cycles, but he could do that. And then?

And then, Ennaris would be his.

37. Trabor and the Ninth

Move faster, Trabor!

He heard the words that were delivered directly inside his head and recognised the voice of Lak. How, he couldn't begin to fathom, but he knew it was Lak. He moved his hrss up to a canter.

Now he could hear the commotion, although he was still quite a distance away. Trabor listened for a moment before a renewed sense of urgency caused him to move his hrss into a gallop, heading towards the noise. He rounded a bend and was confronted with a scene that he thought he had left far behind, thousands of cycles behind.

A rowdy mob clustered around a large tree, just outside the town boundary. In their midst a young woman was being jostled and man-handled as she was forced through the group of mostly men to where a rope hung from a large branch. Trabor's sharp gaze saw that the branch had many gouges in its skin, obviously caused by many similar scenes in its life. Trabor pulled his hrss to a stop, reaching into his travel pack as he did so.

"Stop!" Trabor shouted, enhancing his voice so that it racketed through the hearing of everyone in the mob.

Immediately the crowd turned and stared at the newcomer.

"What's going on here?" Trabor asked, suffusing authority in the tone of voice.

"A witch is dyin'," one of the men snarled.

"There are no witches," Trabor replied sharply.

"There is," a woman shouted, pointing towards the tree, "and there she be!"

"She's a witch," another man shouted.

"How do you know?" Trabor replied. "She doesn't look like any witch I ever heard of, even if they did exist. Which they don't!"

"Stay out o' this, stranger. It ain't nothin' ta do with you." This from a taller man who was standing by the tree with the rope held in his hand. "This woman don't get old and she was here when Davnel's milk beasts died. And we don't stand fer witches here."

The woman does not get old? Trabor's attention sharpened even more.

"Was she the only one here when those beasts died?" Trabor asked.

"She's the only witch was 'ere," the tall man replied.

"I'm no witch," the woman said loudly. "And I have killed no milk beasts."

Trabor shook his head and laughed aloud, to puzzled looks from the crowd. As he did so he examined the woman and, as he had expected, saw an aura that he would expect from someone with gifts.

"Why are you laughing, stranger?" asked one of the crowd, who still were stayed by Trabor's presence.

"I'm laughing because of you, all of you," Trabor said, continuing to force a mirthful laugh. "You're all fools to believe in witches."

"And how do you know? What makes you an expert in witches?" the tall man yelled belligerently as he looked around the crowd that had quieted with Trabor's challenge. "I know what we hav'ta do and that's kill the witch!"

"No, I don't think I'll let you do that," Trabor said as he dismounted and gently slapped his hrss to make it move away to safety. His right hand held his staff, still in the form of a short stub, by his side.

"You can't tell us what to do," the man shouted. "Come on, we got the witch. We gotta kill 'er."

The man took a swift step forward and grabbed hold of the woman's arm, dragging her back and onto a wooden crate just as quickly. He pushed the knotted loop of rope over her head. The loop tightened and he grasped the trailing end while he kicked at the crate. Several in the crowd cheered and Trabor started forward finding his way blocked by others.

The Mage roared in anger. His staff extended and the cerulean light beamed forth, hard edged as it picked up on Trabor's mood. The crowd nearby pushed back even as the one with the rope gave another kick. The box on which the woman stood jerked aside and she fell. The rope tightened around her neck. But even as she grabbed at the rope with panicked hands and the man yelled in triumph, Trabor's staff spat a shot of crimson flame that wrapped itself around the rope, burning through it in an instant so that the man and woman both collapsed to the ground.

Someone in the crowd screamed and others started to run away from the scene. Trabor stalked forward. His expression was forbidding. His eyes were hard like chips of granite. With a thought his staff emitted a gout of brilliant white light that outshone the daylight and caused all there to shut their eyes tight. He reached the woman, lying on the ground where she had fallen, whimpering in fright. She covered her head with both hands.

Trabor stood over her as the light from his staff faded and daylight took over once again. He glared at the man who had been holding the rope. Another thought caused the rope-holder to be raised from the ground and held in the air.

"Hear me," Trabor shouted, his voice magnified so it reached through the entire town. "This abomination will never happen again. I, Trabor, Mage of the Council of Mages of Ennaris, forbid it. Any who is found to have taken a life because of the display of precious gifts will taste my wrath and the wrath of the Guardians."

"What Guardians? And the Mages are dead," the rope-puller sneered, realising that although he was held in the air he had not been harmed.

The crowd gasped and several pointed. Behind the rope-puller a figure took shape, rapidly emerging from a cascade of sparkling motes. The motes swirled and swooped, darted in and out of the gathering shape. Finally, as though emerging from an impressionist painting, Lak stepped from the swirling motes, and walked towards Trabor and the young woman. The crowd gasped again, for Lak walked on air, a tall man's height from the ground. The swirling motes continued to sparkle behind her. And then the crowd took a good look at her face and shrank back. Lak was livid with anger, and even walking through the air she stalked.

"What Guardians? WHAT GUARDIANS? This Guardian!" Lak's voice boomed across the entire town. "I am Lak and I tell you that this practice is outlawed, for ever, everywhere on Ennaris. Any who practice it are condemned. Any who support it are condemned. Any who take up weapons against the Mages of Ennaris are condemned. Is that clear?"

Stunned silence greeted her words. The onlookers stared but none said a word.

"I said, IS THAT CLEAR?" Lak boomed even louder.

This time she received a response, many of the crowd nodding, several of the men and the few women crying, quite a few kneeling. Lak turned to look at the rope-puller, still hanging in the air.

"This," Lak boomed as she pointed to Trabor, "is Trabor of the Council of Mages. This is one who stood against Goroth and his minions to protect Ennaris from total destruction. This Mage and his few remaining comrades have worked tirelessly to rebuild Ennaris and keep *you*" - the depth of loathing she managed to put into the word *you* caused even Trabor to wince - "safe and secure. The Mages are not dead, no thanks to such as you."

Trabor felt a nudge on his hand. He looked to Lak who merely nodded. Trabor released his hold of the rope-puller who stayed suspended in the air, for Lak had taken control. Swiftly, the rope-puller was swept higher and then was taken through the air above the small port town and out over the waters of the small bay against which it sat, crying out all the while. Lak released him and watched impassively as he plummeted into the water. Turning so that only Trabor could see her, Lak winked once and then walked - stalked - back to the sparkling motes. She turned once to look at the stunned crowd, which seemed to have grown larger. Then she stepped back into the swirling lights, or they moved to engulf her. Lak and the light motes disappeared with an audible snap!

Trabor stood ready to defend himself. His staff was held firmly and the stone embedded in the top swirled and sent out its own sparks of light. But there was nothing to fear from this crowd. Suppressing a smile, and thinking that he wished Drewflin could have seen what he had just witnessed, Trabor addressed the crowd, choosing to adopt his Teller voice.

"You have just seen Lak, one of the Guardians of Ennaris. She and her fellow Guardians have returned, as the Prophecy said they would. The time of the Prophecy is at hand. Ennaris will be asked to fight against the ancient evil of Goroth once again. I wonder if you're up to it?"

Deliberately, Trabor turned his back on the crowd, bending down to the woman who cowered at his feet.

"You're safe now," Trabor said gently. "Please stand."

The woman stood, quaking from fear and reaction at her near-death experience.

"So," Trabor said to the young woman, "what is your name? How old are you? When did you come into your gifts? And what are they?"

"I - I - I am Andira," the woman stammered, staring at Trabor with eyes as wide as saucers.

"You need not be afraid, certainly not of me," Trabor said soothingly. "Do you live near here? Do you have parents nearby?"

"N - no, master," Andira managed to get out, visibly calming herself as Trabor's presence gave her confidence. "My parents are long dead and I have no family."

"Ah," Trabor said. "I'm very sorry to hear that. So, how old are you, Andira?"

"I, um, I'm three hundred and forty cycles old."

Trabor stared, his eyes now wide.

"Three hundred and forty cycles?" he breathed.

"About," Andira said, with an uncertain sideways rocking of her head. "I'm not sure exactly."

"About three hundred and forty cycles," Trabor repeated, gathering himself. "And apart from not appearing to get old, what is your gift, Andira?"

"Well, I'm not certain," Andira replied diffidently, "but plants like me and I think I can sense demons."

"Sense demons!" Trabor breathed again. So much for the ever so calm Mage, he thought as the implications of Andira's age and gift washed over him.

"I'm not certain, mind," Andira said hastily. "I mean, I've only ever felt it twice but each time when I got to where it happened there was a dead man and it looked like he had been torn apart. And I've only ever heard of demons doing that in the stories."

"Well, that's one thing that tends to happen when a summoning goes wrong," Trabor said, thoughtfully. "And you had the courage to go to the place where this summoning occurred? But that means you can trace a summoning. Andira, I think I need to get you away from here. There are some people you need to meet."

Varna awoke. She was in a soft bed with a single sheet covering her and soft pillows under her head. She stretched mightily and her muscles stretched and popped as she did so. Lying in the bed she smiled in memory of last night. She decided she needed to get up quickly or she would stay there for ever. And she would take a cold shower if she could find one.

Then she needed to have a word with Flin before he left again as, she gathered, he was planning on doing. He had been coming and going, with regular trips to the Council Chamber to check on events, and had spent a lot of time with Fernis and other Guardians getting a better understanding of past happenings and Ennaris' long history. Varna had sat in on several of those sessions and was amazed at what she heard. Ennaris truly had been a jewel as much as a true power, although it also had suffered from the usual array of wars, diseases and natural disasters before the Ennarisi had been able to exert their own unique forms of control. All of which were lost after the rebellion.

Varna and Dalresar had been with the Guardians for some time now - exactly how long was a little vague - and still they suffered from blockages. Fernis was philosophical about it, but underneath he was concerned. Ogun was less philosophical but felt that Dalresar's blockage needed to be dealt with before he worked with him further. Varna would not be surprised if that situation changed soon and Ogun took more direct action.

She also wanted to understand what Dalresar was going to be doing. Flin had felt - always, according to him - that Dalresar had some form of gifts, and the Council Assistant had confirmed with its genetic scans that he would be expected to have a gift of some nature. The Guardians also, it seemed, had pegged Dalresar for something but she could not work out just what that could be. Maybe it was only to get him past his trauma so that whatever gift he had could be released. Or not, she thought with an unconscious twist of her lips.

For herself, time was passing and she had become aware of a sense of looming events. Something was happening, she knew, but she had no idea of what that may be. Balgor had been spending a lot of time with her, which included attempts to remove her blockage, and she valued that time, but it was coming to an end. Of that, she was sure. The Guardians had been discussing some sort of event in the last days, and only last evening had drawn Flin into those discussions. That may have been what decided him to leave again.

She found a loose robe on a stool at the foot of the bed. Her own clothes had disappeared again - she remembered the alarm she felt when that had first happened, and she had spent a few moments of near frantic search before locating her belt, staff and pack neatly placed on a recessed shelf - but she now knew that Fernis had sent them to be cleaned, no matter that she objected that she could launder her own clothes. She donned the robe, of a neutral beige colour with no additional markings. Of course, her underwear had been taken also and on investigation she found her spare clothes had also been removed. So, the robe and nothing else it would be.

A small basin was in an alcove, fed with hot and cold water from a spigot, so she washed her face to remove the final vestiges of sleep, dried face and hands on a small towel laid close at hand to the basin and turned to leave the room. As though to add impetus, her stomach gave a growl, so she pulled the door open and stepped into a wood-panelled corridor. No, she corrected itself, it was a corridor through wood. She was, of course, in a tree. After a moment of indecision, she turned right and walked down the corridor, rounding a corner to a larger space with both Flin and Dalresar sitting at a table and eating a light breakfast.

A place was set for her at the same table, as usual, as was a bowl of some form of grain and fruit, with what seemed like honey and a berry mixture and a glass of a vibrant pink liquid, which she had not seen before. That, she had reflected on that first morning, was the first glass object she could recall seeing on Ennaris, other than some oddly distorted windows at the Citadel.

Greeting her two companions, she sat and tested the food, finding it all to be to her taste. The drink, a fruit juice she guessed, was fresh and cool, with a zesty taste that she relished.

"What is this?" she asked Flin, gesturing to her glass. "It's wonderful."

"The juice of a pana-fruit," Flin replied. "Usually only found in the Angrew region of the southern continent. The juice spoils if it is not used within the same day of harvesting the fruit, so you won't find it outside that small region."

"Man, if I could get this to Earth, I'd make a killing," Varna said, taking another sip.

Flin laughed, while Dalresar regarded Varna with a wry expression.

"So, what are you going to do next?" Varna asked Flin as she turned her attention to the contents of the bowl. "I heard that you're planning to head off again. Back to the Citadel?"

"Yes. Fernis told me that the norther armies have broken out and are heading towards Escar, so I need to get back to Corm. You both," he said as Dalresar opened his mouth, "are to stay here. Also, Balgor told me last night that there is a working portal in the Citadel, which should mean I can get updates from the Council Chamber that I asked for. I also need to see the twins and I'm betting that Jalor and Blaine want to get updated, assuming they've returned. They may not be aware of the northers, although I understand that they've been trying to build support for Corm." He shrugged slightly. "And I need to check a few things based on the briefing I received in the Chamber. There are some things stored in the Citadel that we will need."

"Oh?" Varna asked, curious.

"I need to get a better understanding of them before I say anything more. Fernis warned me against saying too much yet, because parts of the Prophecy seem to imply different things. He told me that he expected the threads to start to come together as we get closer to the battle, but I need to try to make sense of whatever I can."

"Okay. Do you know how long I'm going to be here?" Varna asked around a spoonful of her breakfast.

"I'm not sure it's a matter of time," Flin said carefully. "I think the Guardians can get around that in some way."

Varna recalled her dreams or visions, where she found herself in a different space, seemingly out of time. She nodded her understanding.

"Like a dimensional shift?"

"Perhaps. I don't really know. I have a much clearer understanding of the Guardians now, but still don't know what they are capable of, or what they may be allowed to do in any fight for Ennaris. I'm not sure they know themselves just yet."

"And Dalresar?"

"No idea," Flin replied, as Dalresar just looked at both of them and shrugged, to indicate that he had no idea either.

"Balgor told me that he had some ideas, and it seems that Eresh will fetch Ogun when she felt the time was right," Dalresar said. "Eresh said that Ogun would add to my skills but that Balgor would work on my block, whatever that means."

"Flin, who is Odruf?" Varna asked softly.

Flin smiled. "Odruf is reputed to be the leader of the Guardians, although if such is the case I'm thinking he would be the first of equals. Why do you ask?"

"Odruf drew me into some sort of dream vision some time ago. That was the first time I was told to come here."

"You never mentioned that," Flin said quietly.

"I was unsure of what it meant, so I kept it to myself. That was while I was having strange episodes, before Balgor did his temporary patch. I apologise for that."

"Hmmpf, no need for apology. I'm guessing that this is all strange enough anyway."

"On Earth, the supernatural, which is what all of this would seem to be, is looked on with a sort of tolerant unbelief. Those who believe are labelled as having a sort of intellectual failure. Even those of us who rated high in psychic ability were taught not to read too much into what that may mean. And in earth's past, those who practised magic, or who claimed to do so, or were thought to have done so - witches, warlocks and such - were persecuted, burned, drowned." Varna looked down to her now empty bowl sadly. "What if they truly had gifts, from their bloodlines? What if those people could have truly done some of those things?"

"I can see no reason for you to dwell on that," Flin replied. "Actions such as those indicate a low level of sophistication, and probably fear of the unknown. I would imagine that was a time of superstition, of uncertainty. Science probably was quite poorly understood so anything out of the ordinary would have been suspicious."

"Yes," Varna nodded, thinking back to her school lessons, "that was in the days before any form of enlightenment, although people believed in spirit beings long after. Who knows, that may have been almost forgotten remnants of the Ennarisi legends that people were remembering."

"It mirrors what happened after the rebellion. Education was one of the first things to suffer as people struggled to live. We ended up having to reduce history to story and legend so people would listen, and the most important things were those that allowed the people to survive. And it was necessary for that to be the case. But at the same time, the memories of the rebellion and the roles of those involved were corrupted, perhaps deliberately, perhaps just by time, and the same things occurred. Gifts were misinterpreted to be dangerous, the gifted were persecuted just as you describe."

At that moment Fernis entered the room, walking over to where the three sat and sitting himself.

"Varna, Dalresar, I trust you had a good night's sleep? You may find the next few days somewhat arduous, to your spirit as much as physically."

Both nodded acceptance. Fernis look to Flin once again.

"Drewflin, I know you will be leaving again. I offer you free access to this, ah, facility, shall we say, for your lifetime, which I hope is long. I regret that this offer could not be made long ago but, as I am sure Balgor has mentioned, we also had constraints placed on us."

Flin was taken aback.

"Why, thank you, Master," he said. "You do me great honour."

"No more than is appropriate, I think. Varna, why do you smile at that?"

Varna found that she was, in fact, smiling slightly, and started.

"Well," she said slowly, "I find it amusing that Flin was not a believer in your existence and now refers to you as 'Master'. That is a turnabout."

"Yes, well," Flin started to say, a little embarrassed. "Before being appointed Mage, I was one of the Arbor Guides." He paused, realising Varna was confused. "The Guides had many gifts among them, but very few had multiple gifts of strength. So, even those of us who did so chose a tribe that represented our greatest passions. The Arbor Guides spent much effort on maintaining and repairing the vegetation, and especially the crops, of Ennaris, and we were the ones who assisted our client civilisations to move beyond very basic hunter-gatherer ways of life to the rudiments of agriculture. My tribe had a symbol, which was held to be dear to our Guardian, Fernis."

"The Tree," Varna guessed, remembering Flin's reaction as they entered the clearing.

"Indeed, the Tree. I have known the shape of this Tree for my entire life, thinking it was merely a representation of an idea. I find in that I was mistaken also." He smiled. "And I find that this is a mistake that I do not mind having corrected."

"In days past the Archmages would have his or her Guide tribe included as part of the Enchara," Fernis said softly. "The Enchara told all that she or he had belonged to a particular tribe, even though members of the tribe would ritually expel the new Archmage from their ranks on her or him being elevated."

"I recall Hardus had his fire-red Enchara emblazoned with a smith's hammer," Flin mused.

"Indeed yes," Fernis replied looking at Flin with a smile. "May I see your Enchara, please?"

"It's but a plain stone," Flin said, reaching under the folds of his long robe and bringing forth a green stone on a chain. "But at least I did manage to get the colour right."

"Ah," Fernis said, taking the offered stone. "Indeed it is, and quite plain also, as you say. This will never do for one of my tribe."

Suddenly the stone blazed. An inner light ignited to shine forth, coating the walls of the common room with a green hue. Varna, and from his reaction Dalresar also, distinctly heard a chime and without warning both Eresh and Balgor popped into the room.

"We heard the Enchara," Eresh said. "Is all well?"

"It is well," Fernis said. "Drewflin was showing me his Enchara, at my request. He has not had the opportunity for his tribe to be etched as yet."

Both of the other Guardians nodded, each wearing a smile. Fernis smiled also, gesturing Flin to his feet. Mystified, Flin stood as bidden. Without warning the room was engulfed in a succession of bright flashes, which, when they had faded, revealed a room full of people, female and male, all wearing similar smiles. Flin's mouth gaped open at the sight.

"Archmage Drewflin," Fernis said, drawing Flin's attention back to him after a moment, his expression slightly wild. "This should have happened long ago. On behalf of the Guardians of Ennaris, assembled here, receive the Enchara of office as Archmage of the Council of Guide Mages of Ennaris. A little late," he concluded ruefully.

With some ceremony Fernis showed the stone to Flin, who gaped anew, and then Fernis lifted the Enchara and draped the chain over Flin's head. The stone centred itself on Flin's forehead while the fine chain somehow arranged itself to be almost invisible on the crown of his head. The stone pulsed with energy and now etched into its surface, clearly visible and pulsing with its own force, was the Tree. A joyous peal rang out, heard by those able to hear such, and in one movement the assembled Guardians of Ennaris bowed to honour the Archmage. With a tear to her eye Varna followed suit, with Dalresar only a moment behind her.

In the Citadel, where they were explaining to Corm how to manage aspects of his interactions with other leaders, Raglin and Ragnor paused as the Enchara's peal rang out. From each forehead a pulse of blue-grey light shone momentarily, causing Corm to stare, and the twins grinned to each other.

In a dirty, dusty tavern deep in the wilds of the southern continent, Trabor stopped to listen, causing Andira to glance at him. His audience, who were fully engaged in the story he was telling, watched in astonishment as a bright cerulean flash erupted and the man sighed and smiled before continuing. "But enough of the old," the Teller said to the scruffy, violent and largely criminal group sitting before him, "now let me you about the return of the Mages to save Ennaris."

On *Starfire*, in her private quarters, Grand Admiral Mavin Serra stood suddenly and a silver flash lit the small space. She gasped. The tears running down her face were belied by the joyful laugh that erupted from her.

On the bridge of the Empire flagship Qorv, speeding towards Ennaris, Likud also stood, a snarl breaking forth as an obsidian flare erupted from his brow. Furiously he turned on his bridge crew and demanded more speed. Time was getting away from him.

In the northlands, Grensor, the Old One of the northers and ghazrak, stumbled and almost fell. He was held upright only by his attendants as a dark flash was emitted from a dark, cracked stone seemingly embedded in his forehead. He lifted his head and looked to the south, and his spirit quailed.

In the nothingness of stasis Goroth shifted as a jet-black light briefly engulfed his prison. His consciousness, which was slowly fighting its way through the bindings, recognised the joyous peal and he grimaced. An Archmage had been appointed. Drewflin? Or another enemy?

In the Hides, Maf heard the peal and the silver-green stone flashed in acknowledgement, causing those gathered for their training session to gape. Most of those listening heard the peal and turned to themselves and Maf with questioning glances. Maf was unsure what had happened, but he knew it was something of significance. He shrugged. He would find out soon enough if it was anything to do with him.

Across Ennaris, select men, women and children awoke or were distracted, some explaining that they heard a sound like someone calling out in joy, but there were none at that time able to interpret for them just what they had heard, and no-one else had heard anything. They shrugged it off and returned to what they were doing.

In the town of Manis Reach, sitting in the tavern with Hunder as they discussed the town's defences, both Jalor and Blaine distinctly heard the peal of the Enchara of the Archmage as it announced to the world and to all who could hear that the Archmage of Ennaris had been anointed to his position. They glanced to each other and then around the tavern common room, realising that they were the only ones to hear anything, and both wondered what it presaged.

In the Council Chamber a low tone sounded. Chambers that had been dark for thousands of cycles were lit, and consoles sprang to life. Around Ennaris portals that had long been dormant re-awoke, going through their restart sequence and making contact with the central AI. Sensor Array 413 recognised the renewed activity. As the cavern behind it re-activated, Senasarra, as it had started to think of itself, sent a request for the rock-fall blocking the entrance to be cleared.

On the larger moon, in a chamber carved from the core of that major satellite long, long ago, a series of huge chambers were lit. Maintenance robots reanimated, received their orders from the base AI and went to work preparing the long line of vessels for use. Attached to service conduits at the back of the moon, away from prying sensor eyes, another set of lights awoke, followed in sequence by a line of lights that illuminated the long vessel that had been idle, dark, for so long, and the maintenance bots commenced evaluating how to finalise repairs to its many injuries while, at the same time, the ship system interfaced with the moon's control systems, established communication with a set of codes common to all ships designed and built by the Ennarisi, and commenced the required upgrades.

In the depths of the ocean Ooshmin, the leviathan, heard the chime as it rolled around the planet. A blue flash emerged from a point in the centre of the bony ridge above his eyes. The leviathan's spirits lifted and he emitted a piercing multi-tone whistle that was heard through all of the oceans of Ennaris. With powerful strokes of its tale, the leviathan surged from the depths and leapt high into the air, crashing down once more on the ocean's surface, whistling in joy once again. An Archmage! Ennaris had an Archmage again! The leviathan dove once more only to breach and crash back again, and then he started his journey, issuing his call to the cubs in training.

On the bridge of *Starfire*, relative calm had ensued for some time, enough to allow the ship's complement to rest. Now Rork stared as his monitoring equipment went haywire. As he watched multiple energy signatures sprang up where there had been nothing moments before, dozens and then hundreds of them. Calling Kiri and Jord over, Rork merely pointed and then transferred his display to the large screen. Node after node of the planetary defence network awoke, established a link and created its part of a barrier. Satellites that had not been detected made their presence known, each orienting on one of the ships of the two fleets arrayed around the planet. From the moon Rork saw two launches of satellites that rapidly took their place in the grid, in place of two that had suffered failure. Within minutes Ennaris was a blaze of energy signatures and an impenetrable shield was in place.

"Mr Rork?" Kiri said, while Jord just stared.

"Colonel," Rork breathed, while the bridge had gone deathly quiet. "I've never seen anything like it. The whole planet just lit up with the most complete defence system I've ever seen. Each ship of each fleet has been targeted."

"It's a planetary defence system like nothing I've seen before either, and it's preparing for something we probably don't want to see," Jord said to the two bridge officers. He leaned over the console the touch a stud. "Admirals Serra and Bard to the bridge," he said calmly, although he felt anything but calm.

Then he looked around the bridge staff, all of whom were watching his every action. He forced himself to remain calm as he continued to speak in a level voice.

"Send to all ships, please. Sound general quarters."

About The Author

James K. McVey is an author living on the New South Wales Central Coast, in Australia. The four novels that comprise *Children of Ennaris* are his first published works.

Visit www.jameskmcvey.com.au for further information and updates on these and other works.

www.ingramcontent.com/pod-product-compliance
Lightning Source LLC
Chambersburg PA
CBHW070346170726
48291CB00001B/198